Jack looke

distracted.

The steam had already begun to destroy Olivia's tight chignon. Golden strands had fallen loose and curled around her throat. "You do need a good wash-up," she said. "Do you want me to get your back?"

He closed his eyes against every image those words provoked. "Dear God, yes. I can't remember the last time I bathed."

Kneeling next to the tub, she picked up a cloth and wet it and laid it against his neck. He swore he'd never felt anything so decadent in his life. Hot water lapping his belly, a warm fire crackling on the hearth, and Livvie bent close. It was all he could do to keep from groaning. His heart was beginning to race. He could smell apples and the faintest musk of arousal. He sat perfectly still, his head resting on his folded arms, investing all his concentration in Livvie's touch.

"Are you all right?" she asked.

"I believe I'm in heaven." He reached up to brush his knuckles across her cheek . . . and saw that her eyes were all but black with desire.

"Please, Liv," he begged, his voice a bare rasp. "Touch me."

Barely A Lady

Eileen Dreyer

FOREVER

NEW YORK BOSTON

Cover design by Claire Brown
Cover illustration by Jon Paul
Hand lettering by Iska Johnson
Book design by Giorgetta Bell McRee

Forever
Hachette Book Group
237 Park Avenue
New York, NY 10017
Visit our website at www.HachetteBookGroup.com.

Forever is an imprint of Grand Central Publishing.
The Forever name and logo is a trademark of Hachette Book Group, Inc.

Printed in the United States of America

First Printing: July 2010

10 9 8 7 6 5 4 3 2

To Melinda Helfer
Since the last thing she said to me was
"Eileen, you need to write a Regency."
I hope this is what you had in mind.

Acknowledgments

For this, my first foray into historical fiction, I have so many people to thank. First, my fans, who have followed faithfully, no matter what road I've taken. Second, the Convocation: Julie Beard, Carol Carson, Shirl Henke, Pat Rice, Karyn Witmer-Gow. The Divas: Kim Bush; Tami Hoag; and Karyn, who did triple duty, the most difficult as midwife. Sally Hawkes, researcher extraordinaire; my temporary assistant (and beautiful daughter), Kate Christlieb. Also, my son Kevin Dreyer for computer repair above and beyond. Jan and Judy and the entire staff at Wired Coffee, who have put up with me at all hours. Special thanks to Andrea Cirillo, who saw the potential, and Amy Pierpont, my ADD sister, who was able to spot the alligators.

One final note: I did a lot of book research, much of which has been covered in better authors' acknowledgments than mine (although I will list them on the research page on my Web site). But one book I would like to single out is *Dancing Toward Waterloo* by Nick Ffolkes, which documented Brussels in the days up to and after Waterloo.

Oh, wait. *Really* finally. My wonderful Rick. 'Nuf said.

Barely A Lady

Prologue

Charleroi, Belgium
Dawn, June 15, 1815

It would take a miracle to get him out of this alive. And he had the feeling he'd long since used up his share of miracles.

Warming his hands on a hot tin of coffee, he took a moment to assess his environment. The plain of Charleroi spread out before him like a green and gold patchwork quilt sewn together with hedgerows. Dawn thinned the summer sky to a watery yellow, and the smoke from a hundred cannons writhed through the morning mist. Relative silence temporarily reigned, but the battlefield was a site of frantic activity.

The air stank of cordite, overridden horses, and unwashed men. As far as the eye could see, men were preparing for battle. Campfires were being doused, weapons checked. The rolling landscape echoed with the rhythmic scraping of swords being honed, the nervous whinnying of horses, the sharp sounds of command.

In his own vicinity, men were stripping their kits of everything they wouldn't need. Uniforms were straightened and checked, bad jokes exchanged, courage exhorted.

No one took any notice of him as he stood beside one of the doused campfires. He was just another officer trying to catch a quick smoke as he waited for the call to arms.

This was it, then. The final battle for Europe. How the hell had he ended up here? He'd only wanted to get back to Brussels. He had a mission to finish, a final gift to deliver, and nothing stood between him and success but the two armies massing to collide like great beasts.

If he had been a different man, or this had been a different time, he probably would have happily stayed to offer his life up on the altar of patriotism. Nothing played quite as well at home as a solemn memorial stone in the village church.

But he wasn't that man. He'd already committed more sins to get here than a soul is allowed, and he couldn't let himself be stopped now. He had to reach Brussels. And when he was finished here, he had to go home to England. He owed it to the people he'd left behind. He owed it to the ones who waited ahead. Most of all, he owed it to himself.

It was time to finally answer old questions. To do that, he needed to face Livvie and Gervaise. He needed to settle things with his family. He needed to get revenge.

Yes, he thought, pulling the cheroot he'd been smoking from his mouth and flipping it onto the grass, that was what he would live for. Revenge.

Whistles sounded up and down the line. Men gathered into the great columns that had terrorized a continent. He dumped his coffee on the ground and buttoned his tunic. Picking up his sword, he sheathed it with a lethal-sounding hiss. He checked the powder and priming on his pistol and retrieved the musket he would reload and fire on the run. He stood alone in the chaos, trying to see if there was any way to avoid this fracas.

A young soldier ran up and greeted him with a breathless salute. "*Mon Capitaine*. The enemy is in sight."

He looked at the anxious young face before him and wished he could laugh. Was this a tragedy or a farce he was caught in? The lad who stood before him hadn't even been introduced to a razor.

"Indeed, Private. And what is our job this morning?"

The boy looked confused. "To harry the enemy flanks, sir."

"And so we shall. But for you, *mon brave,* I have a special mission. You are willing?"

If possible, the boy grew taller. "But of course, sir."

"Excellent." Pulling out a slip of paper and a nub of charcoal, he scribbled a note. "Deliver this request to the quartermaster. And then stay at his command until it is done."

No matter what other sins lay on his soul, he was not going to send this child to be slaughtered. At least not this day.

The boy cast a brief frown over his shoulder to where the red British uniforms were beginning to materialize through the mist. He looked puzzled, but finally he accepted the twist of paper. Then, saluting, he ran for the rear.

Waiting only until he was sure the boy was well out of it, the captain straightened his blue tunic and shot his red cuffs. Then, giving the uniform he'd worked so hard to acquire a final pat, he set his shako on his head.

"Well, then," he snapped to the rest of the men as he pulled out his pistol. "Don't stand there like sheep. The enemy comes!"

As one, the squad of sharpshooters turned to jog through the receding mist. Along the plain, trumpets blared. The great drums began to beat the *pas de charge*. Thousands of strong voices took up the chant, *"Vive l'empereur!"* and the massive columns set off. The Battle for Quatre Bras had begun.

He had no choice but to engage.

God forgive him.

Setting off at a lope, he followed his ragged squad of blue-clad soldiers. A line of sharp, crimson uniforms became visible at the ridge. He raised his pistol and fired.

A soldier in blue jerked and fell.

Tossing away his pistol, he lifted the musket and fired again.

Chapter 1

Brussels
11:00 p.m., Thursday, June 15, 1815

All prey understands the need for concealment. Sitting at the edge of a crowded ballroom, Olivia Grace knew this better than most and kept her attention on the room like a gazelle sidling up to a watering hole.

Olivia couldn't help smiling. *Watering holes.* She'd been reading too many naturalists' journals. Not that there weren't predators here, of course. It would have been impossible to miss them, with their bright plumage, sharp claws, and aggressive posturing. And those were just the mamas.

Olivia was safely tucked away from their notice, though. Camouflaged in serviceable gray bombazine, she occupied a chair along the trellis-papered wall, just another anonymous paid chaperone watching on as her charges danced.

The ballroom, a converted carriage house at the side of the Duke of Richmond's rented home, was full to bursting. Scarlet-clad soldiers whirled by with laughing girls in white. Sharp-eyed dowagers in puce and aubergine committed wholesale slaughter of each others' reputations. Civilian gentlemen in evening black clustered at the edge of the dance floor to argue about the coming battle. Olivia had even had the privilege of seeing the Duke of Wellington himself sweep into the room, his braying laugh lifting over the swell of the orchestra.

It seemed all of London had moved to Brussels these last months. Certainly the well-born military men had come in response to Napoleon's renewed threat. Olivia had already had the Lennox boys, the Duke of Richmond's sons, pointed out to her, and handsome young Lord Hay in his scarlet Guards jacket. Sturdy William Ponsonby was in dragoon green, and the exquisite Diccan Hilliard wore diplomat's black.

With all those eligible young men afoot, it would have been absurd to think that families would have kept their hopeful daughters at home.

Tonight Olivia's employer had insisted on shepherding her own chicks, which left Olivia with nothing to do but watch. And watch she did, storing up every bit of color and pageantry to record for her dear Georgie back in England.

"Oh, there's that devil Uxbridge," the lady next to her whispered in salacious tones. "How he can show his face after eloping with Wellington's sister-in-law..."

Olivia had heard that Uxbridge had been recalled from exile to lead the cavalry in the upcoming fight. She'd also heard he was brilliant and charismatic. Catching sight of him as he sauntered across the room in his flashy hussar's blue and silver, his fur-lined pelisse thrown over his shoulder, she thought that the reports had been woefully inadequate. He was breathtaking.

She was so intent on the sight of him, in fact, that she failed her primary duty. She forgot to watch for danger. She'd just leaned a bit to see whose hand Uxbridge was bending over, when her view was suddenly blocked by a field of gold.

"You don't mind if I sit here, do you?" someone asked.

Olivia looked up to find one of the most beautiful women she'd ever seen standing before her. Even sitting against the wall, Olivia fought the urge to look over her shoulder to see who else the newcomer could be addressing. Women like this never sought her out.

For a second, she flirted with old panic. She'd spent so many years trying to evade exposure that the instinct died hard. But this woman didn't look outraged. In fact, she was smiling.

"It's quite all right," the beauty said with a conspiratorial grin. "Contrary to popular opinion, I rarely bite. In fact, in some circles I'm considered fairly charming."

"I do bite," Olivia found herself answering. "But only when provoked."

She should bite her *tongue*. She knew better.

The woman didn't seem to notice, though, as with a hush of silk, she eased onto the chair to Olivia's left. "Well, let's see who we can get to provoke you, then," she said. "I think what this ball needs is some excitement—more than Jane Lennox making cow-eyes at Wellington over dinner, at any rate."

Olivia actually laughed. "I think you might get some argument from all those men in red."

Her companion took a moment to observe the room through a grotesquely bejeweled lorgnette. "It never occurred to me. This is the perfect place to watch absolutely everything, isn't it?"

"Absolutely."

"I wish I'd been sitting here when those magnificent Highlanders did their reels. I don't suppose you caught a glimpse of what they wore under those kilts."

"Sadly, no. Not for lack of trying, though."

Olivia wondered why this peacock would choose to sit among the house wrens—especially since several of the wrens in question had taken umbrage. One or two sidled away. Olivia even heard the whisper of "harlot." Again she fought the old urge to hide, but the attention was definitely on the newcomer.

As for that petite beauty, she appeared to take no notice. A Pocket Venus, she looked to be no older than Olivia's four and twenty years. As fine-skinned as a porcelain doll, she had thick, curly mahogany hair woven through with diamonds and a heart-shaped face that might have looked innocent but for her slyly amused cat-green eyes. Her dress had been crafted by an artist. Draped in layers of filmy gold tissue, it seemed to flow like water from a barely respectable bodice that exposed quite an expanse of diamond-wrapped throat and high, white breasts.

"I noticed the way you watch everyone," the beauty now said, lazily waving an intricately painted chicken-skin fan under her nose. "And I've been dying to hear what you're thinking."

"Thinking?" Olivia said instinctively. "But I think nothing. Companions aren't paid enough to think."

The lady gave a delighted laugh. "If you only did what you were paid for, my dear, I sincerely doubt you'd ever move farther afield than your front parlor."

"The back parlor, actually. Closer to the servants' stairs."

Olivia knew perfectly well she was being reckless. Exposure was still possible, after all, and one gasp of recognition would destroy her. But it felt so good to smile.

Her new acquaintance laughed. "I *knew* I'd like you. Who is it who benefits from your companionship, might I ask?"

"Mrs. Bottomly and her three daughters." Olivia gestured toward a group on the dance floor. "They felt that passing the season in Brussels might be... advantageous."

The beauty turned to observe the short, knife-lean matron in pea green and peacock feathers smacking a rigid Mr. Hilliard on the arm with her fan as three younger copies of her looked on.

"You mean that flock of underfed crows pecking at my poor Diccan? Good Lord, how did she ever manage to acquire an invitation?"

"Ah, well," Olivia said, "that would involve a well-timed walk along the Allee Verde, an even better-timed ankle twist that obliged the Duchess of Richmond to take Mrs. Bottomly up in her carriage, and Mrs. Bottomly's tenacious confusion as to the nature of the invitations to tonight's event."

Her new acquaintance shook her head in awe. "Why

ever has the creature wasted her time with a mere ball? Let's introduce her to Nosey, and she can help him rout Napoleon."

Olivia wryly considered her employer. "Not unless he has three eligible officers who might be offered in compensation."

Just then, Mrs. Bottomly let off a shrill titter that should have shattered Mr. Hilliard's eardrums. Olivia's companion flinched. "Not something I'd want on my conscience. I'm afraid Wellington will simply have to rely on his own wits."

"Indeed."

"But what of you?" the beauty demanded of Olivia. "Surely you deserve better than service to an overweening mushroom."

Olivia smiled. "I've found that life rarely takes what we deserve into consideration."

For just a moment, her companion's expression grew oddly reflective. Then, abruptly, she brightened. "Well, there are small mercies," she said with a tap of her fan on Olivia's arm. "If that dreadful woman had decamped from Brussels like everyone else who anticipated battle, I never would have met you."

"Indeed you would not. For it is certain we couldn't have met in London. Not even Mrs. Bottomly would dare to aspire so high."

The woman turned her bright eyes on Olivia. "And how do you know that?"

Olivia's smile was placid. "Your gems are real."

Her friend gave a surprisingly full-throated laugh that turned heads. Olivia saw the attention and instinctively ducked.

Her companion suddenly straightened. "Grace!" she called with a wave of her fan. "Over here!"

Olivia looked up to see a tall, almost colorless redhead turn and smile. She was in the same serviceable gray as Olivia, although the cloth was better. A sarcenet, possibly, that did nothing but wash out whatever color the young woman had in her plain features.

Then she began walking toward them, and Olivia realized that she limped badly. Must have danced with the wrong clod, Olivia thought, and moved to offer her seat.

Her companion quietly held her in place. "Grace, my love," she caroled, her hand still on Olivia's arm. "What have you heard?"

The tall redhead lurched to a halt right in front of them and dipped a very fine curtsy. "Word has come, Your Grace. Fighting has commenced in Quatre Bras, south of us."

Your Grace? Oh, sweet God, Olivia thought, feeling the blood drain from her face. What had she done?

Unobtrusively, she searched the room for Mrs. Bottomly and her daughters, but suddenly it seemed the entire crowd was in her way. Many of the officers now milled about uncertainly. Young girls wrung their hands and chattered in high, anxious tones. Wellington himself was speaking to the Duke of Richmond, and both looked worried.

It had begun, then. The great battle they had all been expecting for weeks was upon them. Awfully, Olivia felt a measure of relief. She would be invisible again.

"Ah well, then," the duchess said, climbing to her feet. "It seems our time for frivolity is over. *Noblesse oblige* and all that. Before we go, Grace, come meet my new friend."

Olivia stood and was surprised to see that the duchess came only to her shoulder. And Olivia was only of medium height.

"I'm sorry we didn't have time to share more observations," the petite beauty said to her with a gamine smile. "I think we could have thoroughly skewered this lot."

Olivia dipped a curtsy. "It has been a pleasure, Your Grace."

The duchess lifted a wickedly amused eyebrow. "Of course it has. Although by morning you will be notorious for speaking with me. 'Oh, my dear,' they'll all whisper in outrage, 'did you hear about that nice companion, Miss...'"

The little duchess suddenly looked almost ludicrously surprised. "Good God. I can't introduce you after all."

Olivia froze. Had she finally recognized her?

"We never exchanged names," the duchess said, laughing. "I shall begin. I, for my sins, am Dolores Catherine Anne Hilliard Seaton, Dowager Duchess of Murther." She wafted a lofty hand. "You may respond with proper gravity."

Olivia found herself wondering at such a young dowager as she dipped a curtsy of impeccable depth. "Mrs. Olivia Grace, Your Grace."

"Good Lord," the duchess said, her eyes wide. "I'm a grace, you're a grace, and, of course, Grace is a grace. A *real* grace, mind you, in all ways." She patted the tall girl halfway up her arm. "Introduce yourself and make the irony complete, my love."

With a smile that softened her long face, the redhead dipped a bow. "Miss Grace Fairchild, ma'am."

"Grace is the daughter of that grossly bemedaled Guards general over there with the magnificent white mustache," the duchess said. "General Sir Hillary Fairchild. Grace is one of those indomitable females who has spent her life following the drum. She knows more about foraging for food and creating a billet from a cow byre than I know about Debrett's."

Olivia exchanged curtsies. She liked this plain young woman, who had the kindest gray eyes she'd ever seen. "A pleasure, Miss Fairchild."

"Please," the young woman said. "Call me Grace."

"And I am Kate," the young duchess said. "Lady Kate, if the familiarity sticks in your craw. But never duchess or my lady or Your Grace"—she shot a glare at Grace Fairchild—"for how would we tell each other apart? Which would be unconscionable among friends. And we are friends, are we not?"

Olivia knew better than to agree. "It would please me immensely," she said anyway. "Please call me Olivia."

"Shall we see you later at Madame de Rebaucour's, Olivia?" Grace Fairchild asked. "She is organizing the ladies of the city to help prepare for the anticipated wounded."

"Never let it be said that I am completely without useful skills," Lady Kate boasted. "I've become absolutely mad for rolling lint."

"If my employer gives me leave, you can expect me there," Olivia said, casting an eye out for that lady among the crowd.

Lady Kate gave her a wicked smile. "Oh, I can assure

you she will. Simply tell her you accompany a duchess." Flinging her zephyr shawl around her shoulders, she made to go. "We shall all help, like the heroines we are."

"And sully those exquisite white hands?" a man's voice demanded from behind Olivia.

Olivia froze. Shock skittered across her skin like sleet.

"Since these are the only pair of hands I own," Lady Kate was saying lightly, "I imagine they will just have to adapt."

Olivia couldn't move. Sound suddenly echoed oddly, and movement seemed to slow. Lady Kate was looking just past her to where the man who had addressed her obviously stood, and Olivia knew she should turn.

It wasn't him. It *couldn't* be. She had escaped him. She'd hidden herself so thoroughly that she'd closed even the memory of him away.

"A generation of young exquisites would go into mourning if you suffered so much as a scratch," he was telling the duchess in his charmingly boyish voice.

Still behind her, out of sight. Still possibly someone who only sounded terrifyingly familiar. Olivia desperately wanted to close her eyes, as if it could keep him at bay. *If I don't see him, he won't be there.*

She knew better. Even if she refused the truth, her body recognized him. Her heart sped up. Her hands went clammy. She couldn't seem to get enough air.

And there was no escape. So she did what cornered animals do. She turned to face the threat.

And there he was, one of the most beautiful men God had ever created. A true aristocrat with his butter-blond hair, clear blue eyes, and hawkish Armiston nose, he stood a slim inch below six feet. His corbeau coat and oyster silk smalls were only a bit dandified, with a silver marcella waistcoat, half a dozen fobs, and a ruby glinting from his finger. He was bestowing an impish smile on the duchess, who seemed delighted by it.

Olivia had once thought that his handsome looks reflected a kind soul. She would never make that mistake again.

"Dear Gervaise." Lady Kate was laughing up at him. "How thoughtful to persist in your delusion that I am a fragile flower."

His grin was disarming, his laugh like music. "Been thoroughly put in my place, haven't I? Daresay you'll ignore my heartfelt wish to safeguard your looks, and then where will you be when they're gone?"

Lady Kate laughed again and held out her hand to him. "Doing it up much too brown, Gervaise. You know full well that I'm content simply being outrageous. I'll leave you to hold the torch for natural perfection."

Gervaise bent over Lady Kate's hand, but suddenly he wasn't looking at her. He had just caught sight of Olivia.

She was probably the only one who caught the quickly shuttered surprise in his eyes. The glint of triumph. She wanted to laugh. Here she'd been hiding herself from judgmental mamas, when there had been a viper in the room all along.

"It seems I arrived just in time," he said, straightening with a delighted smile as he shot his cuffs. "As quickly as this place is emptying, I might have missed you all. I know Miss Fairchild, of course, Kate, but who is this?"

"Make your bows to Mrs. Olivia Grace, Gervaise," Lady Kate said. "Olivia, this is Mr. Gervaise Armiston.

He is about to take me over to the door so I can see off our brave soldiers. I have no brave soldiers of my own. Only Gervaise."

Gervaise chuckled good-naturedly and extended an arm. "I also live to serve, Kate," he protested. "It's just that I only serve you." Giving Olivia a quick bow, he nodded. "Mrs. Grace."

Olivia swallowed against rising bile. "Mr. Armiston."

Lady Kate rested a slim white hand on his midnight sleeve. "Excellent. Come, Gervaise. Let us now go and remind our soldiers what they fight for. Grace, Olivia... tomorrow."

The duchess had barely turned away before Olivia's legs gave out from under her, and she sat down hard.

"Olivia?" Grace Fairchild asked, her face creased in concern. "Are you all right?"

Olivia looked up, trying desperately to quell her nausea. Suddenly, from the streets below, military drums shattered the night. Trumpets blared, and the Duchess of Richmond rushed about the ballroom, urging the men not to leave until after dinner had been served.

"Just another hour!" she pleaded.

Officers lined up at the doors to get a farewell kiss from the lovely Duchess of Murther. Some girls wept, while others swept off to dinner with the remaining men. And in the corner where the chaperones sat, Olivia's world collapsed.

Her hands wouldn't stop shaking. She had to warn Georgie. She had to warn them all.

She couldn't. Any contact with them would lead Gervaise right back to them, and that would prove fatal.

Just as it had before.

Oh, Jamie.

Grace touched her shoulder. "Olivia?"

Olivia jumped. "Oh…," she said, trying so hard to smile as she climbed to still unsteady legs. "I'm fine. I suppose it's time to go."

"You're sure you're all right? You're pale."

"Just the news." Gathering her shawl, she avoided Grace's sharp gaze. Pasting on a false smile, she turned. "I wish I were more like Lady Kate. Look how she's making all the men laugh."

Grace looked to where the duchess was lifting on her toes to kiss a hotly blushing boy in rifleman green. "Lady Kate is amazing, isn't she?"

"She's a *disgrace,*" one of the nearby women hissed.

Several other heads nodded enthusiastically.

"Glass houses," snapped a regal older woman at the end of the row.

Everyone looked over at her, but the woman ignored them. Reticule and shawl in hand, she rose imperiously to her feet. She was a tall woman, with exceptional posture and a proud face beneath thick, snowy hair. She'd taken only two steps, though, before she caught her toe and pitched forward, almost landing on her nose. Olivia jumped to help, but Grace was already there.

"Dear Lady Bea," she said, steadying the elegant woman. "Do have a care."

The older woman patted her cheek. "Ah, for the last Samaritan, my child. For the last Samaritan."

"That's *good,* Lady Bea."

"Indeed it is," the older woman agreed. Grace smiled as if she knew what the woman meant and ushered her on her way.

"Lady Kate's companion," Grace confided as they passed.

"Mrs. Grace!" Mrs. Bottomly screeched. She was bearing down on them like a particularly skinny elephant with her calves in tow. "We are leaving."

Peacock feathers bobbing, Mrs. Bottomly herded her hopefuls toward the door. Olivia had no choice but to follow. Lady Kate waved as Olivia passed and then hugged a burly dragoon. Olivia saw that Gervaise wasn't with the duchess anymore and instinctively knew where he would be. She almost turned back for the safety of the ballroom.

He was waiting for her, of course. Olivia had made it only a few steps into the hot night when he stepped out of the crowd.

"I've missed you, Livvie," he said, reaching out a hand. "You'll see me, won't you?"

Not a request. An order wrapped in etiquette. Olivia couldn't prevent the sick cold or trembling that beset her.

She could hold her ground, though. She could face him eye-to-eye. The days of downcast eyes and prayed-for escape were long over. "Why, no, Gervaise," she said just as amiably. "I won't."

And before he could respond, she swept down the steps and into the chaotic night.

Chapter 2

Saturday June 17, 1815

They had gone.

Olivia stood in the foyer of her little pension and stared at the battered portmanteau on the floor in front of her. She'd just run from the Namur Gate, where she'd spent the day caring for the wounded who had begun to flood into town the night before. She felt stupid with exhaustion, standing there in her stained, wet dress and trying to understand what that poor, solitary bag meant.

She'd gone to the medical tents that morning with Mrs. Bottomly's blessing, just as she had the day before. "No, no, my dear," the little woman had said, her mouth full of muffin. "You must help those poor men. We shall make do here until we can arrange transport home. Although I fear it might already be too late to leave."

It was indeed too late, but evidently only for Olivia. Thunder cracked overhead, and rain beat on the windows.

The skies had opened not twenty minutes ago, forcing everyone inside. Olivia had run for the shelter of her lodgings.

No, not her lodgings. Not anymore. Madame La Suire, the landlady, had just made that point clear when she'd briskly informed Olivia that the English madame and her so-stupid daughters had decamped not an hour after Olivia had left that morning. If Olivia chose to stay, she would need to pay the tariff herself.

Gone. While she'd been kneeling on the cobbles giving sips of water to wounded men, her employer had snuck away without her. It made no sense.

"Did Mrs. Bottomly leave anything for me, madame?" Olivia asked as the stout woman set down a pitifully small bandbox next to the portmanteau. "A letter? A small reticule?"

The reticule she'd left behind with Mrs. Bottomly, where it would be safe. Where she couldn't lose it among the crowds of injured and dying who overran the streets, the civilians who clattered about, swinging from excitement to blind panic. She had every ha'penny she'd earned in the last six months in that reticule, ready to send home to Georgie.

"She said nothing, that one," Madame said. "She gave nothing. I packed what you see here, and there is no reticule. She leaves with the oh-so-handsome English lord." Casting a severe eye at her former border, she lifted a blunt finger. "And do not try to accuse me. I thieve of no one."

Olivia couldn't seem to think. She still had blood on her hands from the young dragoon who had spilled his life out on the road not twenty feet from the gates. She'd reached him only moments before he died, gasping and pleading and so very young, just one among hundreds stumbling back from Quatre Bras.

She'd held him in her arms as his lifeblood drained onto the cobbles, and she'd watched his eyes fade and still. She'd closed those eyes—Brown. Hadn't they been brown? She had laid him down as gently as she could and run from the rain. And now she had nowhere to go, and it was all she could seem to think of.

Madame had turned away to leave Olivia in the foyer when she stopped. "The handsome English lord, he had a message, him."

Olivia started. She managed to focus on the sour-faced woman. Lightning lit the room in a blinding blue, briefly stealing her vision.

"An English lord?" she echoed. The awful portent of those three words began to break through her confusion. "What English lord?"

Thunder cracked overhead. Olivia stood dripping all over Madame's tiled floor and waited for the inevitable.

The woman actually smiled like a girl. "But, yes, the nice man, him, who arranged for the Bottomlys. He says you wait right here, and back he comes for you."

There was only one handsome Englishman still in Brussels who knew Olivia.

Suddenly everything made perfect sense. Ignoring the departing Madame La Suire, Olivia spun around and grabbed her portmanteau and bandbox. She straightened to see that rain poured in sheets against the windows. Thunder pounded and growled, and the trees whipped in a frenzy. Lightning shuddered across the lowering sky.

She couldn't go out in that. She'd be drenched in a second. Yet she didn't have a choice. Madame had already disappeared back into the kitchen, and there was no one else she could turn to for help. Besides, the men she'd been caring for were still outside, lying helpless in that deluge. She had to get back to help them.

She had just balanced her things on one arm and reached for the door when it blew open. Before Olivia could react, Gervaise strolled in.

He was dripping wet, his umbrella turned inside out from the wind. Even so, he looked perfectly put together, the rain only making his hair glisten. And he was smiling.

Olivia detested that smile, for it seemed she was the only one who saw past it.

"Excellent," he said happily as he closed the door behind him and set his umbrella against the wall. "You waited for me."

Olivia fought the sheer terror those words incited. "I did no such thing. I was just on my way back to the medical tents."

Gervaise took a considered look out the window. "In this? I think not."

"In the last fires of Armageddon if I have to. Get out of my way, Gervaise."

He stepped closer instead, so close Olivia could smell the tobacco he used, the vetiver cologne he preferred. The mingled scents turned her stomach.

She should have known. The minute she'd recognized him, she should have anticipated this very moment. She should have run.

He let his gaze drift to the neck of her dress. "Are you still wearing it, Livvie?"

It was all she could do to keep from reaching up and laying a protective hand against her chest, where her locket lay hidden beneath her dress.

He smiled. “Does it really help?”

Panic hit, a hot, sweat-producing urge to flee. *Please God, don’t let him know.*

“It’s the least I can do,” she whispered.

He nodded. “He was a beautiful boy. It’s so sad you couldn’t protect him.”

Another well-dressed threat. A reference to what he had done. What he would do again if necessary.

“It’s just one more thing I love about you, Livvie,” he said as if he meant it. “Your strong protective instincts. I could have helped, you know. Don’t you think I can now?”

She thought he’d destroy her, just as he had before.

Reaching up, he stroked a finger down her cheek. “You’re so brave, Livvie,” he said, his voice gentle and confiding. “I have to admit, I’m impressed. Going to the lengths of becoming a companion for one of the most odious cits I’ve ever had the misfortune to meet.” He flashed a mischievous smile. “She was *aux anges* when I happened on her in the Parc Royale. When I offered to help her flee the city, she was so grateful it never occurred to her to wonder why I wasn’t able to include you.”

Olivia was trembling, and it made her furious. She deliberately stepped back. “Do *you* have my reticule?”

“Only because I felt that if you had any money, you might be tempted to make an unfortunate decision. I’m the only choice you have, Livvie. This won’t be like those other times you lost your position because you were exposed. This time you're hundreds of miles from home with no way back. And you know that even if you could get there, you'd find no one to help you. Certainly not your family. As for your friends here, they won't last once they learn who you really are."

She knew he expected her to weep. To plead. She held still.

"You know I love you, Livvie," he said, stepping closer again. "Isn't it better sometimes just to give in?"

Her heart was pounding; he had to hear it. "Not to you. Never to you. Now get out of my way before I knock you down."

"And then what, my dear? Shall you get another position? Shall you throw yourself on the mercy of one of the other crow-faced women I saw you sitting with last night? They'd be more likely to chase you into the streets themselves. You, my love, are a notoriously ruined woman." Horribly, his expression grew sad. He looked so damned sincere. "I offer you so much more. I always have."

"And I have always refused. I haven't changed my mind."

"No, Liv," he said. "Not always."

She had to swallow to force the bile back down her throat.

Then he sighed. *Sighed*. "Oh, Livvie. When are you going to learn that I never give up?"

She saw how benign he looked and knew that even as he expressed nothing but concern, he was really envisioning her stripped and helpless, in his absolute control. And he would never think to question his right to have her there.

No. She had not come to this. She *would* not. Not with this man who had destroyed her life as if it were sport. She had been safe for three years. She would be so again.

If she could just get past him to the door.

He anticipated her. Before she could move, he grabbed her by the arms. Olivia bucked against him, suddenly panicked. She couldn't let him do this. She couldn't surrender after all he'd done to her. To Georgie and Jamie.

"Let me go!"

"Or what?" he asked, leaning closer. "You'll scream?"

She opened her mouth to do just that when the door blew open again, shoving him into her. Struggling for balance, he pulled her closer. She rammed her knee into his groin.

Gervaise howled and crumpled. Lurching back, Olivia took better hold of her bags and bolted for the door. But it was blocked again. Lady Kate was standing in the doorway.

Olivia shuddered to a halt. She thought she was hallucinating. She blinked, expecting the duchess to disappear. What possible reason could Lady Kate have for coming here?

The duchess walked in as if on a morning call and shut the door. Olivia opened her mouth, but she couldn't manage one word.

"Why, Gervaise," Lady Kate crooned as she noticed him curled on the floor, his hands between his legs. "And I thought you had the smoothest address in the *ton*. If this is the best you can do, you should probably return to your lessons."

"It was...an accident," he groaned, still curled in a ball.

She smiled brightly. "I would never assume otherwise."

Then she straightened to take in the sight of Olivia, standing there with her pathetic luggage clutched to her chest. "Isn't it lovely that we actually do have a certain advantage over them, though?" she asked with a conspiratorial grin. "I'm delighted you aren't too nice to attempt it."

"Your Grace—"

"Now, Olivia, haven't we just been standing side by side at the amputation table? Can you truly not call me Kate?"

Olivia still felt so slow and dull-witted; she couldn't think how to answer. All she knew was that she had to get out of this place. Gervaise was still writhing at their feet, but he would recover quickly. And here was the duchess, appearing like a provident angel, still looking sleek and neat in her bishop's blue kerseymere round gown, even after a day of wading through the worst of the wounded and a surprise thunderstorm.

Olivia felt so overwhelmed she thought she might find herself laughing like a lunatic. Could she dare ask the duchess for help? Could she put this lovely woman at risk?

"I'm sorry," she said, knowing how panicked she sounded. "Could you...? I mean, well, I must leave as soon as possible. You see, my patron, Mrs.—"

"Bottomly." The duchess nodded, carefully brushing water droplets from her skirt. "Yes, I heard she'd done a bunk. Left you in a lurch, did she?"

"I'm afraid so. I thought I'd take my things to the tents with me. I will be able to look for another position later, when things . . . when . . ."

"When we know whether we'll be speaking English tomorrow or French," Lady Kate said with a brisk nod. "Yes. Well, you won't have to worry. You have a position now. Amazingly enough, I need a companion. Dreadful having to fetch my own shawls. It's beneath a duchess's dignity, don't you think?"

Olivia gaped like a landed fish. "What of Lady Beatrice?"

Lady Kate patted her like a child. "Oh, no. Bea isn't my companion. She is my dearest friend. I am looking for someone who can help me organize my somewhat chaotic house." Taking one last look at Gervaise, who by now had made it gingerly to his feet, she took hold of Olivia and turned her to the door. "Indeed, I think we should go right now. There is a prodigious amount for you to do. Fetching, carrying, fawning . . ."

"Lady Kate, it distresses me to say this," Gervaise protested, his hand out. "But you don't know who she truly is."

Ah, Olivia thought, feeling her heart shrivel in her chest. *Here it comes.*

But Lady Kate was evidently in an eyebrow-raising mood. "Darling Gervaise, surely you know by now that while I enjoy gossip, I believe very little of it."

"But you should know—"

The duchess glared him back a step. "No. I don't think I should. And, I think I don't want to know from you, most especially if it distresses you. It would sully that beautiful Botticelli mouth of yours. No, I insist you leave it all to me."

Reaching over, she relieved Olivia of her bandbox and pushed her toward the door. "Now, Olivia, let's be on our way. My carriage is here, and we have little time. I have accepted some of the wounded into my house, and they need care."

Olivia should have protested. She should save her new friend the embarrassment of having to dismiss her when the truth came out, since that could be the only outcome. One look at the frustration that darkened Gervaise's eyes made her decision for her. She couldn't risk the truth yet, even to protect Lady Kate. Even to save her own soul.

"Thank you, Lady Kate," she said, dropping a quick curtsy, her bag still clutched close. "I am grateful."

Kate's smile was incandescent. "I'm not sure you will be once you get wind of my household. But you've committed yourself, dearest Olivia. No turning back now."

And with that, she pulled open the door to let in a blast of wind and rain. A footman waited outside with an open umbrella. Lady Kate sailed past him and ushered Olivia into the open door of her carriage, a sleek blue Berlin with ducal lozenges, which was drawn by what were undoubtedly two of the last horses in Brussels. The great shotgun Olivia saw lying across the footman's lap might have had something to do with that.

Olivia was just about to lean back against the soft cream leather squabs when something outside her window caught her attention. A second man waited outside the pension door, huddled under an umbrella against the rain. What about him made her look? she wondered.

Then the pension door opened, and Gervaise walked

out, umbrella up, to meet the man on the steps. Both turned to watch the carriage pass, and Olivia saw the second man's face.

Middle-aged, lean, neat as a pin, with hair Macassarred back into a slick cap. Recognition flared in his eyes, and he quickly ducked, as if he could hide from her.

It was too late. Olivia had already recognized him. Her husband's valet, Edward Chambers. Another unwelcome reminder of her past, another long-unanswered question. It seemed that he was now Gervaise's valet. Answer enough, she supposed.

Turning away, Olivia closed her eyes. She was still shaking with fear.

There was so much at stake. More than her own honor. More than her life. More than any woman could bear. Because Gervaise wouldn't rest until he dug out every one of her secrets to use against her. Until he tracked down the little cottage in Devon where Georgie hid and completely destroyed them all.

But she couldn't put Lady Kate at risk either. She needed to tell her the truth. If she didn't tell Lady Kate her real name, she risked Lady Kate's reputation. If she didn't tell the whole truth, she put that wonderful lady in danger.

But if she did admit the truth, Lady Kate would have to turn her out, and Gervaise hadn't exaggerated—there really was nowhere else to go. No money. No way to evade Gervaise. No way to protect her little family, and everything she had borne the last five years had been for that one purpose.

She would tell Lady Kate the truth.

Tomorrow.

When she was rested. When she could think straight. When she didn't feel such blind panic.

She just hoped Lady Kate didn't suffer for it.

The next afternoon, Olivia found herself standing on the littered, trampled ground outside the massive stone wall that circled Brussels. She had never been so exhausted in her life. Lady Kate had indeed taken eight men into the house she rented on Rue Royale, but their care had been handed over to the house staff. Help was more desperately needed outside, where the situation had grown critical. Medical tents had been erected outside the Namur and Louvain gates, but the wounded had quickly overflowed them, spilling into the narrow cobbled streets and manicured squares of the medieval city. The crisis had left Olivia without a moment to speak to Lady Kate.

Aching in every joint and dizzy with exhaustion, she leaned against the cool ocher stone of the old wall. The late afternoon sun beat unmercifully down, wounded came without cease, and the distant sound of cannon fire came and went with the wind.

The great battle had commenced. Wellington had finally met Napoleon face-to-face in a field to the south of Brussels near the town of Waterloo. Already the list of dead was too long. Handsome young Lord Hay, who had enchanted every girl at the Duchess of Richmond's ball, was gone, lost at Quatre Bras. As was the Duke of Brunswick, whose black-clad soldiers had personally carried him back to the city from the battlefield. And those striking Gordon Highlanders who had danced in their bright kilts three nights earlier slaughtered almost to a man. God knew how many more, either on the field or along the twenty-five miles that stretched from the battlefield to Brussels.

Olivia stepped to the flap of the medical tent to see that Lady Kate was helping one of the surgeons at the amputation table, her brash, bright smiles easing more than one man through the ordeal. Grace Fairchild was bent over a dying boy who clutched a miniature to his shattered chest. Women were doing work no one had ever expected of them this bloody day, and Olivia wasn't sure how they would ever recover from it.

She herself had spent the twenty-four hours since Lady Kate had rescued her bandaging and comforting and carrying until one face melded into another, only their uniforms distinguishing the smoke-smeared men. No, not men. Boys.

They were boys, so brave and so frightened and so alone in the last moments of their lives. She couldn't get around to them fast enough with the water she carried, often the only comfort they got. She couldn't find the right words to ease them. She couldn't stand the sound of crying and groaning. But even worse were the hard silences. Men with terrible injuries who stayed grim-lipped and quiet so they didn't distress their friends.

Anguish burned her throat and churned in her chest. She felt so petty and selfish, worried about escape when these boys had faced so much more. Then she saw Lady Kate looking her way, and she realized there were tears in those magnificent eyes. Olivia deliberately straightened and smiled and walked back out to the narrow cobbled streets where more wounded waited.

It could have been minutes or hours later when suddenly one of the men grabbed her by the arm. “Listen,” he urged.

Olivia wasn’t sure what he meant. She still heard the cries of agony, the pleas for help, for water, for death. She heard...

The cannons.

“They’ve stopped,” she said. She looked down at the young man, a handsome ginger-haired boy from the 20th Light Dragoons who would lose his arm before the hour was out. “Have they? Does that mean it’s over?”

He wasn’t watching her. His eyes were out of focus, as if pouring all his energy into listening. He shook his head. “I don’t know.”

Olivia helped him sip some water and a bit of Lady Kate’s last reserves of brandy. They’d had conflicting reports all day long. Wellington had won. Wellington was in full retreat, and the French were poised to invade Brussels. They’d even had to avoid a full troop of Belgian cavalry thundering through the streets crying defeat. By now, Olivia almost didn’t care who won. As long as the carnage stopped.

“Well, I expect you to ask me for at least one dance at the victory ball,” she said to the boy.

His exhausted, haggard features softened into a smile. “It would be my honor, ma’am. Ensign Charles Gregson at your service.”

Olivia stood and dipped a debutante’s curtsy. “Mrs. Livvie Grace, Ensign. The Boulanger is my favorite.”

“Why, I excel at the Boulanger, ma’am.”

Olivia capped the brandy and smiled back. “ ’Til then, Ensign Gregson,” she said, and turned to the next soldier.

A white-faced Grace Fairchild blocked her way. Grace's sweat-darkened hair was falling in an untidy lump from her bun. Soot smeared her face, and blood stained the apron that covered her practical gray dress.

"Olivia, may I ask a favor?" She looked as if she were holding herself together by the force of will alone. In the three days Olivia had known her, she had learned that Grace never asked for favors. Favors were always asked of Grace.

Olivia took hold of her arm. "Of course, Grace. What is it?"

"My father..." She looked toward the south, where the cannons had been heard all day. "I've had no word from him. He always manages to let me know how he goes. It's been..."

She swallowed, as if the words were caught in her throat. Olivia wanted to put her arms around the girl. She had a feeling, though, that Grace had long since taught herself to withstand the worst. One show of sympathy might well defeat her.

"Do you know where he is?" Olivia asked.

Grace was still looking to the south. "The Guards have been fighting to hold Château Hougoumont. From what I've heard, the battle has been fierce there all day long. Its loss would cost us the western flank, you see."

Olivia didn't see. Her time on these streets was the closest she had ever come to battle. "Is there no one to go for you?" she asked. "You've been on your leg so long, I fear it will make your injury worse."

For a moment, Grace looked confused. Then, gently, she smiled. "Oh, my leg. There's no injury, Olivia. I was born this way. I assure you, it has withstood worse."

Olivia flushed. "Oh. I'm sorry."

Grace's smile grew even softer. "Don't be silly. How could I object to kindness? Would you mind coming along, though? My father's old batman Sergeant Harper will accompany us. He is securing weapons. But he'd prefer I have a friend along in case... well..."

Wiping her hands on her own blood-streaked apron, Olivia cast a nervous glance toward the walls. "Of course. But are you sure you must go tonight? It's already gone seven, and the soldiers say that the road is all but impassable."

And those cannons stopped such a short time ago.

Grace smiled. "Not for an old campaigner." She looked down at her hands, as if they fascinated her. "Don't you see?" she asked with a stiff shrug. "I must know."

Olivia looked up the shadowed ramparts to see the civilians holding still, as if to better assess the silence. She considered the steady procession of wounded who stumbled through the gates. It was hellish here. What could it possibly be like out there where the sounds of carnage had consumed the day?

Before she could give herself the chance to truly consider it, she gave a brisk nod. "Let me tell Lady Kate. With all those young men to charm, I doubt she'll even know I'm gone."

Grace's face came the closest Olivia had ever seen to crumpling. "Thank you, Olivia. Can you fire a weapon?"

For the first time, Olivia smiled. "As a matter of fact, I can. My father had an inordinate fondness for guns. And I can't think of anything I'd rather do right now than shoot anyone who kept us from getting to your father."

Except maybe shooting Gervaise. But he'd been conspicuously absent since the duchess had rescued Olivia. Even he would never be so foolish as to challenge the duchess. She hoped.

No matter what her troubles were, though, Olivia knew they had to wait on Grace's. So she threw her shoulders back, as she'd seen soldiers do before marching away to war. "Shall we arm ourselves like grenadiers, then, and follow Sergeant Harper into the field of battle?" she asked brightly.

Grace managed a smile through the tears in her eyes. "Indeed, yes. Adventure awaits."

Only the fact that Sergeant Harper carried two shotguns across his knee ensured the success of their mission. It certainly wasn't his size. Not much taller than Olivia, he was bandy-legged and had a shock of penny-red hair. But Olivia could see his bond with Grace and knew he'd never let harm come to her.

Lady Kate offered her carriage, her horses, and her coachman. They took the first two; the coachman had gone alarmingly pale when told of their destination.

Grace was the one who drove so the sergeant could have his hands free to defend them. Not anxious to sit alone inside the carriage, Olivia climbed up between them. Even the pepperpot pistol she carried in her big apron pocket didn't soothe her as they crept down the Charleroi Road.

The land was undulating, with fields of wheat, rye, and barley spreading out in a tree-lined checkerboard to the horizon. The road was churned up, clogged with broken carts, dead horses, discarded gear, and wounded soldiers struggling to reach Brussels. Olivia saw more than one who had sat down beneath a tree for the shade and simply died. The smell was indescribable: death and smoke and blood, a stench Olivia knew she would carry in her memory the rest of her life.

She thought she had seen all manner of suffering in Brussels. One look at the men they passed dispelled that notion. To a man, they walked like the dead: haggard, soot-streaked, tattered, and bloody, holding each other up, sitting down right in the middle of the road when they could go no farther. They barely noticed the odd sight of women on their way to a battlefield. Those who did were more interested in the horses, but Sergeant Harper was enough to quell thoughts of theft.

For hours they struggled on, the late summer light guiding them. The rattle of rifle fire peppered the evening, and thick smoke rose here and there along the horizon. Olivia could see tents and lights to the east as they reached Mont St. Jean and turned west on the Nivelles Road.

"Close now, mum," Sergeant Harper said, his head on a constant swivel, his finger never off the trigger as Grace maneuvered past another overturned cart. "See the smoke?"

How could he tell? There was smoke everywhere, blurring a fading sky. The sun had set and dusk was coming on, casting the scene in even greater shadow. Olivia squinted in the direction Harper pointed, and suddenly her heart fell away.

Oh, sweet Jesus, it couldn't be real. How could anyone have survived? The fields of grain were gone. In their place was a carpet of the dead, bodies in red and blue and green, flowers blown over in a storm, lines of them, piles of them. The fading light glinted off swords and breastplates and guns, and hundreds of horses struggled in their death throes, some already bloating and twisted.

And there was screaming. Human. Equine. The awful, unearthly keening of the damned rising through the shattered trees and turning her insides to water.

"Christ preserve us," Sergeant Harper whispered, and even he sounded shaken.

Already people with lanterns were bent over the fallen, and Olivia didn't think they were all there to help. She wanted to leap down with her pistol and chase them off.

"There, I think, Sergeant," Grace said suddenly, pointing, and all their attention was drawn to another column of lethargic smoke that lifted over the trees. "The western flank."

Olivia saw it then too. A red brick wall. Shattered brick and white stucco farm buildings beyond, flames still licking at gaping windows. More bodies, piled along the walls, in among the splintered trees: alive, dead, torn apart like rag dolls. More smoke, blurring the outlines of the scene. Olivia swallowed hard and wiped her hands on her dress. How could they ever find Grace's father? How could they even face such obscenity?

"Here, I think, Sean," Grace said quietly as they reached the north wall of the compound. "By the gates."

The carriage stopped, and Grace laid the reins across the sergeant's legs.

"Let me look," Harper said, taking her hand. "You stay."

Grace patted him. "Nobody will notice women when a carriage and horses wait here."

Olivia wasn't so sure about that. Even so, Grace finally convinced Harper, and he handed Grace and Olivia down.

"We'll stay in range," Grace promised, and accepted one of the lanterns Harper passed down.

Much more slowly, Olivia followed suit. She couldn't do this. She couldn't turn over one of those poor bodies. She couldn't bear to surprise the stiff dead face of that great, mustachioed general and have to tell Grace.

At least the dusk was beginning to camouflage some of the worst. Taking one of the lanterns, Olivia followed Grace to the ragged wall.

The firing had stopped, and men had clustered by the arched wooden gate. Grace approached them and asked for her father. To a man, they shook their heads. The fighting had been too fierce, and the general had been stationed outside in the orchard.

Grace nodded and turned toward the trees. Olivia followed. She saw Grace turn over the first red-coated body and waited. Grace eased him back down, straightened, and moved on. Olivia squeezed her eyes closed a second, praying. Then she bent over her first body, and from then on focused on nothing but trying to identify a white mustache.

Night came on as they searched. A full moon rose, silvering the horrific scene. Her lantern bobbing erratically with her limp, Grace followed the eastern wall south, her movements quick and efficient. Not nearly as quick or efficient, Olivia followed. She didn't know how much later it was when she first heard it.

"My lady."

A man's voice, like so many others. She wiped the

soot off a young guardsman's face and closed his staring eyes before easing him back over.

"Please, my lady."

Olivia looked up, expecting to see a wounded soldier.

He was no wounded soldier.

Olivia blinked, sure there was smoke in her eyes. That she was just too tired. But when she opened her eyes again, he was still there, not five feet away. Chambers, Gervaise's valet. And he was clad in the red coat of a guardsman, as if he belonged on this killing ground.

"Please, my lady," he said to her, his severe face screwed up in something close to terror. "Help me."

"What are you doing here?" she rasped, looking around.

Then she froze. Oh, God. If Chambers was here, where was Gervaise? She realized then how far she'd wandered. She was alone in the trees except for Chambers and the dead and the deepening night.

"It's all right, my lady," he said, as if hearing her. "He is not here."

"Stop calling me that," Olivia snapped. "I am Mrs. Olivia Grace."

"You must help," Chambers begged.

"Who must I help?" Olivia demanded. "You?"

"Him."

"Gervaise?"

Chambers just shook his head. Olivia waited, wondering what the rest of the joke was, ready to tell him that no matter what, she had no intention of helping him. She had walked away from his world five years ago, been chased, like a thief with a purloined apple in her hand. She had closed that time away and had no intention of opening it back up again.

She turned to leave. Chambers was quicker, grabbing her by the wrist.

"Let me *go,*" she demanded, yanking back.

He ignored her. "I stole a horse and followed you here," he said, inexorably pulling her into the trees. "I thank God it was here you were bound. I would have dragged you all the way across the battlefield if needed."

She continued to struggle, even as he guided her over and around the dead who lay beneath the blasted trees.

"Let me *go,*" she demanded again. "I have to help my friend."

"You have to help *me*."

Her heart was beginning to stutter. This couldn't be happening. She was dreaming. She'd fallen asleep in one of the tents, and now she was paying for her loss of control.

Chambers stopped. She almost slammed into his back. They had reached a stretch of woods where the bodies lay thick among the ruined fruit trees. The moonlight bathed them with a cold hand; the smell of cordite was sharp. Chambers grabbed the lantern from Olivia's hand and went on his knees by one of the bodies.

"Look," he commanded.

She looked. She stopped breathing. She was sure her heart had stopped beating.

It couldn't be. It *couldn't*. He was bloody, so bloody, with a ruined neck cloth tied around his upper arm and another around his leg. His hair was matted with the blood that covered his face and neck and chest. He was sitting, leaning against the tree as if he'd fallen asleep there after a prodigious drunk. His eyes, those beautiful blue-green eyes she'd once thought so honest and dear, were closed.

"Is he dead?"

For just a flash of an instant, the thought gave her vicious pleasure. It would serve him right, after what he'd done to her. But the feeling passed, just as it always did, and she was left with the grief that lived in its shadow.

"Not yet," Chambers said, laying a hand against that bloody face. "Please help him, my lady. He needs you."

"I think he'd disagree with you," Olivia corrected him, unable to move, curling her hands against the compulsion to kneel. To take that battered body in her arms, where it belonged. To pummel at him for the pain he'd caused and then sob her heart out over him. "He threw me away, Chambers. He left me in no doubt as to what I meant to him. Nothing has changed."

"He needs you," the valet begged. "He can't be discovered. Not like this."

"Like what?" she demanded. "So he joined up. That's very patriotic of him. Ask one of the other Guards to help."

She squinted, suddenly uncertain. The Guards had defended this place in their bright red jackets and gleaming brass buttons. He was in blue. Only his stock and cuffs were red.

She'd seen those. Seen many of them, piled on the battlefield to the east. "What uniform is that?" she demanded, suddenly praying she was wrong. "I don't recognize..."

But she did. She stopped. Stepped back. Of course

she recognized it. She was surrounded by them, soldiers fallen in an attempt to take the château from the Guards.

French soldiers.

John Phillip William Wyndham, scion of one of the oldest, most respected families in England, a belted earl, lay on an English battlefield clad in a French uniform.

Her husband was a traitor.

Chapter 3

Olivia jumped back. "Jesus!"

A French uniform. Dearest God in heaven.

She hadn't seen Jack in five years. Not since that day he'd slammed the door on her and had his bailiff escort her from Wyndham Abbey.

Alongside her, Chambers was wringing his hands. "I don't know what happened, my lady, and that's the truth."

Olivia couldn't seem to move. Her friend was out there, still combing the dead for her father. Her enemy was back in Brussels waiting for another chance to attack. And she was standing in front of the man she'd once vowed to honor and obey, and he was dressed in a uniform that branded him a turncoat.

"Please, my lady," Chambers begged. "He needs your help."

"Again you mistake me, Chambers," she said, still unable to take her eyes off her husband. "I am no longer anyone's lady." She pointed to the man who had once owned her heart. "He saw to that. You all did."

Five years she'd survived without any help from him. Five long, terrible years, until she had decided that she was finally quit of him. Her hand went instinctively to her locket.

"As God is my witness," Chambers said, "I have no idea how he got here. I got a message to meet him here. By the time I reached him, he was as you see." Chambers motioned. "No one can find him like this."

"Indeed?" Olivia asked. "And you think I should be the one to help him? Why? For the memory of Tristram?"

Tristram, sweet Tris, who had died out on that empty heath at dawn with no one but her to mourn him.

"I suggest you call Jack's cousin Gervaise," she said, only still upright by will alone. "After all, he is your new master."

Chambers looked over at her. "Do you really think Mr. Gervaise is the person to help him right now?"

Olivia squeezed her eyes shut. She clenched her hands into her skirts to keep them still. Of course, Gervaise wouldn't help. Gervaise wouldn't waste a moment to inform the world—most regretfully, of course—that his cousin the earl had been caught in a treasonous position.

His mother was French, you know, he'd say with a sad shake of his head. It would be enough to condemn Jack.

Her heart was thundering. Pain squeezed her temples, and she knew she was sweating. How could Chambers ask this of her?

But she had once loved Jack so. She'd thought it a miracle that he'd asked her to marry him: her, the daughter of a mere vicar who'd relied on Jack's father for his livelihood. She had lived as Jack's wife for eleven months and prayed for another three years that he would come to his senses and bring her home.

But she'd long since gotten over that idiocy. He wasn't going to change his mind. He wasn't going to beg for her return. He wasn't going to ask her forgiveness. She had no reason to help him.

"You really don't know how he got here?" she asked.

"The note he sent was the first I'd heard from him in two years."

She nodded. She tried desperately to fan her outrage.

"What should we do?" Chambers asked, as if he'd already assumed her cooperation.

She couldn't do this. She was already living on a thin edge. God only knew what could happen if she helped Jack.

It didn't matter. She couldn't walk away.

"Get him out of this bedamned uniform," she snapped.

And suddenly she was on her knees, reaching out to touch Jack's cheek. God, how was she ever going to survive this again?

She looked up to see Chambers just staring at her. Probably appalled at her language. She paid him no attention. Laying her fingers against Jack's throat, she checked for a pulse.

Thready, yes, but regular. He was alive. "Strip one of the British dead of his jacket," she ordered. Closing her eyes again, this time in a brief prayer for the sacrilege she was about to commit, she steeled herself to move. "I'll undress Jack."

Reaching out a trembling hand, she began to unbutton the bloodied brass buttons on Jack's coat. The last time she had unbuttoned Jack's coat, they'd been clawing at each other, too impatient to get their hands on each other to worry about popped buttons or ripped seams. He'd been insatiable for her. She'd been mesmerized by him.

It hadn't been enough.

"Get a jacket from someone who suffered a bloody wound," she instructed Chambers. "Nobody can question his appearance."

At least she didn't have to bother with the gray overalls. They were ubiquitous among both armies. But even the coat was a struggle. He was dead weight in her hands.

He was thinner. No matter what else she'd closed away, she had never forgotten his body. He was still as hard, his limbs long and elegant, his shoulders broad. Her hands itched to explore that beloved territory. But the well-tailored jacket hung from his once-broad chest, and his hips jutted.

She couldn't think about that. Nor could she let herself dwell on the fact that this uniform could have been tailored specifically for the Jack he'd been twenty pounds ago.

"There was a dispatch bag on him," Chambers whispered from a few feet away. "I put his personal things in it and hid it under him before I sought you out."

Olivia unearthed the bag when she rolled Jack over. "Did you check its contents?"

"No. Wasn't my business."

Taking a second, she slung the bag over her shoulder beneath her apron. She'd go through it later, when she had time.

"My lady—"

"Don't," she snapped, her arms once again full with Jack's painfully familiar weight. "I'm holding on to my position by my fingernails. One mention of the Countess of Gracechurch, and even the Duchess of Murther will have to show me the street. Now, that might appeal to you, but it won't help Jack at all, will it?"

Chambers stopped a few feet away, a bloody, soot-stained Guards' jacket and officer's sash in his hands. He opened his mouth as if intent on answering. One look at her obviously made him reconsider.

"I'll need help getting him back," he said, handing over the clothing. "The horse is gone."

She shook her head. "No. You can't expect it of me."

"Please," Chambers said, and she heard his desperation.

She squeezed her eyes shut and prayed for strength. "Try and get him to the road. We'll be passing by."

Careful not to further injure him, they slipped his bloody arm into the sleeve and pulled the jacket closed. Olivia was sweating in earnest now. She had to wipe moisture from her eyes as she tied the crimson sash around Jack's waist and shoved the betraying blue jacket away.

"I'm going back to help my friend now," she said, climbing to her feet and rubbing her hands on her apron.

Chambers looked up from where he hovered over his former master. "Thank you...Mrs. Grace. I won't forget it."

Because she couldn't help it, Olivia took one final look at Jack. Then, deliberately crushing a spasm of grief, she turned her back on them both and walked away.

Sergeant Harper was waiting around the corner by the

north gate, the shotguns resting on his knees, his attention beyond the open gate into the château yard.

"I haven't had any luck, Sergeant," Olivia said, hoping he didn't notice how badly her voice shook. "Have you seen Grace?"

"Yes'm," he said, motioning with his head. "She went in there. Would you go to her? I got a bad feeling."

Olivia nodded and walked through the broken, blasted gates into the north courtyard. There were more dead here. More bright red bundles piled in untidy hillocks, more broken hearts. There were others wandering about, blank-faced Guards checking for wounded or just stumbling toward rest. Olivia took a look around, but she didn't see Grace anywhere among the remains of the outbuildings and great house.

"Grace? Where are you, dear?"

There was a moment of silence, the courtyard thick with smoke and the smell of carnage. Olivia thought she'd never see smoke again without returning to this place.

"I'm here," Grace called from beyond the shattered house.

And Olivia knew. It was in the flat tone of Grace's voice. Finality.

Ah, God. Poor thing.

Lifting her skirt away from the blood that puddled in the cobbles, Olivia walked past the still-burning buildings to find another littered courtyard. Grace was there, crouched in the shadow of a little stone chapel, her skirts pooled about her, the hem drenched in more blood. One of the red-coated bodies was in her arms.

She looked up, and Olivia saw the rivers of tears that

had scoured away the smoke and grime from Grace's cheeks. Her expression was calm, though, almost as if she'd finally played out a scene she'd anticipated a thousand times over.

"Oh, Grace," Olivia said, crouching down beside her friend. "I'm so sorry."

Grace lifted a small smile. "He knew I'd come. He waited to bid me good-bye," she said, stroking that lined face that rested so peacefully in her arms. "He was supposed to be back at headquarters, you know. Wellington had detached him to Quartermaster Corps. He was just too old this time. But he wouldn't allow his boys to face this without him."

Olivia laid her hand atop Grace's where it rested on her father's blood-soaked chest. "Do I say he died as he wanted?"

Grace's smile grew, and with it the bittersweet light in her eyes. "Indeed you do," she said. "Thank you."

Olivia wished she could give Grace the time she needed. The hour was getting late, though, and they had a long way to go.

"We need to get him back, dear. I think there are scavengers about."

Grace's attention sharpened, and she looked out toward the gates. "Oh, yes," she said, giving her father a few final pats. "I should have thought of that. You aren't safe here."

"Shall I send the sergeant to you?"

"Would you?"

Olivia reached over to wipe the tears that scoured Grace's cheeks. "I have the most curious urge to wield a shotgun. I think I'll look quite fearsome, don't you?"

When he saw Olivia walk out of the big gate, Sergeant Harper secured the reins and set down the guns. He'd known, of course.

"I'll take over here, Sergeant," Olivia said. "The general needs you."

The little man's eyes were suspiciously bright. "You sure you can manage, ma'am?"

Olivia took a second to stroke the noses of the restless horses. "Mine is not the difficult task, Sergeant. I'll be fine."

He nodded and hopped down. "Thank you, ma'am. I'll be back in a flash, then."

It was then, oddly, that Olivia finally noticed that the sergeant had only one leg. His left foot was made of wood, and it took him a minute to catch his balance on it. She waited until he marched into the courtyard to attend his general one last time, his limp only slight. Then she climbed up to take his place atop the coachman's perch.

It was an excellent vantage point. Too excellent, Olivia realized. The unearthly light of the moon sapped the color from the carnage around her. She could no longer identify the uniforms. The dead had lost their identities. They were no longer friend or enemy, just thousands and thousands of boys who would never go home.

Please don't let Jack be responsible for any of this, she prayed into the darkness. *Don't let me betray these fallen boys by helping him.*

When Grace returned, it was with an honor guard of six of the surviving Guardsmen who gently carried the general's body to the carriage, led by Sergeant Harper. Another officer guided a limping Grace by the elbow and was bent over her, talking. Grace nodded, her gaze never leaving the body of her father.

Olivia tightened the reins to calm the horses. Sergeant Harper opened the carriage door, and the men deposited their general inside. After bestowing parting kisses on each of the men, Grace followed. Sergeant Harper climbed up alongside Olivia, and she could see tear tracks on his homely face.

Ah, to have been mourned like that. To have a daughter with the courage to brave a battlefield to search for you. To have a line of battered, smoke-stained soldiers snap off a salute as your hearse door closed and a faithful friend to see you home.

"If you don't mind, Sergeant," Olivia said, "I'm not a very good whip. I am a deft hand with a weapon, though. My papa insisted we all be able to hunt. It was his obsession."

His eyes glassy, the sergeant nodded and took the reins from her. Olivia settled on the seat and arranged the weapons more fully across her lap.

"I thank you, ma'am," he said. "It's a good thing you're doing this day, all right."

"Nonsense, Sergeant," she said, shoving her straggling hair out of her face before she thumbed the triggers. "I was merely looking for a bit of adventure."

With a small smile on his face, he clucked the horses.

They made it no farther than the edge of the orchard before Harper pulled them to a stop. A group of wounded blocked his way. In the center stood Chambers, a pistol in his hand and Jack at his feet. Olivia blinked, momentarily disoriented. For a fraction of a second, she'd forgotten. She saw Jack and felt her courage falter.

"We need a ride," Chambers said quietly, as if he were indeed an officer who'd bled on this field with the rest. "I'd appreciate your help."

The sergeant bristled. "Don't be pointin' that popper at me, boyo. Lots o' men are needin' help this night."

Chambers lifted the gun. "Good. Then you won't mind taking a few."

"I won't—"

"Please," Olivia begged, her hand on the sergeant's arm. "Surely we can help."

"Olivia?" Grace asked from the carriage, and Olivia turned back to see her friend leaning out of the window.

It was all Olivia could do to look down at that sad, strained face. She could barely speak past the dread of what she had to do.

"These men need a ride," she said. "Couldn't we take them up, at least to the field hospital?"

Grace looked up at her, as if she could discern Olivia's intent by the frail light from the carriage lamps.

"Please, Grace," Olivia begged. "For me."

Grace said not another word. She just opened the door and motioned for Chambers to carry Jack inside. Knowing that she had just sealed her own fate, Olivia hopped down to help.

Chapter 4

He was…he…

Was he dead, then? Was this hell? There was…he was…He couldn't think….Too much pain…too much…

But he had to get on. He had to find…Who did he have to find? What did he have for them?

He couldn't…remember….

"Oh, stop, Sergeant," Olivia begged, her hand out to where he was setting another stitch in Jack's leg. "His eyes just opened. He can feel that."

The sergeant straightened and gave his back a cracking stretch. They'd been in Lady Kate's second-best guest room for the past two hours, cleaning and stitching Jack's wounds, washing his battered body. Olivia felt so drained she was shaking. And Jack had just opened his eyes, even if only for a moment.

Sergeant Harper set down his needle and thread and reached over to pull up Jack's eyelid. "If you'll pardon me sayin', ma'am," he said, his voice gravelly with exhaustion, "I've seen my share of head knocks like this one, and won't the captain be opening and closing his eyes for a few days before we know if they'll stay open? And, sure now, he don't really feel a thing. At least, not as he'll remember later."

Olivia fought a wave of exhausted tears. "You're certain?"

Sergeant Harper obviously saw them and patted her on the shoulder with his wide, callused hand. "You really should be after gettin' a bit of sleep, ma'am. I'm fine here. Really."

Olivia dredged up a stiff smile and gave her hair another shove out of her eyes. She'd never forget this hellish night as long as she lived. It had taken them five hours to travel the nightmarish road to Brussels, to end up with three new wounded in the house, including Jack. Olivia still wasn't quite sure how it had happened. She was certain she'd meant to leave him in the medical tents with Chambers. But Chambers was gone, and Jack was in Lady Kate's second-best bedroom.

"Don't worry, Sergeant," she said to Grace's protector. "I won't fail you."

"Haven't so far, ma'am," he said, and turned back to work.

She hadn't had the courage to let anyone know who Jack was. Not until she had the chance to talk to the duchess. But she'd given up pretending she didn't know him. Given up lying to herself that she cared no more for his welfare than any of the other ten men sleeping in the house. Every time the sergeant had driven the needle through Jack's skin, she'd flinched. When she'd heard the click of Lady Kate's tweezers as he dug out shrapnel from Jack's leg. When she'd counted up the injuries Jack had suffered and seen older scars she didn't recognize.

She wanted to stand stoic and cold against him. But this was the man she had taken into her body, the man she'd worshiped as if he were a young god. The man whose mere touch had ignited a white-hot intoxication in her that had never cooled.

Even now she felt it, as if his skin sizzled with an energy only her body recognized. As if once met, that force could never be broken; fine tendrils that coiled around them and pulled inexorably together, sparking fire and life and want.

She didn't want him. She *couldn't*. But, oh, sweet Lord, she ached for the memory of him.

"Here now, ma'am," Harper interrupted.

Olivia started back to the present. "Of course, Sergeant."

Reaching over, she snipped the ends of a knot. They were sewing an angry slash that stretched from Jack's jaw to his left temple, which was sure to leave a terrible scar. He would never again be the devastating, perfect Jack Wyndham who had cut such a swath through the *ton*. He'd carry this day with him for the rest of his life.

It made no difference to Olivia. She'd fallen in love with him without ever seeing his face.

She'd heard him through the hedges. It had been a Saturday, she remembered, and she'd been on her way to bring flowers to her father's church in Little Wyndham. She knew now it had been Jack's sister Maddie he'd been with. But at the time, all she had heard was his laugh, and it had stopped her in her tracks.

For the longest moment, she'd been unable to do anything but stand there, the flowers clutched to her chest, her eyes closed. His laughter had sounded like church bells to her, a carillon of unfettered joy and strength and freedom. It had been the sound of a man who knew his place in the world and who reveled in it.

Even now she couldn't look down on him without feeling amazed. Of course, she'd fallen in love with him. By the time she'd met him, all of the county and two-thirds of the *ton* had been at his feet. That this man with the laughing sea-green eyes had loved her back had been a miracle.

The only miracle greater than that had been looking down on their baby and seeing those same bright, winsome eyes.

Olivia squeezed her eyes closed. *No.* She would not think about Jamie. He lived in a place she had to keep so tightly closed, she could almost pretend he had never existed.

She was so focused on her thoughts she almost didn't hear the knocks on the door behind her. Turning, she saw Lady Bea walk in, Lady Kate right behind her.

Olivia held her breath. She couldn't believe Lady Kate wouldn't recognize Jack, even as battered and bruised as he looked right now. Lady Kate seemed to know everyone, and Jack had definitely been someone.

But she barely looked toward the bed.

"How is he coming along, Sergeant?" the duchess asked.

Lady Bea said not a word, just stepped up to the bed, her patrician features screwed up in distress as she bent to examine Jack. Olivia couldn't take her eyes off the elegant old woman, terrified she was going to straighten and cry out, *What is this traitor doing in our house?*

Alongside her, Harper straightened. "I'm thinkin' it'll be a long slog for the poor lad, all right," he said.

"Will he live?" Lady Kate asked.

Olivia held her breath.

"Well, now, Your Grace," Harper said, considering the slack features of his patient. "That's something I couldn't say. Sure isn't he due for a fever, after sitting out in the mud and filth of that battle? And then to be afflicted with this great wallop to the head? The best I can say is that we'll have to take it a day at a time."

"You don't think I should call a doctor and have him bled?"

"Punting on River Tick," Lady Bea unaccountably proclaimed, her head tilted like a bright bird.

Olivia was too tired to do anything more than stare. Oddly enough, Lady Kate was nodding. "Indeed, my dear. He is in short supply already. Any idea who he is, Harper?"

Harper shrugged. "A captain of the First Guards."

Olivia still couldn't relax. "He'll tell us when he wakes," she assured them, hoping the duchess would be satisfied and go. She would have to know soon, of course, but Olivia wanted a chance to explain first.

If only she knew what she could possibly say.

"Odysseus!" Lady Bea suddenly chirped as if making a huge discovery. She turned to Lady Kate, as if for validation, then gave Jack a pat on his bruised, filthy cheek.

Lady Kate met Lady Bea's bright smile with a narrowed gaze. "Ah," was all she said.

Olivia felt completely at sea. What did the old woman

mean? Then Lady Bea turned to peer at her, as if trying to place her, and Olivia felt the blood drain from her face.

Please, no. Not yet. Not 'til I'm ready.

Evidently her prayer was answered, because Bea just patted her cheek and made for the door.

"Well, then," Lady Kate stated with a brisk nod. "I'm sure you don't need our help. When you finish, Sergeant, call my butler Finney, and he'll send someone up to watch our patient so you can rest."

Olivia wished she could do just that. Instead, feeling deathly cold, she turned to face the little duchess and her confounding friend. "Not until I speak with you, Lady Kate."

Kate made a perfectly outrageous moue. "Yes, I heard about how you commandeered my coach. All I can say is it's a good thing your patients truly needed us. I'd hate to think you were simply picking up passing officers on a lark."

"Lady Kate, please."

"No, Olivia. Not now. You brought us two other fresh officers, and the wounded keep pouring into town without cease. Now, Grace, Bea, and I have slept. I want you to also. I've put you in the sitting room of my personal suite. It's the only room besides the front parlor and larder that has space, and I didn't think you would want to bed down with the cheese. Finney will show you the way."

"But—"

Lady Kate straightened and donned her mantle of hauteur. "I don't see how I can keep you in my employ if you're always arguing. Come see me after you sleep. Not a moment sooner."

And without another word, she ushered Lady Bea out

and closed the door behind them, leaving Olivia to feel equal parts guilt, relief, and shame. She couldn't put off telling the duchess. Jack's life might depend on it. *All* their lives might depend on it. But still, she couldn't help being grateful for her small reprieve.

"Got another thread to cut, ma'am," Harper said behind her, and she turned back to her work.

Stopping a moment at the top of the stairs, Lady Kate looked into the early morning shadows that defied the forest of candles she always kept lit. Satisfied that there was no one but Bea to witness her behavior, she gave in to the urge for a most unduchesslike stretch. She swore she could hear every bone in her back crack as she arched herself backward like a ballet dancer.

"Oh, Bea," she said, bending over at the waist until she could touch her fingertips to her toes. "I've been wanting to do this for days."

"Princess Caroline," her friend said with a sniff, which made Kate grin.

"If you're saying that a good stretch is unbecoming in a duchess, I already know. It's why I would only do it in front of you, my dear. And only here, where I know I won't destroy any of Monsieur's furniture."

"French," Lady Bea sneered, her fine-honed features smug.

Kate laughed. "A bit ornate for my tastes too," she admitted as she took in the excess around her.

The gentleman from whom she was renting had fallen victim to the excesses of rococo without a murmur of protest. Every available surface of the little town house was frescoed, gilded, and festooned. There wasn't an inch of ceiling that wasn't weighted with ornate plasterwork, and the furniture was so fragile even her twelve-year-old tiger was afraid to sit on it.

A fitting setting for a duchess, old Monsieur Menard had assured her back in March when he'd showed her around the prime location on Rue Royale, right across from the Parc Royale. Kate couldn't help but think that Menard would have an apoplexy if he knew how his fussy, feminine rooms were being put to use.

"It is a unique design for a hospital," Kate mused, thinking of all the wounded who crowded the rooms.

And morgue. She could hardly forget that Grace Fairchild's father waited in the cold little wine cellar.

Shaking her head, she led Lady Bea down the ornate pink marble staircase. *Bloody damn hell,* she thought. She had seen a lot in her life. She'd faced her share of demons and disasters, which her valiant Bea could attest to. But she had never experienced anything like these last few days.

And there was still so much to do. Grace needed to bury her father, and the wounded needed care. The other British visitors in town had to be convinced to ante up desperately needed supplies. And Kate needed to find out just what was going on in her second-best guest room.

"I did understand you correctly upstairs, didn't I?" she asked Bea as they continued down the stairs. "You recognized our guest? That's Jack Wyndham in the flesh or I'm Marie Antoinette."

Lady Bea patted her on the arm. "Odysseus."

Kate slid her hand along the banister. "And our Olivia knew who he was."

Lady Bea nodded emphatically. "Penelope."

Kate skidded to a halt, almost upending her friend. *"What?"*

Lady Bea gave her a hard nod. "Penelope."

Kate gaped. "Good Lord. How can you be sure?"

Lady Bea shrugged.

Kate looked upward, as if she could see inside that room where Jack Wyndham lay unconscious and the woman caring for him wouldn't admit to knowing him.

"Well bless my undeserving soul," she said, shaking her head. "No wonder she wasn't forthcoming about his identity. What do you think we should do?"

Bea took a considered look up the stairs. "Pray."

"Indeed." Kate sighed. "Well, I just hope we can keep everyone in the dark about her identity for a few days. We need her to help with the wounded."

Just then, Finney stepped out from the library, where several of their wounded lay. Kate always smiled at seeing the hulking, stoop-shouldered Finney with his cauliflower ear and prehensile brow. He'd been a mediocre fighter. He wasn't much better at butling. But he provided excellent security.

"The men is all fed, Y'r Grace," he said in a low growl. "Any orders f'r the house?"

"Indeed there are, Finney," she said, retrieving a pair of bonnets from the hall table. "Lady Bea and I are going out. See that Mrs. Grace gets some sleep. Put something in her meal if necessary. I have a feeling she'll be needing her strength in the next few days. As, I fear, shall we."

"She'll never bubble to it, ma'am," Finney said, opening the front door for them.

Smiling brilliantly for him, she turned to slip her arm through a thoughtful Lady Bea's. "I wonder if she'll have the courage to tell us the truth before we have to confront her with it."

"Perilous," Lady Bea answered with a frown.

"Yes it is," Kate assured her, suddenly very serious. "Perilous indeed."

Chapter 5

Olivia had been waiting for three days for the chance to speak to Lady Kate. She was beginning to think the duchess was going out of her way to avoid her. It wasn't that the duchess wasn't busy. They all were. They hadn't even had time to bury Grace's father. His body lay in the cool cellar on a plank, with candles at each end and a staff member to sit with him.

Grace spent most of her hours out at the tents, where the wounded poured in without relief. Lady Kate divided her time between the tents and the homes of British visitors, where she mercilessly bullied them into donating supplies. Olivia supervised the care of the men recuperating in the house. Considering the fact that she'd seen Gervaise loitering outside a few times, she was only too glad to stay in.

Olivia hadn't had much of a chance to sit with Jack. There were too many others who also needed care. But every free minute she had, she spent in his hot, stifling room, waiting for him to wake, fighting the surges of hope when he opened his eyes, even briefly. Surviving the dread and disquiet when he closed them again, never really waking.

She was beginning to feel stretched to the point of breaking. Her hands shook constantly, her stomach roiled, and her heart stuttered at odd sounds and surprises. She had so many secrets to hide. So few options. So little time before Lady Kate would be forced to show her the door.

Every time she tried to rest, she was followed to sleep by dreams of all that she feared, all she'd survived and seen these last days. The wounded, the dying, the mutilated, hundreds of them, all looking to her for help she couldn't give.

And then, always, Jack. Jack reflected in her little Jamie's eyes. In the memories of those last terrible days of her marriage. In the dreadful puzzle he now brought to her door.

He wasn't a traitor. Olivia would swear to it. But she didn't know how to defend him against the evidence. If she claimed that Jack had been found with an Allied regiment, it would take only a matter of hours for the lie to be exposed. Society was simply too closed, all related by blood or school or club. They would know to the day when Jack had enlisted and under whose command.

She had his dispatch bag, but she hadn't had the courage to open it. She knew she was putting everyone in more danger, but shouldn't Jack have the chance to explain first? The battle had been won. The city was still in turmoil, trying to deal with the dead and wounded. Would Jack's secret really make a difference?

She knew it very possibly could. Even so, she waited.

By the third morning, Olivia wondered if he would ever wake. Coming up from her morning rounds among the wounded, she opened the door into his room to find that he still slept, watched over by Sergeant Harper's redoubtable wife. "How are things in here?"

"Ah, mornin' to ya, missus," the broad, platter-faced woman said with a smile as she hefted her considerable self from the frail chair. "The men are all fed and ready f'r the day, then?"

Olivia couldn't quite take her eyes from where Jack slept, his features so curiously still. "They are, and all improving."

"Good on 'em," the woman said, rolling up the socks she'd been darning. "Now, if we can only get this poor *créatúr* here to wake so we know what name to give him, I'd be happy."

Olivia looked up. "Has he woken at all?"

"Not so much woken," Mrs. Harper said, considering Jack a moment. "Mumblin', like. Callin' f'r his lady."

Olivia found herself holding her breath. "Pardon?"

Slanting Olivia a sly smile, Mrs. Harper leaned close. "His fancy piece, I'm thinkin'. Named Mimi. Wasn't he after speakin' French to her an' all? Fair turns a girl's head."

Olivia looked up sharply, but Mrs. Harper didn't appear suspicious. She just looked fierce, as she always did.

"Indeed," Olivia agreed vaguely. "Mimi."

Amazing how one word could send a shaft of pain right through a person.

Mrs. Harper didn't seem to notice. Gathering her things, she turned for the door. "Well, then, now you're here, I'll be off to harass that prissy excuse f'r a cook into makin' some nice potato soup for the lads. Sure and if I don't think himself here is a few pounds shy of fighting weight." She shot Olivia a close look. "You shouldn't turn down some soup y'rself, missus. Won't do to fade away now that all the excitement's over."

"Thank you," Olivia said, settling onto the chair. "It sounds wonderful."

Mrs. Harper shrugged and was turning to leave when the door slammed open. Olivia jumped. A skinny boy with oversized ears, nose, and chin stood in the doorway, wearing a ludicrous powdered wig and spanking-new crimson and gold livery.

"Whatcher think o' this?" he demanded with an engaging grin, arms held wide. "Don't I look the proper tiger?"

"Hush, now!" Mrs. Harper snapped. "Y'r a proper jailbait!"

"'Course I is," he assured her brightly. "You think a name like Thrasher comes from some fancy gentry mort? Me mam was a 'ore, and me dad rode the three-legged mare for being a bridle cull. And afore 'Er Graceship took me up f'r 'er tiger, I were the best cutpurse in the Rookeries."

Olivia had spent enough time in Thrasher's old neighborhood to be able to interpret his cant. His mother had been a whore and his father hanged for a highwayman. She also knew that Lady Kate had hired him when he'd tried to slice her reticule from her arm one night in Covent Garden.

Olivia shook her head. Leave it to Lady Kate. "You look quite distinguished," she told Thrasher gravely.

He grinned down at his sartorial splendor. "'Course, I'll 'ave to ditch the duds when I'm scopin' out the lay f'r her ladyship, won't I? Nobody'd talk to a cove looks like this."

"Have you some scopin' for us now, ya little heathen?" Mrs. Harper demanded. "Or are you just here to harass the ill?"

"Oh, no." He strove to look serious. "Y'r needed in the kitchen, Miz 'Arper. Cook 'as taken y'r curse on him bad and won't come out o' the larder. Says he needs to surround 'isself in chickens to keep his 'air."

Mrs. Harper huffed with visible satisfaction. "Little skint wouldn't let me make a proper broth. Well, he will now, or won't I be forced to put the curse o' the Dubhlainn Sidhe on him."

"Good Lord," Olivia said. "What's that?"

Mrs. Harper grinned, which was more frightening than her scowls. "Nothin' at all. Made it up. But *he* don't know it."

With a full laugh, Thrasher galloped back downstairs. Still smiling, Olivia turned back to a still-silent Jack.

"I've heard that sometimes it helps if you talk to them," Mrs. Harper said suddenly from behind her.

Olivia jumped again. She'd thought Mrs. Harper had already gone. The woman still stood in the doorway, and for the first time appeared less than sanguine. She was looking down at Olivia's hand, which was when Olivia realized she was holding Jack's.

She let go. "Talk?" she asked, her heart thudding.

Mrs. Harper motioned toward Jack. "Them's as is in a sleep like that. When me ole da fell off the roof, sure didn't me mam yell at him all day and all night to get his lazy sorry bones off the bed and see to the cows? And didn't he wake up, sure as Oisín, two days later, sayin' he'd heard the angel of God tormentin' him over his duties." She shrugged. "Might work."

Olivia turned to look at Jack. Talk to him? And just what would she say? She couldn't talk about the two of them. She couldn't speak of Wyndham Abbey and his family as if she still belonged there. It had been five years. She could barely even think of his family without feeling sick.

Except the twins, who had wept for her, and Neddy, who'd tried so hard to help, even if it meant admitting that his older brother was not quite as heroic as he'd thought.

And Georgie. But she would not speak of Georgie. Not here. Not now.

She could not talk to Jack. She *would* not.

She did. For minutes, then hours. Leaning close so only Jack could hear, she spoke of the Abbey she'd known, the nearby town of Little Wyndham, the small Norman church her father had served, where she'd sung in the choir and chaired the fete committee. Where they'd been married that rainy May morning.

She peered at Jack's hand in hers, once so elegant and now scratched and callused. "The lambs and calves are growing," she whispered, rubbing his fingers. "The wheat will be getting high. And the hops for your special ale. Brewer John will be walking the edge of the field to judge it. And Ned will be waiting for you to come home to help him pick a new pair for his curricle. Maude and Maddie will want you to take them to the local assembly so they can show you off, and your father"—she choked a moment, took a breath—"he'll have that new Manton to show off. It's time to go home, Jack. They miss you."

He was so quiet. It was all she could think of as she sat next to him, talking in the dimness of the waning sun. She could never remember him ever being so still. He'd had such energy, such delight in everything he did, be it riding or boxing or fencing, or even, when the mood struck him, stripping off his jacket and helping bring in the crops.

One of Olivia's sweetest memories was of coming upon him in the farthest fields of the home farm, his bare throat golden and gleaming with the sun, his eyes that eerie green of early spring, his shoulders shaking with laughter as he scythed the wheat with two of his childhood friends.

He'd looked like a young god, and so his people had thought him. He hadn't simply been the marquess's son. He'd been "their Master Jack." Every milkmaid within a ten-mile radius had timed her route to his daily rides. Not one farmer's wife could resist filling him with warm meat pies and cool ale. He'd never passed the local inns without stopping to trade outrageous tales with the denizens. He'd been a force of nature, and all the people he'd touched had gloried in him.

Even her. *Especially* her. He'd been like nothing she'd ever encountered in her small, staid life. As a vicar's daughter, she'd been used to moving parishes at the whims of the church and defining her world by her chores. She'd liked the life, for she enjoyed being active too. But she'd been a small brown trout in a slow-moving stream, until Jack Wyndham had seen her and yanked her out into his bright morning sun.

"Oh, Jack," she sighed. "Where have you gone?"

"Right here."

Olivia swore her heart stopped. She rocketed off her

chair, certain she'd imagined the raspy sound of Jack's voice.

But she hadn't. His eyes were open. Mesmerizing, mythical sea-green, all but glowing against the stark pallor of his face.

"Sweet Jesus, Jack," she cried, her hand pressed to her chest, where her heart thundered beneath her locket.

He was awake, looking around the room as if he'd misplaced something. "Where is it?" he asked, fidgeting with the covers. "I can't lose it. I *wouldn't,* I swear."

Olivia instinctively sank back onto the chair. "What, Jack?" she asked, reaching for his hand. "What have you lost?"

He closed his eyes as if in despair. "I have to find her."

Olivia leaned closer. She touched Jack's poor, battered face. "Jack? Talk to me. Tell me what you've lost."

He shook his head and flinched. He frowned, closing his hand around hers. "I don't know... I don't..."

It was Olivia's turn to close her eyes. He wasn't awake at all, just caught in that vague netherworld of dreaming. Looking for something he'd misplaced. Something that might be hidden in the dispatch bag she'd buried in her portmanteau beneath her cot in Lady Kate's boudoir.

"Christ," she heard, and opened her eyes again.

And suddenly, his eyes weren't just open. They were alert. He was staring at her as if he'd seen a ghost. She held her breath.

"Dear God," he rasped, clutching her hand. "You're here. Oh, sweetheart, I've missed you so much."

He smiled, and Olivia lost the strength in her knees. "You missed me?" she dared to ask as she settled onto the side of the bed, closing her other hand around his.

He ran a thumb down her cheek. *"J'étais désolé. Je ne peux pas vivre sans vous."*

Olivia felt herself go cold. He'd told her before that he couldn't live without her. But not in French. Not spoken like a native. Jack's French had always been execrable.

Then another thought pushed forward, and she found herself pulling her hands away.

"Jack," she said, steeling herself for his answer. "Who am I?"

He frowned. "What do you mean?"

"You suffered an injury to your head. Who am I?"

Don't say Mimi.

"Don't be absurd," he rasped, taking her hand back. "Who else could you be but my Livvie?"

And suddenly it was all too much. She couldn't breathe. She couldn't think. She couldn't move her hand from where he held it against his chest.

"Oh, my God, Liv," he groaned, pulling her down to him. "I thought I'd lost you."

And then his arms were around her, and of course her body knew him. She ignited like fireworks, from fingers to toes to the deepest recesses of her soul, too long hungry, too long alone. Too long without Jack, who had missed her.

She rubbed her face against the bristle of his cheek. "Oh, Jack, I thought we'd lost *you*. Where have you been?"

He didn't bother to answer. Tangling his hand in her hair, he pulled her closer, until she was stretched out almost atop him. He kissed her hard, and she found herself answering. Overwhelmed, her senses swamped, she couldn't gather the strength to fight what she had tried so desperately to forget in the secret hours of night.

She felt his mouth open beneath hers, and she opened in welcome. She met his tongue, sliding and curling and invading to lay claim to him. She felt the pure force of him washing through her like spring light, like fire on a cold morning, like life itself. She recognized something she'd never thought to taste on Jack Wyndham.

Need.

Not just the passion that flared when the two of them came close. Not the sweet, bright joy of communion. Need, as if he'd been starving without her, his soul as well as his body. As if he'd walked the same dark roads as she and needed her comfort.

She felt his other hand wrap around her breast, and she arched into it, moaning. Her nipples tightened, and her bones melted. Her skin glowed. Her heart thundered, and her body shook as she sucked in a startled breath. She slid her arms around his sleek shoulders and held him to her.

It was so familiar. So good. So right. His hand, his wonderful elegant hand with its long clever fingers, skimming across her suddenly fever-bright skin, his mouth commanding, controlling, cherishing her lips, her cheek, her throat where she laid it bare for his touch. His hard shoulders and broad back flexing beneath her fingers. The feel of him, the sound of him, the smell of him.

Oh, sweet God, the smell of him. Not trauma or blood or smoke or death. Not even the clean-air perfume of fresh sheets.

Jack.

Somehow through all the work they'd done on him, the bathing and cleaning and bandaging, the filthy clothing they'd removed and the slashes they'd sewn, she could still, miraculously, smell him. Not his cologne, a melange of spice and smoke. His essence, a sharp, dark scent that was so uniquely him that it had set her senses sizzling from the moment she'd met him, a musk of secrets and strength and seduction. She inhaled that cherished scent and succumbed to it.

He slipped his hand beneath her bodice, beneath the frayed lawn of her chemise to set her breasts on fire. He found the peak of her nipple and teased it. Heat pooled deep within her and spread out to every finger and toe, to the roots of her hair, to the juncture of her thighs.

She rubbed against him, desperate for the friction, for the age-old attraction of soft for hard. She pushed the blankets down to bare his chest. She closed her eyes, narrowing her world to the feel of his tongue as it swept her mouth, the texture of his hair-roughened skin beneath her fingertips, the dark seduction of her own arousal, all but forgotten over the years. She wished briefly for the lady's hands she'd once had. She wanted to shatter his control with her soft hands.

She heard him groan, felt the vibration of it against her breasts. She slipped her leg over his to fit more closely and realized that he was surprisingly hard. She wrapped her hands in his thick, curling hair and savored its silk.

"Oh, Jack," she murmured, licking the salt from his throat. "I've missed you so."

She felt him nip at her shoulder and gasped. She felt his hand snaking beneath her skirt and heard her blood sing in her ears. *Yes,* she thought, arching higher, there. *There.*

She felt the air swirl against her thigh and higher, searching out the weeping flesh that ached for him. She arched closer, suddenly shameless, whimpering with the sweet feel of him. Of her Jack. Of the only man she'd ever loved.

The man who had thrown her away.

From one heartbeat to the next, she lurched back, gasping and shaking and stricken. The room was suddenly cold, her heart bereft.

No! her body screamed, the pain acute and disabling. *Let me go back. Let it be like it was before.*

Except it wasn't. It couldn't be.

She lifted a trembling hand to her mouth, as if she could hold in the keening that rose in her soul. Would it always be this way? Could he merely touch her and she'd crumble all over again? Before explanations, before apologies? Just a hot, hungry mating of bodies too long kept apart?

"Livvie," he moaned, his eyes opening, wide and hurt. "What's wrong? What happened?"

He reached his hand out again. She stumbled to her feet to get far enough away. Struggling to right her gaping bodice, she closed her eyes. "I...I can't....You're hurt, Jack."

"Oh, I can't be that hurt...." He ran a shaking hand through his hair and paused, his hand meeting the swath of bandages that circled his head. "Bloody hell. What happened?"

Olivia tried hard to masquerade her distress. "Don't you remember?"

He frowned. She curled her hands into her skirts, where they wouldn't get her into more trouble. Her heart still thundered uselessly. Her senses screamed to regain Jack's touch.

"I must have come a cropper on a horse," he said,

frowning as if he had to search for his words. "Never did that before." Fingering the bandage, he gave a lopsided grin. "I guess this is what happens when I get mad."

"I don't think this happened because you were mad, Jack," she said, suddenly feeling uncertain. "Try to remember."

He laughed. "I am remembering, sweetheart. I remember needing to get away to clear my head. I remember wanting to throttle you. I remember Gervaise being the one to suggest I might benefit from a bit of a cooling-off period."

Olivia gaped. "You call this a *cooling-off* period?"

He blinked, staring as if she had just sprouted horns. "For heaven's sake, Livvie. It's only been two weeks."

Suddenly she was the one struggling for sense. "What?"

Jack was frowning. "Well, what did you expect me to do, Liv? I needed to put a little distance between us until I could forgive you. It was my wedding gift, for God's sake."

She felt as if the world had just been upended beneath her. Suddenly she was sitting. "Your wedding gift? What are you talking about?"

This conversation was so familiar, as if it were a piece of an old dream or memory. But she was too careful with her memories. She would never have let this one loose.

"Your gambling," Jack said, taking hold of her cold hand again, as if that would help. "I've forgiven you. I even paid off your debts. But then you went behind my back and sold my wedding gift to cover your losses. How did you expect me to react, Liv? If Gervaise hadn't found your necklace in that store window, we never would have gotten it back."

Lurching like a drunk, the fragments of memory tumbled into place. Olivia felt her perilous world spin out of control.

"Jack," she said, pulling her hand back. "Tell me what year this is."

He was rubbing at his forehead. "Livvie, don't be ridiculous. You know perfectly well what year it is."

She nodded, her hands knotted together so tightly her fingers had gone numb. "You hurt your head, Jack. I need to know that you know what year it is. What day."

He sighed, as if she were being ridiculous. "Oh, all right. But I promise. I may feel as if I were run over by a field of racehorses, but my brainbox ain't broke. It's 1810."

No. This was not possible.

"1810?" She knew her voice sounded unpardonably shrill. "You're sure?"

"Of course. It's October. No. November. The Harvest Fair was on October twenty-seventh, and Gervaise brought me your necklace two days later. I left the next morning while you and Mother were arguing over the garden."

More accurately, his stepmother had had a three-day tantrum over Olivia's attempt to transplant a rosebush that, according to the marchioness, had been in place since the Conqueror.

Olivia had moved that bush five years ago. Five *years*.

Jack had no idea what had happened since. That he'd killed her cousin Tristram and cast her off with nothing more to support her than the wedding ring he'd forgotten to reclaim in his hurry to throw her off his property. He didn't know about Jamie or Gervaise or any of what had followed.

His smile faded. "Livvie? What's wrong?"

What was *wrong*? What was wrong was that she had spent five years in hell after what he'd done to her, and in his mind he was still her generous husband. What was wrong was that she had risked everything to protect him from exposure. Suddenly she wasn't quite sure why.

She meant to say something; she was sure. She meant to explain, to correct him with calm and logic. She would tell him the truth, quietly, and then she would escape before she could tell him in no uncertain terms what exactly had happened to his precious wedding present and his cousin and his honor.

She opened her mouth.

And she began to laugh.

Appalled, she slapped her hand against her mouth to stop.

She couldn't. Tears welled in her eyes. Her stomach heaved. She kept laughing.

Jack struggled to sit up. "Livvie?"

She reached out a hand as if to ward him off. She fought to regain her composure. She really did.

Instead, laughing even harder, she ran out of the room. And no matter how hard she tried, she couldn't stop.

The Allee Verde was all but empty. A lovely stretch of green lined with trees at the edge of the river, it was where the society of Brussels gathered on fine days to exercise their horses. Now the ground was churned up from all the military wagons, and society stayed inside rather than face the thousands of dead who had been collected on the city ramparts.

Two men had braved the hot afternoon. Giving every evidence that they would succumb to ennui by the end of the day, they walked their horses beneath the thickly leaved trees.

"What have you learned?" the taller one asked impatiently.

His dapper companion shook his head. "Nothing. The battlefield is a hellish mess. They were already carrying on mass burials before I could even get down there. There's even talk of funeral pyres."

"You are certain someone saw him."

"That's what I heard."

"We need to find out for sure. It is imperative."

"You think I don't know? You haven't been the one with his handkerchief to his nose as he turned bodies. I tell you, if he really was where he was supposed to be, he is there no longer."

"Then find him."

For a moment, there was silence. "I did hear something about his wife," the dapper man said. "I wonder if she's involved."

The tall man scowled. "You need to find out for certain."

He received a shrug. "Well, at one time or another, all society meets at Lady Kate's. If I want to catch a rumor on the wind, that's where I'll have to start."

"Do you expect me to help?"

For a moment, the more handsome man seemed to consider it. Then, with a smile full of mischief, he shook his head. "No, I think I'd much prefer to plow that field myself."

He lifted a cambric handkerchief to lazily dab at a bit of perspiration on his forehead. The movement caused the ruby on his signet ring to flash bloodred in the sunlight.

"If you do find him," his companion said, "notify me at once. Our good friend might need a bit of... persuasion to cooperate."

The handsome man actually grew pale. He wanted nothing to do with his associate's idea of persuasion. No one with sense would. Not when the man had such a facility for knives that he had taken to calling himself the Surgeon.

One of his victims had once suggested his name should more rightly be the Butcher. He had carved his response in the man's forehead in perfectly legible copperplate. *Precision is the true mark of genius. The Surgeon.*

The mistake had never been made again.

"I don't have to tell you how vital it is that we find our friend," the Surgeon insisted. "Or how I would feel toward you if we didn't."

Dabbing once more at his damp forehead, the other man tucked his handkerchief away. "No," he said with feeling. "You certainly don't."

Just then, a pretty Bruxellois on a roan mare approached, her groom in tow, and the men turned to doff their hats. After all, there was nothing else to say until Jack Wyndham was found and, if necessary, eliminated.

Chapter 6

Livvie! Damn it, come back here!"

Jack couldn't understand it. Livvie had been here; he couldn't have mistaken that. His body still thrummed with residual sexual energy. He had seen her, tasted her. He had cupped those gorgeous breasts in his hand.

And then she'd fled like a fox hearing bugles. And hadn't returned. He swore he'd been lying here for a good thirty minutes trying to get her attention, without any success, and he was feeling worse by the minute.

It might have just been that he couldn't seem to get off the damn bed. He kept trying, rolling over and throwing his legs over the side. He'd even gotten an arm under him to push himself aloft. But it had proved impossible to move farther. It was as if those moments holding Livvie had completely done him in.

He hurt everywhere. His stomach dipped and rolled like a leaky ship, and every so often, he swore he saw two of everything. His face felt like an overstretched balloon, and his chest ached like the devil. And to top it all, he was abysmally weak. He'd felt like hell before. This was far worse.

He wished he could remember just how he had been injured. It must have been a hell of a story.

Throwing back the bedcovers, he got a good look at himself. He had no mirror with which to see what had happened to his head, but there were bandages wrapping his left thigh, right arm, and chest. He took an experimental breath and gasped. Must have broken a rib or two.

If only his head wasn't such a disaster. The pain wasn't unendurable. He'd suffered more from a five-bottle night. But he felt as if he were caught in a fog.

He couldn't remember anything past the moment he'd arrived at the Wyndham hunting box. He certainly couldn't remember doing something so spectacular to himself that he'd ended up in bed looking like a second-rate mummy.

He felt as if everything he knew was shifting, the colors bleeding, the shapes suspect. He looked around the room and didn't recognize it. It definitely wasn't one of the bedrooms in the hunting box. It wasn't any place he'd be caught dead in, with its fussy gold and white furniture, pink walls, and brocaded fabrics. Where the blazes *was* he?

"Livvie!"

His voice seemed to be fading away like a badly filled bellows, but he knew she could hear him. She was still close. He could feel her, just as he'd always been able to, as if invisible threads connected them. And he could hear the oddest muffled noises out in the hall, as if she were still laughing. Which was ludicrous. As upset as she'd been when he'd walked out two weeks ago, he couldn't imagine her finding any of this funny.

He most certainly didn't.

He needed to hold her again. He needed to make sure she was real.

Why did he have such a sudden sense of dislocation from her? She was his beautiful girl, with her sun-streaked corn-silk hair and doe-brown eyes. He only had to close his eyes to see the sweet sweep of her cheek, the lush lower lip he loved to nibble, the hint of a dimple that peeked out just to the left of her pretty mouth when she laughed.

But something was *different,* and he hadn't realized it until she'd disappeared.

He needed to see her.

"Chambers!"

At least he could count on his valet. Chambers made it a point never to be farther away than ten feet.

But Chambers didn't answer. Instead, a short, bandy-legged gnome with shocking red hair and dressed in a worn Guards jacket clumped into the room. And he looked as confused as Jack felt.

"Who are you?" Jack demanded, and was mortified when his voice came out as nothing but a rasp. "Where's Chambers?"

The little man must have heard him, because after a quick frown over his shoulder toward the hallway, he smiled and limped over. "If that'd be your man, he's not here. I'm after bein' an excellent batman, though. Name's Harper."

"My wife." Why did that sound odd? Just saying the words made Jack's head ache. "Where is she?"

The little man's squashed features scrunched up in a frown. "Now, that I'm afraid I don't know. It's grand to see y'r eyes open, though. Hasn't the house been fair fetched thinking we'd be after buryin' ya next to the general?"

Jack found himself blinking, not sure whether it was his brain or the little man that was having trouble making sense.

"Can you tell us your name then?" the little man asked, making short work of getting Jack comfortably back beneath the covers. "So we can get on with settlin' your affairs 'n all?"

He stared up at the ugly little man, feeling even more disoriented. "My name? How could you not know my name?"

It was the little man's turn to blink. "Well, now, when have we had the chance to ask? Sure, this is the first you've woken."

"Then what the devil has Livvie been doing?"

"Livvie?" the little man echoed uncertainly. "Who...?"

"Harper," Jack heard from the doorway and battled a cowardly impulse to weep in relief. Livvie had come back. She'd tell him what was going on.

She was standing in the doorway, clad in an awful brown gown, her eyes red as if she'd been crying rather than laughing, looking as hesitant as a fox kit on the edge of the woods.

Livvie had never looked like that in her life. It made her look faded somehow. Thinner. Sad.

Had he done that to her? Had she had such an awful time with his mother while he'd escaped to his retreat?

No. Instinctively, he knew this was worse. But how?

And for the love of God, why was she clad in the ugliest gown he'd ever seen?

"I'm sorry, Liv," he apologized, reaching a hand out. "I didn't mean to hurt you. I don't mind about the gambling. I promise." He flashed her a wry grin. "Just tell me you haven't put up the Abbey. I'd rather not have to inform Mother she has to share lodgings with Millicent."

But she didn't smile back. "I've told you before, Jack. I don't gamble."

He laughed. "Since I'm at your mercy, I'll be happy to agree. Now where the hell am I?"

The Irishman shifted. "Language, milord."

Jack glared at him. "What are you still doing here?"

"Protecting the missus, looks like."

"That's *her ladyship,* you repellent little bog trotter," he snapped. "And don't threaten me. I've killed better men than you."

Olivia stared at him as if she didn't recognize him. For a second, Jack thought she might be right. He had the most disorienting feeling that he didn't recognize himself.

But before he could ask why that could be, she turned to the Irishman and laid a hand on his arm. And oddly, she smiled as if the two shared something. "You really think a curse is going to cripple me, Sergeant?"

His answering smile was far too familiar. "Curses are one thing, *a chuisle*. I won't be after havin' you insulted."

Again, Jack battled a surge of confusion. He felt as if he'd walked into the middle of a play he'd never seen.

"Jack," Livvie said, still smiling at the Irishman. "This is ex-regimental sergeant Sean Harper, late of His

Majesty's First Life Guards. He's the one who sewed you up and cared for you when we found you. You can thank him any time."

If it had been anyone but Livvie, or had this little leprechaun been any handsomer, Jack would have given in to jealousy. "My thanks, Sergeant."

"Ah, no, that's *mister* these days," the little man said with a big grin as he gave his leg a knock that thunked.

"Harper," Olivia continued, "I'd like to present Jack Wyndham, the Earl of Gracechurch."

"Well, good," Jack couldn't help saying. "At least I was right about that. Can you tell me what it is you think I don't know?"

He was rubbing at his forehead again, where the pain had seemed to swell with Livvie's return.

Walking over to a table, Olivia poured a glass of water. Adding a few drops of some liquid, she brought it over to him. "You fell," she said, "just as you said. The rest can wait 'til you feel a bit better. Now drink this and get some rest."

Catching her hand, he slipped his fingers beneath the cuff of her brown sleeve. "I think I did overdo it a bit just now, Liv," he said, teasing the soft skin of her wrist with his thumb.

For a second, she hesitated. But she didn't smile back as she tilted the glass to his lips. "I think you did, Jack."

Jack drank, suddenly thirsty. He knew without asking that there was laudanum in the water, but he didn't care. Livvie had pulled her hand away as if he'd hurt her. She wouldn't make eye contact.

Suddenly he felt exhausted. Finishing the water, he lay back. "Promise you'll be here when I wake."

Again she briefly paused. “Yes, Jack. I’ll be close.”

It wasn’t enough, he thought. There was something she wasn’t saying. Something he wasn’t understanding. But for right now, it soothed him to have her take his hand. To know she was there with him.

Feeling somehow saner, he closed his eyes. “There’s a good girl. I knew I could trust you.”

For a second, all he heard was silence.

“Did you?” she finally asked.

But he was too tired to make the speech he’d been working on while he rusticated, about how no matter what, they had each other, and they could weather anything as long as they did it together.

He settled for, “I love you, Olivia Louise Gordon Wyndham. Never doubt that. I’ll always love you....”

This time he got no answer at all.

He was fading quickly to sleep when he finally thought he heard her speak.

“I know you have questions, Harper. But I have to share something with the duchess before I can answer them.”

“O’ course, missus. Anything.”

Jack frowned as he slipped away into the dark.

Olivia knew she had to get up. She had to take the dispatch bag downstairs and wait by the front door so Lady Kate could no longer avoid her. She needed to confess.

In a minute. When she regained her composure.

She would not cry. Not anymore. No matter what it took, she would not cry over Jack Wyndham.

But she was feeling so overwhelmed, tossed into a

cold ocean with the water closing over her head. And now, when she thought she couldn't survive a moment more, here was Jack vowing undying love.

Damn him for doing this to her.

She pressed her clenched fist against her chest, as if it could stop the burning there. She closed her eyes, as if it would help her hide.

It didn't. Instead she saw that high shelf where she'd stacked all the secrets and memories she'd locked away in little boxes where they couldn't hurt her. Only they weren't there anymore. They were all tumbled about her like bricks from a building toppled in a high wind, hundreds of them, all broken open and leaking.

Five years. She hadn't seen Jack in five years. And in that time, she had endured hunger and cold and destitution. She had given birth in a cow byre assisted by a farmer's wife and had carried her baby over hundreds of miles as she sought work, as she sought handouts when nothing else was available. She had withstood Gervaise's scorched-earth campaign and stood tall and dignified as she faced public condemnation from those who should have loved her. She had even survived a mother's most unspeakable agony, that of empty arms. In all that time, she had managed to keep those odd little boxes of hers securely locked away so she could focus on what she needed to do rather than what she had lost.

When Jack had thrown her away, she'd locked him away in one of her most impregnable boxes. She'd spent months disciplining her mind, her heart, her body to forget him. To abolish the sweet joy of his smile, the heady exhilaration of his touch, the very miracle of his love.

She'd made him disappear, like Jamie, because she simply couldn't survive as she must, knowing he still existed.

Until now. Until Jack opened his eyes and swept all those boxes down about her.

Abruptly she straightened. *Enough*. No one needed to see her feeling sorry for herself. Especially in this house, where honorable men suffered worse pain in silence. Stiffening her back, as she had a thousand times before, she stopped her tears by will alone. And then, picking up the torn and bloody dispatch bag, she left her little room and descended the stairs.

In the house of the Dowager Duchess of Murther, disaster was evidently served up over tea and scones. Olivia learned this when she finally ran Lady Kate to earth later that afternoon. Knowing that she could put off her confession no longer, she decided to intercept the duchess before she could again escape. So she took up a post in the foyer on a straight-back chair and waited for the duchess to return from morning visits.

Lady Kate swept in just as the Percier clock struck four, Grace and Lady Bea on her heels. Olivia caught the brief flash of humor in the duchess's eyes when she realized what was afoot.

"Are you certain this can't wait?" Lady Kate asked as she unpinned her rose Oldenburg bonnet and handed it off to Finney. "You'll pardon my saying so, Olivia, but you look perfectly hagged."

Rising to her feet, Olivia dredged up a smile. "Well, since I feel perfectly hagged, I can hardly object. I'm sorry, but I waited as long as I could."

Finney patiently collected the ladies' pelisses, his ham hands making the attire look like doll's clothes. "We all tried to make the lady rest," he whispered to Lady Kate in a scratchy rumble. "Wouldn't budge."

"Miss Olivia is nothing if not perseverant," Lady Kate assured him with a pat to his massive arm. "I'm sure she wouldn't refuse a bit of tea, though, would you, Olivia?"

And without waiting for an answer, Lady Kate sailed into the Lavender Salon, the only public room free of wounded.

Taking up the dispatch bag, Olivia followed.

"Is there anything I can do?" Grace asked, looking as if she meant to put her arm around Olivia's shoulder.

Olivia knew her smile was stiff. "I don't know," she said, carefully stepping away. She hoped Grace understood. Like Grace, she had moments when comfort would shatter her tenuous defenses.

She was hanging on to her composure by a thread, still overwhelmed by the urge to laugh like a lunatic. What in all that was holy was she to do? Where did she start? And how did she survive the inevitable when she and Jack were exposed?

Seating herself on one of the lilac Louis Quinze chairs that bracketed the overcarved marble fireplace, she found herself staring at her hands, as if it would help her understand their treachery. She swore she could still smell Jack on them.

How could they? How could *she*? She'd made a mockery of the terrible sacrifices she'd suffered the last five years. He'd opened his eyes and called her name, and the discipline she'd struggled so hard to gain had simply vanished.

Just the thought sent frissons of need slithering through her. She literally ached with the urge to jump up and run back to him, to gather him close and breathe in his scent. To sweep her hands over every dip and ridge of that body she'd held in her sleep so many nights.

Briefly closing her eyes, she curled her fingers into her palms, as if it would help protect her from herself.

"Just for clarification," Lady Kate said, startling Olivia back to the present. "What is that unhygienic article you've brought into my house?"

Olivia looked down at the dispatch bag she held before her like a rat. "Part of my explanation."

She had searched the dispatch bag after all. It had made things immeasurably worse.

"First things first," Lady Kate said as Lady Bea settled next to her on the plum brocade settee. "I have waited all day for tea."

Olivia nodded, beset by an even greater sense of dislocation. She realized that this was one of the first times she'd seen these women awake since the night of the battle, and they were all perched on fragile seats in a salon decorated in a dozen shades of purple, as if nothing but tea awaited them.

She wasn't sure if they had slept any more than she had. They all looked pulled, although Lady Kate maintained her style, dressed in a lovely cream jaconet walking dress that was trimmed in the same hunter-green ribbon she'd threaded through her mahogany curls. Lady Bea wore silver moiré and lace, with a tidy cap on her neat white hair. Grace was again in serviceable gray, her own dull strawberry hair scraped back into a bun that should have given her a headache.

Olivia wondered briefly whether Grace always wore gray. A practical choice for a woman who spent her life one bullet away from mourning, she imagined, then felt guilty for the thought.

"The patients are all well?" Grace asked, startling Olivia.

"Oh, yes. In fact, the gentleman upstairs has woken."

Lady Kate's head snapped up. "Indeed."

Olivia almost flinched from that perceptive gaze. "Yes. It's what I needed to speak to you about."

Before she could continue, though, the door opened and the tea cart was rolled in by an impossibly young maid who sported a noticeable bulge beneath her apron.

"Ah, thank you, Lizzie," Lady Kate said as the blushing girl stopped before her. "You may close the door on the way out."

"Yes, mum," the girl whispered with a lopsided curtsy.

"Would you care to pour, Bea?" Lady Kate asked when they were left alone. "That will leave me free to speak to Olivia."

Olivia's heart faltered. "Thank you."

Suddenly she felt hollow. Her vision dimmed. She had held her secret to herself for so long. Even after practicing her speech for the last three days, she still wasn't sure she'd have the words to explain it.

"I know who the man upstairs is," she said before she could falter. "I should have told you before, but...well, that is part of my problem. He is John Wyndham, Earl of Gracechurch."

"Is he?" Lady Kate asked evenly as she accepted her tea.

Olivia nodded, her hands clenched. "I assume you've heard of the Countess of Gracechurch."

Lady Kate smiled. "Oh, my dear, who hasn't?"

Olivia swallowed. She wished she could close her eyes, but that would make her even more craven than she was. "*I* am the Countess of Gracechurch. I go by Olivia Grace in order to secure employment."

She braced herself for sneers. Outrage. Lady Kate laughed, and she felt upended.

"Well, thank heavens," the little duchess said with a pat to Lady Bea's hand. "We were hoping you'd admit it yourself."

Olivia stared, stricken. "You knew?"

Lady Kate nodded. "I recognized Jack, of course. He's a friend of my cousin Diccan. But it was Lady Bea who sussed *you* out."

Olivia gaped. "Lady Bea?"

"Oh, yes," Lady Kate said. "Didn't you hear her? She called Jack *Odysseus*. A man in exile. And then she called you Penelope—well, that was later. The long-suffering wife, of course."

She stopped, as if that was explanation enough. Olivia felt more disoriented than ever.

It was Grace who interceded, her face softening to a smile as she helped Lady Bea hand around cups. "I don't believe Olivia quite understands yet."

"Oh, dear." Lady Kate chuckled. "Of course. You're having trouble understanding my lovely Bea."

Olivia blushed furiously. "I, well..."

Lady Kate waved away her discomfort. "It's quite all right. Bea doesn't mind speaking of it. A few years ago, she lost the ability to communicate normally."

"Untangling yarn," Bea said with a nod.

Olivia couldn't help glancing at Lady Bea, but the old woman never looked up from pouring tea. "An apoplexy?"

Lady Kate shook her head. "Heroism." She turned suspiciously bright eyes on her friend. "Bea suffered an injury trying to protect a helpless friend, and her speech was affected by it. She is just as sharp and thoughtful as before, but because of the injury, she can't speak literally. She speaks in, oh, metaphors. Symbols. 'Untangling yarn.' She's telling you that sometimes you have to unravel her thoughts from her speech. You see?"

Olivia slowly nodded. "Indeed, I do. I just hope I haven't insulted you in any way by not knowing, Lady Bea."

Lady Bea looked up and smiled. "Impossible," she said in her clipped way. "Eat." And she handed Olivia her cup.

Olivia couldn't help but smile as she accepted.

"Well, then, Olivia," Kate said, sipping from her paper-thin Sevres cup. "What are we to do with you?"

Olivia carefully set her own cup on the satinwood table beside her chair. Her reprieve was over, then. "I will leave, of course."

"Before I can toss you out onto the cobbles in full daylight so all may know your shame?"

Olivia shrugged. "It's happened before."

She thought she heard Grace suck in a startled breath. As for Lady Kate, oddly enough, she bristled. "Well, I've been insulted before," the little duchess snapped, "but I have never once been called *proper.* Next you'll say I remind you of an Almack's patroness." She said this in the same way she might have said *vermin*. "And I don't abandon a friend just because she threatens to be more notorious than I." She gave a quick grin. "Although I do admit to some jealousy. You were quite the scandal for an entire season."

Olivia struggled to stay calm. "Actually, it was two."

"We've all read and heard the official version of what happened, of course," Lady Kate said, snatching a biscuit from the tray. "But I think no one has heard your side of the story. Surely Bea and Grace and I have the right to be the first."

Lady Bea gave a definite nod. "Family."

Feeling more than slightly overwhelmed, Olivia recovered her tea and sipped, as if that could give her inspiration.

"Grace," Lady Kate said, never looking away from Olivia. "Do you know who the Countess of Gracechurch is?"

"I'm afraid I must confess my ignorance," Grace admitted. "But, then, I've spent most of the last twenty years out of the country. Is it very bad?"

"*Very* bad." Lady Kate grinned. "At least according to Jack's cousin Gervaise, it is."

Olivia couldn't help flinching at Gervaise's name.

"Doesn't Gervaise have the right story?" the duchess asked.

"I'm sure Gervaise has a perfectly delicious story," Olivia said. Finally giving up on her tea, she set her cup back on the table to keep it safe. "Gervaise loves nothing more than a good story."

Lady Kate tilted her head a bit. "Except this time the story was perhaps a bit biased?"

The only response Olivia could give was a stiff shrug. "I'd hoped I could be gone before anyone could connect you with the notorious Olivia Wyndham."

"Notorious?" Grace asked, sitting very still.

"Scarlet," Lady Bea said.

Lady Kate leaned close to Grace. "Divorced," she whispered. "One of the most salacious crim.con. cases of the decade."

Grace's eyes widened. "Ah."

"What Olivia doesn't understand, though," Kate said with a sip of her tea, "is that hosting her would serve my purposes perfectly. I can't think of anything I'd rather do than set up the backs of the Wyndhams. Except for Jack, I bear a particular aversion to a family whose favorite sport is giving me the cut direct. I am too...outré, don't you know."

Olivia gave a little hiccuping chuckle. "My dear Lady Kate, Queen Charlotte is too outré for them. You can imagine how the daughter of a vicar fared against them."

"You ran away to marry?"

"Heavens, no. My family was thrilled beyond bearing. My father married us himself, right in the parish church."

"Without a member of his family to represent Jack?"

"Gervaise was his best man."

It was Kate's turn to look surprised. "Ah."

Grace was looking back and forth between them. "I hope you don't think me dense..."

"Try and keep up, dear," Lady Kate said with a pat to her hand. "What our Olivia is telling us is that she, a vicar's daughter, fell madly in love with our mystery man upstairs, Jack Wyndham, heir to *her* father's patron, the Marquess of Dourne. The family, one of the oldest titles in the kingdom, predictably did not favor the match and...what, attempted for an annulment?"

Olivia nodded. "It was their first strategy, certainly."

"Round two must have been the rumors that began to circulate about a certain countess's gambling habits."

Olivia remembered Jack's outrage and fought to hold on to her dignity. "Much more effective."

Kate nodded. "Not effective enough, evidently, for in short order came news of Olivia's long-standing affair with her first cousin Tristram Gordon. This was evidently too much for our impulsive young Jack, because within a matter of weeks, he had initiated divorce proceedings and killed poor Tristram in a duel."

Gervaise's tour de force, Olivia almost said. But even with the support Lady Kate had already offered, Olivia simply didn't know the duchess well enough to know what she really thought of the beautiful, laughing Gervaise. "Yes," she said baldly.

"Petulant brat," Lady Bea snapped.

"Heavens," Grace murmured.

Lady Kate nodded. "Straight out of a Minerva Press novel, isn't it? Although they lost me when they tried to make Tristram the scapegoat. Of all the absurdities."

Olivia went still. "You knew Tris?"

Lady Kate faced Olivia squarely. "I know his real lover."

Olivia had made it through five years of hell without weeping. Lady Kate's words almost broke her. Then Lady Bea reached over to pat her hand, and she lost her breath entirely.

"I met Tristram, too, of course," the little duchess

continued, her eyes softening. "I was very sorry when he died."

Olivia swallowed the hard lump in her throat. "As was I."

Dearest Tris, who had been her shadow as a child, her best friend as a girl, her confidante as an adult. Offered up on the altar of expediency and mourned by none but her. And, evidently, this self-possessed little duchess who adopted pregnant maids.

"Because of the duel, Jack was forced to flee the country," Lady Kate continued. "Oh, what, Olivia, four years ago now?"

"Five. Jack discovered Tris and me in what he thought was a compromising position, challenged Tris, and threw me off the property all in a single day."

"How very efficient of him. You returned to your parents?"

"For another week, until my father could strike my name from the family Bible at weekly services."

Grace gasped. Lady Kate's mouth thinned.

"Brimstone!" Lady Bea snapped, and Olivia thought her father's ears should be burning.

"It's all right," she said as evenly as she could. "I managed." She would never tell them how, though. Those were not memories she shared with anyone. Not even Georgie, who knew more than anyone.

"And Gervaise recognized you at the ball," Lady Kate said. "I didn't mistake that, did I?"

"No," Olivia said, standing, as if it could help her avoid Kate's discerning eye. She focused instead on a flock of voluptuous little china shepherdesses who crowded the mantel. "He was one of my most vocal critics at the end."

"Yes, he was," Lady Kate agreed. "Was he threatening you when I came upon you at your pension?"

"Gervaise?" Olivia echoed, the thought of his silkenly woven coercion forcing bile up her throat. "I guess you could say that. He was...angry at how things turned out."

Angry. What a lovely euphemism. He had been murderous.

"I also heard," Lady Kate said gently, "that your little boy died."

Olivia forced herself not to move, not to betray the searing pain those words set loose. Her most precious, shut-away memory, the most perilous. Her Jamie. Resting her hand against her locket, she focused hard on the laughing porcelain shepherdess before her. "It was a very bad time."

Silence stretched taut behind her. She so wanted to say more, but she didn't know how.

"I'm so sorry," Grace quietly said.

"Celestial choirs," Lady Bea whispered, and it sounded like prayer.

After all this time, Olivia still didn't know how to respond. "Thank you," was all she could manage.

"What now?" Lady Kate asked, her own voice suspiciously subdued.

Olivia faced her friends. "I should leave," she said again, ashamed to admit that she hoped Lady Kate turned down her offer.

After a moment's consideration, Lady Kate granted her wish. "Oh, I don't think so, Olivia," she finally said. "I think you have to stay right here where we can enjoy each other's disrepute. Besides, I'm probably the only person who can keep Gervaise's tongue between his teeth."

Olivia must have looked skeptical, because Lady Kate offered a rather savage smile. "My family might not think much of me. In fact, they think so little of me they tend to have me watched so they can send dire warnings about the state of my social standing and soul, in that order." She leaned close, grinning. "But I am still the daughter and widow of dukes, and no matter what my brother says, that still counts for something. What do you say, Olivia, shall we set all of Belgium and London on their ears?"

Again Olivia was surprised by the burn of tears. It had been so very long since anyone had been kind to her. She fought back a surge of useless hope and reached over to squeeze her friends' hands in gratitude. In that moment, she almost threw caution to the wind and told them the rest of her story.

She didn't. She sat back down and picked up her tea and pretended that she had found a haven.

"Jack's family does need to know that he's alive," Lady Kate said, pouring more tea. "Since Gervaise already knows who you are, I don't see why we can't tell him."

Olivia almost spilled her tea. She looked down at that dingy, telltale bag that now lay on the floor and sighed.

"We can't tell Gervaise," she said, swallowing her disappointment. "We can't tell anyone. I'm afraid this is all a bit more complicated than just my notoriety."

"Oh, my dear, notoriety isn't complicated at all," Lady Kate assured her with a blithe wave of the hand. "In fact, it's the simplest thing in society. I earned mine by telling Sally Jersey she looked dreadful in puce. By the time I danced in the Carlton House fountain in nothing but muslin, I was old hat."

"This is serious, Lady Kate. What I'm about to tell you puts you at more risk than ruin."

"Good Lord," Lady Kate said, looking intrigued. "What could be worse than ruin?"

Olivia held her breath. She faced her friend with cold-eyed purpose. "Treason."

Chapter 7

Lady Kate lifted an eyebrow. "Are you a French spy, then, Olivia?"

Olivia battled an absurd sense of disloyalty. "It's Jack."

Lady Kate's teacup hit the floor and rolled across the rug. *"Jack?"*

"Maybe," Olivia hedged. "I didn't think so. I..."

"Should explain before we jump to conclusions," Grace said quietly.

Lady Kate actually looked a bit abashed. "No wonder I asked you to stay, Grace. You remind me of my manners."

Recovering her cup, she sank gracefully back onto the damask settee, the picture of a perfect duchess.

Olivia focused on her own fingers where they lay twined against the serviceable gray of her gown. Gray like Grace's. Just as appropriate, she supposed.

"When we found Jack out at Hougoumont—" she said.

"*You* found him?" Grace interrupted.

Olivia nodded and focused on Lady Kate, who held all their futures in her hands. "He was carrying this."

And before she could talk herself out of it, she dug into the dispatch bag and produced the crumpled paper she'd found inside, twisted like a lover's note.

Kate accepted the paper with a frown. The rest of them waited, only Olivia knowing how dangerous that note was.

"It's...in French," Kate said. "To somebody named General Grouchy. 'Advance at once on Papelotte. Do not'...um, 'delay. Your emperor commands you.'" Her eyes growing almost comically wide, she lifted the paper as if it had caught fire. "It's signed 'N.' Are we talking about *that* N? The little one who only recently tried to conquer the world?"

"The earl must have intercepted it," Grace offered, reaching out to see the note herself.

"He was wearing a French uniform," Olivia blurted out.

Grace's head snapped up. "What? Who?"

Olivia did her best to meet that stony gaze. "Jack."

Lady Kate seemed to freeze. "*What?* You're certain?"

Olivia nodded. "Believe me. There was no mistake."

"He was wearing Guards red when we came across him," Grace accused, suddenly on her feet. "A captain's jacket and sash."

Olivia so wanted to close her eyes against the accusation she knew she'd see in Grace's. "I changed the jacket."

She explained to the best of her ability what she'd done in those insane moments after finding Jack. She faced the disgust on Grace's gentle face and knew she deserved it. She felt soiled and small before that grieving girl's reproach.

"Did you see how many of our men fell at the château?" Grace demanded softly, her eyes suddenly swimming in tears. "How many more wounded needed our transport?"

"Of course I did. But he was so badly wounded. I couldn't let anybody find him until I knew why he'd—"

"Betrayed his country?" Grace said, rigid and cold.

Lady Kate rose to lay a hand on the girl's arm. "Peace, Grace. There's more to this than we're seeing. A Wyndham would *never*..." Shaking her head, she sank back onto the settee. "His mother *was* French...."

"And dead long before he could remember her," Olivia retorted as she and Grace sat as well. "But it's been so long since I've seen him. Do you know what happened after he left England?"

"I always assumed he went to Jamaica," Kate mused. "The family has plantations there. I saw him, not, oh, two years ago. I simply cannot believe Jack Wyndham would do something so..."

"Heinous," Grace rasped, as stark and hard as a statue. As justice, when what Jack needed was mercy.

Lady Bea patted the girl's hand, shaking her head. Even she couldn't seem to come up with a reasonable response.

"Good God." The duchess shook her head, staring blindly out the window that faced the Parc. "Well, we'll just have to ask him."

Olivia rubbed at the headache that had taken root in her temple. "We can't."

All three women stared at her.

"Why?" Grace demanded. "You said he was awake."

"He is." Olivia struggled with that insane urge to laugh again. "He was. But he has no memory of the last five years. He thinks it's 1810."

This silence was even more stark. Lady Bea's mouth sagged. Grace looked flummoxed.

"He doesn't think you're still married," Lady Kate finally protested.

Olivia's smile was painful. "Oh, but he does."

Silence returned, taut with every question the women longed to ask. Then, suddenly, Lady Kate began to laugh.

"Oh, this is too delicious. And I can't...tell... anyone!"

"He doesn't remember where he is?" Grace demanded.

Olivia lifted her hands in helplessness. "He thinks he fell off a horse at a hunting box in Leicestershire."

Lady Kate wiped at her eyes with a lacy bit of cambric and kept chuckling. "I'm sorry, Olivia. It is unconscionably insensitive of me. But even Mrs. Radcliffe couldn't have come up with something this absurd."

"Believe me," Olivia said, "I've had much the same thought."

Grace was still staring. "He thinks you're still married."

Olivia kept rubbing at her temple. The headache had blossomed. "He does. He thinks we just had an argument over my alleged gambling, and he ran off for a 'cooling-off' period."

"Bow Street," Lady Bea said with a nod.

Lady Kate nodded, still wiping her eyes. "Indeed. We need to unlock Jack's secrets."

"How?" Olivia asked. "What if we do the wrong thing? Couldn't we hurt him more?"

"Darling Olivia," Lady Kate said with an amazed shake of her head. "If I were you, I'd be more inclined to drop him on his head, not protect it."

Olivia managed a smile. "I have had that thought as well."

"I agree with Olivia," Grace said suddenly. "We can't act until we understand the consequences."

Olivia frowned. "Then what do we do?"

"Would you like me to ask Dr. Hume what to do?" Grace offered. "He's the army's chief surgeon."

Olivia hesitated. "He can't know…"

Grace's smile was painfully dry. "Believe me, Olivia. I have no intentions of spreading such a tale. No one would believe it. I can speak with Dr. Hume once my father's funeral is over."

"It's time, then?" Lady Kate asked, suddenly sober.

Grace nodded, her attention suddenly on a fraying ribbon on her sleeve. "Yes. Tomorrow. I've arranged to have him buried with his men on the battlefield."

Lady Kate nodded. "We will join you, if it's all right."

Looking suddenly anxious, Lady Bea plucked at Lady Kate's skirt. "Evensong?"

Lady Kate smiled at the woman. "Yes, dear. Grace, my lovely Bea would consider it an honor to sing for your father."

It seemed Grace was incapable of destroying the fragile hope in the old woman's eyes. "I would be honored."

Lady Kate nodded. "And until we speak to the doctor?"

"Status quo," Lady Bea said, beaming with relief.

"I can't leave things as they are," Olivia protested. "Jack thinks we're still married."

"It's only until tomorrow," Grace assured her.

She had no idea what she was asking. Olivia could feel the ground slipping out from under her. "I'll do my best," she finally said. "But I don't think we can wait much longer. We don't know that Jack hasn't already been recognized. We don't know what danger he's in. What danger *we're* in."

Grace nodded. "I understand."

"I have to ask again that you say nothing to Gervaise," Olivia said. "*Especially* Gervaise."

"Of course not," Lady Kate agreed. "He'd never be able to keep a story like this to himself." Quietly she turned to face Grace. "It is Grace who must ultimately decide. As impulsive as he is, I for one would trust Jack Wyndham with my life. But I'll not risk another person's neck for my own convictions."

"What about your staff?" Olivia asked.

Lady Kate waved a hand, completely unconcerned. "Oh, I'll tell them. But no one would accuse a staff for their mistress's misconduct." Her smile grew. "Especially mine. Now, then. Grace?"

Olivia waited for Grace to pass sentence. When she failed to speak, Olivia looked up at her to find those soft gray eyes bright with unshed tears.

"Have you ever seen a battle before these last few days, Olivia?" Grace asked.

Olivia frowned, taken aback by the non sequitur. "Pardon? Oh. No. Nothing worse than a good tavern brawl, I imagine."

Grace looked down at her, and Olivia could see the

conflict in those gray eyes. "And yet you went out there with me."

Olivia shrugged, uncomfortable with her friend's regard. "That doesn't change the danger to any of you. I should take Jack away before anything can happen to you."

Lady Bea surged to her feet. Lady Kate held her still.

Grace shook her head and took Olivia's hand to stop her. "You need to stay where you're safe," she said. "Which you could have done when I asked you to help me find my father. Instead you crossed a battlefield to help me. I can never repay you for that act of courage, Olivia."

Olivia fought the burn of tears. "But Jack might have betrayed everything your father stood for."

"Well," Grace said, squeezing Olivia's hand as if restoring herself, "when he remembers, we'll just have to ask him."

It was time to dress for dinner. Grace Fairchild had other business to attend to first. Rather than follow the duchess up the stairs, she descended into the cellar where her father lay.

The stone cellar was cool and dark, her father resting in a coffin Harper had built, with candles burning at his head and feet. Next to him, the little pregnant maid Lizzie sat hunched over in a chair scribbling something on a slate.

"Thank you, Lizzie," Grace greeted her. "If you'd like to get something to eat, I'll stay for a bit."

Lizzie shot to her feet, her freckles standing out in the flickering light. "Oh, ma'am, it's no problem. Wasn't I the one sat for my gran and granfer when their time came? I find it peaceful and all. Y'r da looks to have been a great man."

Grace looked over to where her father lay in the same smoke-stained, bloody uniform he'd worn into battle. She'd thought of changing him into his best uniform for burial, but he would never have understood. He had always been prouder of his battle-worn tunics than the ones with the shine on the buttons. He did look peaceful too. As if comfortable in a job well done.

"He *was* a great man, Lizzie," she said, and smiled.

She waited until Lizzie found her way up the stairs before taking her seat. "I have to tell you, sir," she said, gathering up his cold hand. "I'm about to do something you would be heartily disgusted at. But I hope you'll understand my reasons."

She expected no answer, of course. But she told him, anyway, of the long hours spent recovering him and the role Olivia Grace had played. Of the danger the two of them had brought back in the duchess's fancy carriage. And of the fact that Grace could not turn away from the injured earl or his divorced wife, even in the face of his possible transgressions.

Grace had had so little family in her nomadic life. Real family. The Harpers had stood by her, of course, and the men of her father's company had considered her their little sister. But her relationships with those young men had been battle-born and surely wouldn't last past her separation from them.

It hadn't been until the little duchess had inexplicably

taken her up that she'd felt a real connection. Until Olivia, untested on a battlefield, had risked her life to help her.

Grace couldn't bear the thought of turning away now, of once again being alone. A cowardly thought, she knew, one the general would have scoffed at. *Been alone weeks at a time, girl*, he would have said. *What's new of that*?

What was new was that she could no longer count on the moment he would blow through the front door like a brisk wind, all his laughing, roughhousing young men trailing in his wake so she could pamper them all and briefly feel they needed her.

"I hope you'll forgive me," she whispered, and bent to kiss him good-bye.

Olivia should have expected it. By the time she finally lay her head down on her pillow, she was trembling with exhaustion. Even with the soothing effects of Mrs. Harper's famous posset, she felt battered and overwhelmed, her emotions rolling about like a leaky merchantman in a storm. Everything she'd seen and done in the last days followed her to sleep. And then she finally curled up on her side and slipped her hands beneath her cheek, and she smelled him again.

Jack. As if it were five years ago, and she had just discovered the miracle of making love. Her skin heated. Her heart stumbled, and her breasts grew heavy. Instinctively, she snuggled closer to his scent, savoring it like warm cognac, as if just breathing it in could calm her overwrought senses.

It didn't. It woke them. From one second to the next, her body ignited, every long-silent nerve ending sparking like fireworks. Memory became reality, and she found herself back at Wyndham Abbey.

Jack's house. *Their* house, although it wouldn't be for another week or so. It was just at dusk, and she was standing in the shadowy library looking out to where Jack's family was gathered on the back terrace. The girls were battling with a shuttlecock, their bright shrieks muffled by the thick glass in the mullioned windows, the rest of the family lazily waving away the late afternoon heat from the lawn chairs and blankets that had been spread across the back lawn.

She'd been out there with them until just a few minutes ago, trying her best to fit into a family that wanted nothing to do with her. She stood here now thinking about what her life would be like in a week. Wondering if she would finally feel as if she belonged. Overwhelmed by the strength of her love for Jack and praying that would be enough to hold her through the difficulties she knew lay in store for them both.

She smelled him before she heard him. A breeze of his cologne, and then, stepping up to her, Jack. Just Jack, that special spice of heat and night and secret desires. She smiled to the window without turning. Her body exploded into life, just as it always did when he came near.

"You're so beautiful," he whispered into her hair, reaching up from behind her to pull out one of her hairpins. "Your hair is like corn silk, and you smell like apples and vanilla."

"I've been baking." She shivered down to her toes

with the scent of him. With the barest touch of his fingers. "Stop that."

Hunger woke, just like always, her heart racing, her breasts swelling against her stays. With only a scent. But, oh Lord, how it wove through her, promising sensations she still only imagined. Hoped for.

"I can't stop." His voice was strained, and he laid his mouth against the skin behind her ear. Another pin eased away and the heavy weight of her hair began to slip. "I love you." Slipping his finger into her hair, he slowly unwound it. "We'll be wed in a week. I just can't wait, Livvie. I *can't*."

She found herself leaning back against him, just to feel the heat of his body against her. *Touch me*, she thought, too impatient, too suddenly hungry to stand still. *Love me*.

They had been learning together, touching and whispering and kissing until they couldn't breathe. Tucked furtively away in shadows where no one would see, once on the moors above the village. Olivia swore she could still feel the sun on her skin. She could taste the sharp frustration of stopping. Gasping, wide-eyed, resistance wearing thin.

It had been like that since they'd set eyes on each other. Ravenous for each other, obsessed by the need for privacy where they could ease their hunger. Consumed by the smell and touch and taste of each other.

He stepped up against her, his hard shaft pressing right against her bottom, his breath fast and hot against her ear. She groaned, leaning her head back. "You're a very . . . bad man."

She felt his smile against her skin. "*Very* bad."

Licking the salt from her neck, he wrapped his arms around her, resting his hands just underneath the swell of her breasts. She jumped, gasped, his touch striking lightning, sparking a hotter need, a darker yearning. She wanted him to do unimaginable things to her, things she didn't even know how to ask for. More than they'd managed in the stolen moments they had shared. More than was right, even this close to her wedding. She wanted.

She *wanted.*

"They'll see us," she objected, knowing it was only a token protest. Afraid of this need that kept her standing where she knew she shouldn't be. Wanting to experience whatever surprise Jack had in store for her, when she knew it must be wrong.

He was behind her.

Behind her, so she couldn't see his eyes to know he brought love with this heat. Behind her where she couldn't touch him back, where he constrained her there against the window.

She couldn't move. Worse, she didn't want to, and it terrified her.

It was wrong. But it felt so right.

"No, they won't see us." He ran his tongue around the shell of her ear and sapped the strength in her knees. "Too dark in here. Besides, Maudie and Mad are making too much racket."

He leaned closer, his lips brushing her skin, setting off another waterfall of chills. "Lean forward. Put your hands on the windows."

She shook with the effort of trying to hold still. "Don't be silly. They'd surely see then."

He was shaking too. It made her smile.

"Not at all," he coaxed. "Don't you want to feel that cool glass against your palms?"

It would be the only cool thing she felt, she thought, and before she could talk herself out of it, she leaned forward just a little. She laid her palms against the slick chill of the windows at shoulder height, and opened herself up to his touch.

He began slowly, circling his thumbs along the bottom curve of her breast, nibbling at her shoulder, molding his body against her. "I want to take my time," he murmured. "I want you to have the same pleasure I do."

"I have... ah, pleasure," she protested, her head falling back with the nip of his teeth at her shoulder. Lord, she swore she was melting, a terrible heat that poured deep into her belly, into the core of her, that place Jack had first touched with tentative fingers just the day before. That secret spot even she hadn't known about.

"I want to give you more," he insisted, sweeping his hands up to cup her breasts. "I want to give you everything."

She arched against him, desperate for his touch. She moaned when he pulled her laces loose. She giggled when he slipped his hand into her dress, right there where, if they looked, his parents could see him pull her breasts free. She could see it herself, faint in the glass that was struck by a setting sun: her face, flushed and anxious, her arms stretched out before her, her breasts standing out like pale moons in the dusk, and Jack, a shadow behind her, his dark hands a compelling counterpoint to the white of her dress, of her breasts. A suggestion of sin in the staid library.

"This is not right," she groaned.

He said not a word, just watched over her shoulder as he wrapped his elegant hands around her breasts. As he took her nipples between finger and thumb, as he rolled them and tugged them and aroused them to a tight pucker. She wasn't going to survive this. She swore she wasn't.

"Jack..."

"It is right," he soothed, his breath fanning across her neck. "We love each other."

He took away one of his hands, and she almost cried out. Until he slid that hand down her back, over her bottom, slowly, so slowly she thought she was going to die, because she knew where he was going, what prize he sought. Right there in front of his mother. Oh, sweet Lord, she was going to hell.

She didn't think she could stop him even if his mother turned their way. If she leaped to her feet screaming and pointing. If her own father walked onto the lawn and condemned her for a harlot.

"Tell me you can't wait, either, Liv," Jack begged. "Please, tell me."

"I can't... wait, either, Jack. I love you so much."

She tried to pull her hands back so she could touch him, too, but he stopped her. "No. No, stay just like you are."

"What?" She laid her hands back against the window. "Why?"

"Do you trust me?"

Not at all, she should have said. But he was working the buttons loose on the placket of his pantaloons. He was reaching for the hem of her dress and drawing it up. He was *behind* her.

She couldn't breathe. She couldn't think.

"I trust you."

"You want this," he said. "I promise."

"I…I do."

His hands. Oh, sweet God, his hands, one on her breast, one slipping between her legs, where she was so wet it mortified her. He dipped his fingers in her juices and chuckled.

"Oh, yes," he said, pressing his naked shaft against her bare bottom. "Oh, yes, Livvie. Spread your legs for me, sweet. Let me love you."

She couldn't think to question. His fingers were *there*, and he was stroking her, setting off firestorms. Taking her vision and dimming her ears, her body reduced to the place his hands touched. She couldn't tolerate much more. She couldn't wait. Her eyes drifted closed, and she knew her legs wouldn't be able to hold her upright much longer.

"I can't wait," he groaned, and she was the one who chuckled this time, her voice breathy and uncertain.

"Are you sure?"

"Oh, yes. I'm sure. Look at me, Livvie. Let me kiss you."

She never questioned him. Keeping her hands flat against the glass where anybody could see them, she arched her body, preparing to turn her face for his kiss. She opened her eyes, hungry for the love in his sea-soft eyes.

And then, somehow, the scene began to feel wrong. To slip away.

"I knew you'd finally come to me," he whispered against her ear. "I knew you wanted me too."

And even before she turned, somehow she knew. She opened her eyes and opened her mouth, even before disaster struck.

Because when she turned, it wasn't Jack she saw smiling over her shoulder, his face sheened with perspiration, his hair mussed and his eyes dilated and feral.

It was Gervaise.

She screamed.

Chapter 8

Olivia? Olivia!"

Shaking, sobbing, Olivia flinched away from the hand that touched her shoulder.

"Dear, it's me. Come on now, wake up."

Breathe. She had to breathe. She had to get away from the images in her head. She had to...

Wake up.

Finally able to get her eyes open, she was mortified to find an anxious-looking Grace bent over her.

Grace. It's only Grace.

"Everything's all right," her friend assured her, her soft eyes narrowed with concern. "It was only a dream."

Olivia lurched up. Swinging her feet over the side of the bed, she laid her head in her hands. Grace immediately sat next to her and wrapped an arm around her shoulder. This time Olivia welcomed it. She was still feeling disoriented and nauseous.

Gervaise. Oh, God.

The door into Lady Kate's bedroom swung open.

Olivia looked up to see Lady Kate standing there in the most amazing dressing gown she'd ever seen, her glorious hair tumbled like a courtesan's down her back. "Are you all right in here?" the duchess demanded.

"Yes, I'm fine," Olivia assured her, completely distracted by Kate's bright crimson attire. "Thank you. It was just a dream."

Lady Kate gave a brisk nod. "Too much time in the medical tents."

As good an excuse as any, Olivia imagined. Certainly she wasn't going to tell them the truth. "Too much time in the medical tents," she agreed unevenly. "I'm . . . I'm sor—"

"I sincerely hope you don't mean to say you're sorry," Lady Kate genially suggested. "I live by the firm rule that guilt is pointless. If you can't follow that simple axiom, I doubt you'll last in my employ. Now, would you like to try again?"

Olivia hiccuped on a surprised laugh and wiped at her eyes with shaking hands. "Thank you, yes." Gervaise lingered at the back of her mind, threatening her stomach again. But she'd survived that before. "At least allow me to hope I didn't disturb your sleep."

"Not at all," Lady Kate assured her with a wave of the arm that set scores of bright red feathers fluttering madly along her neck and wrist. "Nothing like a bit of a fright to get the blood moving. Now, I will see you both in the morning."

Even Grace grinned at that. "Of course."

Lady Kate bid them adieu and disappeared back into her room, leaving the two women to stare at the closed door.

"Were those marabou feathers?" Olivia asked, her voice suspiciously high.

Grace shook her head. "I don't know. They were certainly…"

"Outrageous?"

Grace giggled. *"Red."*

Olivia gave a sage nod. "Very restful."

"If you're a parrot."

"Or an opera dancer."

Grace shook her head. "Not one self-respecting opera dancer I've ever met would be seen dead in that thing."

This time Olivia stared at Grace. "You've *met* opera dancers?"

Grace's grin was unrepentant. "I was with the army. I've met a spectacular assortment of people."

Olivia found herself grinning back. "Oh, how wonderful. I want to hear about every one."

Climbing to her feet, she took a few moments to splash her face with cold water. She was just about to return to bed, when she heard a scratching on the door.

She opened the door to find Thrasher bouncing on his feet, his uniform half on. "Pardon, miss," he said with a big grin. "But the earl's askin' f'r ya. 'Eard you, he says."

Oh, Lord. She had woken Jack. Hoping she could keep Jack from disturbing the rest of the house, she shrugged into her own faded, worn dressing gown and followed Thrasher out the door.

She wished she didn't have to see Jack yet. The memory of that day in the library was still too sharp: his touch, his scent, his power over her. She could still see him reflected behind her in those mullioned windows, a dream within a dream, and thought of how that day had really ended.

He had loved her. Oh, how he had loved her, teaching her how adventurous love could be. How surrender could be victory. How wonder could be woven with fingertips. She could still feel the moment he'd entered her, his chest tight against her back, his breath at her ear, the full, hot, hard length of him slipping into her as he'd held her captive against the window. It had been magic. It was only in dreams now that the memory was perverted.

Her heart galloping in her chest, she stepped into Jack's room. *Please,* she thought, *don't make me have to touch him. I won't be able to bear it.*

She was destined to be disappointed. The dolt was sitting up on the side of his bed looking as if he was a heartbeat from collapse.

"Are you all right?" he demanded, peering up at her in the uncertain candlelight. "I thought I heard..."

He was chalk white, with a sheen of perspiration on his forehead. He was also naked, the sheet covering only his lap. Olivia had helped bathe him and treat him. She had watched him while he slept. But after what she'd just been through, the sight of his well-honed body paralyzed her. Even five feet away, her skin had begun to hum, as if a swarm of bees had been caught underneath.

"A mouse," she said, curling her fingers into her itching palms, unable to move from the doorway. "Ran over my foot."

Even pasty white, Jack had quite a look of scorn on him. "Believe me, my love. I know the difference between a mouse scream and what I heard."

There was such a wealth of meaning in those words. In his tone. As if he had screamed like that himself more than once.

Olivia didn't want to know. She didn't want to care.

It was all she could do to remain in the room with him. "Well, I'm sorry, but it was a mouse."

Somehow the pragmatic words unfroze her feet, and she walked into the room.

"Lie down, Jack. Do." Fighting her inevitable reaction to him, she reached out to steady him. "You're going to go face-first onto the floor, and I won't be able to stop you."

He grinned up at her, and she struggled even more. His pale green eyes seemed to glow in the dim light. "Forgive a man his pride, dear heart," he begged, catching one of her hands and kissing her palm. "You know I can't abide being helpless."

She tried to quell the frissons his touch set off. "I know no such thing. You haven't been helpless a day in your life."

He closed his eyes. "A lot you know."

Olivia heard that tone of voice again, as if dark sins had sullied his soul. What could they have been? She'd seen his physical scars, brands from injuries she'd never seen. What brands could have been burned into his psyche? What traumas had he misplaced inside that fractured brain that could have compelled him to don a French uniform?

"Besides," he said, rubbing at his bristly chin, "I need to bathe. I smell worse than Tannus after a long hunt. I have a feeling I must look twice as charming."

"But it's after midnight, Jack."

"And I'm awake. You're saying your friend Harper wouldn't like a healthy tip to help a man rid himself of his dirt?"

"I'm saying I won't ask. He's asleep. And you can wait."

"No, I can't," he retorted, and leaned closer. "How am I supposed to make love to you when I smell like an uncleaned stable?"

It had never bothered them before. She almost made the huge mistake of reminding him.

"Well, don't worry about that," she said instead. "You're barely up to kissing."

He reclaimed her hand. "Then kiss me."

She shivered. His touch seared her. "Tomorrow," she said, pulling away. "After you bathe."

He was about to reply when the sound of laughter and shouting drifted up from the street. He turned to it, frowning. "Is my head completely shattered, or do I keep hearing French being spoken out there?"

Olivia's knees almost gave out on her. Oh, Lord. Couldn't he give her even five minutes without turning her on her ear? She had no idea what to say. What to give away.

"I'm hosting émigrés," she suddenly heard behind her.

Kate swept in, still clad in her crimson dressing gown, the feathers fluttering from neck to toe. "Hullo, Jack," she greeted him. "I heard you were finally up."

"Kate!" he cried, grinning like a schoolboy. "Don't tell me I'm at *your* hunting box. I won't believe it."

She cast a look at the insipid pink walls and shuddered. "I should say not. Remember anything yet?"

"I remember guns," he said, frowning, as if this were a surprise. He grinned at Lady Kate. "Good Lord. Murther didn't mistake me for a quail, did he?"

"Maybe a buck." She grinned. "Never a quail. But, no."

"Well, good. It wouldn't do his heart any good."

Olivia saw a queer flinching in Kate's expression that disappeared before she could wonder at it.

"I didn't mean to wake anybody," Jack said. "I just thought I heard Livvie."

"And now you're going back to sleep," Olivia said.

"What émigrés?" he asked suddenly, as if it just occurred to him. "And how many? It sounds as if we're in a city of them."

Lady Kate hesitated just a bit too long.

Olivia sighed. "We are," she said, not knowing how to keep lying. Even Lady Kate stared at her. "We're in Brussels, Jack."

Jack gaped. "Brussels? What the deuce are we doing here?"

"Visiting. Lady Kate has been kind enough to host us."

Jack frowned, as if trying to solve unsolvable problems. "I don't remember ever being in Brussels."

"It will come back to you," Olivia said. "Now, get back to sleep. That's what you need."

He gave her another sly smile. "I could tell you exactly what I need if the duchess weren't here. No offense, Kate."

"No offense taken, Jack."

Olivia glared at him. "I told you," she said. "No."

He managed to catch her hand again before she could pull away. "Give me a kiss on account. You're being very stingy, you know."

Olivia started at his touch. She looked down. "Why, you're warm, Jack," she said, hoping to distract him.

He gave her a halfhearted leer. "Only for you."

She laid the back of her hand against his forehead and then his temples, a mother's sure gauge, and realized her ploy had revealed a real problem. "You're running a fever."

He scowled. "I won't accept that as an excuse."

She told herself she did it to shut him up. But when she leaned in to kiss him, it was all she could do to keep from wrapping her hands into his tangled hair and holding on. The bristles on his face tickled her cheek. His lips molded perfectly to hers. His scent enveloped her. Her body remembered.

Barely withstanding the urge to surrender, she yanked away. "There. Now, can we deal with this fever?"

He smiled slowly, looking thoroughly debauched. "Oh, you mean the other one."

She almost pinched him.

"Might be my leg," he finally admitted, looking down. "Feels like the devil." Ruefully he grinned. "Sorry. The deuce."

It didn't take long to prove Jack right. Pushing up the sheet, Olivia cut away the bandage to find the stitches seeping and straining against angry swelling.

"Really, Liv," Jack quipped. "You put me to the blush. Move that sheet another inch and Lady Kate will know all my secrets." He made the mistake of looking down. "Good God, what *is* that? It looks as if I were gored by a bull."

"Nothing so romantic," Olivia said, struggling to maintain her poise. "Maybe I should get Harper."

"Nonsense," Lady Kate said briskly. "I'll get Grace."

Grace must have anticipated the call, because by the time Jack gave in and laid back down, she was there in a wrapper much like Olivia's, her pale hair in a braid down her back. Not bothering with civilities, she flipped back the covers again.

"Ah," she said, seeing the wound. "Harps warned me."

It didn't occur to Olivia to introduce Jack until Grace laid her hand against Jack's thigh to test it for heat. Jack grabbed Grace's hand. "My apologies, ma'am, but usually I'm at least introduced to a lady before showing her so many of my charms."

Grace blushed a brick red. Olivia found herself staring and speechless. Jack never would have said that. Not in front of her.

But then, he'd lived an entire life without her.

"Heavens, Jack." Lady Kate laughed, unconsciously echoing Olivia's thoughts. "You've grown quite a smooth tongue."

She got another smile. "Practice, Kate. Practice."

Olivia just shook her head. Lady Kate introduced Grace.

"My pleasure," Jack said, giving Grace's hand a salute before letting it go. "You received medical training at which university?"

Busy evaluating his wound, Grace gave an absent smile. "The university of Peninsular Wars."

Jack nodded. "My apologies, ma'am. My leg is completely at your disposal."

"Honey," Grace announced.

He cocked an eyebrow. "Sweetheart."

Grace smiled. "No, I mean we should lather honey

on the wound and wrap it. It works wonderfully against infection."

"I lay at your mercy, Miss Fairchild. Will you sit and hold my hand while it does its magic, Liv?"

"I will sit a while," she said, disgracefully grateful for the fever. It might actually delay the inevitable confrontation.

"I hate to say this," Grace said a few moments later as the three women headed down to the stillroom for ingredients. "But even with the honey, he's in for a touch of rough weather."

Olivia cast her a sharp look. "He'll be all right?"

"He'd better be," Lady Kate quipped. "I think Monsieur would object if he found a body buried in his garden."

"The earl will have a fever for the next few days," Grace said. "But I found a woman who can supply willow bark. With that and the honey, I believe he'll weather it." She gave a look upstairs. "As long as he doesn't try and do anything stupid."

"He's a man," Lady Kate snorted. "Of course he'll try and do something stupid."

Suddenly, all three women stopped and turned to look back up the stairs to where Jack lay.

"He was already sitting up," Lady Kate all but accused.

Olivia rubbed at her forehead. "Which means he'll soon push himself to stand. And then walk."

"And, being a man, won't be satisfied 'til he's strolling down the street looking for his friends."

Olivia pressed her fingers against her temples, thinking that she needed to get some headache powders for herself when they got Jack's draught. "Where anyone might recognize him and ask questions. Where he'll ask questions in return. Questions we can't answer."

"I certainly hope you can speak with Dr. Hume tomorrow," Lady Kate said to Grace, "or Jack might walk right into a noose."

And those who'd cared for him, Olivia thought, looking at her two friends, *would follow right behind.*

The next morning, the little group of women accompanied Grace back down to the battlefield to bury her father. Olivia had been to many interments. It had been one of her duties, especially for parishioners with no one else to mourn them. But she doubted she'd ever attended a more poignant service.

Following right behind the coffin, her hand on Harper's arm, Grace carried herself with quiet dignity. The general's surviving men formed an honor guard, and the Guards chaplain performed the simple, moving service. A Highlander piped the general home, as he'd always loved the fierce, barbaric sound. And then, as the last keening notes faded into the morning air, Lady Bea stepped forward, lifted her face to the morning sky, and began to sing the Twenty-third Psalm.

"My shepherd is the Lord,

I shall not be in want..."

And every person in that battered, bloody place stilled before a miracle. Olivia felt the chills rise at the first note, so pure it must have made God weep. So soaring that the usually tongue-tied old woman turned a grief-soaked battlefield into a site of celebration for the life of this blustery old general and his grieving daughter.

Lady Bea's voice echoed away over the low hills, and the general's men snapped off a seven-gun salute. Grace quietly thanked everyone for the honor done her father. And Olivia stood silent a few minutes longer and thought again how rich Grace was in her life. How vastly wealthy her father had been, in the love and respect of his men and his child.

But then, from what Olivia had learned, he had earned it. He had been loyal and protective and kind in his brusque way. He hadn't condemned his own child when she'd needed him the most.

Ah, but that wasn't a memory that belonged at the burial of a brave man. Impatient that she could still feel the loss, Olivia decided to wait for Grace back at the carriage.

Lady Kate was already there, giving Lady Bea a long, hard hug.

"You continue to astonish and delight me, my love," the duchess was saying as she swiped tears from both their cheeks. "That was a lovely gift you gave Grace and her father."

Lady Bea, bright red and bobbing her head in some distress, huffed a bit. "Laurel... laurel wreath..."

"Indeed, he does deserve honor. I'm just glad you were here to offer it, for you know that the last time I sang, every cat in the neighborhood thought one of their own was being strangled."

Olivia helped settle the old woman into the coach.

"Poor dear," Lady Kate said as she shut the door. "She really feels so deeply."

"But her singing," Olivia said with an awed shake of her head. "Who could imagine?"

Lady Kate beamed. "Miraculous, isn't it? For some reason, it was unaffected. She can remember every lyric and note she ever learned. Not only that, but if she truly gets agitated, sometimes the only way to get any sense out of her is to have her sing it. She has no problem then." Lady Kate looked over to where Lady Bea waited inside the carriage, plucking nervously at her gloves. "Isn't the mind an amazing thing? I don't know what I would have done if I'd lost her."

"She's been your companion a long while?"

Lady Kate smiled. "Oh, didn't you know? She is my husband's youngest sister."

Olivia tried not to stare. Lady Bea was surely four decades older than Lady Kate. Not knowing how to respond, she merely nodded. "Well, we should get her back, as well as Grace."

She turned to see Grace surrounded by soldiers, smiling at them as an older sister would.

"That presents a problem I hadn't anticipated before," Lady Kate said, sounding unusually reluctant.

Olivia looked up. "What?"

Lady Kate waved toward Grace's friends. "They will assuredly wish to follow Grace home to continue the general's tribute. And once I have been seen opening my house to them..."

"There will be no reason to exclude it to everyone else." Olivia closed her eyes a moment. If the house was opened up to visitors, how could they keep Jack a secret until they could prove his loyalty? How could they uncover the truth about Jack's actions without betraying him? Without betraying themselves?

It was inevitable that Gervaise would come. And Jack was straining at the bit to get up. How were they going to keep the two of them apart?

"We have less time than we'd thought, don't we?"

Chapter 9

They got a reprieve. By the time they returned to the house, Grace's prediction had come true. Jack wasn't going to be walking anywhere soon. His fever was rising. While Grace accepted condolences in the Lavender Salon, Olivia cared for an increasingly irritable Jack on the second floor. But nothing she did seemed to make an impact on the fever.

"I don't want this," he snapped, his voice growing thin as he pushed away the gruel Olivia had brought. "Devil take it, I don't want *anything*."

"You have mentioned that," Olivia said, rescuing the bowl.

He shook his head as if he hadn't heard her. "I need to get up. I've wasted enough time as it is. I need to find it."

Olivia's head snapped up. "Find it?"

He'd said much the same before, when he'd woken the first time.

Jack was rubbing his fingertips against his eyes. "I can't have lost it. I have to find it."

"Jack?" She remained very still, her heart beating hard. "What are you talking about?"

Jack's eyes popped open. "What?"

"What is it you think you've lost?"

Now he looked impatient. "Lost? I haven't lost anything. Except," he all but snarled, "my bloody memory. Which my wife hasn't seen fit to help me recover."

"Only some of your memory," Olivia answered, feeling increasingly unsettled.

Her Jack would never have used profanity before her. He never would have used this tone of voice, which made it sound as if he were being fueled by a core of fury.

"It's time for a bit more willow bark, I think," she said, looking away from the harsh light in his eyes.

"I'm sorry, Liv," he suddenly said, reaching out to brush a hand across her cheek. "It's just I bloody well hate being ill. Especially after I'd just started to feel better."

"Yes," she said, sidling away from him and toward the medicine. "I gathered that as well."

"You'll find it for me, won't you? You'll find her?"

It went on like that for hours, as Olivia fretted and Jack slowly succumbed to the fever. One minute he was lucid, the next caught between two disparate worlds, and then finally he slipped into a place she didn't know. Grace stopped by to check the wound and told Olivia that this should be the worst night of it. Lady Kate suggested someone else spell Olivia. But she couldn't let them. She couldn't seem to walk away while Jack was so ill.

By ten o'clock, she was mentally and physically drained. Jack slept fitfully, a cool cloth draped across his forehead. The room was stifling. Needing air, Olivia lifted the window and stood before the tepid breeze.

The window looked out over the wide, elegant Rue Royale and the Parc beyond, where couples strolled beneath the lush trees and flickering lanterns. Somewhere church bells tolled the hour. It had been six days since the battle, and normal street sounds had begun to return: the rattle of cart wheels, the clop of horse hoofs, the singsong cadence of flower-sellers, the sound of conversations punctuated by the musical laughter of women.

Olivia desperately wanted to be out there. No, she admitted. What she really wanted was just to be away. To maybe run back to her little cottage in Devon, where she could regain her distance. Where she could recover her sanity. She wanted to be gone before she succumbed to this insane ride of emotions and made an irredeemable mistake.

She couldn't afford to fall in love again. Jack's memory would return, and he would once again abandon her. And this time, it might just destroy her.

She didn't leave, though. She stayed where she was, listening to Jack toss restlessly in the bed, plucking at his blanket, patting where his pockets would have been, searching for something.

For someone.

"Mimi!" Jack called, just as he had been all evening.

"Probably his old pony," Olivia heard behind her.

Olivia turned to see Lady Kate standing at the door. "If it is, she's a blond pony with breasts like pomegranates."

The little duchess stepped in, and Olivia saw that she was wearing another dressing gown, this one of shimmery peacock silk decorated in gold dragons that writhed across her shoulders.

"Pomegranates?" she echoed, staring down at Jack.

"Good Lord. I know he's changed, but who knew he'd grown poetic?"

Olivia considered Jack a moment. "He has changed, hasn't he?"

Lady Kate did her own assessment. "He isn't really our golden Jack anymore. I think life caught up with him."

Olivia shook her head. "Something did." Returning to her seat, she retrieved the now-warm rag from Jack's forehead. "I just wish he'd cease being such a nuisance and tell us he's innocent."

"Well, he'd better," Lady Kate said with a grimace. "If he doesn't, I haven't a clue what we're to do with him."

Olivia looked down on his poor, battered face and sighed. "If you'd asked me before Waterloo, I would have had quite a few suggestions."

Lady Kate smiled. "It does play hell with your self-righteous indignation when they go and get themselves half killed, doesn't it?"

Olivia dipped her rag and wrung it out. "It does." She grimaced. "Until they begin calling for another woman anyway."

Lady Kate huffed. "Well, then, he doesn't deserve your devoted attention. You should take the afternoon off tomorrow and rejoin the living."

"I might," she said. "If I haven't smothered him with a pillow and been carted off to gaol first."

Lady Kate actually laid a hand on her shoulder. "I'm not easing your burden, you know. I need you to help with visitors."

Olivia shut her eyes against the instinctive panic. She didn't want to face those people. Especially Gervaise. She knew as certain as sin that he'd be there.

But would it be any easier up here?

"Someone will sit with Jack," Lady Kate said, "and Grace will join us. It seems she can't consult with Dr. Hume for at least another day, and she doesn't trust anyone else."

Olivia felt a bubble of anxiety well in her chest.

"I've quite a notorious circle of friends," Lady Kate continued in light tones. "You'll undoubtedly be offended."

"Nonsense," Olivia retorted, lifting a trembling hand to wipe Jack's face. "I'm a divorced countess who is sheltering a possible traitor. I imagine they all pale in comparison."

Lady Kate's response was serious. "I think you need to attend, Olivia. You need to help us evaluate anything we hear about Jack."

Not from Gervaise. She couldn't face Gervaise.

"If Jack is better."

"Even if he isn't. I don't think we can wait."

Olivia sighed, knowing that Kate was right. "If Jack doesn't remember soon, we'll need to ask for help. But I don't know who we can trust with the truth."

"Funny you should say that," Lady Kate said. "I was just about to suggest my cousin Diccan. He's in the diplomatic corps, which should mean he can discover if there is any kind of official investigation. And I know for a fact he's able to keep a secret."

Olivia lifted an eyebrow. "Even if it jeopardizes the safety of his nation?"

For once, Lady Kate didn't have a glib answer. "I don't know," she admitted. "But you can see what you think tomorrow. He's promised to attend my at-home. If nothing else, he should keep us entertained. He's raised condescension to an art form."

That undoubtedly sounded better to Lady Kate than it did to Olivia. "Fine."

Kate had turned to leave when Jack began to toss again.

"Mimi!" he called. "*Ah, mignonne, je trouver vous!*"

Lady Kate stopped. "That's French."

Olivia nodded. "He seems quite fluent."

Lady Kate stared. "His French is appalling! I've heard it."

"Not anymore."

"Mimi..."

"*Ici*, Jack," she crooned until he quieted. "*Je suis Mimi. Soyez facile.*"

Be easy. As if it were that simple. Olivia thought the words would burn a hole through her chest.

Lady Kate stared. "I don't suppose he's said anything at all...important."

"Like whether he was in the French Army or sold secrets to Napoleon? No. I've asked in English *and* French. All he'll say is that he's searching for something he swears he had. I thought it might have been that dispatch, so I gave him a twist of paper. He dropped it. So I think he's missing something else."

"Mimi," he repeated. "*Où êtes-vous.*" *Where are you?*

"Besides Mimi, of course, which I consider careless of him." Her smile was hard. "A man should never misplace his mistress."

She lasted another two hours. She'd been trying to dribble willow bark tea down Jack's parched throat, when suddenly he grabbed her, knocking the cup over and splashing her.

"Tell me I didn't lose her," he demanded, grabbing her hand. "It's all I have of..." His eyes were open, and they looked haunted. "*Tell* me."

"You didn't lose her," she said so he would calm.

And, by degrees, he did. His breathing deepened. His grasp on her slackened, and his eyes closed. "I had it..."

He began to pick at his cover again, resuming his endless search. And suddenly it was too much. She couldn't stay.

She rang for Harper. When the sergeant arrived, still tucking his shirt into his pants, Olivia handed Jack's care over without a backward glance.

She didn't know where she meant to go. She was exhausted, but she knew she wouldn't be able to sleep. As she walked down the hall, what Jack had said kept replaying itself over and over in her head. *He'd had it.* Something he kept searching for. Something that might help him rest.

Suddenly she thought of the dispatch bag. The dispatches themselves rested in Lady Kate's safe. But Olivia had returned the bag to her portmanteau. Could she have overlooked something? She hadn't removed Jack's personal items. What if she had missed something there?

Well, she'd get no rest until she looked. Carrying her candle with her, she returned to the room she shared with Grace.

Grace lay on her side, fast asleep, and Olivia heard the faintest whisper of snoring through Lady Kate's bedroom door. No time like the present.

Setting down her candle, she knelt and retrieved the bag from where she'd stored it in her luggage, wrapped in muslin to keep Jack's blood from staining her clothes. And then for endless minutes, she just stared at it, her hand instinctively against her locket.

She needed to put more space between her and Jack, not less. She should give this to Lady Kate to search. But even Lady Kate didn't know Jack's things as Olivia did. So she grabbed the bag and candle and fled to the kitchen, where she'd be alone.

The cook's domain was pristine, every pot shining, every surface cleaned. Setting the bag on a scarred oak table, Olivia lit a lamp. The room beyond receded into darkness.

Taking a breath, she upended the bag. There was a clinking as the items rolled out. She ignored them and examined the bag. She turned it inside out and patted it to see if there were secret hiding places. She didn't find any. Which meant she was left with Jack's things.

She'd felt them before, identified them. Now she had to examine them in the light.

A snuffbox. A flask. Jack's signet ring.

Oh...

She loved that ring. Jack had slipped it onto her finger when he'd proposed, an ancient gold signet with the Wyndham griffin rampant etched across the face and the motto *Summum Laude* beneath. *The highest honor.* Jack had always laughed about the family motto, coined according to legend by a stiff-necked crusader. Meaning not the greatest accolades, but the perfect virtue. Jack had delighted in telling her that generations of Wyndhams had decided that since it was impossible to live up to the motto, they'd done their best to live it down.

They hadn't, of course. They had been exemplary

landlords and responsible members of parliament. Olivia rubbed the old gold of the ring, as if conjuring the truth of Jack's place in that line. Then, deliberately, she set it aside.

The gold and enamel snuffbox was uninteresting, except it carried with it fresh memories with the scent of Macouba and Spanish Bran, Jack's favorite mix. After a quick examination, she set that aside, too, and picked up the flask.

Typical. She could easily imagine Jack taking a last swig of brandy as he rode into battle. It was a beautiful thing, a flat square of chased silver, but it was nothing that should have explained his anxiety. She turned it over and unscrewed the top to sniff at it, but smelled nothing but brandy.

She was just about to put it down when her thumbnail caught on the long edge. Her heart picked up. She turned the flask over to examine it more closely, sliding her thumb over its edges.

There. An almost imperceptible seam. Slipping her nail into the minute crack, she worked at it until with a little *snap* the casing hinged open.

And she had her answer.

Blond. With breasts like pomegranates, perfectly visible through the scandalous lawn of her chemisette. Beautifully painted on an oval ivory inset, the miniature was of an exquisite, doe-eyed beauty wearing little more than a smile. It reminded Olivia of Romney's paintings of Emma Hamilton, a face of sunlight and whimsy, a body to inspire poetry, hair the color of sunlight.

And there, at the bottom of the picture, in perfect English: *Is not the first fruit sweet, my love?*

So this was Mimi. Faced with the possibility that this was what Jack had been seeking, Olivia could do no more than stare, sick at heart.

But just to be sure, she stood up and carried the flask back up to Jack's room. Sergeant Harper looked up when she opened the door, but she didn't have the composure to speak. She just reached over and placed the flask in Jack's searching hand. And watched as he abruptly stilled.

He brought the flask up to his chest and laid it there. And then he went soundly to sleep, as if relieved. Olivia turned away and closed the door behind her.

At any other time, Olivia would have delighted in Lady Kate's at-home. Seated alongside the duchess on the settee, she met the famous and infamous as they came to ingest gossip and tea. Lady Uxbridge, who had hurried to Belgium to be with her lord, came with Lady Somerset, both women pale and distracted by their husbands' injuries. Mr. Creevey shared Wellington's agony over the loss of so many men, and Fanny Burney skewered those civilians who'd been too timid to stay.

Each visited a precise fifteen minutes over tea or Madeira. Lady Kate's cook provided stacks of tea cakes and biscuits. Lizzie kept the tea service filled, and Olivia poured. She was happy to do so, since it kept her too busy to converse. And since Lady Bea took up the last place on the settee, there was no room on the settee for Gervaise's close company when he inevitably arrived.

He walked into the crowded salon on the heels of Lady Kate's cousin Diccan Hilliard. Diccan was everything the duchess had promised. Not a handsome man, Olivia thought, his features too broad to be classically aristocratic. He was tall and well formed, though, with a wide forehead, strong jaw, and deceptively lazy gray eyes beneath straight eyebrows. His sable hair was thick, and his nose looked as if it had been broken.

He was everything that was languid and witty. Even dressed in unrelieved black with no more ornamentation than one gold fob and a ruby signet ring, he effectively cast even the golden Gervaise into the shade.

"So, Katie," he drawled, his gold quizzing glass lifted between two fingers as he scanned Olivia and Grace. "These are the newest additions to your little family. They seem a bit...oh, shall we say, *naïf* for you, infant."

Olivia found him amusing, just as Lady Kate had said. Poor Grace succumbed to an unattractive blush.

Lady Kate paused as she listened to the impassioned whispers of an ardent suitor named Tommy with pomaded hair and vivid yellow inexpressibles to wave a dismissive hand at her cousin. "I have many faults, Diccan," she said. "Happily, deceit is not one of them. Olivia and Grace are well aware of my sins."

"You, Mrs. Grace?" he asked Olivia.

She handed off his cup of tea and smiled. "I was assured I would become quite as notorious as Her Grace if I entered her employ. Please don't tell me I was mistaken."

He raised an elegant eyebrow. There was a gleam in his eyes that reminded Olivia of Lady Kate. "You frighten me, ma'am."

She smiled. "Then it has been a profitable afternoon."

"En garde," Lady Bea abruptly barked from her place at Lady Kate's opposite side.

Diccan beamed on the old woman. "A palpable hit, indeed, Lady Bea. I suspect Mrs. Grace of being a worthy opponent."

"Really?" Gervaise asked as he waited for his own tea. "I have found Mrs. Grace to be quite shy. Submissive, even."

Olivia did her level best to remain calm. He wanted her to react. Before the battle, she would have. Today she focused on everyone who relied on her to keep her head. Today when Gervaise asked her to pour for him, she nodded and picked up a cup.

"You're having *tea*, Gervaise?" Lady Kate demanded with patent disbelief. "Is my Madeira all drunk, then?"

"Bit of a sore head," he admitted with attractive chagrin. "Besides, I consider it an honor to be served by Mrs. Grace."

Biting her tongue, Olivia asked his preferences, as if she didn't know, and handed over his cup. No one noticed him slide his fingers up her wrist. They noticed her almost drop the hot tea in his lap. Fortunately for the peace of the room, he grabbed hold of the cup just as she yanked her hand back. She turned away, never betraying her revulsion at his touch.

Next to her, Lady Kate addressed another newcomer, a broad-shouldered gentleman with sharp hazel eyes and salted black hair who had been introduced as Lord Drake. "You seem in fine fettle today, Marcus."

"And why shouldn't I be?" he asked, balancing cup and cake plate on his stockinette-clad knee. "Napoleon is finished, I won a pony from Armiston at faro last night, and I am allowed to spend the afternoon basking in your celestial presence, Kate."

Lady Kate frowned. "Are you saying I'm a moon, Marcus?"

He grinned. "A star. A sun. A comet streaking across the sky."

"Oh, no. Not a comet. It is far too farouche to be seen streaking anywhere."

"Very sensible," Diccan agreed. "Be a star, Kate. They don't even have to expend the energy of orbiting."

"And would still be the center of a universe," Gervaise agreed. "What do you think, Mrs. Grace?" he asked, turning on her. "Would you like to be the center of a universe?"

Olivia managed to keep her face impassive. "Heavens, no. I haven't the stamina for it."

Gervaise made sure only Olivia could see his smile. "You could easily be the center of *my* universe, Mrs. G."

Lady Kate tapped his arm. "One does not court a companion, Gervaise. You'll ruin her for hard work."

Lord Drake chuckled. "If you don't want anyone to notice your companion, Kate, hire one with a squint."

"Ah, thank you, Marcus. You reminded me of a task I've overlooked. Grace, Olivia, be warned. Marcus here is the leader of the notorious Drake's Rakes. Dangerous libertines all."

"Not so, not so," Lord Drake demurred with an easy grin. "Merely men who enjoy life to the fullest."

Kate's smile was wry. "Indeed. Well, you'll not be 'enjoying' anyone here. We're far too busy caring for our brave wounded to have time for even so much as a scandalous thought."

"Brave goddess," young Tommy of the yellow inexpressibles trilled.

"Fiddle. It's Olivia and Grace do the actual care. Although I did sacrifice my best carriage to ferry Grace back and forth to the battlefield."

"Oh, the battlefield," the sharply thin Lady Thornton said with a shiver. "We went just yesterday, didn't we, Thorny?"

"Perfectly awful place," her doughy lord sniffed. "Though I did manage to come away with a brilliant French saber."

"I was not collecting souvenirs," Grace said, her soft voice chilly, "but wounded soldiers."

"No place for a lady," Lady Thornton stated with disdain.

"No place for anyone at all," Diccan assured her with a straight face. "Perfectly hideous places, battlefields."

Grace went rigid. "Particularly for the men still lying there," she snapped. "Especially if they must watch souvenir hunters drive by without stopping while they—"

She stopped, blushing into blotches. Olivia froze in amazement. She'd never seen Grace raise her voice before.

"Brava!" Diccan drawled with a lazy clap of the hands. "The fair Boadicea puts us park saunterers in our place."

"Don't be absurd, Hilliard." Lord Thornton chuckled, his thick neck purpling above his high shirt points. "She don't actually expect us to stop and pick anyone up."

"She most certainly does," Diccan assured him, never taking his eyes from Grace. "Only think how people would talk if we did. Why, it might become all the rage, what, Miss Fairchild?"

Grace glared at him, but it seemed that she had

reached her limit. With a muttered excuse to Lady Kate, she gained her feet and limped from the room. Right behind her, Lady Bea rose like a duchess and followed, never bothering to take her leave.

"Hyenas," she muttered, much to Diccan's delight.

"Surely not, old thing. You must mean jackals."

Lady Bea stopped short and leveled her own glare on him. "Jackals," she said in awful tones, "don't laugh." And swept from the room, as if she hadn't spoken her first coherent words in five years.

"Rather churlish of you, Diccan," Lady Kate agreed.

He was still smiling. "Well, how was I to know Miss Fairchild would take exception to a bit of banter?"

"You might have remembered she just buried her father."

His eyes widened with real shock. "That tartar with the magnificent mustache?" He shook his head. "I didn't know. Just got back from helping deliver the victory news to London."

"An apology wouldn't go amiss," Lady Kate suggested.

"Apologize?" Gervaise countered with a big grin. "*Hilliard?* By Jupiter, just let me know when, and I'll have an audience to rival the Cribbs-Molyneaux bout."

"I'll lay you a monkey he never does," Thornton challenged.

Gervaise waved a spoon. "No one would take that bet."

"Stubble it, both of you," Diccan snapped.

"No need anyway," Thornton said. "Nothing more ridiculous. *You* don't travel to the battlefield, do you, Mrs. Grace?"

Olivia blinked at the sudden attention. "Oh, I'm not that intrepid. I care for the men here."

"Who are they?" Drake spoke up. "Anyone I should greet?"

Olivia's heart all but stopped beating.

"Excellent idea," Lady Thornton said, setting down her cup. "It would be unconscionable to overlook someone we know."

Lady Kate laughed. "I wouldn't worry," she said, picking a lemon biscuit from the tray. "We were somehow overlooked when it came time to dole out influential people. I believe our senior guest is a mere baronet."

"We should still visit them," young Tommy demanded. "Patriotic duty, you know."

"Excellent idea," Gervaise said. "Hasn't Miss Fairchild just chastised us for not doing our duty by our brave lads? What better way than to visit them on their sickbeds?"

He spoke to the room, but his eyes were suddenly on Olivia. It was all she could do to remain still. He was threatening her again. And he didn't even realize how great a threat it was.

"Another day, Gervaise," Lady Kate spoke up. "When they're strong enough to withstand the excitement."

"I believe I'll make a point of it," he said. "Frequently."

Olivia felt cold. She saw the glint of triumph in his eyes and battled a flush of dismay.

Just then, Finney lumbered into the room. "'Scuse me, Y'r Grace. Mrs. Grace be wanted upstairs."

Jack. Olivia knew it without his saying it. His fever had receded nicely, and she'd left him sleeping. But now she could hear a faint rumble of voices, one of them Harper's. She had to get up there. One shout from Jack and they were ruined.

One look at Lady Kate kept her from jumping up.

"Thank you, Finney," she said, rising and shaking out her skirts. "I'm on my way. My apologies, Lady Kate. I've left you with the teapot."

Olivia doubted anyone but Gervaise would have noted her departure. She made it a point to walk quietly out the door. The minute she was out of sight, though, she ran as fast as she could up the stairs.

Chapter 10

At first he thought it was a dream. He could see himself in bed with her, his sun-darkened hand a stark contrast against her milk-white thigh. He could smell the fresh air on the sheets. He could taste the morning sun on her skin. She was giggling as he tickled her, high, breathy notes of delight. She loved to be tickled, right there behind her beautifully dimpled knee. And every time he tickled her, she dropped the sheets she held so tightly to her throat in a simulated show of virtue.

Ah, success. She shrieked with glee and the sheet fell away, bestowing those perfect, luscious breasts for his sole delectation. They bounced a little with her mirth, and her rose nipples puckered with the sudden chill—and with the heat in his gaze. He couldn't look away from those perfect, pert breasts.

Before she could roll away in another display of maidenly reticence, he fell on them like a starving man, and, ah, the taste of them. The delicious texture of those long, hard nipples in his mouth as he sucked and nibbled and licked his way to heaven. The mysteries that just waited for his exploration beneath that lovely patch of blond hair. The charming music of her coos and sighs and moans as she lifted to meet his thrusts.

"Oh," she gasped, "surely you will kill me."

He laughed at her impish smile. "Surely I'll try."

And he'd tried very hard. But inevitably, he'd had to leave her in that warm, soft bed and return to duty. She was still giggling, threatening to give away all his secrets if he didn't return to her. So he rolled her over and slapped her pretty bottom. Then he lifted his uniform jacket from the bedpost and walked over to the chipped mirror that hung above her dresser.

"I don't love you, me," she pouted, showing him just a peek of those perfect breasts.

"Of course you do," he retorted, offering her a gallant bow. "And I, Mimi, love you to distraction."

Turning, he buttoned his jacket.

His uniform jacket.

His blue uniform jacket. With red facings and cuffs.

Jack lurched up in bed so fast his ribs screeched. Who was Mimi? Where had he been? And dear God, why had he been donning a French uniform?

How did he know it was French?

He shook his head. He had no idea. He just knew it as surely as his name. He dropped his head into his hands. "What have I done?"

"Problem, m'lord?" Harper asked from the doorway.

He was gasping for air. "Yes. No."

How did he ask? *Who* did he ask?

Jack looked up at the solid little man who still wore a tattered Guards jacket and wondered if he knew. But if he did, surely he would have said something. "Get my wife," he snapped.

It hadn't been a dream. He had been in that bedroom, with that woman. He'd been laughing, as if he had not had a trouble in the world. And he had been donning the uniform of the enemy as if he were used to it.

He understood now why he remembered guns.

Lying back, he stared at the plaster swags that criss-crossed the ceiling like elaborate spiderwebs. He tested the memory of that other bedroom, tried to bring it into focus. To bring *her* into focus.

Mimi.

He'd been happy with her. Without Livvie. Oddly enough, that thought brought a flush of resentment. And right behind it, a hot wash of shame.

What did it mean? What had he done?

He needed to talk to Livvie.

He must have spoken out loud, because in only minutes she was there.

"Jack?" She stood in the doorway, not quite entering the room. He noticed again how tired she looked. Her drab gray dress hung from her frame, as if she'd suffered deprivation, which made no sense. She was a countess, for God's sake. They were one of the wealthiest families in Britain.

"Why didn't you tell me I fought in a battle?" he demanded.

She stiffened. Her skin paled. Nodding to Harper, who'd followed her, she waited until he left before shutting herself in with Jack. She was so thin, was all he could think.

"You would have remembered soon," she said. "It seems you have."

"No, I haven't!" He closed his eyes and pressed his hands against them to try and shut out the images that still tumbled through his mind. Suddenly his world was upside down and all of his memories lies. He didn't even know what to *ask*.

So he went on the attack. "How much weight have you lost?"

He opened his eyes to see her standing still, her hands clenched at her waist. "I don't know. A stone, maybe."

"Maybe two. Why? And what are you doing wearing that execrable dress? You're a countess, damn it. Why do you look like an underfed governess? What aren't you telling me?"

She shrugged. "Quite a bit, I imagine."

He'd hurt her. He could see it in her eyes. He'd never hurt Livvie in his life. But if he hadn't, who the hell was Mimi?

He must have spoken out loud, because Livvie flinched.

"You remember her, then?" she asked.

He stared at her, stunned. "You're not surprised."

She never looked away. "When your fever was high, you kept calling out to her."

"But that's absurd. I don't know anybody named Mimi."

With breasts that should have odes written to them. With a gamine smile that embraced the universe. He was getting hard again just remembering. What the hell was wrong with him?

"I think you do know her," Livvie said, and sat in the chair by the bed. "Can you tell me about the memory?"

It was then that Jack realized how tightly her hands

were clasped. "No." He rubbed again at his forehead, as if it could erase the pictures. "It's not possible. I would never…never…"

And yet he felt guilty and ashamed. And wished like hell he could reclaim that laughing young face.

But he was not about to discuss that with Livvie.

As if she'd heard him again, Livvie sighed. "You and I had been having some problems," she said, her voice flat. She looked away. "You've been…away for a while."

"How long?"

She shrugged again without looking at him. "A while."

He could read the rest in her posture. *Long enough to take up with Mimi, whoever she was.*

"What do you remember of the battle?" Livvie asked, a curious stillness to her face, which made him feel even worse.

He remembered that he'd worn a French uniform and heard the boom of cannons, the stutter of a thousand muskets. Horses.

"Guns," he said, unable to tell the truth. "Big guns. Did I join the Hussars?"

"I don't think so."

"What do you mean? You must know. I'm here, aren't I? How did I get here?"

"Chambers found you and brought you to us."

He braced himself. "Well, what uniform was I wearing?"

For a second, she said nothing. Then she shrugged. "When you got to us? Life Guards."

"Life Guards? Don't be ridiculous. I never would have joined the Life Guards. If I finally convinced my father to let me join, it would have been the Hussars."

She shook her head. "I don't know, Jack."

"And you haven't *asked*? Someone has to know. My commander. My friends. Find Drake or Lidge. Hell, ask Gervaise."

"We've been told it's safer for you to remember yourself."

He opened his mouth and closed it again. Dear God. She couldn't tell him whether or not he'd...

He couldn't even think it. He saw himself again, smiling as he adjusted those damning red cuffs. Setting his shako on his head and whistling as he left Mimi's atelier.

He closed his eyes against the shaft of white-hot pain that pierced his temple and knew that he had to change directions.

"Chambers," he said, opening his eyes. "Ask him. Come to think of it, where the hell is he?"

She shrugged. "He left right away. He, uh, doesn't valet for you anymore."

Jack felt another linchpin in his life slip free. "Why?"

She shrugged. "I'm afraid I don't know that either."

Suddenly he was furious. With Livvie. With himself. With whatever fate had landed him in this bed with a head that didn't work.

He wanted answers. He wanted to be absolved of treason, and he didn't know how.

"Tell me about the battle," he said. "You can do that, can't you?"

She nodded. Settling back a bit into her chair, she told him of a field now called Waterloo. She talked of valor and carnage and the piles of dead, mown down like flowers in a storm. She mentioned Wellington and Uxbridge and Blucher, Napoleon and Ney and somebody named Grouchy, as if Jack should recognize it all.

Please, God, tell him he hadn't participated in such carnage. Tell him he hadn't turned against everything he believed in. Let there be another explanation.

He found himself reaching for Livvie's hand; suddenly, desperate in a way he'd never known just for the comfort of her touch. He held back. He had no right to her comfort. Not yet. Not until he knew for certain.

He looked down on her bowed head and thought how the sunlight set her hair afire, how she hummed as she became aroused. How free and open her smiles were. *Had* been.

What had he done to her? What had he done to himself?

"How?" he asked, and Livvie looked up. "How do I get my memory back?"

She seemed to search his eyes for something. "Grace is going to speak to a doctor tomorrow. We need to wait until she does before we try anything. You've been very ill, Jack. We can't take any chances."

If she only knew.

"My family," he said, clutching at anything familiar. "Do they know?"

"Not yet."

Absently he nodded. There was no way he could have betrayed his family. His name. His parents were far too proud and his older sisters a right pain. But how could he hurt young Ned and Georgie? He was their hero. Their teacher. And Maddie and Maude, poised on the brink of adulthood. He would ruin them all.

"Jack?" Livvie suddenly sounded so hesitant.

He shook his head. "Does your friend Grace have anything for a headache?"

In an instant, Livvie was on her feet, resting the back

of her hand against his temple. That simple touch seared him, stealing his breath and obliterating Mimi's face. He almost shoved Livvie's hand away.

"No temperature," she said. "But a headache can be a warning of brain fever. You mustn't fret so, Jack. You'll remember."

He looked up to see a vast uncertainty in her eyes. What was it she was afraid of? What memory? Could it be a French uniform? Or something worse? Could he bear to lose her regard if it was?

He should gather his courage and just ask.

He couldn't. He couldn't bear being unworthy of her.

"Why are you here?" he asked instead. "I don't think I've been very good to you lately."

She lifted a hand, as if she meant to touch him. But just as he had done, she let it fall. "What else could I do?"

"I'm sorry, Liv."

Her head snapped up and she glared. "Don't, Jack. Don't apologize until you know what it's for."

"I think I should get it done before I know how bad it is."

Her expression stiff and unrevealing, she got to her feet. "I think I should get your headache powder now."

All he could do in response was nod. "I think you should."

Olivia walked out without looking back, and he felt her dismissal in his chest. What was it he had lost back in the darker reaches of his mind? Something to do with the two of them, something crucial.

Could they really have bungled their marriage so badly? Was there someone who could tell him how? All he knew was that he'd been disporting himself with Mimi as if he had no one waiting for him back home. And how could that be?

He was still thinking about it twenty minutes later when Livvie stepped back into the room carrying a glass of liquid. Her back was straight and her expression calm, as if she hadn't just heard him speak of his mistress. She was brave, his Livvie. She had the strength of a soldier. And she carried the injuries he'd inflicted on her like battle wounds.

She was wrong. He could apologize before he knew exactly what injury he'd caused her. The problem was, she wouldn't accept it. So he took the glass and drank his medicine and allowed her to help him lie back down and rest, all the while knowing that he wouldn't rest at all. Not until he knew for certain what had brought him to this house in Belgium.

For the first time in weeks, Grace Fairchild allowed herself to enjoy a leisurely stroll through the Parc. It had taken another day, but she'd finally tracked down Dr. Hume to speak with him about the earl. She knew she should get the physician's advice back to Olivia, but the wait wouldn't make the news any better. Besides, she needed a moment to herself.

She was bone weary. There was still so much to do for the wounded, and she knew she had yet to face her future without her father. But for these few minutes, she needed to lift her face to the sun.

The day was warm, and the sky a perfect azure. A light breeze ruffled the trees. The smell of death had faded, replaced by the faint whiff of roses from the Parc Royale.

It had been so long since she'd been able to enjoy this lovely city with its winding cobbled streets and soaring Gothic churches. She loved the tall, gable-topped houses and the quaint old shops. She wished her leg was feeling well enough to climb the bell tower of St. Gudula's so she could look out on the jumbled red-tiled roofs of the medieval city. She wished she could simply wander the narrow streets and sit in one of the coffeehouses. But she knew that would have to wait.

She had just settled onto a bench beneath the broad limbs of a linden tree when she heard voices nearby.

"I'm telling you it's absurd. What would Gracechurch be doing in Brussels?"

Grace went perfectly still. The speaker was Lord Thornton. It was hard to mistake that petulant voice.

"*You* must know, Hilliard," someone else said. "You're in the government."

"I haven't the least clue," Mr. Hilliard replied. "Last I heard, he was sharing rum punch with the natives in the West Indies somewhere."

Their voices were coming closer.

"Heard he was seen on the battlefield with a weapon."

"Well I imagine if he was actually on a battlefield," Mr. Hilliard drawled, "a weapon would have come in handy."

"But nobody at headquarters seems to have heard of him," Mr. Armiston protested.

"Dear boy," Mr. Hilliard protested. "Right now, headquarters can't be relied on to count their own toes. I wouldn't rely on them to do any serious detective work. And why is it so vital you find out?"

"Why, he's family. Can't just ignore him."

Grace knew she should leave. Olivia needed to hear this.

She lurched to her feet so fast that her bad leg screeched in protest. Gritting her teeth, she grabbed the bench for balance and held on to her knee, afraid it would give out. She must have made a noise, because suddenly she heard footsteps.

"Why, if it isn't my Boadicea," Diccan Hilliard said, sauntering down the path toward her.

Grace blushed with shame. Of all times for him to come across her. She couldn't make a polite retreat. Her leg was still too seized up to function. And there, behind him, followed Gervaise Armiston and the florid, overstuffed Lord Thornton.

Grace didn't know which one she liked less. Thornton was an ass, and Armiston too.

There was no question who intimidated her more. One look at Diccan Hilliard had her heart stuttering around like one of Whinyate's rockets. She was sure she was already blushing like a child caught in a misdeed, just as she did every time she met Mr. Hilliard.

It wasn't just that she found him handsome. Most of her father's officers were handsome. It wasn't that she wished he would look on her with approval. Grace never expected that from any man. She knew exactly what she was and was comfortable with it.

Diccan Hilliard, though, had an unnerving ability to remind her of just what she wasn't. He strolled up to her like a suave god, clad in impeccable black, his curly brim beaver tilted just so, a gold-headed walking stick in hand, the epitome of elegance.

Reaching her, he bowed. "You present me the perfect opportunity to fulfill a most necessary duty, ma'am."

Grace felt a blush spread across her chest like a rash. "Indeed?"

Without waiting for her permission, he set her hand on his arm and held it with the other, concealing his support of her dicey leg. And suddenly he was looking at her. Really looking, his icy gray eyes oddly warm. "May I speak with you, Miss Fairchild? These jobberknolls will wait a moment for us."

"I don't think we will," Gervaise protested with a grin.

Mr. Hilliard stared him down. "But of course you will."

Before Grace could protest, he guided her a few steps away.

Grace had the most disconcerting feeling he was as uncomfortable as she. She was shriveling with embarrassment.

"Miss Fairchild," he said, tilting his head close so as to exclude the others. "Would you accept my sincere apologies? I had no idea your father had died when I made my thoughtless remarks yesterday. He was a gentleman and a fine soldier."

Grace felt as if she'd stumbled into a dream. Could he be sincere? Or was he merely setting her up to be the brunt of another joke?

His eyes lit with a wry smile. "I quite understand if you cannot completely believe me. I am not precisely known for any of the finer virtues. But I am serious. It was unconscionable of me to make sport like that."

She had never seen him look serious. But he did now, offering a half-smile that curled through her like smoke. And he was waiting for an answer.

"I will, gladly," she said, and found herself softening. "Thank you."

His smile reached his eyes, if only for a moment, before he lifted her hand and dropped a kiss on it. Blinking like a dolt, Grace could think of nothing to do but nod.

"Please consider me at your service," he told her, and oddly, she thought him sincere. "Now," he said, leaning even closer. "Would you help me protect my reputation?"

She thought she said yes. Winking, he returned her to where the others waited.

"Ah, fair Boadicea," he said, his voice once again languid. "It would please me, pon rep it would, if you'd accept my apologies."

Grace barely prevented herself from gaping. It was as if he felt it necessary to camouflage his thoughtfulness with a veneer of artifice. And oddly, she understood.

"If you will desist in calling me Boadicea," she retorted.

His smile was wicked. "But who more resembles that redoubtable woman?"

"Indeed? Boadicea stood six feet in her stockings and had a deformed leg?"

Could she actually be bantering with Diccan Hilliard?

"Don't know about the leg. Must have been about your size, though. Vanquished Rome, after all." He gave her a slow perusal that made her weak-kneed. "Or would you rather be an Amazon?"

"Thank you, no." She knew her face was flaming. "I see no need to sacrifice a breast just to chuck a javelin at someone."

Lord Thornton flushed. "Here, I say!"

Mr. Hilliard stilled, and Grace saw his surprise. Then, abruptly, he threw back his head and laughed. "Odious wench."

She grinned. "Toplofty snob."

"I say," Thornton whispered to Armiston. "Did he apologize or not?"

Mr. Hilliard leveled his glass on them. "You owe me a monkey, Thornton. And now, Miss Fairchild, it would please me to accompany you on your walk."

Was he being kind? Did he realize how badly her leg hurt?

"Oh, I say, Hilliard," Thornton protested. "You can't mean to waste my afternoon babysitting a companion?"

Mr. Hilliard's smile slowly froze. "Sometimes, Thorny, I wonder why I waste my time with you. Good day."

Grace didn't know what to say. At that moment, it was all she could seem to do to put one foot in front of the other.

And it wasn't to be her only surprise of the afternoon. They had reached the gate almost across from Lady Kate's house, when Grace was hailed from across the street.

"Gracie!" A gentleman in the buff and blue jacket of the 11th Light Bobs was waving from Lady Kate's doorstep.

Grace came to an ungainly halt, only Mr. Hilliard's arm keeping her upright. "Kit!" she called back, delighted.

Major Christopher Braxton ran to intercept her. As he loped across the busy street, one noticed that his left sleeve was empty and his face scarred from burns.

"Gracie!" he greeted her, pulling her away from Diccan with his good arm and giving her a twirl. "I tried to get here sooner, but I was all the way to Paris before I heard about the general. You know I would have seen him off if I could."

Grace hugged him back. "Of course I do. I didn't even know you were back. I thought you'd sold out after Toulouse."

His grimace was telling. "Quartermaster Corps. No one trusts a one-armed dragoon."

She shook her head. "Fools." And she meant it. Kit was one of the most daring soldiers she'd ever known.

It was at that point she suddenly remembered Mr. Hilliard. Giving way to another furious blush, she presented him.

Mr. Hilliard bowed. "You are acquainted with this lady?"

Kit returned the gesture, his expression cautious. "Charter member of Gracie's Grenadiers."

Mr. Hilliard became his most supercilious, quizzing glass lifted. "Egad, that sounds perfectly martial."

"And so it is," Kit assured him. "It is our sworn duty to always protect and be of service to our magnificent Grace."

"Excellent. Then I may safely leave her in your care. I must catch up with my friends." And with that devilish grin, Mr. Hilliard tipped his hat and sauntered away.

Grace turned to Kit, embarrassed. "That was not well done, my dear."

"Of course it was," Kit disagreed with a grin. "Don't want the bounder thinkin' our Grace is unprotected."

She couldn't help laughing. "Kit, your Grace has been protecting herself since she was ten, when Harry Lidge tried to run her over with an elephant. Shall you join me for tea?"

"Can't." He scowled. "Maybe tomorrow?"

She smiled, suddenly happy. "You know where I'm staying."

He tipped his head. "Flying high, my girl."

Grace frowned. "Her Grace has been all that is kind. I think she knew I would not have done well alone right now."

"Point taken. You'll call if you need anything."

And not thinking how quickly she might have to do that very thing, she bid him good-bye.

It was when she entered the house to find Lady Kate, Lady Bea, and Olivia waiting to leave that she remembered just what news she had to impart.

"The word is out," she said baldly. "Someone spotted Lord Gracechurch and knows he's in Brussels."

Olivia immediately began stripping off her gloves. "Then we need to help him remember the truth before he's discovered."

Grace completely forgot she was standing in the middle of Lady Kate's foyer. "We can't," she said. "It would kill him."

Chapter 11

Olivia froze in place, her glove hanging from her fingers.

"Do you still feel like a walk, Olivia?" Lady Kate asked.

"We might want to stay here," Grace said, stepping completely inside and closing the door. "You'd be surprised what can be overheard in the Parc."

Lady Kate immediately handed off her bonnet. "Finney, we'll be in the garden."

Adding Olivia's garments to Finney's pile, Lady Kate steered everyone toward the back of the house. Olivia almost balked when she realized they would pass through a room that held three of their wounded.

"Don't get up, lads," Lady Kate trilled as she stopped on her way through the library to grab the sherry decanter and pass three glasses to Olivia. "We're just off to see the flowers."

"A pleasure to havc you in our humble barracks, Your Grace," one of the soldiers assured her from his cot by the bookcases.

"And smell you," the blind lieutenant next to him said with a grin. "You are flowers yourselves when you waft through. Especially you, Lady Bea."

Lady Bea stopped to kiss each man on the top of the head on the way by. One of the men had lost his sight, another his leg. Another had been caught beneath his fatally stricken charger and suffered broken ribs. Olivia saw them as an indictment on her own actions. They had fought honorably and suffered terribly. And yet, she protected Jack at their expense.

"Now," Lady Kate said after they had successfully escaped to the quiet of the tiny garden and sherry was handed around. "Spill your budget, Grace."

Grace eased down next to Lady Bea on one of the wrought-iron benches as if her leg was bothering her, making Olivia feel even worse. But she couldn't wait for her friend to get comfortable.

"What do you mean we can't tell him?" she demanded.

"I've spoken to Dr. Hume," Grace said, staring down at her sherry as if for advice. "And he told me that we simply can't force the earl's memories on him."

"But why?"

"Because Dr. Hume fears it could bring on brain fever. The earl's condition is called *amnesia*. It is common after head injuries to briefly forget some time before the trauma."

"Briefly?" Lady Kate demanded.

"He will most likely recover all but the hours before the injury. But there is no way to predict how much of the memory will return. Or when. And there might always be gaps."

Olivia stared at nothing for a moment, unable to

comprehend the scope of the disaster. For some reason, she got caught on one fact. "He could have married again and not know it."

Grace nodded. "I'm afraid so."

"Most men's fantasy," Lady Kate quipped.

"Not his." Olivia shook her head, then whispered, "Not the Jack I knew."

Lady Kate frowned. "I'm not sure the Jack in there *is* the one you knew."

Olivia opened her mouth to disagree but stopped. Lady Kate was right. Jack was different. Darker, harder, more complex. Her Jack was still there. But he had gained layers she didn't recognize.

"Caterpillar," Lady Bea blurted out.

"Indeed," Lady Kate answered. "But I'm not perfectly certain he means to come out a butterfly, Bea."

"Then we need to find out," Olivia said. "You're certain we can't ask him about his lost time?"

Grace did not look happy, but she shook her head. "It could prove fatal. Headaches are a symptom, and he has had some."

Lady Kate snorted unkindly. "I'd have a headache, too, if I just told my wife about my mistress."

Olivia felt panic climb her throat. "But then what do I do?"

"Family!" Lady Bea snapped.

Lady Kate nodded. "What do *we* do?"

"Offer support," Grace said. "We can acknowledge returned memories, but that is all. But"—Grace stopped, and Olivia looked up to see that her friend hated to continue—"he must not under any circumstances be reminded of traumatic events."

"He already knows he fought in a battle," Lady Kate said. "What could be more traumatic than that?"

Olivia just stared at her.

"Oh," Lady Kate responded sheepishly. "Of course."

"He must rediscover those memories on his own," Grace said.

Olivia felt the impact of Grace's words sink like a rock in her chest. "So I'm to continue pretending we're still married."

Grace looked distressed. "Yes."

That brought her to her feet. "No." She knew she sounded shrill. "I won't. I *can't*."

"You have no choice," Lady Kate said very quietly. "Whatever else has happened, we must be able to prove his innocence."

"No, we don't," Olivia snapped. "He doesn't deserve my loyalty or my help. He certainly doesn't deserve my sympathy."

Lady Kate lifted a wry eyebrow. "Then why did you save him at all?"

Olivia closed her eyes against a fresh surge of impotent resentment. There was no good answer to that question, and she knew it. "He's going to keep asking questions," she protested.

Lady Kate nodded. "Hopefully he'll remember the rest soon."

It took a moment, but Olivia finally shook her head. "No. We can't wait. We have to find another way."

"I'm afraid you're right," Grace said. "When I was in the Parc just now, I heard Mr. Hilliard speaking with Lord Thornton and Mr. Armiston. They're looking for Lord Gracechurch."

"Well, we can't move him," Lady Kate protested.

"We can't keep him here either," Olivia retorted, beginning to pace. "Our patients are about to be shipped home."

Which meant Jack would lose his camouflage. They would lose their excuse for staying behind in Brussels where they could keep him sequestered.

She tipped up her glass and drained her sherry. "Jack and I need to leave."

Lady Kate scowled. "And refuse me my adventure? Don't be a looby. Give us another answer. Who else knows about Jack?"

"Chambers," Olivia said before thinking of it.

Lady Kate lifted an eyebrow. "Gervaise's valet?"

Olivia looked up, shocked that she hadn't thought of it before. "He used to be Jack's valet. He's the one who found him at Hougoumont. Said he got a message from him."

"Turncoat," Lady Bea snorted.

Lady Kate turned to her. "Chambers? Yes. But a handy turncoat, dear." Rising, she began to gather glasses. "I'll send him a note."

"No." Olivia protested, grabbing her arm. "I told you. Gervaise can't know."

Everyone turned toward her. Olivia knew how shrill she sounded.

"Are you finally going to tell me why you have such a particular aversion to him?" Lady Kate asked. "It is more than just a loathing to mix with Jack's family I think."

This was moving too fast. Olivia wasn't sure she had the courage for it. "Will you believe me?"

Lady Kate lifted a languid hand. "Gervaise is a charming dinner companion. But you will remember that I braved a thunderstorm to pry you out of his hands."

Olivia stared at her. "You knew he was there?"

The little woman shrugged. "Someone might have mentioned how quick he was to get Mrs. Bottomly out of town. I thought it...exceptional. Especially when he went back for you himself."

So Lady Kate's offer of sanctuary hadn't been as capricious as Olivia had thought.

Lady Kate sat back down and poured another round of sherry. Pulling in an unsteady breath, Olivia joined her.

After all this time, the words were so difficult. "Gervaise," she said finally, her hand clenched around her glass, "is singularly focused on what he wants. For him, the ends always justify the means."

"What was it he wanted?" Grace asked.

"What Jack had."

Lady Kate frowned. "But he could never inherit."

"Truly? That never seemed to matter. But I think he saw Jack's advantages as shiny new toys. Money. Talent. Power."

"You?"

Olivia was picking at her dress now. "Please understand. It isn't that I am so desirable. My looks are at most middling and my talents few. But I think Gervaise saw that Jack was smitten" —she shrugged—"and suddenly I was the shiny new toy."

For a moment, there was stark silence.

"Are you telling me that Gervaise orchestrated all that nonsense five years ago?" Lady Kate demanded.

Olivia almost laughed out loud. Only Lady Kate

would define a divorce, a duel, and a death as "nonsense." "Gervaise was very persuasive. And Jack and I were so young. Maybe if we'd had more time together. Maybe—"

The duchess snorted. "Maybe nothing. Jack was always the golden child. He'd never been truly challenged in his life." She shook her head. "I'm just sorry he failed at his first fence."

Olivia shook her head, almost amused that suddenly she was the one defending Jack. "Gervaise did present a convincing case."

"Willingly aided by the Wyndhams, I assume?"

"Spiders," Lady Bea muttered.

"Can you blame them?" Olivia asked. "I am hardly what they expected for the next marchioness."

"Certainly not," Kate said. "You have spirit, wit, and compassion."

Olivia sighed. "And a former husband who might be hanged as a traitor. Which would absolutely delight Gervaise."

Lady Kate got to her feet. "Then he shall never know."

Olivia blinked. "It's that simple?"

Lady Kate's smile was rapacious. "Indeed it is. In fact, I believe I shall enjoy the game of confounding him."

Olivia jumped up again. "This is no game, Kate. Gervaise is dangerous."

"Oh, now, Olivia."

At that moment, Olivia had a choice. She could be honest, or she could be expedient. She considered telling Kate the truth. All of it. Even the most dangerous, the most awful truth of all.

But the moment passed. She didn't have the right.

"How do you think I lost my child?" she asked instead, for it, too, was a truth.

For the first time, she saw honest astonishment on Lady Kate's face. "You can't possibly mean..."

"Don't you see? Gervaise convinced Jack that the baby wasn't his. But one look at Jamie would have revealed the truth. Gervaise couldn't chance that."

"Oh, Olivia..."

"He poisoned a nine-month-old baby!" Olivia cried. "He found us where we were hiding and slipped henbane into my baby's pap."

She could see it on their faces. The charge was one too many, the idea too inconceivable. Even Lady Bea looked skeptical.

"How can you be certain?" Grace asked.

Olivia sat back down, suddenly unbearably weary.

"He told me. He made it a point to when he came to pay his condolences. I've been on the run ever since."

Lady Kate spent some long moments considering the bloodred roses that lined the garden wall. Olivia held her breath, terrified that her friends, like everyone else, would find it too hard to believe Gervaise could be such a monster.

But Lady Kate, one hand up to massage the bridge of her nose, began to shake her head. "All right, then," she said, coming to her feet in what Olivia thought of as her duchess pose. "I can set Finney to contacting Chambers without Gervaise finding out. What else?"

Olivia felt light-headed with relief. It was her turn to show courage. "It's time to trust someone else," she said, and stood, as if that would give her extra courage. "We need to speak to your cousin Diccan."

* * *

They lost four of their patients the next day, sent off on rumbling carts with smiles and hampers of food. By the time the move was accomplished, noon had come and gone, and Olivia still hadn't seen Jack again. She knew she was avoiding him, but each visit took more out of her. Each moment of opening that door, of hearing his voice, of seeing him catch sight of her and break into that wide, boyish grin. Of steeling herself against the inevitable shock of contact when she finally had to touch him.

She was losing her hard-won distance. Her precious control. She knew that there would be an afterward to this brief rift in her life. She knew she would have to walk away alone. It had taken her five years to learn how to do so with equanimity. After only a few days, she would have to start all over again.

The church bells were striking one by the time she collected enough courage to present herself. Her body had begun to sing the minute she'd climbed the first step. Her heart had begun to speed up, her hands gone clammy. She was afraid. She was excited. She was so churned up with ambivalence that she wasn't sure she'd ever be able to rest again.

He was seated in a wingback chair by the window, playing cards with Thrasher. Harper must have lent him clothing, because he wore an oversized shirt and trousers. Thrasher had obviously lent his wig, which sat perched atop Jack's head like a furry beret, his thick sable hair curling ludicrously beneath it. Olivia found herself fighting a smile at the sight.

"That, sir," Jack accused his small challenger, "is cheating."

Thrasher looked up from his discard. "'Course it is," he admitted brightly. "Only way to win against toffs."

"Don't be a brat," Jack suggested, scooping up the cards and shuffling. "And I resent being called a toff, you guttersnipe."

Thrasher laughed as if Jack had tickled him. Jumping up to retrieve his wig, he plopped it on his own head. "Now I'm a toff too."

"Oh, good," Jack retorted. "Now *I* can cheat."

"I think I got here just in time," Olivia said, stepping into the room. "I fear the house is about to fall prey to scoundrels."

"Scoundrels." Thrasher nodded. "That's us, all right."

"It occurs to me, my lady," Jack said, leaning his head back against the chair and raising pleading eyes to her, "that you have not kissed me today."

Harper had removed Jack's headwrap that morning, exposing the still-swollen and bruised injury along the side of his face. Olivia caught herself wanting to kiss the length of it. She wondered if her smile looked as strained as it felt.

"It occurs to *me,*" she retorted, hands on hips, "that you haven't eaten your dinner. Shall I get you some gruel?"

The face he made would have once had her in giggles. "Only if you want to finish the job of killing me. I beg you, Livvie. No more gruel."

"Soup, then. A bit of bread."

"A kiss."

"You have been very ill, Jack."

He pouted. "The last I heard, nobody died from a kiss. In fact, it's been proven a kiss can wake a person from death."

"Only in fairy tales."

"Who says they're fairy tales? Maybe they're true stories that have been exaggerated a bit, like *ton* gossip."

Olivia felt the old thrill of his infectious humor and fought against it. "Oh, like that fable of the gambling countess."

His grin was wry. "I certainly hope so."

She nodded. "So you'd have it that if I'd just kissed you before now, you would not have been rendered unconscious."

"No. I just would have wakened sooner." He grinned again, his green eyes preternaturally bright against his pale, bruised face. "Can you really think I could stay away from you, Liv?"

Olivia was proud of herself. She held her place against the sudden blast of anger that buffeted her. Imagine his staying away from her? Of course she could imagine it. She could imagine it, because he *had* managed to stay away.

Something must have showed on her face, because Jack frowned. "I wouldn't have stayed away. If there is anything I do know, it's that."

For a long moment, all she could do was open and close a fist in an effort to control herself. She ached to batter him with the truth. To make him face what he'd done to her.

But that kind of truth had no place in her life right now. She couldn't afford it. If she let one real memory out of the box, the rest could well sneak out behind it, and that she couldn't bear.

She almost laughed at that lie. The memories were already out, churning emotions she feared she couldn't control. But Jack wouldn't understand that now. And she couldn't force it on him, not until he understood her anger. Her grief. Her years of despair.

If only he didn't still keep that damned flask beneath his pillow. She could see a corner glint beneath the snowy linen.

"It's all right," she said, careful to keep any tremors from her voice. "How is your leg?"

He looked down as if surprised to see it there. "Much better. It seems honey is good for something besides crumpets."

She nodded, careful to keep her hands to herself. "Thrasher, would you be so kind as to get this churl a bit of roast beef?"

Thrasher jumped up from his chair. "I can cadge him a bit of chocolate, too, 'f ya want. Them Belgians make it real proper. Easy as pie to snatch."

"Keep your famblers to yourself, you scamp," Jack warned.

Thrasher had barely made it out the door before Jack turned back to Livvie. "I said something wrong just now," he said, reaching out a hand.

She took it rather than risk his wondering. "Not really." Her resistance began to melt just with his touch. "It's just... well, you were so hurt. You almost did stay away."

God forgive her for such a facile lie. God forgive her for hating him even more for the need of it.

"I'm sorry, Liv," he said, looking absolutely sincere. "I would never upset you for the world."

"But you did," she said before she could stop herself.

"That's not all," he said quietly, watching her too closely. "Is it? I know that it's been longer than two weeks since I've seen you. I can't imagine it, I swear to you. But... evidence doesn't lie. What happened between us, Liv?"

For a moment, she couldn't even breathe. She was so afraid she would blurt out the truth. *You threw me away like last night's garbage. You listened to a liar and damned your own child, and then you made a new life with someone named Mimi.* "Oh, I think we were simply too young and precipitate when we married. We didn't give ourselves time to know each other well enough to withstand troubles. And then..."

"I joined up."

She blinked. Swallowed. "Yes."

"What about Gervaise? Did he join with me?"

She laughed. "Are you mad? Can you really imagine Gervaise slogging about in the mud?"

He rediscovered his grin. "You're right. I hope I am not in considerable debt to him by now over your little card games. Or have you finally allowed me to cover your losses?"

Olivia felt those words like a punch. He still didn't believe her. "If you want me to stay," she said, letting go of his hand, "you will never mention gambling to me again."

"Oh, I know you got in over your head, Liv," he said, reaching for her again. "It's perfectly understandable. You'd never had that kind of blunt to throw about before."

Evading his clasp, she stepped back. "I mean it, Jack. I will tell you this one time and then never again. I. Never. Gambled. If you cannot believe me, we have nothing more to say, and I will leave you in Sergeant Harper's capable hands."

"But Gervaise—"

"Lied."

"Oh, don't be absurd, Livvie. Why would Gervaise lie?"

Again, she fought for reason. One word of truth here and the rest would pour out like poison. Drawing in a slow breath, she was proud of how calm she sounded. "It is one of the troubles I spoke of, Jack. You found it easier to believe everyone but me. Your lack of trust began to eat at us."

"How can I trust you when I don't remember what happened?" he demanded, oddly angry.

"You do remember that I made a vow that I didn't gamble. You knew I would never break a vow. But you never questioned what anyone said about me. You never defended me." Tears welled in her chest, but she refused to let them gain ground. "I won't allow that to happen again."

She saw the distress in his eyes and desperately wanted it to be real. "Give me a chance, Liv," he begged, once again trying to take her hand. "I probably don't deserve it, but I want to make it up to you. Let us get to know each other again. Please."

She'd meant to keep a safe distance from him. She meant to pull away. Instead, somehow she found herself taking his hand. She found herself sitting back down.

"I'll try."

He leaned back in his chair, as if the last few minutes had exhausted him. "I've been trying so hard to remember," he said, and suddenly she saw that he really was plagued by his uncertain memory. His eyes were dark with it. "It feels as if it's all just out of my reach, as if I could recover it by merely closing my eyes. But I try, and it skips away, and I feel...furious. Frightened. Upended.

There is something bad lurking in the fog, and I simply can't see it." He looked up at her then, and the pain in his eyes pierced her. "What is it I'm afraid of, Liv? What have I done?"

And suddenly she wanted to lie for him. She wanted to hold him to her and promise it would be all right, when she knew it couldn't. Obeying old instincts, she reached over and gently pushed back that rogue lock of hair. "We'll find out," she told him. "I promise. What has fallen out of the fog so far?"

"Well," he said, fingers pressed to his injury, "I know this is going to sound odd, but"—he shrugged—"lions."

Olivia stared at him. He was frowning, as if waiting for her to laugh. "Lions?"

"Yes. They're looking in the wrong direction."

She blinked. "Who? The lions?"

His answering smile was a bit lopsided. "Odd, isn't it? But I have this thought suddenly stuck in my brain, and it won't let loose. Lions. And the conviction that they're looking the wrong way, whatever that means." His smile grew. "I don't suppose Lady Kate has a menagerie I've been hearing in my sleep? I certainly wouldn't put it past her."

"She is a good friend," Olivia retorted more hotly than she'd intended.

Jack's eyebrow rose. "Do you believe I think less of you because you've taken refuge with her?"

"The point is, I don't care. She is my friend, and nothing will change that."

He lifted her hand and kissed it. "Then she shall be. I'm the last person to choose your friends, Liv." Again, he stopped. Frowned. Closed his eyes, as if the memories were teasing him again. "I remember being cold. And hungry. God, I was so hungry. We must have been on a fast march."

"You have lost weight."

He rubbed at his stitches. "I can't tolerate this. I want so badly to remember, and every time I try, I end up with a ferocious headache."

She instinctively clutched his hand. "Well, then, stop. You'll remember when your brain is recovered enough."

He shook his head, holding her hand as if afraid he'd fall. "Sit with me for a bit, Liv. Please."

So she sat. She pulled Thrasher's chair close and watched as emotions alien to Jack Wyndham flickered across his eyes: fear, anxiety, loss. Vulnerability. She saw and knew that Lady Kate was right. The Jack Wyndham who had come back to her wasn't the one who had walked away.

Jack had never needed her before. He had *wanted* her. He had loved her. But he had never sought her out when he felt unsure or sad or frightened. But then, she had never believed he'd ever really felt such things.

Lady Kate had also been right about him having been a golden boy. It had been such a blessing to bask in his light. Olivia had a terrible feeling that it would be an even greater privilege to be his light when he faced darkness.

She wondered, suddenly, whether that playfulness Jack showed with Thrasher, the playfulness that would have once been the sum total of Jack, was now only a mask hiding what he couldn't allow anyone else to see. What he now asked her to see.

It frightened her so badly she almost pulled away. She didn't want to love him again. She didn't want to be the repository of his dreams and fears and sins. She had enough to carry on her own.

But, oh, how could she turn from such pain?

Keeping hold of his hand, she went down on her knees beside his chair. "Tell me, Jack. Tell me what you're thinking."

His smile was so strained. "I'm still thinking about that kiss," he teased, his voice sore and tired. "I know I don't deserve it. But, please, Liv. I have the most absurd feeling I'll perish without it."

She saw sincerity in his eyes. She felt the almost frantic clasp of his hand, as if he was afraid to let her go. She realized in that moment just how much danger she was in. She simply couldn't tell him no.

Getting up, she leaned over the chair and laid a hand against his battered cheek. She briefly closed her eyes and inhaled the secret scent of Jack. She felt the tug of that unbreakable tether that still held her to him. Sighing, she brushed her fingertips against the rough stubble of his beard.

"You're right," she whispered. "You do need a bath."

And then she kissed him.

Where had the anger gone? All she could feel was a worn kind of joy, swirling through her like the attar of long-dead roses. All she could think was how she had missed him. How she had lost the comfort of his arms when she needed them, how she'd lost the exquisite pleasure of his touch.

She knew better. Didn't she know better? But blind to everything but his mouth and his scent and the delicious rasp of his fingers against her skin, she realized that she should have known that this was inevitable. His eyes were so sweet, so grateful, as if heat and hunger were miles away. As if, for once, the two of them met as imperfect humans who needed each other for solace. For communion. For support. She closed her eyes again and met him mouth to mouth, and she was lost.

It was no different. No. It was better. Deeper, the taste of him harsher, hungrier. She was the one this time to let her hands wander. She spread them against his chest to tease herself with the soft crinkles of hair that peeked out of the open collar of his soft cotton shirt, to taunt herself with the memory of how that hair narrowed to an arrow that bisected his belly. She rediscovered the sleek power of his muscles and the hard lines of his arms. She melted against him when he wrapped his arms around her and pulled her more fully onto his lap.

"Your leg," she protested, pulling her mouth away.

He tangled his hand into her hair, sending pins flying, and pulled her back to him, and she heard him sigh. She felt the warm lift of his breath against her lips, and she opened to him.

He nuzzled at her neck, that little hollow at its base, where his touch had always sent a waterfall of chills down her body, where it did now, settling deep in her belly, down where the heat in her had died so long ago, where the woman in her waited for resurrection.

She felt his shaft, astonishingly hard against her thigh, and rubbed herself against it. She knew that part of him even more intimately than any other, and her body craved it like air.

He had once filled her. He had taken away her loneliness and replaced it with wonder. She could still feel the burn of him as he drove into her, the slick friction of his thrusts, deep and sure, all the way to her now-empty womb, which was suddenly hollow with need. She could feel the slick slide of skin against skin, the moist secrets of mouths meeting. She could remember companionship and communion and love.

She felt his hand sweep down her arm, down her leg, like lightning, like daybreak, and she arched closer to his touch. She wanted to keen and wail and sob for the lost beauty of their lovemaking, for the hard, hungry matings and the soul-shattering hours when they challenged themselves on to higher, more exquisite pleasure. The early mornings met in friendship and the late nights in surprise.

She missed him. Sweet God, she missed him, and she hadn't allowed herself to admit that for years. She shouldn't allow it now, because it would make it so much harder later when he left again. But it was as if her body had been waiting for his hands to waken it. For his mouth to bless it. For his body to meet it.

She stretched into his hands, his touch setting her skin afire. She sent her hands searching over him, hand and hip and the corded thighs of a horseman. She closed her ears to everything but the thunder of their hearts. She closed her eyes to everything but the terrible beauty of his body, his eyes, the unbearably soft pillow of his mouth. For immeasurable minutes, she gave herself up to the whirlpool of sensation, her mind a thousand miles from despair.

It was Jack, finally, who broke the kiss. She hovered, uncertain, his hands on her shoulders, his breath caught against her throat. She looked down and was shocked to see his eyes closed. He pushed her away as if she were contaminated.

"That was a terrible idea," he muttered, shaking his head.

Olivia's stomach clenched with shame. Her heart battered at her ribs. It had been so good. It had been revisiting what she had lost, and it hurt so deeply she couldn't even reach it.

Looking down at Jack's upturned face, she saw that he'd felt the same sweet communion and was appalled by it.

She brushed off her skirts with shaking hands. "Thrasher will bring your meal," she said, not able to look at him. "I'm sure it will be better if I don't return."

And again she walked out on him.

Chapter 12

What had he done? God, he knew better. He had no right to make love to Livvie. Not now. Not before he knew for certain what he had lost in the chasm of his memory.

Closing his eyes, he listened as Thrasher clattered about setting up the tray of food he suddenly didn't want. He could still smell Olivia's scent, the faint breath of apples and spring, as if she'd been wandering barefoot through an orchard on a summer's day. He could still hear the surprise in her sighs, as if lovemaking were something unfamiliar.

She had looked so hesitant when she'd opened that door, as if poised for flight. She'd looked just as she had when they had first faced their passion, those times she'd accepted him on nothing but love and trust in the days before their marriage. Before he'd proven to her that he always kept his promises.

It had never been enough to merely worship her body like an acolyte. He'd promised to protect and honor her, no matter what his family said. He'd sworn that every time they came together, it would be a sacred thing.

Suddenly she didn't believe him. He could tell by her expression, by the strain in her voice. By the very fact that she insisted on wearing those horrible high-necked rags.

She knew him so well. She knew that even though he loved her entire body, every hidden freckle and each strand of sun-streaked hair, there was just something special about her throat. About that notch just above its base. The sight of it alone could make him hard. Even in his dreams he could feel it against his tongue, that seductive little dip, that perfect repository for a single tear, for a drop of perspiration. It was there he could taste her salt on a summer's day, sip her tears like dew on a dawn rose.

And yet now when she saw him, she stood as if she'd never felt his mouth on her. As if her body didn't know his hands better than her own. And she dressed to hide that sweet little hollow.

He shouldn't have begged her for that kiss. He shouldn't have compelled her when he knew she was unsure. He knew, sitting there in the prison of his room, that there was something terrible between them. Something she couldn't quite get past.

He had to find out what it was. He simply couldn't go on, seeing the pain in her eyes when she looked at him. He needed to understand what Mimi meant to him and how he could ever have thought to replace Livvie with her.

"Y'r lordness?" Thrasher hesitantly said.

Jack opened his eyes to see a plate of roast beef and mushrooms before him, along with a large frothing pint of porter. He should have been ecstatic. He nodded and picked up a fork. If nothing else, he needed his strength.

"Thrasher," he said, taking a bite. "What year is it?"

Thrasher walked over to the dresser and picked up a vase. "Can't tell you that. Lady Kate said so."

Jack almost smiled at the sound of absolute devotion in the boy's voice. He needed to gain that kind of loyalty. He needed to find someone who wouldn't hesitate to help him find out what he'd forgotten. And what those damning red cuffs had meant.

Just the thought swamped him with guilt. Shame. Fury. Fear. The emotions felt familiar, as if this wasn't the first time he'd felt them. As if, in fact, they were old friends.

It was maddening. He had no memory of what he'd done before he'd woken, but he was beset by emotions that had to reflect *something*. It was as if his memory had been amputated, like a leg, leaving behind only the phantom pain. Which, he thought ruefully, meant he had phantom guilt. Phantom despair.

It certainly felt real enough. Which made him wonder why he was in such a blazing hurry to get the memories back. No memory that came seasoned with that kind of grief could be good.

Even so, he had to find out what it all meant. And he had to do it before he made an unpardonable mistake around Livvie. God help him, he couldn't keep his hands off of her. He couldn't seem to think when she was gone, but he couldn't think of anything but her when she was with him.

He might be a danger to her, and she wouldn't know. He might have done something so terrible that he would have no choice but to break any contact with her, if only for her sake. And he would never be able to do that if he didn't do it soon.

"Thrasher," he said, passing a slice of bread over to the too-skinny lad. "Did I hear you're good at finding out things?"

" 'S right," the boy said, pacing again, as if he had too much energy for the room. "I c'n find out anyfing."

"Even here in Brussels? They don't even speak English here."

"Aw, sure. 'Nough do. 'Specially with all the army 'ere."

Jack nodded absently as he mechanically put food in his mouth and washed it down with the bitter drink. "How would you like to earn a bit of coin?"

The boy stopped by the bed and bent to check something by the pillow. "Suit me to a cow's thumb."

Jack nodded to himself, struggling to recall even one fact he could send the boy off on. It was so frustrating. He hated the weakness, the uncertainty, the terrible suspicion that whatever lay beyond that opaque veil would hurt him.

Did he even have the right to send this boy out for him?

"What's this?" Thrasher asked. "Private stash?"

He pulled something out from beneath Jack's pillow. Jack looked back to see that he held something silver. A flask. "I have no idea. Put it back."

Thrasher shrugged and obeyed.

"Can you find out something for me?" Jack asked.

Reaching over to cadge a piece of beef, the boy huffed. "Wouldn't say it if I couldn't."

"Can you help me find out how I got to Belgium?"

The boy looked up at him and frowned. "Prob'ly."

"Will you keep it between us?" Jack asked, looking down at those too-wise brown eyes. "I don't want to worry Lady Kate."

The boy seemed to consider Jack's offer. "I won't lie."

And Jack couldn't ask it of him. "I just want to protect the women. Something bad might have happened."

That seemed to settle the matter. "Well, can't argue with you there. 'Eard some coves is lookin' for ya, and I don't think they wanna shake 'ands."

Jack stopped cold. "What do you mean?"

Thrasher shrugged his skinny shoulders. "'Aven't 'eard much. Whispers, like. Ifn y're really the Earl o' Gracechurch, 'eard a coupla coves sayin' ya did somethin' bad. Seein' as 'ow they's bad themselves, wasn't so sure I b'lieved 'em."

Something bad. Like fight for the French army? He felt nauseous with the possibility.

"Have you warned the duchess about this? Surely those men know I'm here."

Thrasher shook his head. "Nope. Y're a secret. 'Til you know y'rself what happened, they're not lettin' anybody else near you what might give it away."

Jack was taken aback. Did that make sense? Why would Livvie keep him from his friends, if any were near? What did she fear?

"Can you find out who's looking for me without putting yourself in any danger?"

At that the boy laughed as if Jack were the funniest thing on earth. "Lord luv ya, Y'r Majesty, I grew up in the Rookeries. Ain't nobody in all o' bleedin' Belgium worse 'n that!"

"I wouldn't be so cocksure if I were you," he said, and suddenly a memory flashed.

An alley. Noisome, wet, the cobbles oily in the distant lamplight. The fetid stink of a slum and the lap of a nearby river. Panic. Exhilaration.

A knife, curved perfectly for his palm, cool against hot fingers. The round, thick silhouette of a man. Was he facing him? He couldn't tell. But he saw the glint of another knife as it raised in the dim light, and he struck.

He felt it then, as if the memory lived in his hand. The slick ease of a thrust, the scrape of bone. He heard the gasp. The gurgle. He felt the drag of that heavy body on his hands.

"Guvn'r?"

He startled, blinked. Lifted his hand to his suddenly aching head to realize he was shaking.

He had killed a man.

"I may have murdered someone."

"Well, sure," Thrasher said. "You was at Waterloo."

But this hadn't been Waterloo. Bile crowded Jack's throat, and sweat broke out on his brow. For a moment, he couldn't even see the skinny, jug-eared boy he'd just confessed to.

"Not in battle," he said. "In an alley."

"Wouldn't be surprised," the boy said with a hesitant pat to the shoulder. "Ya got that look. But you got the look of a righteous cove. Wouldn't worry 'bout it none."

Blinking, Jack pulled the boy's complacent face into focus and almost laughed. Didn't it just figure he'd confess to the one person in this house who would take it with such equanimity?

"I don't know who it was," he said, his voice shaking almost as badly as his hands. "I don't know where. A city. A river." Searching hard for more, he suffered another blinding flash of pain to his head. He pressed a fist against it. "I just wish I could remember."

"Well, I 'ope ya does," his conspirator agreed, grabbing a couple of mushrooms and popping them into his mouth. "I 'as this sneaky feelin' we're gonna be leavin' soon, and it won't be near as easy to do in Lun'on. Bigger place."

Jack almost laughed again. How had Kate found this unbelievable urchin? "All right, then. I'll make it worth your while if you can find out who it is who's looking for me."

Thrasher nodded. "Piece o' cake."

"No," Jack disagreed, grabbing the boy's hand so he'd listen. "It's not a piece of cake. It's dangerous. And if there was anybody else I could send out, I'd damn well do it."

Finally the boy lost his grin. "I know, y'r worship. But I've lived through dangerous afore."

Not this kind of dangerous, Jack thought, wondering how the hell he knew. Not this kind of dangerous at all.

When she left Jack's room, Olivia stopped only long enough to retrieve her bonnet before she fled the house. She needed to walk, and she needed to do it alone. Suddenly the Parc seemed very inviting.

At first her thoughts matched her flight; she couldn't settle on anything. Her body was still thrumming from Jack's touch. Her hands curled in on themselves for want of something to touch—for want of *Jack* to touch. Her brain skittered around, seeking purchase, but there were too many memories suddenly let loose, and they all seemed to be about Jack.

His beautiful green eyes, his hands, his work-hardened body. The secret scent of him, the sound of his laughter early on a Sunday morning when the two of them lay buried beneath the covers. The wonder in his eyes when he'd laid his hand on her belly to feel the first whisper of their babe.

His passion.

Jack had taught her sensuality. He had woken her to the intense delight a body could experience at the hands of an ardent and considerate lover, and he had encouraged her to revel in it. He had been like flint to her tinder. He'd been impetuous and generous and imaginative, and he'd opened a world of shared delight to her. He'd taught her that trust was the greatest aphrodisiac of all.

She remembered a time when Jack had been out working with the field hands, building up a sweat and, evidently, a hunger. His clothes caked with mud and sticky with perspiration, he'd swaggered into Olivia's private parlor like a pirate boarding a helpless merchantman.

"You smell like three-day-old fish," she'd accused, laughing, knowing it didn't matter. Her breasts had pebbled hard at the mere sight of him. Her belly had gone tight with need.

He laughed back, his eyes hot, and pulled her into his arms, not caring that her beautiful new muslin dress would be ruined.

"Surprise, Livvie," he whispered in her ear, his voice full of laughter. "Look what I brought you."

She felt it, felt *him,* hard against her belly, and her own body ignited in response. He backed her against the silk-papered wall and demanded she open her mouth to him. She did, gladly. Inhaling the pungent sweat scent off him like exotic perfume, she wrapped herself around him. She took his tongue deep into her mouth and met it with her own. Frantically fumbling with his muddy clothes, she managed to free his already stone-hard cock. She helped as he lifted her against the wall with his callused, grimy hands, trapping her high off the floor as he fisted her skirts and shoved them high, baring her legs to the air and sending lightning exploding through her.

And there, without smile or whisper or plea, he impaled her. She bit his neck as he slammed into her. She gloried in it, a hot, quick, hard consummation that left them both breathless and even hungrier for more.

And when it was done, when she hung limp against his shoulder, damp and sated, with him hardening again inside her, he hesitated. She saw it in his eyes, the fear that he had shown her disrespect. That he'd taken her, a sheltered gentlewoman, hard and fast against a wall like a Covent Garden whore. His concern had made her fall in love for at least the tenth time that day.

Laying her hand against his chest, where his heart still thundered, she'd leaned up to whisper into his ear. And because it was the only way she could convince him how delicious he had made the moment, she used a word that should have been anathema to a vicarage-raised girl.

"I love it," she panted, "when you fuck me."

It was scandalous. It was frightening. It was right, and she knew it. And it was only Jack she could say it to, only Jack she trusted enough to hear it.

In answer, he kissed her thoroughly, as if softening the word to wonder. "You don't mind?" he asked against her neck.

She yanked at his sweat-soaked shirt until it came free, then slid her hands up his bare torso. "I know I should never admit it," she said with a siren's smile, "but it excites me."

He kissed her again. He devoured her with his tongue and his teeth and his hot, wonderful mouth. "As long as you never admit that to another man as long as you live."

She remembered laughing again. "Why would I ever need to?"

Why, indeed?

She had struggled so hard to create a new image of herself, one that was independent of Jack—of needing him. Out of ashes and ruin, she had crafted a life she was proud of. No matter what she had faced, no matter how tempted she had been to succumb to despair, she hadn't. She had stayed true to herself, and she thought she had grown into a strong, worthy woman. If she had never seen Jack again, she would have survived.

But all Jack had to do was touch her, and suddenly she was scrambling to shore up her defenses. She had trusted him once. She had believed he would hold her heart as carefully as she'd held his. But she hadn't realized how fragile a thing trust was. Now it was the most precious gift she bestowed.

She trusted Georgie. She trusted Lady Kate and Grace

and Lady Bea. But Jack? She loved Jack. No matter how hard she tried, she couldn't escape that. Whatever else she felt for him, she had never stopped loving him.

But trust? No. She no longer trusted him. And as she'd learned to her distress, love without trust was an empty vessel. And passion without either was pointless.

But, oh, sweet heaven, she wished she could convince her body that were true.

She was so lost in thought that she didn't anticipate company. She should have expected him, of course. This was, after all, the first time she'd been far enough from Lady Kate to be vulnerable. And God knew his best talent was sniffing out vulnerability.

He slid down next to her on the bench. "Hullo, Livvie."

It might have been because she was still so distracted. It might have been that the control she maintained over her memories had slipped. For whatever reason, the sight of Gervaise only irritated her.

She found she could look at him without going pale. In fact, for the first time in her life, she could see him for what he was. An infant in a man's body. A spoiled little boy who simply didn't understand that he couldn't always have his way.

"Hullo, Gervaise."

His sunny hair glowed in the dappled light, and his eyes crinkled with humor. He was golden. He was breathtaking. "How did you let yourself get so far from safety, Liv? Aren't you afraid I'll snatch you right off the path and run off with you?"

Olivia didn't have the patience for him right now. "Good heavens, no. There are too many witnesses. It might prove difficult to maintain an air of innocence when fifteen soldiers, three nannies, and a cleric watch you commit a crime."

His laugh was delighted. "Not a crime, surely, unless it's a crime of the heart."

"Clichés, Gervaise? I'm disappointed."

"Oh, Livvie," he said, reaching out a finger to stroke her cheek. "And you wonder why I've never been able to forget you."

"You never forgot me," she said, cold with the crawling dread of his touch, "because I'm the only one who said no."

"Not true," he said with a conspirator's smile, "and we both know it. We had wonderful times together, Liv."

"Obviously your definition of *wonderful* differs from mine."

He studied her for a moment, as if trying to understand her behavior. "You'd rather be a paid lackey."

She studied him back and realized that his face was completely unlined by worry. Gervaise never worried. It never occurred to him that he should have to. "Why, yes, Gervaise," she said. "I would rather be a paid lackey."

His smile cooled. "Ah, but what happens when people learn there never was a Mr. Grace?"

A surprise bubble of laughter caught in her chest. "Oh, for heaven's sake. You think I'll be ruined for using my sister-in-law's name?"

"You did get it from Georgie, then? I wondered."

She shrugged, as if it mattered not at all. "She and James helped me when I needed it."

"Why aren't you still with them?"

"I've done quite well on my own."

"Not as fine as you could have with me."

Wearily, she shook her head. "Again, my definition differs a bit from yours. I am perfectly comfortable where I am."

And there, finally, she saw it. Just a flash, no more, for he would never give himself away in public. But the petulant boy was in a rage. His pupils dilated. His nostrils flared just a bit.

"Please, Livvie," he begged, his voice silk-soft. "Don't make me hurt you again. You don't know how it distresses me."

Olivia knew perfectly well how pernicious he was. But suddenly all the threats made him seem small and petty. So she stood. "You hurt anyone I love again," she said, leaning close, "*anyone*, I will kill you."

He burst out laughing, until he looked more carefully into her eyes. "Don't be absurd."

She straightened and pulled at her gloves. "Don't doubt me, Gervaise. I believe I've finally had enough."

And without waiting for his answer, she walked away.

She was almost to the street when she remembered that Gervaise had been looking for Jack. He might even know Jack was in the city. Olivia stopped at the edge of the bustling street, her courage faltering badly. She thought she was hidden well enough, but what about Jack?

And why hadn't Gervaise just mentioned him? He had to know Jack's return would be a perfect threat.

She almost turned around. She almost looked to see what Gervaise was doing. But she knew he expected it. So, dragging in a calming breath, she finally crossed the street and went home.

She came across Grace in the foyer. "I need to speak with you all."

"Later," Grace said, linking arms. "Lady Kate has guests, and Mrs. Harper is looking for you."

Olivia set aside her bonnet. "Of course."

She followed Grace to the kitchen to find Mrs. Harper feeding a plate of scones to one of their remaining patients, a young hussar who had lost his left leg. He sat at the scarred oak table with a dragoon she didn't recognize.

"I'd take it a bit easy on those scones, Peter," she advised, smiling, "or you'll be too heavy to mount a horse."

After hearing how Lord Uxbridge had laughed off the loss of his own leg, Peter had vowed to be back in the saddle by the end of the month.

"Ah, leave off, ma'am," Mrs. Harper said with a grin. "Aren't these lads still growin' an' needin' their sustenance?"

"I'm growing all right," Peter agreed, patting his belly. "Sideways." Waving a scone, he indicated his guest. "Like you to meet a friend, ma'am. Kit Braxton, late of Kent, like me."

The blond dragoon stood to reveal a pinned-up sleeve on the right and a puckered burn scar up the side of his face that pulled at his mouth. But his smile was strong and his bow courtly. "Pleasure, ma'am. The little colonel has mentioned you. You performed a great service for her."

Olivia frowned. "The little colonel?"

"Gracie," Braxton said, looking to Grace. "Term of affection, you know."

Olivia turned to see that her friend was blushing like a debutante. "I imagine our Grace is quite a managing female, Major."

Braxton chuckled. "The veriest tartar, ma'am. But the best of comrades."

Yes, Olivia thought sadly. It was exactly how most men would see Grace, overlooking the deliciously dry wit and dear heart that hid beneath that plain facade.

"She is also the very best of friends," Olivia assured him with a smile for the embarrassed Grace.

As if aware how mortified her charge was, Mrs. Harper quickly turned the conversation. "The garden, ma'am."

Olivia lifted an eyebrow, but when no answer was forthcoming, she stepped out into the small walled garden.

It was another warm day, but clouds had moved in to blunt the sun. The few trees present shaded the begonias that edged the path and lent the garden its sense of privacy. The shadows were spicy with the scent of roses. Stopping on the path, Olivia looked around for whatever it was she was to see.

He was standing back in the shadows. Olivia checked the windows to make sure no one was watching, and then approached.

"Chambers," she greeted the fastidious middle-aged man.

Chambers gave her a brisk nod of his ruthlessly groomed, graying head. "Mrs. Grace. I am glad to see you looking well."

"And you. May we sit?"

They settled on the bench tucked away beneath a drooping birch.

"I have spoken with Mr. Finney," Chambers began. "The earl truly can't remember anything?"

"No. He can't. Can you tell me how he knew where to find you?"

"It is something I have thought much of, ma'am. I have no answer. Of course, he knew I was Mr. Gervaise's man, and he possibly knew that we were in Brussels. Beyond that I cannot say."

"Do you still have the message he sent?"

He shook his head. "Oh, no. I burned it immediately. But I can tell you what it said. 'Chambers. Need help. Meet me on Nivelles Road two miles south of Mont St. Jean.'" He looked up, frowning. "It was actually serendipitous that I tripped over him. He was not where he was supposed to be."

"He never spoke to you?"

"Never." Chambers shuddered. "I was so afraid he was..."

She nodded, trying to piece the story together. "Would you tell me what happened five years ago after the duel with my cousin? I thought the earl went to the West Indies."

The little man nodded. "We did. The earl spent a year managing his father's plantations on Jamaica."

A year. Olivia ruthlessly quelled memories of that same time. "And then?"

The valet shrugged, looking very uncomfortable. "He released me. We returned home in the fall of 1811, and the master called me into his office and handed me a severance payment and a letter of recommendation. Said his cousin was looking for a man and would be happy to take me."

"You don't know why he released you?"

He drew himself up. "It was not my place to ask. I think he never recovered from...uh, the duel. He dismissed his entire staff, although many of them went to work for his family."

"You don't know where he went?"

"There was some talk of the fur trade in Canada."

Olivia shook her head, frustrated. This was no help at all. "And you haven't seen him since?"

"Maybe two years ago. Mr. Gervaise met Master Jack in London. Something about family business."

She nodded. "Yes, the Duchess of Murther remembers seeing him then. You don't know what the business was?"

"Mr. Gervaise only said it was good to see his cousin in such a situation. He seemed delighted by it."

If it had been anyone else, Olivia might have thought he'd meant that Jack was well set up. With Gervaise, she wasn't so sure. "And he didn't tell you anything more?"

"Oh, no, ma'am. Only that the earl seemed to benefit from his adventures, whatever that might mean."

Olivia nodded. "The earl's family never said anything about him in your presence?"

Chambers looked away. "Only to blame you for his absence, I'm sorry to say."

Olivia smiled. "Oh, that is no surprise, Chambers."

"There is one thing, ma'am." When he looked up, Olivia saw how troubled he was. "Please do not misunderstand. Mr. Gervaise has been a good employer. But he has talked about that time. The duel and...all. I wanted you to know that I am sorry for my part in it.

Mr. Gervaise has since boasted to me about his schemes."

He really did look distressed, something Olivia never thought she'd see. She patted his small, tidy hand. "You weren't the only one who believed him, Chambers."

He flushed and dipped his head. "Is there anything I can do now? I bear much affection for his lordship."

Olivia thought hard. "I wonder if seeing you might pry loose a few memories."

"I would be delighted to help, ma'am."

She got to her feet. "Follow me."

Returning to the house, she led him back through the kitchen, where Mrs. Harper stood alone now, pounding out bread dough. Poor Cook must have been frightened back into the root cellar again. "Mrs. Harper..."

The big woman never looked up. "Mr. Gervaise has arrived."

Which meant that Chambers was in danger of being discovered. "You'll return?" she asked the suddenly nervous man.

"Indeed, ma'am," Chambers agreed, casting anxious glances toward the front of the house. "Please give his lordship my best wishes."

Olivia ushered him back out through the garden. "One more thing, Chambers. Was there ever anyone in Jamaica named Mimi?"

Chambers frowned a moment, then shook his head. "No, ma'am. Not to my knowledge. And the community was a small one."

Olivia held out her hand. "Thank you, then."

With all the hesitation of a well-mannered servant, Chambers shook her hand and departed. Olivia was left with more questions than answers. Could anyone else tell them where Jack had been? Could she really trust Mr. Hilliard to help? And where was he?

As she stood alone in the shade of the garden, she noticed through the kitchen window that two of her other patients had arrived to sample the fresh scones. She could hear them teasing Mrs. Harper. By this evening, they would all be gone, and Lady Kate would have to think about returning to London. Somehow they had to take Jack along without exposing him. And Olivia found herself loath to let him go without her.

Depressed, she sighed. No woman in her right mind would think to reconcile with a man who had treated her as Jack had. She would be a fool to risk her heart, her very life, to him again. After all, she was not who he called to in his sleep.

For now, though, she couldn't escape. Plastering a bright smile on her face, she opened the door into the kitchen, where brave men reminded her how high the stakes were in the game she played.

Tucked into a corner of the adjoining garden, the Surgeon watched Chambers take his leave of Mrs. Grace. *Finally,* he thought complacently. *Something interesting.*

Gracechurch's ex-valet was speaking to his ex-wife. Just what would those two have to say to each other? How would he find out?

He allowed himself a satisfied smile. How would he find out, indeed? He could think of a dozen ways, each one more delicious than the last.

He would enjoy convincing the valet to cooperate. But he already had a towering cockstand thinking about what he would do to the earl's wife. There was surely a quote worthy of being carved into her soft white belly. Maybe something about the price of loyalty.

Yes, he thought, following the valet down the street. She would definitely be his best work yet.

He just hoped she didn't succumb too quickly.

Chapter 13

There were days when Kate thought that being a duchess was highly overrated. This day was turning out to be one of them.

It had started out well enough. She had managed to escape the house for a bit of shopping and had actually thought she might have some blessed time alone. It was a lovely, cool summer day, and she risked her reputation once again by walking.

Her first stop was the Grand Place. Kate loved the great cobbled square with its gold-dipped medieval guild halls and inevitable clock tower. Today the wounded had gone and the flower sellers returned, and the quaintly gabled shops were open for business. Kate took great advantage of both, especially a cunning little shop that sold the most exquisite lace.

From there, she visited several friends, ending with the Uxbridges, who were putting up with the Marquis d'Assche around the Parc from her house. She left them with the flowers she'd just bought and the *on dits* she'd been collecting.

It was on the way home that she had her first inkling that the day was about to go wrong. Stepping onto the Rue de la Loi, she was brought up short by the sight of a man standing on the Parc side of the boulevard. He was nondescript, a tall, thin man dressed by Nugee, who loitered as if he were merely enjoying the sun. She had seen him before, she realized, and not too long ago. He'd been in the Grand Place. He'd also been on the street the day before when she'd walked to the Capels for tea.

It still might not have registered if he hadn't smiled and tipped his hat when he saw her looking his way. She knew every face in the *ton* and a good portion of European aristocracy. She knew to a name those to whom she'd been introduced. She did not know this man.

"Bivens," she said to her abigail, who walked alongside. "Do you recognize that very forward gentleman over there?"

Bivens, who prided herself on knowing just as many people as her mistress, shook her head. "Forward piece of business," she huffed. Of course, coming from an ex–Covent Garden dancer, the pejorative was ironic at best.

"I saw him in Grand Place as we walked out of the lace shop. And I've seen him before."

"Well, if you don't know how to give him what he deserves, Miss Kate," she said with the familiarity of one who'd grown up not four miles from her mistress, "I don't know who does."

Lady Kate was forced to smile. "Indeed, Bivens." But something set her teeth on edge about this man. Could it be her family after her again? Murther's? Or, more disturbing, could it have something to do with the guest in her second-best bedroom?

When she came across Diccan a few moments later, she almost made the mistake of asking him. Finally, she thought, someone to share her little problem.

She took a quick peek at her mystery man to see that he had turned into the Parc. She was about to bring Diccan's attention to him when she realized that her cousin wasn't alone. In fact, he was inconsiderate enough to be accompanied by the very people she'd ushered from her parlor not three hours earlier.

Gervaise Armiston might keep her interested for a few moments, especially considering the dramatic allegations Olivia had been making, but the Thorntons provoked nothing but paralytic boredom.

"*Uxbridge*?" Lady Thornton demanded with an outraged sniff when she heard of Kate's visit. "I could support visiting such a hero, but *that woman* has joined him."

Kate set her hand on Diccan's arm. "You mean his wife, Char? It would have been insupportable if she *hadn't*."

"But she is a pariah," Lord Thornton objected as they turned onto one of the leafy Parc lanes. "Bad *ton*, Lady Kate. Bad *ton*."

"Like that Lady Gracechurch," Lady Thornton said with a nod of the head that had her orange egret feathers tickling her husband's nose. "Brazen-faced hussy."

And sometimes, Kate thought, it was good to be a duchess. That training alone kept Kate from gaping like a nitwit. "You mean Jack Wyndham's wife?" she asked with marked indifference. "Good Lord. What makes you bring *her* up? That story is so old it gathers dust. It's been what, three years?"

"Five," said Gervaise, and Kate turned an assessing eye on him. Hmm. Could Olivia's tale be true? Gervaise was venal, yes. Certainly self-centered. But a murderer? She wouldn't have thought so. But if anyone knew about masks, it was she.

"Why, I thought of Gracechurch's wife because of the latest *on dit*," Lady Thornton said. "Surely you've heard."

"I must have been too busy doing my Christian duty by our brave wounded," Kate drawled to hide her sudden discomfort.

It was, of all people, Diccan who supplied the news. "Word is that Gracechurch and his wife have both been seen in Brussels, if you believe it. I keep hearing he was at Waterloo."

"Have you heard this, Gervaise?" Kate asked.

His smile was all that was innocent. "Gad, no. Thought he was in Jamaica. Hasn't felt much like returning home."

"All that wife's fault," Thornton huffed. "Woman was a slut. Proved it in court."

"It did make an entertaining season," Diccan said. "Haven't heard that many salacious stories since Sheridan's last play."

Kate was startled by a rare rush of rage. How dare they? Even Diccan, passing such a capricious judgment on something they knew nothing about. But, of course, she knew how. There was no beast more carnivorous than the *ton,* and five years ago, Olivia had been the meat of the moment.

"Oh, so you knew her?" she asked Thornton in a drawl. "Biblically, I mean?"

Thornton flushed an unflattering red. "Here, I say!"

"You, Gervaise?" Kate asked. "Diccan? You knew Jack better than I. Did you also tup his wife?"

"Certainly not. The only wives who interest me are the available ones. Until the duel, I had no idea Jack's was among them."

"Who told you she was?"

Diccan laughed. "My darling girl. Everyone."

Yes, Kate remembered. The rumors had spread like wildfire, almost on the heels of the surprise wedding. "Ah, yes. Gervaise, it seems to me you dined off that story for months."

"It was my cousin who was ruined," he reminded her gently.

Which sounded perfectly understandable, on the surface.

"So you don't know the countess?" Diccan asked her.

"No, of course not. Why should I?"

He shrugged. "Armiston here thought you might."

Kate went very still. "Really, Gervaise?" she asked, suddenly certain he would never suspect Olivia of having had the courage to tell her the truth. "Why is that?"

Gervaise looked completely unconcerned. "You know everyone."

"As I do. Just not her, although after the way she's been treated, I do find I have quite a bit of sympathy for her. But you've met her, surely."

"Only a time or two. Jack was much taken with the country during those months, if you remember. And I gladly confess to being a town mouse."

"Still," Diccan mused absently. "Wouldn't mind seeing Jack again. See how he's going on."

Lady Thornton gave a portentous nod. "Paid his price for the duel. The jade wasn't worth it, no matter what you say."

Kate ached to take her to account. But this wasn't the moment to teach old tabbies new tricks.

"Speaking of available wives," she said in an attempt to distract them from their prey. "Which lovely blond wife did I see you with at the theater this week, Diccan?"

Diccan playfully slapped her hand. "You know perfectly well you saw me with no one, you odious brat. It is simply not done."

"Oh, please. Absolve me of society's more quaint notions. She was quite pretty. And very...attached to you."

He grinned. "You must mean Madam Ferrar. A lovely bit of fluff. The perfect light quaff to take the taste of diplomacy off the tongue at the end of the day."

"She does have a most...musical giggle."

He shot her a glance that let her know he understood just what she was doing, but he played along. Dear Diccan, always the perfect diplomat. Kate just hoped he could play the perfect conspirator.

"Did you still want me to stop by, brat?" he asked.

"Afraid so." For the audience, she gave a moue. "Deadly dull family matters."

"Which means the dear pater has once again expressed his displeasure," Diccan said. "I am rarely in the good bishop's graces."

It was enough to detach the rest of their party. As Kate turned toward the Rue Royale, she caught sight of that strange gentleman again.

"Diccan," she said very quietly. "Do you recognize the chap down the lane there? The one in the green Nugee coat."

As if hearing the caution in her voice, he refrained from looking through his quizzing glass. "Can't say as I do. Looks vaguely familiar, though."

"Still has no right oglin' the duchess like that," Bivens protested from behind them.

Diccan laughed. "Dear Bivens, if we chastised every man who ogled my cousin, the entire male population of Europe would be sent to their rooms without pudding."

"He does seem to have been following us," Kate mused.

This time Diccan must have heard something more. "Do you want me to speak to him?"

"No. I want you to respond to my request and join my houseguests and me for a bit."

His bow of acquiescence was everything it should have been. "It was ever my intention."

Kate, though, knew that Diccan was now on alert. However, after the last conversation about Olivia, she hoped she hadn't made a serious mistake in asking for his help.

Lady Kate wasn't the only one who hoped she hadn't made a mistake. The minute Olivia saw Diccan Hilliard, she thought the same thing.

"Why am I put in mind of the bigwig's office at Trinity?" he was asking as he followed Lady Kate into the morning room.

Olivia took a seat beside Grace on one of the chintz

sofas by the fireplace. Now that there were open rooms in the house, Lady Kate had moved her little flock into the lemon-hued parlor at the rear of the first floor. And just as Mr. Hilliard said, the women were lined up behind the tea tray like a jury.

Olivia was fast losing her confidence in Mr. Hilliard. Surely he was too self-interested to wish involvement in this. Too aloof. How could they possibly expect discretion from a man who wielded his tongue like a rapier?

"Sad to say," Lady Kate said as she offered him one of the Louis Quinze chairs, "we are not here for badinage. We have a rare problem I thought you might delight in sinking your teeth into. I've had Finney broach that ninety-eight amontillado you like."

Diccan's eyebrows soared. "This must be serious indeed." Flipping his coattails, he settled on an ornate gilt chair that should have looked designed to hold him. Oddly, it only looked fussy and small. It reminded Olivia that Diccan Hilliard was physically more substantial than his character.

"Good to see you all looking so well," he said as he poured his brandy. "Sorry I couldn't get here any quicker. For some reason, Ambassador Stuart likes to keep me occupied."

"How appropriate," his cousin said, "as what we need from you will be your diplomatic skills."

"Valor," Lady Bea said with a nod as she handed out the ubiquitous tea.

Lady Kate nodded. "Yes, Bea. Definitely discretion."

Sipping his brandy, he leaned back. "I'm all ears."

Lady Kate seemed to assess his sincerity. "Olivia has a

story for you," she said, and Olivia felt her heart speed up.

"Indeed," he said. "I do so love a good story."

Again Olivia was struck by the feeling that something about Kate's cousin didn't add up. She couldn't decide what, though, and it made her nervous.

"She'll be happy to tell you," Kate was saying, "after I introduce her to you."

Diccan made a point to look between them. "I might be a bit confused, but haven't you already done that? I remember, because I particularly recall thinking how well her name fit her."

"Her real name does as well. Diccan, may I introduce Olivia Louise Gordon Wyndham, former countess of Gracechurch."

For the first time since she'd met him, Olivia saw Diccan Hilliard stunned to silence. She thought he actually might have gone pale.

It was only seconds, though. Suddenly he grinned. "Fiend seize it! Hiding in plain sight, are you, ma'am?"

She shrugged. "I often find that to be the most effective tactic."

"Joan of Arc," Lady Bea blurted out again.

Diccan allowed an eyebrow to rise. "If you mean pure of heart, dear thing, I'll take your word for it. If she's hearing voices, however..."

"You can imagine why Olivia's identity is proprietary," Lady Kate said in a deceptively lazy voice.

Olivia saw a slight flush on Diccan's face. He shot a rueful grin at his cousin and sipped at his brandy. "I imagine you've had quite enough of unfounded rumors, Countess."

"I am no countess, Mr. Hilliard. Plain Mrs. Grace will do."

He raised his snifter in a salute. "Of course. Can you tell me why you chose this moment to reveal yourself? And why to me?"

"Because of recent events." Drawing a steadying breath, she did her best to maintain eye contact. "And because I heard that you knew of the rumors about Jack."

"Being on the battlefield, you mean? I'm not sure I'm the man to verify them. I, for one, did not see him."

Olivia held his gaze. "I did."

Diccan's smile was a bit stiff. "Egad. You didn't leave him out there, did you? Understand the urge, of course. But not done."

"No, Mr. Hilliard, I didn't."

"She brought him here," Lady Kate said.

That stopped him again. He stared at Lady Kate as if he didn't know her. "Why not tell someone? His commander, for one."

"Even if his commander was French?"

Olivia wasn't sure how she'd expected him to react. Surely either outrage or disbelief. Instead, he again went very still. "Well," he finally mused, leaning back and crossing his legs. "It sounds as if this is going to be a very good story indeed."

"Worthy of Sophocles himself," Lady Kate assured him. "Before we begin, you, of course, understand that we must demand your silence."

"That bad, is it?"

"That's the problem. We don't know."

He spent a moment swirling the brandy in his snifter.

"Well, it is well known that I'll do almost anything for a good afternoon's entertainment. You have my word."

Olivia wasn't sure if that was enough. But Lady Kate nodded, as if relieved, and she felt reassured. "Accept my story or not as you will. But please reserve judgment until you've heard me out."

"Oh, I never judge," he assured her. "It would severely limit the gossip I'm privy to."

For the first time, she smiled with him. "Thank you."

She had to look away, since so much of her story was painful. So she focused on the once-lovely handkerchief she had shredded in her hands. And as sparely as she could, she told her story all the way back to the moment she'd met Jack.

Mr. Hilliard interrupted her only once, when she told him about the dispatch Jack had been carrying.

"General Grouchy, you say?" he asked, distractedly swinging his quizzing glass. "Intriguing. From the reports we've received, Grouchy never did advance. It might have made the difference in the outcome of the battle. And I believe his position was clear across the battlefield from Hougoumont."

For the first time since she'd discovered Jack, Olivia felt a small spark of hope. "Then he might have simply intercepted the message so it couldn't be delivered," she said. "Isn't it possible Jack was working for the British government? Oh, I don't know, as a traveling officer or something?"

He shook his head. "Beyond the fact that traveling officers are fairly well known, they make it a point to do their behind-the-lines reconnaissance in full British uniform."

Another half-formed hope dashed. "I see."

"But surely he's told you himself."

Which was when Olivia told him about Jack's amnesia. She was reminded that Mr. Hilliard was a diplomat when he received the news with no more reaction than a raised eyebrow. "And my place in this fascinating tale?"

Olivia looked up. "Is there any way you can help us find out the truth? We don't know who else to turn to."

Cradling the brandy snifter in his palm, he lazily rose to his feet and walked to the windows. "Hmm," he murmured. "A challenge. How intriguing."

"We don't have much time, Diccan," Lady Kate informed him. "You've heard the rumors. I think we've overstayed our welcome."

"Home is where the heart is," Bea said.

He nodded absently. "Certainly no good can come from remaining in a thinning society. You begin to stand out, and there are too many sharp eyes who remain."

Lady Kate nodded. "Our thoughts exactly."

"Do you think the gentleman you pointed out today could be part of this group looking for Gracechurch?" he asked Lady Kate.

"Gentleman?" Livvie asked. "What gentleman?"

"Possibly just a shy admirer," Mr. Hilliard demurred.

Lady Kate shrugged. "Or a spy sent from one of the dukes to see if I'm behaving. You remember I told you how they love to keep current on my bad behavior."

"But you don't think so."

Lady Kate smiled. "No. Their tactics are usually much more confrontational."

Diccan nodded absently, still swinging his quizzing

glass and sipping his brandy. "Mrs. Grace, do you think Jack innocent?"

"Don't you?" Olivia asked, aware how terse her voice sounded.

He turned fully to consider her. "His mother *was* French…."

She came to her feet. "You know perfectly well she had no influence on him. Please, Mr. Hilliard. He needs to know the truth. And he needs to be protected. At least until his memory returns."

At that, Diccan turned and lifted his glass to give her a good look.

It made her bristle. "What are you doing, sir?"

"Looking my fill at the last honorable woman in Europe," he said with an impish grin. "Strike me if you ain't incomprehensible, ma'am. You sure you don't want to serve him up just a tiny bit of revenge?"

Olivia couldn't help but chuckle. "Oh, probably. But I imagine it won't be truly satisfying until Jack knows exactly why I'm doing it."

That got a laugh from him. "Excellent. In that case, I believe I will help." Striding over, he reclaimed his seat, and Olivia followed suit. "Can't see why I can't call in a few markers. Sadly, I wouldn't know if Gracechurch turned coat if I saw his seams, but I might know someone who dabbles in all that cloak-and-dagger business. And, if I say so myself, I'm a dab hand at sneaking people away from tense situations. Quite a talent of mine in the trade."

"How?"

"Sleight of hand, my girl. Is there another person you can trust? Preferably male. Even more preferably military."

"Why?" Lady Kate asked.

"Patience, infant. Anyone? I thought I saw Major Braxton here yesterday. He's done some messenger work for us recently."

"Braxton," Lady Bea agreed. "Good boy."

Grace was already smiling. "I agree. Kit is a good friend, and completely trustworthy. Or we could ask Harry Lidge. I just saw him, and he's heading home."

"Lidge?" Olivia asked. "I think he's a friend of Jack's."

"Not," Lady Kate suddenly said, "Lidge." Before Diccan could raise his quizzing glass, she pointed a finger at him. "And if you lift that odious thing at me, you coxcomb, I swear I'll feed it to you."

Olivia found herself staring at the duchess. She saw Grace open her mouth, but another glare from Lady Kate silenced them both. Who was Lidge, Olivia wondered? And what had he done to earn Kate's disapprobation? It was obvious, however, that Lady Kate had said all she would on the subject.

Diccan turned back to Grace. "Braxton it is, then. Can you contact him?"

Grace nodded. "Easily."

"Good. Bring him by tomorrow and we can set our plans in motion."

"At what?" Olivia demanded.

Diccan's smile was quite smug. "Why, smuggling your husband—well, Gracechurch—home, of course. Just in case someone really is looking for him, we'll give them Kate and her entourage to look at instead. You go one way, and Gracechurch will go the other. That's if Braxton agrees, of course."

Lady Kate nodded. Grace nodded. Olivia felt as if she were swimming through murky water. "Do you want to speak with Jack, Mr. Hilliard?"

"Please, Mrs. Grace. Co-conspirators deserve first names. But not just yet. The last time Jack saw me was as he was raising a gun on your cousin on Finchley Commons at dawn. I'm not sure that's the first memory you want him to recover."

Olivia all but shuddered. "Yes. I thank you, Mr. Hilliard. You don't know what it means that you're willing to help us."

His sudden grin was blinding. "My dear lady, do you know what you called me away from? Listening to Slender Billy alternately gloat about his heroic injury and whine about his lost command. The Prince of Orange wears thin."

"He *will* be the next king of the Netherlands," Grace reminded him.

"Even if he is a twelve-year-old in a man's body." Diccan leaned close to Grace, as if imparting a secret. "I know it's not my lot to question, my Boadicea, but it's almost worth more than my career to simply stuff a gag in his mouth."

Grace maintained an admirable calm. "It could be worse. You could be negotiating with a victorious Napoleon."

He laughed. "Just what I needed. A dash of perspective." Downing the rest of his brandy, he gained his feet. "Now, then, ladies, I must be off to assure Belgium's goodwill. When Braxton arrives, alert me. 'Til then, keep good heart. I'll whisper a suggestion in an ear or two that they might keep an eye out for suspicious lurkers in the area. Inform your house staff as well. And for heaven's sake, keep Gracechurch locked up tighter than a lunatic."

They followed him out into the foyer, where Finney waited with Diccan's high-top beaver. Retrieving it, Diccan set it on his head at a definite slant. "No more worries, Bea," he said, giving her a smacking kiss on the cheek. "Hilliard is in charge."

She huffed in indignation. "Heaven help us."

Chapter 14

Thrasher was back. Jack looked up from another circuit of the room to see the imp sneak through the door as if being chased by runners, his spotless uniform traded in for stained and torn rags and a disreputable-looking cap.

"Don't tell me," Jack said from where he stopped by the window to look out at the darkening sky. "You couldn't help it if those snuffboxes fell into your pocket."

Thrasher drew himself up as if Jack had accused him of treason. "I'll 'ave you know, y'r worshipness, that I stays on the windy side of the law these days. 'Er Grace wouldn't like it above 'alf ifn I didn't."

Jack gave a formal bow. "My apologies, lad. How was your afternoon?" Not waiting for the answer, he took off again, forcing his still-wobbly legs to keep moving him forward. He had to get back on his feet as soon as he could. Something tucked away in his memory felt dangerous, and he had the feeling he was going to need to be solidly on his feet to face it.

Stepping up next to him as if accompanying him on

the stroll, Thrasher scratched at his chest. "Amazin' what coves'll say round a street sweep. You know some cully named Surgeon?"

Jack shuddered to a halt. Surgeon. It sounded familiar, and not as in 'do you know a doctor?' He frowned, searching his memory like a cloudy crystal ball.

He could hear himself yelling. But he wasn't yelling *Surgeon!* He was yelling *Chirurgien!*

French.

He must have spoken out loud, because Thrasher frowned. "What?"

Jack snapped back to attention. "Sorry. Must have been woolgathering."

The boy huffed impatiently. "Sounded like you was talkin' to a Frenchie."

For a moment, Jack could only stare at him. He was right. But did he want to know why?

"Weren't no Frenchie," the boy was saying, bending over to peek at Jack's bed. "Was a English toff, sure as shift."

"Is he someone I would wish to know?"

Thrasher's laugh was far too old. "Cor, luv ya, guv. With a name like the Surgeon? Nah. Skinny toff what 'as a phiz like a lizard and a nasty habit o' playin' with his pocketknife. Seems ta think you might be somewhere near somebody 'e called the 'cyprian countess.' Know the mort?"

Jack shook his head. "Doesn't sound familiar at all."

Could that have been Mimi? He didn't think so. It didn't sound right.

"The Surgeon also said as 'ow you was in trouble with the lions." The boy shot Jack a cheeky grin. "You sure you wasn't lost in a zoo?"

Jack came to a halt by his bed. "Lions. I do know lions." Grabbing hold of a bedpost, he shook his head. "I know something about them. *British* lions." Again he struggled for clarity. All that came to him was that odd thought that they were looking the wrong way. Who? The lions? The British?

Squeezing his eyes shut, he pressed a fist to his temple. God, if only he could remember!

"I don't suppose he was thoughtful enough to explain himself?" he asked.

"Nup. Not to Axman Billy, leastwise."

Jack gaped at him. "Axman Billy?"

Thrasher nodded, for once not looking very cheeky. "Nasty bit o' business from the Dials. Don't know 'ow he got over 'ere, but I'd sure run shy of 'im, I was you."

"Axman Billy and the Surgeon are looking for me?" Jack demanded. "I am the popular fellow. Did they mention anyone named...Mimi?"

Thrasher tilted his head to the side. "There *was* some flash mort they was talkin' about, but I thought it was that cyprian thing. Said she'd been invitin' the wrong folk over." Losing interest, the boy shrugged. "That's it."

Jack nodded, still distracted. "And you still won't tell me what year it is."

"Not on y'r life. Why don't you ask the ladies? Tell 'em 'bout this Surgeon cove."

Jack rubbed again at the reawakened headache. "No. It would just worry them needlessly."

"You think anyfing's more worrisome than some cove named Axman?"

He managed a small smile. "All right. Tell them you

heard there's someone looking for me. But I wouldn't mention names if I were you."

The boy shrugged. "Suit y'rself."

"I'd appreciate it if you could see if any of my friends are in town, though. They might help. Lord Drake, Sir Harry Lidge, Mr. Gervaise Armiston."

"Cor, lumme. You know that nib cove?"

Jack was just about to ask what Thrasher meant when the door opened behind them.

"What do you think you're doing?" Olivia demanded.

Looking up, Jack saw her standing in the doorway, arms akimbo, eyes flashing. She was in another high-necked dress, and it suddenly made him angry.

"Isn't she something?" he asked Thrasher.

Thrasher nodded. "As flash a mort as ever I seed."

"I won't be distracted by blatant Spanish coin," she snapped, arms crossed. "Jack, you have no business being up."

"I am tired of that bed," he said, and straightened his protesting body. "I needed to move around a bit."

He needed to get outside, but she didn't need to hear that right now. Then she settled her soft brown gaze on him, and he lost all other thought.

He'd spent the entire afternoon telling himself that he had no business wanting her. One look at her, one faint whiff of apple, and he was lost. He had no right, but God, he ached to hold her. To bury himself so deep in her he could forget how afraid he was. He needed to strip off that offensive dress and fill his hands with her unforgettable body. He needed to unpin her hair and see it curl like a living thing over her bare breasts.

He should get the hell away before he destroyed her, but he knew he wouldn't be able to.

Oblivious to his distress, she stalked into the room like an avenging angel. "You need to lie down before you fall."

He gave her a self-conscious grin. "I need a bath, and I don't think I can wait any longer. I stink, Liv. I'm sure you noticed."

"*I* noticed," Thrasher assured them in an aggrieved voice.

Jack cuffed him. "That's enough out of you."

Olivia reached out, only to suddenly stop. Instead, she clasped her hands at her waist, a nun with no habit. Jack felt that withdrawal all the way to his gut.

"The staff might have time now," she said stiffly. "The other ladies have just left for the opera. I'll get you some water and a cloth."

He was sure she didn't realize the reaction that suggestion incited. His cock sought her like true north. He shook his head. "A hip bath or nothing. I'll walk to the river if I need to. I can't stand myself any longer. Thrasher, go on down and tell someone."

Livvie didn't see the sly grin Thrasher flashed Jack on his way out the door.

"Yes, yes," she snapped. "Fine. A hip bath. Anything to get you horizontal."

Also the wrong thing to say. Jack shuddered with memory, real memory. A memory that should have had Livvie blushing. "Ah, Liv," he rasped. "You're not thinking of the easiest way in the world to get me horizontal."

She froze, her eyes widening just a bit. Jack knew a direct hit when he saw one. He wished he could enjoy it more.

"Not 'til you get that bath," she snapped, and finally took hold of his arm.

"Sure you want to wait?" he asked, leaning close. "We didn't used to."

Again, he felt his words impact her. He knew he shouldn't do it, but he couldn't seem to help it. He suddenly couldn't tolerate her distance. He needed her to remember. To share at least something with him, when he felt as if he'd lost everything else.

And she did remember. He could feel it in the stiffness of her body. He could see it in the ready flush of her skin.

Her distress made him feel like a heel. What was he thinking?

He was thinking that he was afraid. He was imprisoned, even if the prison had clean sheets and a window. He was kept in the dark like an irresponsible child, and he couldn't allow it to continue.

He let her guide him to the chair, all the while praying for a new flash of memory that would be good. That wouldn't walk dark streets and taste like despair.

"You actually caught me on my way back to bed," he boasted like a five-year-old caught sliding down the banister. "I've quite mastered the room. The view out the window is fine. By the way, who were the soldiers decamping just now?"

"The rest of our injured. You're the last."

He frowned down at her. "You had other soldiers here? Why didn't I know?"

"Because you were the most severely wounded. You didn't need the annoyance."

"What I need is—"

"A bath. Yes, I know. As soon as I can get some help." Not even looking at him, she fled.

Jack didn't blame her. If she was beset by the same memories he was, she should have been weak at the knees.

It had once been such a game between them, the wonders of the bath. The first time, of course, she had blushed like a young girl. She'd opened the wrong door to find him wet and smiling, his knees tucked up and his hair curling in the steam.

"Oh, good." He'd grinned. "I hate to scrub my back."

She'd gulped like a fish. They had been engaged only a week, and she'd obviously never seen a gentleman missing so much as a neck cloth. She was seeing one then. He knew he didn't look like an ordinary gentleman. He spent far too much time outside working with his tenants. He had muscles no gentleman should exhibit and a tan across his chest. Jack saw her take it all in. He watched as her embarrassment turned to curiosity, and then slowly to fascination.

Laying his washcloth right over his aching groin, he gave her a full view and the most carnal smile he knew.

"Come along, Livvie," he said, spreading his arms, "you can't be afraid of this. After all, in another two weeks, you'll have rights to every square inch of it."

She hadn't moved, but Jack had seen the possibilities overtaking her. Right there in her expressive eyes, in the way her hands opened and closed at her sides, as if instinctively grabbing for him. He saw the flush of arousal climb her chest and sweep up her long, elegant throat to wash over ivory cheeks. He heard the quickening of her breath. And then he saw her eyes drop from his chest to the washcloth, which was predictably changing form before her eyes.

Hers. Hers to do with as she pleased. To explore, to claim, to tease and torment until both of them gasped with exhaustion.

Hers.

It had been the most erotic thought he'd ever had.

He was so caught up in his memories that he didn't even realize that he'd once again gotten to his feet. A chilly breeze reminded him the window was open, and he wandered over to it.

Immediately his attention was caught. Was that somebody watching the house? Without thinking about it, he stepped to the side so he could look without being seen. A thin man in decent attire was standing at the Parc gate, lighting a cigarillo, the spark flaring yellow in the graying light. Jack couldn't see his face. For some reason, though, the man's casual position alerted him in a way that seemed familiar.

"I thought I told you to sit," Livvie said, walking back into the room.

Jack pointed out the window. "Is there any reason someone would be watching this house?" he asked.

She strode over to check for herself. By the time she got there, though, the man was gone.

"I don't know," she said, frowning as she looked outside. "Let me tell Sergeant Harper when he brings up the water."

They stood there for a bit, side by side, thinking separate thoughts. "Thrasher told you?" Jack asked.

She startled. "That you've attracted questionable attention? Yes. Do you have any idea why?"

Now. Tell her now. “No. You?”

She didn’t look at him. “No.”

He absently nodded and returned to his chair.

“Are you sure you’re up to this?” she asked.

His body seemed to not care that the household might be in danger. One unintentionally suggestive word from Livvie and it reacted with amazing predictability.

“Oh, I’m up for something,” he assured her, casting a quick glance down to where his cock was stirring. “At least I know *that* wasn’t injured. I’ve been tenting the sheets like a fifteen-year-old with his first housemaid.”

He peeked up to see her casting a frantic glance at his lap. He saw it again on her face, that beautiful flush of arousal. The pinched frown of distress. He’d be a cad to urge her on, especially now. But when she turned away, he could see the sweet slope of her behind as her dress swirled around her, and his body refused to behave. Heat speared his gut, settling with unerring accuracy in his groin. His fingers tingled. His chest tightened. The once-loose pantaloons Sergeant Harper had lent him again grew tight. He suspected he was going to spend this night with balls that ached like fury.

He didn’t care. He had the most unsettling feeling he hadn’t had the chance to enjoy this view much recently, and he couldn’t bear to miss it.

“We found another set of clothing for you,” she was saying, looking out the door for the sergeant. “One that might fit better.”

“I sincerely doubt it,” he muttered.

She whipped around. “Pardon?”

“Thank you, Liv.” He forced a smile. “I appreciate it.”

Have you ever heard of anyone called the Surgeon?

Axman Billy? Should he really ask her? Should he risk her peace of mind, maybe her life, by forcing that darkness on her?

How else would he be able to get the answers he needed? He couldn't merely rely on a twelve-year-old pickpocket.

Before he could decide, Harper knocked on the door and led in footmen with the tub and water. While the tub was being filled, Livvie acquainted Harper with Jack's suspicions. Harper made it a point to check out the window himself.

"Don't ya be worryin' none, lass. We'll keep an eye out."

Jack didn't wait to pull his shirt off over his head. "Oh, Lord, Liv," he groaned when he caught a whiff of himself. "I'll need a lot of soap."

Levering himself up off the chair, he began to unbutton the placket on his trousers. Livvie took an anxious step his way. "Jack, you shouldn't..."

He couldn't believe it. She was as fretful as a maiden aunt, her eyes skittering around the room—anywhere but at his body. The last time he remembered them together, they'd spent an entire day tumbling about in a field before God and most of the sheep in North Riding. Now she looked as if she'd never seen him naked.

How long *had* it been since they'd made love?

He hesitated, his hands holding up his gaping pants. "I wouldn't mind a bit of help balancing, Liv."

She shot him a quick glance and actually stepped away. "Would you like Harper to help you?"

It only took another look at her expression to

understand. It hung between them like a sword. Mimi. How could he expect his wife to welcome him when she believed he was involved with another woman?

How did he know he wasn't?

Jack stood where he was while Harper orchestrated the scene around the tub. The footmen poured water in and tested it, and then left supplies on a chair. Setting two cans of hot water by the fireplace, they exited, which left Harper waiting in the middle of the room.

"Thank you, Harper," Jack said. "But I'll be fine. My wife will help me."

Harper had the brass to stand right where he was. "Ma'am?"

She looked up, a bath sheet clutched to her chest like a shield, her eyes wide and dark. Jack held his breath, mentally begging for mercy.

It was when she sighed that he knew he'd won. "Thank you, Harper. I'll call for the tub's removal when my husband is finished."

Jack waited for the door to close before dropping his drawers. He was not surprised to see that he was as stiff as a post.

Livvie glared at it as if accusing it. "And you can put that thing away," she told him briskly. "You're not going to be using it tonight."

He looked down past the bruises and scrapes and cuts to where his rod seemed to be waving greetings and offered a tired smile. "Sorry to say, it has a mind of its own. As long as it thinks it's going to be entertained, it'll be on the alert."

Livvie sniffed like a chaperone and bent to line the tub with a bath sheet. "Well, disabuse it of that notion. There isn't the time, I haven't the energy, and you haven't the stamina."

His smile grew wry. "Well, there you have me. Will you help me into the tub?"

She helped him in, and Jack had to remind himself that he needed this bath more than he needed sex. Well, more urgently anyway.

He slid into the water with a heartfelt sigh, sure he'd never take hot water for granted again. It was positively life-giving. He would never overlook the sweetness of a woman's scent or the softness of her hand. Although it occurred to him that Livvie's wasn't so soft. She had calluses.

He looked up, intent on asking why, and was immediately distracted. The steam had already begun to destroy her tight chignon. Golden strands had fallen loose and curled around her throat. Her skin was rosy, and her breasts strained against the worn gray of her gown. Her forehead, though, was pursed and her mouth tight.

She met his gaze, and he saw the flood of emotions she had dammed up inside. For just a moment, he thought he understood them. For a moment, he thought he would remember what it was that had robbed her of her joy and whimsy. He thought he might just be able to find the words to recover them.

But that moment passed, and he was still lost in the dark.

"You're still not listening," she snapped, her voice not quite as forceful. Her hands were shaking.

Jack shook his head. It was all so funny. She was afraid of him, he was trying his damnedest to be a gentleman, and his John Thomas had obviously decided to ignore them both.

"Pay no attention to it," he advised, pulling a washcloth from her hand and dropping it over his blatant erection. "If you ignore it, it might just go away."

And he might decide to join the priesthood.

"I have a feeling I should apologize again," he said, reaching up to take her hand. She didn't pull away this time. "You seem so uncomfortable, and it's something I never thought to see in you. Not anymore."

And she didn't even know the worst.

That thought took the rest of his humor. He had no right to insist she be here. He should chase her out of the room and make sure she didn't come back until he could explain that alley near the river and the people looking for him and the man who might be watching the house. Until he could come to her with a free heart.

But it was so difficult. Giving her hand a tender salute, he let go.

"I'm sorry we couldn't get to this sooner," she said, her voice uncertain. "You do need a good wash-up. Do you want me to get your back?"

He closed his eyes against every image those words provoked. "Dear God, yes. I can't remember the last time I bathed."

Kneeling next to the tub, she picked up another cloth and wet it. "You have so many scars," she said quietly. "Wherever you were, you fought hard."

He twisted a bit to look over his shoulder. "Yes. Harper told me I looked like I'd been flogged like a sailor."

"Caught with the wrong wife?"

"I don't have a taste for wives, Livvie."

She paused, as if surprised. "Glad to hear it."

And he felt worse.

Lathering the rag, she pushed on his shoulder. "Can you bend forward a bit?"

He did, and she laid that cloth against his neck. He swore he'd never felt anything so decadent in his life. Hot water lapping his belly, a warm breeze wafting in through the window, and Livvie bent close, her hand encased in a soft cloth, scrubbing away all the grime he'd collected. She was rubbing hard, as if scraping away years' worth of dirt, and Jack felt pathetically grateful. Every time she pushed forward, her breasts brushed against his bare back, and he could smell her perfume.

It was all he could do to keep from groaning. His heart was beginning to race. His groin was tight enough to explode. He could smell apples. Apples and the faintest musk of arousal. He sat perfectly still, his head resting on his folded arms, investing all his concentration in Livvie's touch.

"Are you all right?" she asked.

"I believe I'm in heaven. You can't imagine how important this simple thing is if you're forbidden it, Liv."

"Forbidden? Why? Were you marching too fast?"

"No. It was dark."

She stopped suddenly. "Dark? What do you mean?"

He lifted his head, blinking. "What?"

"You said you couldn't bathe because it was dark. Why?"

He didn't move. It was there, hovering just out of sight. Something sinister. Something foul and frightening. He clenched his hands, as if to help drag it closer, but it didn't help.

Feeling absurdly helpless, he laughed as if it didn't

matter. "I'm sure there was a good reason." He reached up to brush his knuckles across her cheek. "But right now I'd much rather think about how wonderful this feels."

He knew she didn't believe him. All she had to do was feel how his heart was racing to know he wasn't unaffected. He saw the uncertainty in her eyes, the glint of fear, and hated it.

"All right, Jack," she said, and returned to her scrubbing.

His shoulders. His neck. Each knob on his long spine. Each rib and the slope of his waist and hip, the strokes sending heat spiraling out through his limbs. The warmth of her body against his back lit fires in his belly. He was shaking with the power of his arousal.

"Lean back."

He leaned back and looked up to see her staring at that washcloth over his groin, which wasn't doing such a good job of covering anything anymore. Just her gaze had it twitching, as if it was trying to reach her. Jack gritted his teeth against the pain of it, the urgency. The hunger that exploded through him.

"You're only half finished," he ground out. "Do you want me to take that rag now?"

She turned to him, and he saw that her eyes were all but black with desire, that they were roiling with distress. He wanted to reassure her. He couldn't seem to get the words out.

Without answering him, she began to wash his chest, and Jack thought he'd simply die on the spot. She lingered this time, forgetting to scrub, the rag sliding across his collarbones, over the notch in his throat, down the slope of his sternum. She soaped up his shoulders and then lifted his arms to scrub beneath, from his wrist to his armpit to his waist.

He couldn't watch anymore. He couldn't bear it. Livvie was washing his body as if it were fragile. As if it were explosive and too rough a touch could set it off. He thought she might be right.

He lay in the water, his body boneless, his world diminished to a cooling cloth in a small hand. Water trickled down his ribs, and it felt like ice against his fevered skin. He felt Olivia sweep the cloth down to his belly. He stopped breathing. She paused, an inch away from bliss. He waited. He hoped. He finally opened his eyes to see her watching him, her hand stilled, her pulse throbbing at her throat.

Caught in the heat of her eyes, he let his conscience go quiet. "Please, Liv," he begged, his voice a bare rasp. "Please. Touch me."

He heard her suck in a startled breath. He saw her stiffen, as if she would flee, and he fought the urge to just pull her into the tub with him. It had to be her choice. It had to be her move, but sweet God, he was going to die if she didn't.

Without taking her gaze from his, finally she reached down and lifted away the insufficient washcloth. She looked to where her hand hovered just above his straining cock, and she seemed to sigh. And then, with exquisite slowness, she dipped her hand into the water and wrapped it around him.

He almost exploded right into her hand. He braced himself, every muscle clenched so tightly he thought he'd seize, his eyes squeezed shut. He could smell the flower scent of her hair as she eased close to him. He could hear the quick, small panting of her breath and knew her mouth was open just enough to slip his tongue into if he wanted. He felt the tremor in her fingers as she began to slide them along his shaft and thought that she was as close to climax as he was.

"Sweet...Jesus," he gasped, balanced on a shattering edge, his hands wrapped around the edge of the tub to keep him from yanking her to him. "I can't..."

Her fingers swept over his quivering tip, measured the length of him, then dipped lower to cup his balls. Teasing, tormenting, taunting. "I forgot...," she whispered, and he thought how tortured her voice sounded.

She was so close he could feel the heat lift off her skin. He couldn't help it. He had to touch her. With one hand, he reached up to cup her breast, her full, luscious breast he had once spent a full day mapping. Caressing, suckling, tickling. Laughing when she'd objected to his calling her birthmark the X that marked the perfect spot.

She was so hot, so soft, so ripe. She was everything any man could want.

Why had he wanted more?

It was almost enough to ruin him. If she hadn't still had hold of him, he might have faltered. If he didn't have the most disturbing suspicion that he wasn't the only one who had forgotten how this felt.

"I need a kiss, Liv," he managed, wanting to hold her. Wanting to ask her if she would take him into her, if she would be his comfort. His resting place. His peace. "I need you."

She lifted her head and looked bemused, as if waking from a dream she couldn't quite remember. "I love it...," she whispered, as if it were being dragged out of her, "when you..."

She didn't have to finish the sentence. Jack knew it like a brand on his heart. He heard it again, just as she'd whispered it in his ear last spring. Last spring? He wasn't sure anymore. But he was sure of what she'd said. What gift she'd given him.

Before she could finish, he reached up to cup her face in his hands and brought her to him. And then, without understanding why, without even hearing it until she froze, he murmured into her mouth, "How could I love Mimi more than this?"

Livvie yanked back so fast water splashed all over the floor.

"What?" she asked, her voice deadly quiet.

Jack stared, appalled.

He never got the chance to answer. Suddenly, from the floor below, came a great clattering and the slamming of doors. And then, the bellowing of Sergeant Harper.

"Fire! Fire! Everybody out of the house!"

Olivia jumped to her feet so fast she tipped over a chair. Jack struggled to get out of the tub. Livvie yanked the door open, and Jack caught the smell of smoke. He could hear the commotion of running, raised voices, the crash of something shattering against the floor. And beneath the commotion, he heard something far worse: the crackle of flames.

The house was on fire.

Chapter 15

By the time Olivia got the door open, there was smoke curling over the lip of the hall from the main staircase.

"Harper!" she yelled. "Can we get down the back stairs?"

"If you hurry!"

"Is everybody else out?"

"We're workin' on it. Come on, then, lass!"

She slammed the door closed and spun around to find Jack struggling with his pants. Taking only long enough to grab his shirt, she ran over to assist.

"Livvie..."

She slapped his shirt against his dripping chest. "If you apologize, Jack Wyndham, so help me God I'll march you right into the flames."

She couldn't comprehend what had just happened. Not what Jack had said. She should have anticipated that. What *she* had done. The distress of it knotted up her throat and weighted her belly. It made her want to just sit down right here and wait for the smoke to come. It made her want to bash Jack over the head and leave him on the floor.

"I have neck cloths," she snapped, handing them over. "Bind your feet. You have no shoes."

"Don't worry about that," he retorted, buttoning his pants and shrugging on his shirt. "Wet some towels for our noses and mouths. Did you see which way the smoke was coming from?"

Her laugh was edged with panic. "Everywhere."

He nodded, as if this were something he did every day. "Remember to bend low. Smoke rises." Then, before she could shake him off, he grabbed her hand. "Time to go, Liv."

Bending over the tub, he helped her wet the towels. She could see that he was hurting. She prayed she could get him downstairs.

She needn't have worried. Jack was the one who led the way. Her hand in his, he checked the doorknob, then turned it to open the door. In the few minutes they had taken, the smoke had grown worse, oily and black and thick. Olivia could hear the definite crackle of flames now, and muffled shouts and clangs.

"Keep low," Jack reminded her, and bent himself.

She heard his grunt of pain and tried not to notice. "You don't have shoes," she reminded him, following. "Be careful."

His grin was a bit wild. "I'd hoped we would be anyway. Now get the towel over your face. Looks to be a long way down."

Hands clasped, they checked the front hall to see orange light flicker against the foyer walls. Without a word, they turned toward the servants' stairs. It was impossible to see, and the smoke stung eyes and lungs. Olivia felt it collect in her chest, even through the thick towel she held over her face. She wanted to cough. She wanted to cry. She just prayed that Jack's strength held out until they escaped.

Jack seemed to be able to see in the dark. The stairs were steep and narrow, but he navigated them easily. By the time they reached the first-floor landing, though, he was panting and weaving. Struggling to get in a clear breath, Olivia slipped her arm around his waist.

She was just about to start down the next flight when she heard an odd whimper.

"Jack," she said. "Stop."

He did. "What?" Even his voice sounded strained.

She tilted her head, trying to hear over all the noise. It came again, from one of the drawing rooms.

"Who's there?" she yelled, hanging on to Jack for dear life.

"I'm afraid..." came a thin voice.

"Thrasher?" she demanded. "Thrasher, get out here now!"

"Can't...can't..."

She moved to lean Jack against the wall. "I have to get him."

Jack wouldn't let her go. "Thrasher?" he called, limping toward the drawing room. "Come on, lad. Time to go!"

And suddenly Olivia thought Jack might well have been in the military. How could anyone ignore that voice of command? But he was coughing, clutching at his ribs. Running up, she slid her arm around him.

"Don't make me!" Thrasher cried, his voice sounding horrifically young. "I'll burn up!"

Jack straightened and stared into the parlor, as if he could see the boy. “If you can’t see, crawl to my voice!” he called. “It’s not a real fire, boy. Just a diversion. If you use it as camouflage, they’ll never see us!”

Jack’s words stopped Olivia where she stood. He was bent over, searching the smoke. She knew he hadn’t realized what he’d said.

“You promise?” Thrasher asked.

“Connors, come out here!” he yelled. “Hurry up! No time!”

“I...can’t...”

“We’ll be caught!” Jack barked. “Now move!”

And before Olivia could catch him, Jack dove into the room.

“Jack!”

She lurched forward, only to run into him as he ran back toward her, Thrasher tight in his clasp. The boy’s eyes were running, and he was fish-belly white beneath the soot. It seemed their fearless Thrasher was terrified of fire.

“I’m sorry,” he sobbed. “I looked and looked but I swear I didn’t see nothing ’til it ’appened. I woulda told. I woulda.”

Olivia had no idea what he was babbling about. “I believe you, Thrasher. Now come along.”

“Watch the floor, now,” the urchin cautioned. “That’s ’ow me mam died. Went right through like it was water.”

And Olivia understood. “Master Jack needs a hand,” she urged, trying to break through his terror. “Can you take hold of his other side?”

“Hurry,” Jack was muttering. “I don’t know what will happen if they find out what I’ve done.”

The boy slid in under Jack's arm. "What'd he say?"

It took Olivia a second to understand the boy's confusion. Then it dawned on her that Jack had spoken the last in French.

"He says hurry, Thrasher. Now come along."

By the time they reached the ground floor, Jack was barely conscious. Olivia's heart was hammering in her chest, and she couldn't take a full breath without coughing, but Thrasher had begun a steady monologue that kept them going.

"Jus' a few more steps now," he rasped. "Good thing I'm 'ere, ain't it? This'll sure be a story to tell back 'ome."

"Indeed it... will," Jack responded, panting. "Someone should set it... to... music."

They reached the kitchen to find Harper heading their way.

"There you are," he called, looking relieved. "Let me take his nibs now. We're after gatherin' in the garden."

"Buckets," Jack gasped.

"Already swingin' away, milord," Harper said, and without apologies, slung him over his shoulder.

Olivia tried to ignore Jack's *umph* of pain. Thrasher trotted off after them, leaving Olivia to follow, skirting footmen in various liveries who passed with buckets. Reaching the garden, she took a moment to fill her lungs with clean air before showing Harper where to lay Jack on the grass.

The cool air hit her like a punch, making her cough harder. But it smelled sweet and clear. Harper gently settled Jack, and Thrasher plopped himself down alongside like an underfed guard dog.

"Is everyone out, Harper?" Olivia asked, still gasping.

"All that's here. I sent a messenger for Lady Kate."

Olivia nodded, glancing around to see that Harper and Finney had handily organized the work. "I don't suppose there's a way to get inside and rescue some brandy for the earl."

The sergeant grinned. "Ah, sure, ma'am, there's always a way to procure a drop—for medicinal purposes, of course."

She grinned back and patted his arm. Then she turned her focus to Jack. He lay sprawled in the grass, his sides heaving, his good arm wrapped around his middle as he coughed, his skin waxy and pale. Coughing herself, Olivia dropped down next to him and lifted him against her chest so he could breathe more easily.

"Thrasher?" he asked, not opening his eyes.

"Right 'ere, y'r 'eroship," Thrasher responded with a toothy grin. "Imagine a flash cove like you savin' my groats. Cor."

"Nonsense," Jack rasped, his eyes still closed. "You walked out yourself. We just gave a push to guide you."

"Well, you guided me pretty good."

"How are your ribs, Jack?" Olivia asked, feeling him split them at each breath.

His grin was pure Jack. "Reminding me that I'm breathing."

And so they sat, the three of them, coughing and wheezing as the rest of the staff and a few neighbors mingled dazedly on the lawn and the bucket brigade put out the last of the fire. Harper managed to secure brandy, which Olivia fed in sips to Jack, taking one good gulp herself. She even gave a bit to Thrasher, who, even though he continued to entertain them with a running monologue of what was happening, still shivered like an ague victim. Without a word, she wrapped her free arm around him and let him rest against her other side. She barely noticed that she was shivering even harder herself.

That was how Grace, Bea, and Lady Kate found them when they arrived some minutes later, still dressed in their finery.

"Devil take it, Olivia," Lady Kate snapped. "I can't leave you alone for a minute." She looked furious, but Olivia could see the real distress in her eyes.

"We didn't want you to have all the fun," Jack said from where he still rested against Olivia's breast.

Lady Kate huffed at him. "You have an odd definition of *fun,* sir. Harper? What's to do?"

Olivia hadn't seen Harper approach. He gave Lady Kate a little bow and rubbed the back of his sooty neck. "Well, now, it's thick with smoke in there and all, but, sure, didn't we get to the fire before there was much damage? Might have been somebody who spilled an oil lamp. There was oil all down the curtains in the dining room."

"An oil lamp? What fool did that?"

"Wouldn't that be what I'm after trying to find out? Seemed like an awful lot of smoke for such a little fire. We didn't even lose all the drapes. Looked like the smoke screens we used to use to confuse the froggies."

Olivia looked at Jack, who wasn't attending. Then she looked at Lady Kate, who was. "That doesn't make any sense."

"Bees," Lady Bea abruptly announced, her hands clutched around her gold-beaded reticule.

Everybody turned to Lady Bea, but it was Grace who gave a slow nod. "Beekeepers use smoke to drive the bees out of their hives. Literally, 'smoking them out.'"

"Are you saying somebody did this deliberately?" she asked, and suddenly remembered that man Jack had seen from the window.

Harper was staring at Lady Bea in astonishment. "Faith, if I don't believe that isn't just what happened?"

As if choreographed, one by one, each of them turned to Jack, who was lying against Olivia, his eyes closed.

Outside. In the open. Where anyone could see where he was.

"Jesus, Mary, and Joseph," Harper whispered.

"Get him inside," Lady Kate urged. "I don't care where you put him."

For the first time, Olivia realized that the little yard was crowded with strangers.

"What?" Jack demanded, startling awake as Harper bent over him. "What's wrong?"

"Go with Harper," Olivia said quietly, helping him up.

Jack protested, but he never stood a chance, especially with Thrasher helping to chivy him along. Olivia wanted to stay and search the crowd, as if she could recognize the villain who might have done this. Lady Kate had different ideas.

"Come along, ladies," she announced, reaching for Olivia. "I believe we've provided enough of a raree-show for this evening. This calls for one of Mrs. Harper's famous tisanes."

"Bollocks," Bea retorted, leading the way. "Brandy."

All four women laughed. "You're right," Lady Kate said, and reached into her reticule. "Here, Livvie. You look like you should be first."

Gaining her feet, Olivia instinctively reached out her hand to see that Kate was setting a flask onto her palm. *The* flask. Jack's flask. Holding Lady Kate back with a hand, she let Grace and Lady Bea precede them.

"How did you get this?" she asked the little duchess.

Lady Kate's smile was mischievous. "Jack had it when I went to see him this afternoon. He was looking a might bemused and asked if it was mine. I told him yes. Don't you think it will enhance my image?"

"Taking snuff from a gentleman's wrist isn't enough anymore?"

"So passé. I'm quite smitten with the idea of carrying my own brandy. Do you mind if I keep it?"

Olivia laughed. "On the contrary. I insist." She reached out her hand. "Here. Allow me to complete the jest."

Olivia took the flask and slid her nail beneath the seam. It snicked open, and she handed it back.

Lady Kate took one look and whistled. "Why, it's the pony."

"That, my dear Lady Kate," Olivia disagreed dryly, "is nothing less than a show horse from Astley's."

A show horse Jack had spoken of in a moment of ecstasy.

"'Is not the first fruit sweet, my love?'" Lady Kate read from the flask, then frowned. "That's not right."

Olivia stared. "You recognize it? I certainly don't."

"Hmm." She shook her head. "Well, no matter."

Snapping the flask closed, she slipped it into her pocket. "I will set *such* a trend."

From the back of the crowd, Gervaise Armiston saw the little exchange and grinned. "Well, well, well."

He had been in the box next to Kate at the opera when she'd received the urgent message to return home, and he'd never been one to waste an opportunity. Wouldn't it be a bit of a lark if he could separate Olivia from her friends and maybe imply that he'd started the fire? She'd believe him, of course. By now she undoubtedly thought he was responsible for everything but the king's madness. She'd be terrified and, very possibly, pliable.

But this was even better. She'd had enough, had she? He chuckled. It was nice to have the upper hand again. With what he'd just learned, he would have it all. Livvie, real wealth, Jack's demise.

The flask. Gervaise couldn't wait to see who wanted it.

Venice, he thought. *Maybe Rome. Yes. Livvie would love Rome.*

Whistling, he slipped his hands in his pockets and walked off like any other buck about town.

Olivia followed Lady Kate inside to find Lady Bea comforting a distraught Lizzie.

"What's this?" Lady Kate demanded. "Tears? You didn't drop that lamp, Lizzie. Besides, sobbing is bad for the baby."

"That's not the problem," Finney said, stepping up

to them. "I think you'd better come upstairs."

Lady Kate exchanged glances with Olivia, but she followed in Finney's wake.

"We found it when we was checkin' the rooms f'r damage," Finney was saying, climbing the stairs to the second floor.

He reached Lady Kate's suite and threw open the doors, and Olivia gasped.

The ornate little boudoir was in ruins. Furniture was tossed over, paintings pulled from walls, clothing tossed about as if a high wind had swept through. The pillows had even been eviscerated, feathers still drifting over the room like snow.

"So far there's four bedrooms and the library look like this," Finney told them.

"You've checked for intruders?" Lady Kate asked.

"Sergeant Harper asked f'r that duty particular-like. He seems right upset."

"As am I. I don't suppose my jewel box remains unscathed."

"Well, that's what's off," Finney said, scratching an ear. "Bivens says as how nothin's missin'. Not so much as a brooch."

Olivia dropped to search for her portmanteau, where she'd hidden Jack's ring and snuffbox. They were all sitting safe in the middle of the floor. She felt a coil of dread snake through her. "Someone was here while we were in the garden."

They might have been waiting in the house as she and Thrasher struggled to get Jack down the stairs.

"What could they be looking for?" Lady Kate asked.

"Me," Olivia heard, and turned to see Jack standing

behind them in the doorway. He had arrived with Thrasher, listing and soot-stained but looking very much in command.

"Not unless you can fit in a pillowcase," Finney retorted. "This was as thorough a job as I seen."

"Axman Billy," Thrasher piped up. "Bears 'is stamp."

Lady Kate actually paled a bit. "We've been burgled by someone named *Axman*? I'm not at all certain I like that."

Olivia was more than certain she didn't like it. She found herself looking around, as if expecting the intruder—*Axman*—to materialize from beneath the beds.

"How do you know?" she asked Thrasher.

It was Jack who answered. "Thrasher has been doing some investigating for me. He told me today that this Axman Billy was looking for me. He and somebody named the Surgeon."

And Olivia had thought she couldn't feel more frightened.

"The Surgeon?" Lady Kate echoed, eyes wide. "You're being followed by someone named the Surgeon? Is this someone you know socially, Jack, or have you been dabbling in vivisection?"

Jack sighed. "I have no idea. I'm sorry, Kate. I've put you all in danger."

"Don't be absurd," she retorted. "A little excitement once in a while keeps the blood flowing."

"But what did he tear the house apart for?" Olivia asked.

He shook his head. "Was I carrying anything when you found me? Something small, I'd have to guess."

Turning away, she retrieved his snuffbox and signet

ring and handed them to him. "These," she said. "And a flask."

One warning look from Grace was enough to keep her from mentioning the dispatch to General Grouchy.

"A flask?" Jack's eyebrows rose as he turned to Kate. "Must have been mine after all."

"Do you want it back?"

"No. I doubt somebody would destroy a house just to get his hands on my brandy." He stood there a moment, shaking his head as he turned the snuffbox this way and that. "I can't see how any of these would be of interest to anyone."

"The question is what to do about it," Lady Kate said.

"Blockade," Lady Bea piped up, her voice a little thin.

Lady Kate immediately walked over to put an arm around her friend. "We won't let anyone else in, darling. I promise."

"Me 'n Harper'll set the lads to watchin'," Finney said. "Maids'll clean. I'll get repairs started."

"And I'll leave," Jack said. "Kate, is Diccan Hilliard in town? He's attached to the embassy here, isn't he?"

Everybody seemed to stop breathing. "Diccan?" Lady Kate asked with admirable nonchalance. "Whatever for?"

Jack's smile was old and knowing. "Because he specializes in the discreet removal of problems. And I'd have to say that right now, I qualify as a problem."

Her arm still around a pale Lady Bea, Lady Kate nodded absently. "Probably an excellent idea. I'll send someone out for him in the morning."

"No, Kate. I need to leave as quickly as possible. I won't risk your safety another moment."

Kate straightened, and Olivia couldn't help smiling

at how the tiny duchess seemed to meet towering Jack Wyndham eye-to-eye. "It must be an excess of smoke distorting your reason, Jack, or you'd consider the fact that someone named *Axman* is undoubtedly right now waiting in the shadows for you to come scrambling out my back door. Besides, I refuse to move without at least five hours of sleep. We might be desperate, but we are not barbaric."

"I don't think we can say the same for Axman," Jack suggested.

Lady Kate shook her head. "We're all safer right here until we speak with Diccan. Besides"—she cast a telling look at her butler—"Finney would never let you out the door. Would you, Finney?"

The hulking butler smiled. "Not 'til Y'r Grace told me to."

Jack considered the duchess for a long moment. Finally, he seemed unable to do more than shake his head. "All right," he agreed, and bent to kiss her hand. "First thing in the morning, then."

He must truly have been exhausted, because he allowed Thrasher to help him to his new bedroom.

Jack had no sooner disappeared into the master suite than Lady Kate spoke up. "It would seem Diccan has lost his chance to remain anonymous."

"Paphian," Bea said, startling Olivia back to attention.

Lady Kate gave a thoughtful nod. "Diccan's mistress? Yes, I agree. Finney, we need to find one Madame Ferrar. A tiny blond relict of some Belgian colonel, if memory serves. I believe you'll find our Diccan worshiping at her dainty feet. We'll see him at eight."

Finney's eyes disappeared into his grin. "I'll put

Thrasher on it. The boy needs to be doin'. He's feelin' a mite low."

"He didn't see anything at all?" Lady Kate asked. "It's why I left him behind."

"Aye, so he did, Y'r Grace. Was him give the alert when he heard the glass break. He tried to help everybody out, but then he smelled the smoke...."

"Poor little beast. His whole family." She nodded. "Go ahead and send him, then."

"I'll tell him," Olivia said, still trying to comprehend the scope of the disaster. "I need to check on Jack."

If Lady Kate's room was ornate, the master suite was obscene, a veritable explosion of gilt, from Fragonard paintings to pedimented doorways to robin's-egg-blue walls festooned in ornate plasterwork. It was one room Axman had failed to destroy.

Olivia followed the raspy sound of Jack's voice into the bedroom, where she found him sitting on a gold brocaded settee speaking to a much diminished Thrasher. Just the sight of them brought back the terror of those endless minutes in the dark stairwell, and she found herself trembling again.

"I shoulda tole the ladies," Thrasher was saying.

Olivia saw the real distress in the boy's eyes and knew it wasn't time for serious intent. "Please don't tell me there's more. Someone named Blackbeard, maybe?"

Both of them looked up, their faces almost comically soot-stained. But what caught Olivia was how pale and drawn Jack looked. He'd definitely used up his budget of energy tonight.

"Blimey, guv," Thrasher whispered. "We's caught it now."

"Exactly correct, you scamp," Olivia retorted. "Now, off you go. Finney has a particular mission for you, and Master Jack has to get his rest. As for me, I'm proper knackered."

Giving her a bright giggle, Thrasher took himself off.

"You really must stop hanging about with street urchins, Liv," Jack said with a shake of his head. "Your language."

She gave her best grin, even as she clenched her hands to still the trembling. "Don't be silly. I got that from the duchess."

Stepping up, she brushed back his hair. "Now come along. It's bed for you, my lad. You have performed quite enough heroics for one evening."

Before she could step away, Jack took hold of her hand. Clutching it in both of his, he raised a troubled face. "Stay with me, Liv."

She froze, a great hollow opening in her chest. Why hadn't she anticipated this? Not making love. Even more dangerous—comfort.

It was as if he'd heard her. "I won't touch you, Liv. Not like that. I don't have that right, and I'm sorry I let things go so far earlier. But, Liv, how can you bear to sleep alone? Don't you need me anymore?"

How dare he? In one fell swoop, he set loose all those emotions she'd battened down like a ship in a storm. Did she need him? Of course she bloody well needed him. Just as she'd needed him when he'd been with her, when he'd condemned her, when he'd disappeared as if he'd never existed.

Of course she needed him. She wanted him. She feared him. She hungered for him.

She *hated* him.

And yet, standing in this absurd room with her hands clutched in his, she couldn't muster the strength to leave him. Not this time. Not when she was so cold and so afraid, and he was hurting. For just a moment, she closed her eyes, terrified Jack would see every roiling emotion, every pain and sin. But her greatest fear was that he would see the inevitable despair of surrender.

"Yes, Jack," she said, gently disengaging her hands. "I'll sleep here tonight. But there is still too much between us for me to simply pick up our lives where we left off."

She truly almost laughed at that. At which point would he pick up? When he'd called her a slut, or when he'd slammed that great door in her face and watched her disgrace from the window?

For a very long few minutes, she was terrified she would let all that rancor loose on him. But this Jack still wouldn't understand. And he needed her. Even worse, she needed him.

She wished with all her heart she could have said that she hated the long hours of that night. She wished she could have at least held on to her fast-dissolving pride by waiting for Jack to fall into an exhausted sleep before disentangling herself from him so she could retire to her own bed.

She didn't. She lay wrapped in his arms, her ear against his chest, where she could soak in the hypnotic rhythm of his heart, and she watched the shadows crawl across the wall until they were chased away by the first pearlescent light of dawn.

She held perfectly still, lest any movement woke Jack. She bathed in the warmth of his embrace like a window cat soaking up the sunlight, and she called herself every kind of fool for enjoying it.

She knew better. She was being inexcusably weak, and she had no excuse. And yet, she didn't move until she heard the house begin to stir.

Even then, Jack slept on. Olivia stood at the foot of the bed, seeing the warming light creep across the angles and planes of his handsome face, and she held her fist to her chest, suddenly sure she would simply crumble beneath the pain. She dreaded having to face everyone else in the house, certain they would never understand.

It took only one step into the breakfast room to make her realize there were far bigger threats to her than embarrassment.

They were all there: Lady Kate and Grace and Bea, and even Harper. But they were gathered in a cluster near Finney, who was standing hunched over as if he'd just lost a bout. Lady Kate was pressing a glass of whisky on him, and he was shaking. Olivia thought he might have been crying.

It brought her to a dead halt. "What's wrong?"

Lady Kate stepped forward. "Sit down, Livvie."

Olivia looked around at the grim expressions and shook her head. "Oh, no. I think I'd better take this standing. What happened? Did you find out something bad? Is it about Jack?"

Grace looked up, and Olivia saw she looked stricken. "It's Chambers."

Olivia blinked, confused. “Chambers?” She said it as if she’d never met the man. “What about him?”

Lady Kate drew a breath. “He’s dead.”

Olivia suddenly felt stupid and slow. She knew she couldn’t have heard those words correctly. “I don’t…”

“Last night while we were fighting our fire, somebody slit his throat.”

Chapter 16

Olivia sat down so fast she almost missed the chair. She knew Grace had jumped to help her. She thought Bea might have pulled a vinaigrette from her reticule. She didn't need a vinaigrette. She needed something to vomit into. She kept swallowing, and the bile kept rising.

Dead. No. That wasn't possible. She'd spoken to Chambers just the day before. He had promised to help Jack regain his memory. He couldn't be dead.

He couldn't be dead because of *her*.

"Olivia," Lady Kate said, and Olivia looked up to see that her friend looked uncharacteristically pale. "I'm so sorry."

Olivia turned away, unable to focus on anything but that anxious, tidy little man. "I didn't like him, you know. Not really. He helped Jack throw me out. But then, he was always Jack's man…well, until he was Gervaise's anyway." She found herself laughing, a high, thin sound. "Oh, God, what am I going to tell Jack?"

There seemed to be no answer. Grace sat down beside

her and laid a gentle hand on her arm. Olivia looked up at her. "Do you think it was because he came to see me?"

"I don't think we can discount it," Lady Kate admitted. "Finney. What did the authorities say?"

"They said it were robbery." Finney's voice wobbled suspiciously, and he kept blinking. "He sent me a note yesterday to meet him. I thought it was just to have a pint. I'm not so sure now. They…they found him in an alley."

"Thank you," Lady Kate said, finally sitting down. "Why don't you see if Mrs. Harper has one of her tonics?"

The huge man kept nodding, as if that would help cement the news in his mind. "I believe I will." And without waiting for a proper dismissal, he picked up his whisky and walked out.

"I don't believe our Finney is spy material," Lady Kate mused, although her voice lacked its usual edge.

Olivia couldn't seem to think. Odd bits of information kept swirling around in her head like a kaleidoscope, jagged colors and sharp edges bumping into each other, forming and re-forming patterns that made no sense. Except one. Chambers was dead.

"Poor Diccan," Lady Kate said with a wry shake of the head. "The only thing he expects to deal with is a minor fire and some vandalism. By the time he gets here, we might have already upped the ante to invasion and plague."

Olivia looked at the three indomitable ladies who surrounded her. They were her friends. They had risked their reputations to shelter her, and she had responded by bringing murder and violence to their door. She almost laughed. She'd thought her greatest threat would be from Gervaise.

"Jack's right," she said. "The only way to keep you safe is for us to leave."

Lady Bea turned pleading eyes to Lady Kate. "Anathema."

"Indeed," Lady Kate responded, her expression formidable. "The idea is inconceivable. I will, however, consider other options."

Olivia knew she should be ashamed of herself. She felt nothing but relief at Lady Kate's reprieve. "Maybe Mr. Hilliard has some information that can help us understand what's going on," she suggested. "Especially about"—she swallowed past the knot in her throat—"Chambers."

"You can't tell the earl about him," Grace warned.

With a weary sigh, Olivia levered herself to her feet. "I wouldn't dare. If bad news can give him brain fever, the news about Chambers would kill him on the spot."

Jack stood looking out the window as if he could recognize his attackers strolling in the Parc. Thc sun was up, the hawkers and housewives out. It looked so bloody normal down there, and the stench of smoke still hovered in this fussy, fancy house.

What had he done to incite such a thing? How could he have ever crossed paths with someone named Axman, who thought nothing of starting fires and destroying whatever was in his way?

He couldn't wait up in this room anymore, hoping his memory would simply miraculously reappear. He couldn't survive another night like last night when he'd spent those long, terrible moments trying to get Livvie safely down the stairs.

What if something had happened to her? How could he have lived with that?

And then, in a moment so generous it shattered him, she'd slept in his arms, giving him the first rest he'd had since first waking.

She was protecting him from something. He could see the shadow it cast every time she refused to answer one of his questions.

He could no longer allow her to bear that burden. If he demanded to take it on, she had no right to refuse.

He'd been standing by the window long enough to see a gentleman climb the steps below him to the front door and gain entrance. He wished he could identify him, but the angle was too severe. He was considering going down to find out, when suddenly he caught a whiff of clean air and apples.

Livvie had come.

"Thank you, Liv," he said, his focus still on the Parc. "I slept better last night than I have since I've woken."

It actually took her a moment to answer. "I didn't stay to be thanked," she objected stiffly.

He couldn't blame her. Finally, because he didn't know what else to do, he turned to face her. "Liv," he said, caught by her expression. "What's wrong?"

Her beautiful brown eyes were dark with distress. She stood so stiffly, as if barely holding herself together. Not knowing what else to do, he stepped up and wrapped his arms around her. "What is it?"

At first she remained rigid. But when he wouldn't

release her, she briefly laid her head against his chest. "Someone died," she said in a wavery whisper. "One of our soldiers. We'd thought he'd recover."

"I'm sorry, sweetheart. Especially with everything else that's been happening."

She couldn't seem to do more than nod. "Thank you, Jack."

He gave in to the temptation to glide his fingers over her hair. He wanted to pull it down. He wanted to muss it. To shake her up so she wasn't so unnaturally contained.

He couldn't. He'd asked too much of her already. So when she stepped out of his arms, he let her.

"Has Kate heard from Diccan yet?" he asked.

She seemed fascinated by her own hands. "He should be here later this morning."

He nodded, wishing he could pull her back to him, if only to pretend that he had her support in what he was about to do. "It's time to face the truth, Liv," he said.

She started as if he'd shouted. "Truth?"

He sighed and guided her back to the settee he'd occupied the evening before, taking her hand to hold her there. "This can't go on. I'm a danger to you, and I won't allow it any longer."

She looked as if she was holding her breath. "But you're going to speak with Diccan."

"It's not enough. I need the rest of my memory. Don't you see that?"

She looked away, as if afraid to betray some truth. "You were remembering something last night. In the fire. You spoke as if you'd been…oh, I don't know. Imprisoned. As if you'd escaped by starting a fire. And you mentioned someone named Connors. Is it familiar?"

He tested his memory and recovered only a few disconnected bits. A fight. Gray stone that bled rainwater. The feeling that he could hear death and betrayal whisper in the dark.

He was cold again, as if he could never warm. But just as always, memory was swept away by a sharp headache, and the headache did nothing but increase his frustration.

He shook his head. "I don't know. And we've run out of time. You have all been generous and patient, but the truth is that something I've done is a threat to you. We must find a way to provoke my memory. You have to tell me everything."

Livvie tried to yank back her hand. "No, Jack. We've discussed this. You have to remember on your own or you could suffer permanent damage."

He found himself on his feet. "What if I never remember? My God, Liv, I'm missing great expanses of my life, and you won't tell me what they are. And I know that whatever I've forgotten is significant. More than that, it's dangerous. I need to know before somebody gets hurt. What did I do, Liv? What are you protecting me from?"

She shook her head. "Oh, Jack. I wish I could tell you."

"Why won't you? Don't you want to tell me what happened?"

"I don't *know* what happened."

Her words stopped him cold. He looked down to see her eyes closed, as if she could hide from her own admission.

"What do you mean you don't know?" he demanded, suddenly sure he didn't want to find out. "Surely the men in my unit can tell you. My commanding officers."

She just kept shaking her head, her eyes down. "I...we're not sure who your commanding officers were. I don't know where you've been, Jack. When Chambers found you, you were...naked."

He couldn't quite breathe. "I don't understand. You said I was in a Guards uniform."

"The looters had already been by. We put the uniform on to keep you warm. We hoped that you would explain where you'd been when you woke."

"I was fighting with the Hussars!" he snapped, shoving her hand away. "It's what I've wanted since I was in leading strings. How could you not know that, for God's sake? Ask someone in charge. Ask Horse Guards. Ask bloody Wellington!"

But the moment he said it, he knew it was wrong. Wellington would not know about him. Nor would the Hussars. He got to his feet, his entire body trembling. "I don't understand."

She must have heard the desperation in his voice, because she was suddenly on her feet, her hands on his arms.

He turned his sore eyes on her. Sharp shards of glass seemed to be lodged in his head. "What if I've done something—"

"You haven't." She looked just as upset. "When you remember, you'll know that. Maybe you saw something on the battlefield that is dangerous to someone. Maybe you know something someone doesn't want you to tell or stumbled over something they want."

Rubbing his head again, he turned away. "Why haven't you asked someone?"

"Because of everything we *didn't* know. We couldn't

just stroll into headquarters and ask if anyone knows what you've been doing for the last four—"

Too late, she stopped. Jack swung around, almost losing his balance. "Four what? Days? Weeks? Months? What did I do, just walk out one day and not come back?"

She drew a deep breath, but she faced him. "Yes."

He laughed. "Oh, Livvie. Don't be ridiculous."

She offered an unhappy shrug. "I swear to you, Jack. If I could tell you where you've been, I would. But I can't."

He kept shaking his head. "That's—"

"Absurd. I know. Nothing has made sense since the moment we found you. But all we can do is keep you safe until you remember. We'll be leaving for London soon. That might help."

"No," he insisted, "it's not enough. You're keeping something else from me. Something you know will hurt me, or you wouldn't be afraid. Well, damn it, Livvie, I have to know. Don't you understand?" He fought against that inexorable band of pain. "How can I rest when I know something I did is putting you in jeopardy? You have to tell me."

"No! It could kill you."

"I don't care!" Even if his skull felt as if it would shatter.

"Well, I do care," she snapped. "I am not going to kill you. Please, Jack. Don't ask it of me."

And before he could protest, she turned and left.

For a long time, Olivia just stood there in the hallway, her hand fisted against her mouth, eyes closed, struggling to swallow that hard knot of tears that seemed to be growing. She couldn't keep on this way. She couldn't bear another moment of it.

Unconsciously, her hand snuck up to lay against her hidden locket, and she thought of what she had already borne. Of what she still had to live for. Of how very, very much harder it would be now.

Jack had given her a choice. She could have told him and been done with it. Laid it all out before him and taken her chances. But when it had come down to it, she'd simply been unable to put Jack at risk.

The sound of familiar footsteps alerted her. "Yes, Lizzie?" she asked, knowing her voice was trembling and sharp.

"Lady Kate sent me, ma'am. Mr. Hilliard's come."

Nodding, she scrubbed at her face with her hands, just in case any tears had escaped, and followed the girl back down the stairs.

She found Mr. Hilliard already in the Yellow Salon with her friends.

When he saw her, he rose from the Louis Quinze chair and offered an elegant bow. "I do hope you are anxious to shake the soil of Belgium from your shoes, Mrs. Grace."

He was, for once, not in black but wore a blue superfine coat, biscuit pantaloons, and gleaming Hessians. The look of a man come to pay a cousin a casual call.

"You are very efficient, sir," she said.

He waved a gentle hand. "It's a particular talent. Now, Kate has had a smashing time filling me in on your latest adventures, which simply supports my belief that we must act quickly. Once Major Braxton arrives, we can put my brilliant plan into action. But you must be ready to leave on the moment. Will you?"

She looked around to see that Kate was delighted, Grace hesitant, and Bea busy picking the currants from a bun. Olivia took her usual seat next to Lady Kate.

"Oh," Diccan added. "One more thing. You must be willing to impersonate a bargeman's wife."

Olivia couldn't help laughing. "Oh, why not? I have certainly impersonated worse things."

"Capital. Then we are on. You and Gracechurch will be gone by morning."

Olivia froze. "Jack and I? No. Someone else should go with him."

And for the first time, she saw compassion in Diccan Hilliard's eyes. "I'm afraid not, ma'am. It will take at least seven days for you to reach London, and to separate you for that long would, I fear, be detrimental to the cause."

She could only stare at him, appalled. "You said it would be best for us to travel separately."

"For *Kate* to travel separately. I had always intended you to travel with your husband. I'm afraid you are his best chance for recovering his memory."

She shook her head. "I'm not so sure it would do him any good to stay with me and remember."

"I don't think we have a choice," she heard behind her.

Olivia whipped around to see Jack standing in the doorway. He seemed to look larger, stronger, clad in clothes that reminded her so much of those long-ago days bringing in the harvest. He was looking on her with something akin to regret, and she knew he'd heard her.

Before she could correct him, he looked past her. "Hallo, Hilliard," he greeted his friend, and strode in.

Everyone in the room froze. What would he remember?

Olivia battled an insane urge to drag him back out of the room before it occurred to him that Diccan had witnessed that fatal duel with Tristram.

For Diccan's part, he rose calmly to his feet, lifting his quizzing glass for a good perusal. "Look as if you'd been in a prime mill, old son."

Jack smiled and offered his hand. "It seems I have. Anything you can tell me about it?"

Diccan took Jack's hand in a surprisingly strong grip. "With the resources left behind here, I couldn't tell you what Wellington had been up to. It's a sore trial, to be sure."

Jack cast a quick look to Olivia, and she saw that he wasn't happy. "Besides, your hostesses would have your liver and lights if you told me."

Diccan's smile was telling. "Kate's terrifying enough. The four of them together positively put me in a quake. But with a bit of help, we should be able to collect some resources once you return to home soil."

"You don't think I should stay where I was found?"

"Too much chaos. Far too much opportunity to do you mischief before you can find your answers."

"Do *you* have any idea what this is all about?"

Diccan's expression softened a bit. "Afraid not. And, yes, before you ask, Kate," he informed his cousin, "I did do a bit of discreet asking around. Came up empty."

Jack nodded. "Then fill me in on your plan."

The two of them walked over to the drinks table as if the women had suddenly disappeared. Olivia saw Lady Kate bristle, but she for one was thankful. She was relieved to have no demands made on her right now. She was still trying to come to grips with the idea of spending seven days with Jack. Seven days alone, bound by danger and isolation. Seven days with no one to rely on but each other.

Swamped by dread, she closed her eyes. It would be too much; she knew it. She knew, too, that Mr. Hilliard had left her no choice. And she still couldn't tell Jack the truth about their marriage.

And then, as if she'd heard Olivia's internal monologue, Lady Kate leaned over. "It might just be perfect, Olivia."

Olivia startled, seeing both the duchess and Lady Bea watching her very closely. "Pardon?"

Lady Kate took a quick look toward Jack, but he was involved with Diccan's explanations. "He loves you, Olivia," she whispered. "Spend your time together reminding him of how much."

Olivia thought she'd survived quite enough shocks in her lifetime already. Somehow the insidious logic of Lady Kate's suggestion stunned her to her toes. Not because it was so outrageous, but because she was suddenly so tempted by it, a serpent's whisper in a primeval garden.

"No. I can't."

"Stuff," Lady Bea huffed, although Olivia had no idea to whom she was responding. Then Bea's gaze rose, and Olivia was caught by the purpose in the old woman's gray eyes. "Yoicks and away," the lady said quite clearly.

Olivia should have laughed. Lady Bea had just given her the cry for the sighting of the fox. But the purpose in those wise old eyes sent Olivia's pulse skittering. How could these women know what it would cost her to take such a chance? How could they possibly encourage her to do something so foolish?

Because they knew how much she wanted to.

"This is a different Jack," Lady Kate insisted. "This Jack will understand."

"I can't take that chance," was all she could say, because she couldn't tell them why. She couldn't even think it.

She'd won and lost Jack once. If it happened again, the consequences would be immeasurably worse. Unthinkably worse.

She never got the chance to speak. Suddenly, Finney was standing in the doorway, the picture of a proper butler.

"Major Kit Braxton," he announced.

Grace's handsome friend stepped through the doorway, his expression a bit guarded. He saw Grace, though, and began to smile.

He'd taken no more than four or five steps into the room when suddenly he came to a shuddering halt, his attention no longer on his friend. For a moment, he just gaped. Then he laughed, striding right past Grace to where Jack and Diccan were sharing a drink.

"By God, Gracechurch," he said with a relieved laugh. "What are you doing here? Don't you know that we've been looking for you?"

Chapter 17

Olivia found herself on her feet. "What do you mean, you've been looking for him?"

Over by the wall, Jack was staring at the newcomer. "Do I know you?"

"Of course you do, you gudgeon!" the young man said with a grin. "I was supposed to collect you. Leave it to you to be hiding out with four beautiful women."

By now everyone was on their feet. Diccan once again had his quizzing glass up, but Braxton paid no heed. He was too intent on shaking Jack's hand.

"But why were you looking for him?" Olivia asked.

She had just begun to hope he might have the answers they needed. But when he heard the question, Braxton turned to her as if suddenly realizing she was there. He opened his mouth and shut it again, turning astonished eyes back to Jack.

"Good Lord," he said, as if trying to take it in. "Don't you recognize me?"

"No, I don't." Jack looked suddenly wary, as if

expecting attack. "Can you tell me where I've been?"

Confused, Braxton looked around the room, ending with Diccan.

"Morning, Braxton," Diccan greeted him with a perfect bow. "I assume you've been looking for our wayward friend here."

"Well, yes." He frowned at Jack. "I don't understand."

"Jack suffered a head injury. His memory was affected. Do you know where he's been?"

Olivia thought he might have swallowed.

"Uh, no," he finally said, suddenly sounding much less sanguine. "Not really."

"Then why were you looking for me?" Jack demanded.

"Why don't we all sit?" Lady Kate offered smoothly. "I'll ring for more refreshments."

"Comin' right up, Y'r Grace," Finney called from the doorway.

Lady Kate didn't acknowledge his impudence by so much as a look. She simply gestured to the gentlemen to resume their seats. Braxton took a chair by Grace, and Jack took one next to Olivia.

"Is this what you wanted me for, Grace?" Braxton was asking as he took his own seat. "Jack?"

"Well," she hedged. "Yes and no. The earl needs your help, but we had no idea you were already looking for him."

"Why *were* you looking for him?" Olivia repeated, unhappy with the suspicion that Braxton was stalling for time.

His expression didn't help. He had such a handsome, open face. Why did she think she saw calculation going on behind his soft blue eyes? Why did she think he was going to lie? Maybe because he seemed unable to look at her.

"Why, his family has been trying to find him, of course," he said. "He's been abroad a while, and he was needed at home."

"And why would you be the one searching?"

He looked around, as if surprised at her ignorance. "I'm cousin to Sussford." At the silence, he looked over at Jack. "Your sister Madeline's husband."

Olivia felt her stomach drop. She hadn't told him yet.

Jack swung on her. "Maddie? She's *married*?"

"You don't remember," Braxton said. "I didn't know."

Olivia opened her mouth, all the information she could have given him tumbling around inside. In the end, it was Lady Kate who answered for her. "You remember Sussford, Jack," she said. "Bright young puppy with that brilliant stable. Last I heard, he and Lady Madeline were intent on raising prime hunters."

Jack turned Livvie's way. "Is he telling the truth, Liv? Is he related to Maddie?"

How could she know? She hadn't seen his sister in five years.

"Of course I am," Braxton insisted. "Why would I lie?"

And suddenly, as if a light had been extinguished, Jack's eyes went cold. He didn't move so much as a muscle, but Olivia thought he suddenly looked dangerous. There was a predatory tautness to him she didn't recognize, and it unnerved her.

"You'll pardon my caution," he said, his voice colder

than his expression, "but I find blind trust to be a sometimes fatal error in judgment."

Olivia shivered. How could those beautiful, sweet eyes look so lethal? What had forged the new steel in him? He looked so bleak, as if the memory he'd lost was nothing more than a wasteland.

"You remember something?" Lady Kate asked him.

"No. But I don't think you'd argue my point, would you, Your Grace?"

Lady Kate offered an answering smile. "Not at all. But then, with several key exceptions, I've never trusted anyone. This, I think, is a new twist for you."

He shrugged. "That may be. I do know that I am not acquainted with this man, and he is in a position to harm not only me, but also my wife and her friends."

Kit startled. "Your wife?"

Olivia held her breath.

Grace reached out to take Braxton's hand. "Yes, didn't you know? Olivia is Lady Gracechurch. Oddly enough, the only thing the earl does remember is that he is married. To Olivia."

Kit nodded a few times, his eyes wide. "Indeed."

"How could you not know that?" Jack demanded.

Braxton almost squirmed. "I never actually got to meet her, Jack. Been on campaign, don't you know."

Grace, unruffled, turned to Jack. "I'm not sure if you will accept my word, my lord, but Kit is a dear friend. He served honorably under my father and was injured at Toulouse. I believe you can trust him."

Even the new Jack couldn't seem to gainsay her. But Grace had that effect on people. "Thank you, Miss Fairchild. Your word is enough. But how could my family not know where I was? Haven't I been in touch?"

Braxton shook his head. "Not since that stint in Salerno with the Neapolitan Court two years ago. It's certainly the last time I saw you."

Jack just stared at him, unable, evidently, to speak.

"Why did his family need him home?" Olivia asked.

She had to wait for her answer, as the inevitable parade arrived to dispense tea. Finney supervised the flawless ritual and then backed out, closing the doors behind him. All the while, Olivia felt her tension increase as Braxton accepted a glass of Madeira.

"They asked me to look because the marquess was gravely ill," he said. "Better now, but the family felt Gracechurch should be home."

Jack nodded, his eyes closed a moment. "I assume the marchioness was as helpful as usual."

"She was...distraught."

He only grunted. "Another reason to hurry home, I imagine."

"You're going home?" Kit asked, looking around as if for verification.

"Not immediately," Diccan suggested evenly.

Jack shook his head and opened his eyes. "No. No need to put the family in any danger. I'll contact them as soon as I've cleared up this mess."

Braxton looked at Grace. "Mess?"

"Indeed," Diccan answered instead. "It was why Miss Fairchild contacted you. She recommended you for a delicate operation we have in mind. Jack does need to get back to England, but it's proving a bit more involved than just hiring a place on a packet boat, and we need your help."

Braxton nodded. "You have it, gladly. I can't tell you

how glad his family is going to be to know we've found him."

The words brought Jack back to his feet. "No," he said, and looked straight at Olivia. "They can't know yet. Not until I've been to Horse Guards. I'll be going the minute I get to London."

Olivia was on her feet before she knew it. "No!"

Jack stepped up and laid a hand on her cheek. "Yes, Liv. I don't know how I got here. You don't know. There is only one way to find out, and I have to do it."

She knew he saw the stark fear in her eyes. She thought surely he would ask her why. But he didn't. He just dropped a kiss on her lips and smiled. "Trust me. The sooner I speak to the officials, the sooner this will be over. You'll arrange it for me, Diccan?"

Olivia heard Diccan sigh as if he were the most put-upon person in Europe. "Yes, Jack. I'll arrange it. But until I do, you must promise me to behave yourself and not go running off to solve this puzzle yourself."

Jack smiled over at him. "I would if I could, Diccan. But I don't know what I'll remember between now and then, do I? I can only promise to do my utmost to protect these ladies until I find out."

Tell him, Olivia thought. *Show him the dispatch. Make him realize that he might be signing a death warrant if he goes to the government.*

She turned to Grace, hoping to see encouragement. But Grace shook her head. The danger to Jack's health had not changed.

Beset by the growing conviction that she was condemning Jack no matter what she did, Olivia kept her silence.

* * *

Later that evening, Diccan Hilliard found himself sharing a dimly lit library with one of the sources he'd culled for his infamous plan. The Baron Thirsk was a nondescript man. Medium height, medium build, medium coloring, the kind of man people couldn't quite describe even after just seeing him.

At the moment, the baron was enjoying his cognac. "Everything is in place for tomorrow?" he asked.

Crossing his legs and settling into the tufted leather chair, Diccan made a point to contemplate the pale Delamain cognac Thirsk had poured for him. "They should be in London by next week."

"Excellent."

Frowning, Diccan looked up. "You still insist on sending them to Lady Kate's."

"It is the tidiest solution."

"For you, perhaps. Don't you think they deserve to know that you're using them as bait?"

Thirsk waved off Diccan's concern. "The house will be well watched. Why worry them needlessly?"

"Because we don't know what information Chambers gave away. You didn't see him. I did, and believe me, he didn't die easily. And Gracechurch has inadvertently set a deadline by demanding an appointment with Whitehall. His enemies have evaded us thus far. I don't want to run the risk they'll slip by us again."

"We will be on our own playing field now. Fear not, Hilliard. All is in place. Now, I thank you for bringing this to me, but you need not worry any longer."

Diccan wasn't so sure. But his hands were tied.

If something happened to his Kate, though, he would

never forgive Thirsk. Or himself for bringing Thirsk into this.

Before dawn the next morning, the plan was put into effect. Decoys were sent on a seemingly panicked flight to Ostend, where they would catch a fishing boat to Margate. Thrasher, stationed at the upper-front window, was able to report that the bait had been taken. The minute the substitute couple set forth in Lady Kate's coach, men separated themselves from the deep shadows to follow. They, in turn, would be trailed by Major Braxton as far as Ghent to make sure they didn't double back.

Lady Kate publicly dispatched a portion of her staff home to open her Mayfair town house while she took the more leisurely route via one of the pleasure barges to Antwerp and then a packet home. Decked out in homespun and clogs, Olivia and Jack accompanied the staff as far as the canal, where they climbed aboard a grain barge. They were not watched.

It wasn't until later that afternoon that the Surgeon received the news that his prey had escaped.

"We've looked everywhere," a thin, weasel-faced man assured him. "They are not in Brussels. No one knows where they've gone."

He'd found the Surgeon in his rented room, packing as if he were headed off on a hunting weekend. "No matter," the Surgeon assured him. "I know exactly where they will end up."

The thin man seemed to shrink in size. "And?"

The Surgeon slipped several extra knives into the false bottom of his portmanteau. "And the little valet ended up being a wellspring of information. Gracechurch does indeed have what we want. But the valet no longer knew where it was. He was, however, able to tell us that Gracechurch's wife is now in possession of everything our friend was carrying on the battlefield." Lifting a stack of cravats, he packed them in a precise stack. "I also just learned that Gracechurch is going to be suicidal enough to present himself to Whitehall, which means he still doesn't remember anything. If he did, he wouldn't go anywhere near that place." Smoothing his clothing, he closed the case. "I don't believe he will be successful."

The little man shivered. "How can you be sure?"

The Surgeon smiled. "I understand he loves his wife very much."

"His wife?"

"Why, yes." Lifting his curly beaver hat from the bureau, he set it atop his head at a precise angle. "What do you think of this quote, Fernier? 'The penalty we pay for our acts of foolishness is that someone else always suffers for them.' Appropriate, don't you think?"

The smaller man frowned. "For what?"

The Surgeon tapped him on the cheek. "For carving onto a woman's lovely belly, of course. It is time the earl learns that there are consequences for his actions."

Maybe Olivia could have come out of the trip heart-whole if it had been shorter. If life on the barge hadn't seemed like a place out of time, separated from the past and balanced on the edge of an unknown future. If she and Jack hadn't relied on each other when the sense of danger became too acute.

She might even have been saved if they had been able to find separate berths. But the one-room cabin was small and low-ceilinged, with the entire crew piled in like hounds by a fire. She and Jack had been forced to share a pallet.

They didn't make love: not in a room of strange men. But they touched. They comforted. They settled into old sleeping patterns, tucked up together like spoons in a drawer.

And every second of that time was colored by the memory of the moment they'd slipped out of Lady Kate's house. Catching Olivia by the arm, the duchess had leaned close and whispered, "Remember. This is your chance."

It took five days to reach Bruges, lazy days spent working side by side with the real bargemen as fields of grain slipped by and church bells tolled the hour from village spires.

"I didn't know you could cook," Jack praised her when he finished their first dinner.

Laughing, she shook her head. "We really didn't know each other at all, did we?"

He frowned, and Olivia thought he looked even more handsome as a peasant, his skin sunburned and his hair tousled by wind. "What do you mean?"

Her smile was dry. "If you remember my father, he was the most cheese-paring man in North Riding. And my mother could never get along with cooks. So I did most of the cooking."

Which had saved her more than once in the years that

followed. She had been a welcome addition to inns and bakeries, even with a babe in her belly.

Leaning back on the deck where the two of them had been watching the waning moon reflect on the water, Jack shook his head. "That's right. You had such a way with peach tarts. Every kind of sweet, come to think of it. It's too bad Cook won't allow you in his domain at the Abbey."

Two days earlier, she would have had to bite back a sharp retort. Somehow the barge eased her. The more time she spent with Jack away from the tension of that house, from the reality that awaited them in London, the more she found herself settling into a too-comfortable pattern.

They worked together in harmony, be it cooking or cleaning or leading the great golden Belgian horses that drew the barge along the canals. They began to laugh at the same jokes again, to reach for each other to share the silence of sunrise or the soaring architecture of Ghent's famous three towers. Unforgivably, she began to expect the harmony to continue. Worse, she began to anticipate it.

Then, like a harsh wind, Kit Braxton appeared. The barge was slipping through early-morning Bruges, the sun barely kissing the top of the medieval Belfry that soared over the city. Taking a moment after serving breakfast, Olivia had been seated at the front of the barge watching the morning light creep down the curious stair-step chimneys of the tidy houses that lined the water. She was wishing she'd had more of a chance to enjoy the whimsical Belgian architecture.

She felt Jack step up behind her. "Trouble," he muttered.

She saw Kit immediately. He was waiting ahead on a

restive chestnut, two other mounts in tow. He hadn't spoken a word, and yet Olivia felt the first rush of fear.

"Braxton," Jack greeted him with admirable calm. "You're a surprise."

The young dragoon flashed a grin. "No hope for it. Your destination's being watched. How do you feel about a bit of a ride ventre à terre?"

Olivia's first instinct was to protest. Jack wasn't ready for such exertion. He could hurt himself again.

She looked over to see Jack grinning like a boy. "Can't think of a better way to shake off the doldrums." Turning to her, he held out a hand. "Liv?"

There was no way she could admit she hadn't sat a horse in five years. At least she had once been proficient. Something else besides weaponry to thank her father for, she supposed.

"Certainly," she said, surreptitiously wiping her hands on her skirts, "especially since you didn't force me onto a sidesaddle."

Kit looked a bit abashed. "It would be expected, you see. They're looking for a man and a woman. Can you manage?"

It was Jack who laughed. "Livvie successfully avoided sidesaddles until her fifteenth birthday."

She frowned, trying hard to keep up the banter. "Can't hunt properly from a sidesaddle. You're left behind with the sluggards. Do you wish me to don breeches?"

He did. Ten minutes later, clad in a smaller version of Jack's attire, she bid farewell to the bargemen and let Kit give her a leg up onto her gray.

"I assume you know the route," Jack said, settling onto his big bay gelding.

"Just came from there," Kit said. "I hope you like fishing smacks."

Olivia settled into her saddle and gathered her reins. She hadn't been allowed to ride in men's attire in years. It might be the only benefit of this mad dash to the coast. "Please tell me we're not expected to work the next boat too," she begged, a strange sense of exhilaration sweeping through her. "I detest the smell of fish on my hands."

Nudging his horse across the low canal bridge, Kit looked back at her. "Never fear. You are honored guests. Ready?"

The ride was harrowing. Olivia expected ambush at every turn and the sound of gunshots at her back. Her legs began to cramp and her thighs chafe. But she kept her silence. She wasn't sure that the men would understand that she was having the time of her life. She wasn't sure *she* understood it.

In the end, there were no further alarms. They found their way to a deserted stretch of beach, where they were met by a rascally-looking Belgian with a johnboat. The fishing smack waited out in the water.

"I'll be along a day or two behind you," Kit promised. "Need to finish laying a false trail first."

He gave Olivia a kiss on the hand and turned back for Bruges. Jack helped Olivia onto the boat, and they were rowed out to a suspiciously unfishy fishing vessel.

In the end, the trip seemed more adventure than flight, a thrilling escapade rather than a desperate escape. And Olivia shared that feeling of adventure with Jack, eyes meeting, hands touching, bodics instinctively seeking each other for balance and comfort and rest.

And each touch, each met glance, each shared breath

and inadvertent embrace served only to intensify their barely banked hunger.

She tried so desperately to shore up her defenses against him. She wanted to hate him as surely as she had in the spring. That hate had kept her alive for five years. It had given her purpose and pride and direction.

He had wronged her. He had discarded her without a thought, this husband who should have loved her. He might have been exiled, but he hadn't been abandoned without a penny to his name and a babe in his belly.

No, she thought as she watched the cliffs of England rise over the horizon from the bobbing deck of the little boat. That box with Jamie stayed locked. She couldn't bear to think about him. Not when she could barely deal with Jack.

But that box, like all the others, was damaged, and she knew that soon—too soon—she would have to face what she'd hidden away inside.

Maybe she could have held on to her hate better if the trip hadn't ended like a Sunday afternoon lark, with the two of them stepping hand in hand off the boat in Wapping as if they'd been on a Greenwich cruise. Maybe if they hadn't been met by a thin stick of a young man who was so precise and dour that he provoked laughter. Maybe if Lady Kate and Grace had been waiting for them when they arrived.

But Lady Kate wasn't there. It was Finney who met them, and the housekeeper who begged they treat the house as their own home.

Maybe if none of those things had happened, it would have been different.

But Olivia didn't think so.

* * *

She had to admit that she was surprised by Kate's house. Whereas the one in Brussels had been an explosion of ornamentation, this house on unexciting Curzon Street was almost painfully plain, five stories of redbrick without so much as a pediment to enhance the fanlighted doorway. The windows, although there were many, were long, plain rectangles with white casements, relieved only by wrought-iron balconies on the first and second floors. All in all, an exercise in tasteful restraint one wouldn't associate with the Dowager Duchess of Murther.

The housekeeper, a thin sparrow of a woman named Mrs. Willett, with bristly gray hair and a surprisingly substantial bust, made it a point to personally greet them at the kitchen door and usher them into the upstairs side of the house.

"We've had word from Her Grace," she confided in them. "They are spending a few days in Bruges before continuing on to Antwerp and home."

Such innocuous words to incite giddiness.

Alone. She and Jack would be alone for at least three days before anybody interfered.

It wasn't sensible. It wasn't sane. Olivia knew that she would only suffer for what she was about to do. But suddenly, it seemed inevitable.

Maybe Kate was right. Maybe it could turn out differently this time. She didn't know. All she knew was that she could barely hear the housekeeper for the blood rushing through her ears.

As the housekeeper explained household policy, Olivia looked past her to see that Jack was already watching her. Already at the decision she hadn't even realized she'd made. She and Jack were alone, and whatever else happened, they would make love.

"Well, we've prepared the room Lady Kate reserved for you," Mrs. Willett was saying as she led them across to the sleekly banistered stairs that swept up from the back of the house. "Baths have been prepared, and a tea tray with all of Her Grace's favorite cakes. Dinner will be at eight."

Jack surreptitiously reached over and curled his hand around Olivia's and stole her breath. It still felt unreal, as if nothing that happened here counted, as if they were being given a small window of opportunity to find each other again. The thought fluttered in her chest like a trapped bird.

Mrs. Willett climbed to the second floor and turned left down a short hall to open a set of double doors. "The sitting room. The bedrooms connect through it, of course. I'll leave you here, just as Lady Kate suggested."

And before they could question her, she curtsied and trotted back down the hall.

"Lady Kate is very suggestive," Jack said, ushering Olivia through the door. "I wonder what she can be about."

Olivia pulled her hand free and walked around the elegant eggshell sitting room. "For a notorious woman, she seems to enjoy matchmaking."

Jack stepped up behind her. "A hobby I highly approve of."

He kissed the nape of her neck. Olivia closed her eyes against the wash of weakness that gesture provoked.

She shouldn't be here. She should beg for a different room. She should barricade herself in a distant tower Jack wouldn't be able to find.

She leaned back against his touch. "You are wicked."

"Aye, wicked," he murmured in her ear. "That's me."

Then he turned her around, and suddenly this was her Jack, just back from the fields, his smile relieved and hungry, his laugh as light as wind.

"Oh, Livvie," he greeted her, sweeping her into a close embrace. "I've missed you."

She found herself laughing and breathless as she wrapped her arms around him. "You've been right next to me."

He growled into her hair. "I want to be *in* you." His voice was strained, his muscles taut. Olivia could feel every thought he had before he had it. "We shouldn't, Liv. We should wait until we have all our answers. But, God, I just can't. I feel as if it's been forever."

She closed her eyes and savored the feel of him, the scent of him, the perfect fit of him around her. God forgive her, she wanted nothing more at that moment than to stay exactly where she was.

She *wanted* to hope.

"Say yes, Liv," he whispered against her ear in that wonderful raspy voice that betrayed his arousal. "Sweet God, say yes."

Suddenly, briefly, madly, she wanted to try. Not just to reclaim the magic of lovemaking. She wanted to see if Jack might love her again, really love her. And this, she knew, would be the first step.

She chuckled, the sound breathy and afraid. It had been so long. And yet, her body was already reacting, flames licking along her belly as if he'd touched her with a slow match. She met his gaze to see how hot that beautiful sea-green could be. She felt his hands at the back of her dress and nestled closer. She arched her neck so he could nibble at it. "Yes, Jack," she whispered. "Yes."

He groaned against her skin and raised goose bumps all the way to her toes. "Oh, Livvie..."

He was dropping kisses down her neck when he suddenly straightened. "I remember something."

She went still, his words all but dousing her excitement. "What?"

He never loosened his hold on her. "I remember sitting at a gambling house somewhere playing deep basset and thinking how few places there could have been for you to gamble. How *did* you lose your pearls, Liv?"

She battled a hot wave of hope. "They were taken from my jewelry box. I never knew they were missing until Gervaise appeared with them and said he'd recovered them from the pawnbrokers."

Absently stroking her cheek with his thumb, he nodded. "You never did gamble, did you?"

Olivia fought the burn of tears. "No, Jack. I didn't."

Holding her even more tightly, he dropped a slow kiss on her forehead. "I think I've known that. I think my sisters might have been conspiring to separate us. I'm so sorry, Liv. I should have trusted you."

She lifted a hand to stroke his dear face. He hadn't shaved in six days, so he looked rough, especially with that cruel scar down his temple. She thought she could grow to love the look. "We can talk about it later," she assured him. "I'm just glad you believe me now."

"Of course I do. You'd never lie to me. I know that. After all these years, it's what I've held on to."

She held her breath. *All these years.* Should she

press? Her body was telling her to ignore everything but his hands, where they rested on her waist, his lips, which had begun to trace her ear. A shower of chills was racing along her nerve endings and demanding attention.

"I'm glad," she finally whispered, ashamed of her cowardice.

His life could depend on these returning memories. She should help him pry them loose. But if he remembered too soon, she would never have another chance to win him.

"Take me, Jack," she begged, lifting her face to see the hunger in his sweet, sea-deep eyes. "Be my husband again."

And, as if she had never known regret, she reached up to undo her dress and let it slide to her feet.

He didn't bother with words. Lifting his hands to cup her face, he bent his open mouth over hers. She melted with the first taste of him, with the first invasion of his tongue, rasping against the sensitive roof of her mouth. She held on as he plundered well-remembered territory, and her mind, usually so careful, so protective, could focus on nothing but her need for him to hurry.

Hurry, I need you. Hurry, I can't live another moment without your hands on me, with you inside me.

Want me again. Please.

He noticed her tears but thought they were of joy. He sipped them away, dipping his tongue into that little hollow at the base of her throat and sending a cascade of chills through her. He bestowed his old smile on her, the one that closed them off from the world, that promised a union that would lift them beyond life. She helped him slip out of his shirt and trousers and then knelt, her heart caught in her throat as she untied his smalls and eased them away.

He waited hard and ready for her, jutting from that nest of dark curls and pearled with a drop of juice. She wept over the tip of him, because he was so lovely to her. So long remembered, deep in the darkest reaches of night where no one could blame her for her yearning.

She touched him and was savagely glad at his gasp. She bent to taste him and heard him growl deep in his throat. She drew a breath, just to fill herself with the night-and-sea scent of him, and began to hum in the back of her throat.

"Oh, God, Liv, I do love you."

She closed her eyes, trying so hard not to be stricken by those words. There might be no love left once he remembered. There might be recriminations and abandonment and, if she allowed it, the final death of her heart, that sore, sad organ that had survived so much only to be tossed at his feet yet again.

But kneeling there before him, where her choice should have been obvious, where she should have spurned him as he'd spurned her, if only for the ragged remnants of her self-respect, she knew she wouldn't. She would take what she could now and hold her trust for those who deserved it.

"Livvie?"

She drew an unsteady breath. With slow, deliberate movements, she rose to meet him as the wife she'd once been. As the lover he'd once hungered for. And blinking back tears, she opened her arms to receive him.

Chapter 18

"You're still dressed," he rasped, his eyes dark, his hands clenched at his side.

He had a point. He stood before her splendidly naked, his magnificent body just a bit leaner, more honed. More mature than the mostly formed lad she had so loved. This was a man's body, but she still knew every inch of it: touched, tasted, and savored. She noted the new scars and thought that they only enhanced his formidable beauty. A beauty that had once belonged to her alone.

Another box to put away, right now before it could stop her. Mimi had no place in her bedroom.

"What do you want me to do?" she asked him.

His smile was pure deviltry. "That doesn't look like a very good chemise."

Her skin skittered before the heat in his eyes, swirls and eddies of excitement spilling through her. "It has seen better days."

Beneath it, her nipples tightened. Her stomach clenched with anticipation. Her heart started to race. She bent to take the hem of her chemise in her hands and began to draw it up. Slowly enough that he growled with impatience, she raised it, revealing her knees, then the long line of her thighs, and then, with deliberately lazy movements, the first peek of that triangle of blond curls he had once worshiped.

He let her get no farther. With a strangled curse, he wrapped his hands around the embroidered neckline of her chemise and tore. The old lawn ripped as easily as paper, leaving her panting and ready before him, her only ornament the simple locket he had given her so many years ago.

She froze. Would he recognize it? Would he reach out and say, *Oh, look, Liv. It's the locket I got you for our engagement. Is my picture still there? The lock of hair I gave you?*

And if he did, what would she say?

He nuzzled her throat as if the locket wasn't even there. "I suppose you expect me to carry you to bed," he murmured with a dry smile. "Lazy creature."

And she was laughing, his words bubbling in her like champagne. She climbed onto the bed and turned on her knees to receive him. She thought how brave she was, exposing herself to him this way, even her secret sex open and vulnerable. She saw his naked body and thought again how his new scars stood out to taunt her with the secrets he carried to her.

Slowly he slid a hand up from the ankle she'd tucked beneath her to her calf, to her knee, never once taking his gaze from hers, smiling like a voyager returning home. He slipped his finger beneath her garter, and her body shuddered with need. She knew then that if only for now, she belonged here in his cherished hands.

"Come here," she begged, and he did. "Love me," she pleaded, and he laughed down into her eyes, his face suddenly, belovedly familiar. He was young and happy and carefree again as he settled them both back on the bed, skin to skin, nose to nose, his scent filling her nostrils and melting her insides. She was wet for him. Her heart was skipping, her skin on fire. She felt the languor of desire seep through her and steal her will.

"Remember the time we made love on the moor?" he asked, dipping down to kiss her, a long, slow union of lips and tongues and teeth that incited more than memory.

"I remember the rash I got from the nettles," she protested, cupping his face in her hands and tangling her fingers into his thick mahogany hair.

He allowed her to pull him down for another kiss. "You were sunburned in the most interesting places."

She arched to receive his touch and groaned when she finally felt it. He cupped her breasts in his hands, the pads of his fingers abrading her sensitive skin and sparking lightning. She ached so deeply for him that she thought she would never find ease. She hungered like a mad thing, her body moving without her will to meet him. She quested with her own hands and tongue and lips to rediscover every inch of his beautiful body.

"This is new," she murmured as she kissed a puckered scar on his shoulder. "And this." She bent to the ragged line where they'd stitched his thigh that terrible night of Waterloo.

"This isn't," he assured her, nudging his magnificent cock against her. "Wherever else I've been, I've always wanted you."

Again she fought the urge to pull away. *No words,* she

wanted to beg. *Don't ruin the only moments of pleasure I might have left with you.* Instead she focused on the feel of his hands on her, the rasp of his breathing.

It was as if he heard her. From that moment, he spoke only with his hands, with his tenderness and hunger and joy. He nuzzled and nipped and stroked every inch of her, even turning her at one point so he could drop kisses down the curve of her spine and playfully slap the hills of her bottom. He left love bites everywhere he passed, from her thighs to her throat to the tender skin on the inside of her elbows. He suckled her breasts as if she could restore his life.

He was inciting madness. No matter how wonderful his touch and attention, it wasn't enough. She wanted him in her. She *needed* him in her, where she could hold the feel of him to her after he was gone.

She whimpered as he dipped his fingers into her. She heard the slip of her own juices on his fingers and thought she would go mad.

"Now, Jack," she begged, twisting under the torture of his relentless touch. *"Now."*

He licked the rim of her ear and chuckled. "No," he said. "Not yet. Not 'til you're a puddle."

"I'm a pool," she pleaded, pulling at him. "An ocean. *Please...*"

He slipped his finger into her sheath and stroked until she thought she would simply fly apart. "All right, Liv," he rasped against her ear. "Open for me, sweetheart. Let me see those lovely pink lips."

She let her knees fall apart. She opened her eyes to see him smiling down at the sight of his fingers plunging deep between her netherlips, his eyes almost black with arousal. "Ah, yes," he murmured, still stroking, still driving her wild. "This is what I've missed."

She gasped and bucked against his hand. "Not me?" she was barely able to demand.

She was so close now, the pleasure spiraling to explosion. She was grasping at him, her body arched in an impossible bow. She pleaded, she whimpered. She wept. And then, bending to kiss her, slipping his tongue into her mouth, he raised himself over her and, without another word, plunged deep.

Crying out, she came off the bed. It hurt. He was too full to fit. It was unbearably sweet. He pulled back and drove home again, his body slick with sweat, his mouth fused to hers, his eyes open to her, as they had always been when they met this way. Urging her on, daring her to be more than she thought she could be.

And she took him, all of him, squirming to fit better, wrapping her hands around his buttocks to pull him deeper. She lifted as he cupped her to him, as he drove into her and drove into her until she couldn't think, couldn't see, couldn't imagine anything but this pounding, coursing pleasure. Until, yes, there, *yes*, the hard invasion of him sparked the conflagration, fanned it, fueled it into a wild, keening disintegration, and she wept and pleaded and laughed. Until she milked him to his own climax and he shuddered with a harsh growl, the sound of her name like a benediction to his lips.

Finally, spent and sweat-sheened, they fell into exhausted silence, tangled around each other like old vines, panting and laughing and weeping. And then, as if afraid of what would happen if they let go of each other, they fell asleep in each other's arms.

All that night and well into the next morning, they exhausted each other, rediscovering old pleasures, familiar patterns, cherished harmonies. Olivia slept a while tucked beneath Jack's shoulder in the place she'd always thought would protect her from the world. Twice he woke her during the night to make love, once by the expediency of simply slipping into her while she slept.

She woke with a smile, already moving, her hands instinctively seeking the sleek lines of his arms, his shoulder, his back, her body exploding so quickly she could have dreamed it.

Except she no longer had dreams like this. When she needed to, when tension rose too high and loneliness wore too hard, she took care of her own release, curled into her lonely bed without so much as a word to soothe her. But since she'd seen Jack, her body had remembered how to want a man's touch. After this night, she knew it would remember too well.

Eventually they had breakfast. Exhausted, replete, they finally remembered that there were other hungers that needed to be satisfied. As if she'd heard them trying to gather the energy to descend the stairs, Mrs. Willett knocked on the door, holding a tray loaded with eggs and rolls and gammon.

Jack answered the door in nothing but his inexpressibles, which made Mrs. Willett giggle. She assured Olivia that she wouldn't have let such a strapping man go to waste either, which made Olivia blush furiously and Jack chuckle.

"We should get up," Jack said as he licked strawberry jam from her breast a while later. "Figure out what we should do before we're overrun with well-meaning friends."

Olivia closed her eyes and hummed. "I thought at least Kit would be here."

Jack chuckled against her belly. "A man of discretion."

She laughed back, because she couldn't seem to stop. "He'll be here. If nothing else, he'd never desert Grace. She seems to have secured the devotion of every man who served under her father."

Jack laid his head on her stomach and continued nibbling on his scone. "From the little time I've spent in her company, I imagine she's quite a formidable woman."

Olivia blinked. "Grace? Formidable?"

"Like water against rock. She doesn't batter against opposition. I imagine she just quietly wears it away. Do you know where she goes from here? If she doesn't want to stay with the duchess, maybe she'd like to come with us."

Olivia frowned a bit, impressed by Jack's perception. "She said something about a home she hadn't seen in too long. I imagine that after things settle, she'll move on."

"Ah, too bad. I think she might have made an excellent governess for our children." He was grinning. "Just think of what she could teach them. Riding, shooting, foraging."

Olivia stared at him to see that he was only half joking. He was talking about a future: a home, children, a family. There was a curious longing in his eyes, and his smile carried a hint of wistfulness that curled right around Olivia's heart.

"I wish we already had a child, Liv," he said, picking up her hand. "I think I've been wishing I could see you big with my babe, to lay my head against your belly and tell him what a beautiful mother he has."

He wanted her to assure him that it was possible. That

she wanted it as much as he. What she wanted clogged up in her throat and choked her.

Olivia's idyll lasted only three days, but they were days filled with laughter and passion and companionship. They were days that seduced her as certainly as a rake with an eye for a virgin.

She knew better. She had spent days like this once before, and it had come to naught. But Jack was so different this time. Quieter, more considered, more thoughtful.

It wasn't that he hadn't been considerate before. But his acts had always seemed to have been born of whim rather than deliberation. A flower picked from a field they passed through, a kitten caught in a barn loft. Kisses when he saw her and roses when he left. But in between, she'd always had a sneaking suspicion that the memory of her had disappeared beyond the matter of the moment.

Much later, when she had regained the presence of mind to be able to reflect on Jack's quick defection, she'd come to believe that he had abandoned her as recklessly as he'd loved her, as he'd done everything in his life. Impulsively, all of his emotions engaged and none of his intellect.

Maybe now it would be different. Maybe now when she left him, she would no longer simply disappear from his mind to be recovered later, like a knapsack. Maybe this time when he finally retrieved his past, he would take the time to turn those terrible days over in his mind and realize how wrong he'd been.

More and more, she toyed with the idea of permanence. Of trust. More than once, she caught herself fingering her locket and thinking that it might be time to tell Jack everything.

But hadn't she made that wish too often already? It was like a litany in her head: *Trust him. He won't leave. He won't hurt you.*

The cautious side of her fought the urge to believe. She fought against anticipation and expectation. She fought against expecting miracles. Mostly she fought against hope.

But hope, she found, was an insidious foe.

When the end came, it came fast. Lady Kate had been home all of twenty-four hours, still settling her retinue into the house. Upon arrival, she'd taken one look at Olivia and broken into whoops of laughter. Then she'd hugged her as if she'd produced flowers out of the air. She'd said nothing about the fact that Olivia was still sleeping in the same room with Jack. She didn't have to. Bea just patted Olivia on the cheek and whispered, "Orange blossoms."

Olivia didn't know what to do but continue as she had been. She helped Lady Kate's household, and Jack helped Harper and Finney, their first order of business being to secure the property against surprises. Their second order of business was to send Thrasher to listen on the wind for rumors and surprises. The fact that he came up empty-handed eased no one's nerves. In the meantime, sequestered away from visitors, Jack spent his time sending missives to anyone he knew in hopes of getting an appointment at Whitehall.

On the third afternoon, Olivia found herself in the

stillroom helping Mrs. Harper store herbs. Lady Kate was having an at-home, and Olivia knew to keep away.

She was working by rote, her mind on the memory of how wonderful the morning had been. It had been unusually clear for London, cooler, with a capricious breeze drifting in through the open windows. That first sunlight, so soft and faintly coral, had crept across Jack's face to caress each angle and hollow with warmth. Olivia had awakened with the first sounds of the house, as she had every morning here, just for that moment.

Jack never knew. He slept soundly until she all but kicked him awake. Dawn was Olivia's private time, the only moments she could hold her beautiful husband wholly to herself. When she could be perfectly selfish and unforgivably happy, because for that brief, brightening moment at dawn, Jack was hers.

"Olivia?"

Startled, Olivia turned to see Grace standing in the doorway. She was frowning, and suddenly Olivia felt nervous.

"Does Lady Kate need me?"

Grace shifted on her feet. "She wanted me to warn you."

Her hands deep in feverfew, Olivia stilled. "Is Gervaise here?"

"Worse." Grace's smile was painful. "Mrs. Drummond-Burrell."

"The Almack's patroness? From everything I've heard about her, I believe I'm more than happy not to meet her."

Alongside her, Mrs. Harper set down her mortar and pestle and wiped her hands on her apron. "Well, that'll mean a tea tray, now, won't it? I'd better go light a fire under that prissy Belgian's arse."

Olivia grinned as she watched the big woman leave. "Poor Cook. Mrs. Harper does so love to rile him. Now, then, Grace. Which room do I need to keep clear of? The green sitting room?"

"She'd prefer, um, that you"—Grace took a breath—"stay where you are."

Olivia nodded. "It's all right. I can understand that Lady Kate doesn't want her guest to see me. Most people don't know my face, but..." There was no real change in Grace's face, but Olivia knew she'd tensed. "What?"

Grace looked absolutely miserable. "I'm afraid that Mrs. Drummond-Burrell knows who you are. She has just informed Lady Kate that she's been told your real name."

Olivia didn't think to answer. She just pulled off her apron and started to walk out.

"Olivia!" Grace protested, hurrying after her.

Olivia shook her head. Her heart was thundering, and she felt sick with inevitability. "Stay here."

Grace grabbed her arm. "You can't mean to confront her."

"Of course not." Olivia knew her smile was terrible. "Not unless she becomes unreasonable."

And with her chin raised to battle levels, she stalked out.

Memory was such an odd thing. Jack had never thought to question it. It was just there, coloring everything that came after it. That place was lovely, because he and Livvie had snuck off to cuddle beneath the oak tree.

This food was awful, because his old nurse had forced it on him when he was ill. But now, with his memory sputtering like a spent candle, he couldn't trust the memories that came to him or the ones others said he should have.

For instance, he remembered Mimi. He remembered thinking that his time with her was better than it had ever been with Livvie, and how could that have been? Especially after the three nights he'd just passed, wrapped so tightly about Livvie that he shouldn't have had enough room to breathe. How could any joy have outmatched his when she'd first come apart in his arms after what seemed to be years?

And even though he knew better, he distinctly felt it to be autumn of 1810. There had to be at least a year missing, a giant hole that undoubtedly colored what had come after. Like the word *lions*. It felt important, but he didn't know why. Like the fact that he felt strangely anxious to find out what had happened to Mimi, as if he'd held her in his hand and misplaced her.

It should have been enough that he hadn't forgotten Livvie. That his family was well. That he was back on British soil. Somehow, it wasn't. And all he knew was that it had something to do with his missing memory.

Well, he couldn't wait any longer to recover it. Even without Braxton, he had to contact Whitehall. He had to speak with his family. But he could do neither without basic information, like what the real date was. What he'd been doing since that time at the hunting box. Why he had new scars and odd bits of insight. Until he found out, he continued to pose a risk to everyone in this house.

Somewhere in the last months, he must have learned to care for himself, because it didn't even occur to him to wait for Harper to help him dress and shave. He must have overcome the small pride he had in his own looks—good Wyndham features—because the sight of his scars didn't distress him. Or maybe he'd only needed to see Livvie's reaction to know how little they meant.

She hadn't wept or flinched. She'd kissed him, down the length of each and every scar she'd found. She'd assured him that they must have come honorably, for he was one of the most honorable men she'd ever known.

Why did that make him feel even worse?

Stealthily he opened his door. Satisfied that he wouldn't be seen, he took the servants' stairs down to the kitchens. He had to admit he was impressed by Lady Kate's home. Not just the Sheraton and Chippendale with which she furnished it but with the pragmatism in which she kept it. She'd even painted the servants' hallway and stairs a lemony yellow with the trim picked out in white, which made it easier to see down the steep stairwell.

The kitchen, when he pushed his way into it, spread across the back of the ground floor, an arching, echoing room painted in soft blue to repel flies and fitted with the latest closed stoves. He could even hear the potboy humming as he worked.

"My lord?" the cook asked, stepping forward.

A thin, intense Belgian with bulging eyes and bristling mustache, the man appeared to be defending hard-fought ground. Jack eyed the cleaver he clutched to his chest and smiled.

"I was just escaping from what sounded like a flock of ladies up in the drawing room, Maurice. Would you mind if I snuck a couple of ginger cakes and a cup of tea?"

For so thin a man, the cook had a magnificent frown. "You are too skinny, you, and tea is *pffft*." He gave a wave with the cleaver. "I give you ale. Build you up. And cheese. Good cheese from Belgium I have none. So we settle for this cheddar, yes?"

Jack situated himself on the bench and allowed the chef to fuss. "How long have you been with the duchess?" he asked.

"Since my last master, the toad of a *comte*, thought himself poisoned." The cleaver hit the table with a thump. "The magnificent duchess, she take me right away before I am doing damage to the old dog's house."

Jack fought hard to hold in a smile. "Good of her."

Maurice slapped a mug of ale in front of him. "Only for her do I stay. A man of Maurice's talent should not have to fight off witches."

"He means me." Mrs. Harper suddenly spoke up from the larder, sounding suspiciously amused.

Maurice jumped as if he'd been poked and flashed the sign of the evil eye before turning away. "Witch, be bringing his lordship some cheese."

Jack thought he heard her rumbling laugh. "Ah, and won't it be a treat to see you walkin' on y'r hands, Mr. Maurice, if you call me witch one more time?"

At that, Maurice stiffened. "Four years I stay with the dowager, since her *cochon* of a duke die, and I say nothing of anything. But no more, you evil woman. You I will not endure."

"Ah, don't fesh y'rself, little man," Mrs. Harper said as she clumped in with a board of cheese and bread in her hands. "We'll be gone soon as Miss Grace has enough of y'r snooty ways."

"Then Miss Fairchild does have a home?" Jack asked, eyeing the cheese with delight.

Good cheddar. God, he couldn't remember the last time…

His head shot up. "Four *years*?" he demanded, on his feet before he realized it.

Both Maurice and Mrs. Harper were staring. It was Maurice who nodded. "*Oui*. Four years. Do I not count every day in my gratitude?"

"Since the duke died."

The two actually looked at each other. This time Maurice looked less sanguine. "*Oui*."

Four years.

The last Jack remembered, the old duke had been hale, hearty, and unhesitatingly belligerent. Jack had never understood how the gorgeous duchess had settled for such a gargoyle. She was, after all, the daughter of a duke herself. Considering how powerful her father had been, it had undoubtedly been a dynastic connection.

Which had been over for *four years*.

Suddenly, he sat down. "What year is this?"

"1815," Maurice said.

"Now you be shuttin' y'r gob, you heathen," Mrs. Harper demanded, striding up. "You'll do injury to the lad."

But Jack wasn't listening. The words sparked a sense of panic. 1815. It was 1815. He'd been having enough trouble understanding that he'd lost a year or two. But *five*?

"You're sure?" he asked needlessly.

Mrs. Harper considered him a moment. "Oh, aye," she finally said. "For haven't I spent every day of those years following Miss Grace and her da across the battlefields of Europe?"

Absently he nodded. "What else can you tell me about the last five years?"

Which was, evidently, too much for the good lady. "I think you should ask the missus, sir. No offense and all. But it'd be worth more than my job to go against their wishes."

Jack stared at the table, trying desperately to justify the real time that had passed with the remembered time. He gulped down his ale and ate his beloved cheddar and didn't taste a thing. And then, realizing that the kitchen staff thought him absolutely mad, he walked stonily out of the room and through the baize door, intent on confronting his wife.

He didn't see her at first. He opened the door into the first-floor hallway to find it deserted of everyone but a suspiciously stiff Finney, who stood by the open door of the Green Sitting Room as if ready to jump to someone's defense. Jack was about to ask what was going on inside when he heard the voices of women who made no effort to be discreet.

"My dear duchess," came the cloying sound of aristocratic hypocrisy at its best, "You must understand that when the news came to me this morning, I was forced to venture forth."

"I understand no such thing," Lady Kate drawled. "How is my household of any concern to you, Lady Brightly?"

"Cat," he distinctly heard Lady Bea sniff.

There was a titter and a shuffling as if someone were ill at ease. "It is the concern of every Christian woman to alert a friend that she harbors a fallen woman beneath her roof."

Jack, standing in the shadows, suddenly felt cold. Something awful waited in that room, and he didn't want to hear it. And yet, he couldn't seem to move away.

"Fallen?" Lady Kate asked. "From what? I've heard of no such accident."

Then a new voice, thinner, sterner. It sounded just like Mrs. Drummond-Burrell. God knew that harridan loved nothing better than looking down on her fellow woman. "Levity can hardly benefit you, Your Grace. You must know the consequences of taking in someone as notorious as Lady Gracechurch. Why, the divorce alone puts her outside the bounds of good society. Considering everything else..."

Divorce? Suddenly Jack couldn't breathe. He started rubbing at the ache that had bloomed beneath his injured temple.

"Indeed," Lady Kate was saying. "I don't suppose Gervaise Armiston shared this diverting tale with you."

"Why, it's in every drawing room in London. Dear Duchess, if you thought your newest companion was respectable, you have been cruelly deceived. Nothing could be further from the truth."

"Pharisee," Lady Bea snapped.

"Indeed, dear," Kate said. Jack heard the impatient rustle of fabric. "As much as I appreciate your doing your civic duty," the duchess said, her voice as cold as winter, "I'm afraid you've gone to all this trouble in vain. Lady Gracechurch made it a point to alert me as to who she was back in Brussels. That would have been while she was caring for wounded from the battle. Something I can only assume puts her further beyond your notice, since it was a most charitable act of great courage."

"But she cuckolded her husband with her own cousin!"

For some reason, this sent Lady Kate off into peals of laughter. But Jack was no longer paying attention.

Olivia's cousin? *Tristram*?

Suddenly, he remembered. Only a bit, a slice of time caught against the jagged edges of fury. Him slamming open the door of the old crofter's cottage where he and Olivia escaped to when they wanted to be alone.

Only Olivia wasn't alone. He saw her standing with her arms around Tristram. He heard foul obscenities coming out of his own mouth. He saw Livvie, his Livvie, the love of his life, just where they'd said she would be. With whom they said she'd be.

She'd reached out a hand to him, he remembered, her face deathly pale, tears streaking her cheeks, her sherry-brown eyes huge with entreaty. But her hair had been tumbling down, that exquisite corn silk he couldn't keep his hands out of, and her dress was pulled awry. And her cousin, her loathsome cousin, whom he'd trusted in his home, was shouting at him.

From one moment to the next, the image disintegrated, but it had been enough. The pain sharpened in his head, and he clutched at a door handle to keep himself upright.

It was something straight out of a melodrama, he thought distractedly, still seeing the alarm in Livvie's eyes, the stark whiteness of her skin. *If I had seen it presented at a theater, I would have done an injury to myself laughing*.

But he didn't feel like laughing. He felt old rage break loose, like a badly healed wound. He felt revulsion and shame and humiliation, their taste so well remembered he had no need to question them.

How could she lie so easily? How could she make him believe that she loved him? He'd thought she'd been keeping him in the dark to protect him from some terrible thing he'd done. She'd only been protecting herself. She'd been giving herself time to worm her way back into his affections before she was exposed.

He was just turning away, trying to decide where he could go, when he saw her. As pale as a specter, she stood tucked back in the shadowy library across the hall from the sitting room. As if drawn inexorably to him, she turned.

There were no tears this time. No sobbed pleas. Only, if he could believe it, a desolation so deep it should have scored her. Only, if he could trust it, resignation.

She looked at him for a long moment. Then, without another word, she simply turned into the library.

She must have known he would follow. He did, ready to slam the library door behind him until he realized that it would only alert the harpies across the hall.

"*This* is what you couldn't tell me?" he demanded, shutting the door, thinking how badly the hard edge of his voice seemed to fit. "I've been killing myself with guilt, and all this time you were just protecting *yourself*?"

Standing very still, she frowned down at her hands, as if surprised to see them. He wasn't even sure she knew he was in the room.

Suddenly furious, he stalked up and grabbed her by the arm. "Damn it, Olivia, *listen* to me."

She startled, as if coming out of a sleep. "Oh. Jack. Yes, I was coming to talk to you."

"I'm sure you were," he sneered. "May I assume it's to explain what I just heard?"

She blinked. "Explain?"

He saw red. "Don't lie to me, Liv. I know what I just heard. In fact, I remember it. I remember catching you and Tristram making love in our cottage. I remember that you had no excuse—although I'm not exactly sure what would be sufficient reason for my wife to be disporting herself like a back-alley whore." He shook her, the hot wash of betrayal choking him. "Try and explain it away, Liv. I dare you."

She just looked at him. She didn't apologize. She didn't explain. Instead, astonishingly, every hint of warmth bled away from her expression. "Thank heavens those two shrews didn't take any longer to get here with their rumors," she said, actually sounding sad. "I'd almost begun to trust you again."

"Me?" he retorted. "Trust *me*? Who are you to speak of trust? You've been with me for weeks now, pretending to be my loving wife, seducing me back into your bed, and all this time it was a lie." He barely kept from shaking her again. "Well? Wasn't it? *Are* we married, Livvie?"

She pulled her arm free, but she never retreated. She stood there like a man before a firing squad, her certain doom visible in her eyes. "No, Jack. We aren't. But you knew that when you followed me in here. Now, what do you really want to know?"

"Why you didn't tell me!"

She lifted her chin, as if bracing herself for injury. "We didn't tell you because the doctor warned us that if we told you anything that distressed you, we could kill you."

He was swamped with disgust. His stomach curled with it. His head pounded. "Ah, I see. Altruism. Not an attempt to get into my good graces."

Good God, now he was the one who sounded as if he were in a bad melodrama. Why did he feel such an urge to apologize?

She was rubbing her eyes, as if too tired to go on. "I don't suppose you could keep your voice down until the leaders of the *ton* get out the front door? All things being equal, I'd rather not be forced to meet them."

He barely heard her. He wanted to demolish something. He wanted to *understand*. "At least tell me that I called the makebate out."

She was so suddenly silent it forced him to look up. Her eyes were bright with unshed tears, her hands clenched by her sides, her posture unbearably rigid. "Yes, Jack," she said, her voice as flat as her expression. "You called him out. You killed him."

Jack felt that blow all the way to his gut. Had he really wanted Tristram Gordon dead, that insignificant failure of a poet?

"It is why you've been gone," Olivia went relentlessly on. "You were forced to flee ahead of the law."

Was the ground shifting? He rubbed at his eyes, fury and frustration battling with grief. Old injuries, older, festering emotions that seemed to batter at his head without relief.

"Are you going to tell me now where I've been?" he asked.

She sighed. "I told you. I don't know."

He glared at her, but it was plain she was finished. "Well, if you can't tell me," he finally said, "I'm sure my family can. If you will call one of the servants to help me, I'll be gone within the hour."

He expected her to plead for leniency. For forgiveness.

Instead, she reached over to a pedestal desk and picked up a grimy, blood-spattered musette bag. "Not," she said, "until you can explain this."

At the sight of the filthy, foul thing that dangled from Livvie's fingers, Jack's head seemed to explode and his sight disappeared. He hit the floor like a falling tree.

Chapter 19

"Oh, bloody hell," Olivia muttered.

The thump of Jack's falling body still reverberated through the room. She was sure that the brace of shrikes in Lady Kate's salon had heard it and were even now wondering what new bit of salacious news they could carry away from Lady Kate's.

Damn. She was going to have to meet them after all. She couldn't take the chance that they'd feel compelled to investigate.

For a very long, searing moment, she was tempted to let them. *Here. Here is your darling Jack Wyndham, betrayed innocent and noble son. Would you like me to tell you just why he's lying unconscious on the floor?*

She wished, if only for that moment, that she'd felled him with her fists. She actually ached with the impulse. But she'd undoubtedly done enough damage by surprising him with that bag.

Dragging in a deep breath, she sought to calm herself. She imagined she should bend down and see if he lived.

She should return the dispatch bag to Lady Kate's safe and beg Jack's pardon for startling him so badly.

Maybe he really hadn't meant what he said. He could have simply been repeating remembered emotions, his reaction no more than an echo of that moment in the cottage. Maybe when he woke, he would apologize.

She almost laughed out loud. Even when he had come upon her with Tris, he'd never called her a whore.

Sod him. Let him apologize to her for believing—a second time—the lies he'd been fed about her. Let him think about the promises he'd made and how quickly he'd forgotten them. Again.

First things first. She had to protect Lady Kate. Her hands shaking, she carefully opened the door and peeked out. Finney stood in the hallway, one eye on her and one on the suspiciously silent parlor.

"C'n I help any?" he whispered.

"There's a small problem in the library," she murmured, her voice thin with strain. "One of Lady Kate's paintings fell on the floor. I'll tell her." She saw Finney's lifted eyebrow and flashed him a wry smile. "A very large painting."

Finney grinned back and headed past her into the room. She didn't wait for him. She refused to look back at Jack, where he lay sprawled on the floor. She was just too angry. Too bitterly disappointed. Too perilously close to shattering like dropped ice. Much easier to brave the lion's den.

"Excuse me, Lady Kate," she said as she stepped into the salon with a quick curtsy. "I thought you should know that there has been a small accident in the library. I'm afraid that the landscape of Green Park is resting on the floor."

Lady Kate's smile was gracious. "No matter, Olivia. You know I detest the thing. It will give me an excuse to donate it to a jumble sale. Have I introduced you to my guests?"

Olivia stared at her. "There is no need, Your Grace."

"There is every need, Olivia. Come in."

The last thing Olivia wanted to do right then was face those two dragons. One was a plum pudding away from exploding out of her corset, a red-faced, suspiciously black-haired middle-aged woman in all-over pink. The other bore a striking resemblance to a ship of the line. The very self-important Mrs. Drummond-Burrell, if she had to guess. The woman already had the obligatory quizzing glass up to her eye.

Olivia clenched her hands against a sudden urge to grab the glass and grind it under her heel. She'd been on the wrong end of those things too many times in the last years, lifted in just that way, as if being used to assess a stinking pool of refuse.

Do it, she heard in her head. *Just this once, pay them back.*

It was as if Jack's accusation had frayed the last tether on her control. Suddenly she wanted to strike out, to hurt others the way they'd hurt her. To destroy every person who thought it was their right to call her a whore.

"I see no reason," Mrs. Drummond-Burrell objected icily.

Olivia came so close to slapping her, she actually clenched her hands to keep them still. She had to get away before she disgraced Lady Kate.

Lady Kate didn't seem to notice. Never taking her eyes from her guests, she came to her feet with the kind of grace intrinsic to the daughters and wives of dukes. "Ah, but I do see a reason. I insist that all my friends meet. My dear Olivia, may I introduce you to Mrs. Drummond-Burrell and Lady Brightly. Ladies, my very dearest friend—except for Lady Bea, of course—Olivia Wyndham. Make your curtsies, my dear."

There was no ignoring that kind of order. Battling a wild urge to run, Olivia dropped another quick curtsy. "My lady. Ma'am."

"Well!" the puce-faced Lady Brightly huffed, jumping to her feet as if a mouse had scuttled beneath them. "I never!"

"Nor will you," Lady Kate advised her softly, "if you do not sit back down. I'm afraid I would never be able to welcome into my home anyone who lacks the basic civilities."

Any other time, Olivia might have enjoyed watching Kate wield her power. Not today. Today she could barely see past the rage that suddenly swamped her.

"I'll just help Finney," she said, and backed out the door.

She made it no farther than the hallway. Trembling so badly she couldn't move, she found herself leaning against the wall not five feet from the open door, her eyes squeezed shut, her hands fisted against her mouth.

The other shoe had dropped. The truth was out, and what she should have felt was fear. She should have curled over with humiliation at the snub those women had tried to serve her.

She didn't. She trembled with fury. Her chest was suddenly thick with it, a foul miasma of every betrayal and indignity and loss she'd ever suffered, every snide comment and closed door and gloating condemnation. Every mile walked and every day spent without her baby. Without a home. Without hope.

She had kept all that poison locked away for so long. She'd convinced herself that it didn't matter. That she was bigger than that. That she would survive no matter what, just to spite them.

Suddenly she was afraid that her control was irretrievably lost. Like an ocean pushing at a faulty dam, all that venom she had locked inside for five long years threatened to spill out over everything around her.

Just in time, Finney peeked out the library door. Olivia knew she should speak to him, at least to warn him. She was suddenly sure, though, that if she opened her mouth, she would let loose a scream that would shake the chandeliers.

Finney, bless him, took one look at her and nodded. "She still keepin' them gentry morts busy?"

Struggling to take slow breaths, she nodded.

Finney gave a sage nod. "This time o' day, I'd try the garden," he suggested. "Nobody there to hear you curse."

She let loose an abrupt gurgle and smiled, not trusting herself to say more.

"But if you needs to throw summit, try and save the windows."

She nodded. Finney disappeared for a moment and returned with Jack slung over his shoulder like a sack of grain.

"Harper 'n me'll take care of 'im," Finney whispered. Then, leaning close, he gave her a buss on the cheek.

"Though truth to tell, I'd rather just dump 'im out the back window. As the sergeant'd say, the man's a feckin' eedjet to believe that pack o' lies."

Looking up at the hulking ex-prizefighter, Olivia felt her precarious control weaken. "Thank you, Finney," she rasped. "And thank Harper."

"So say we all, lass. Now go on. We'll take care of 'im."

She went. She hadn't spent any time in the garden before, but the minute she stepped outside the library windows, she realized it was perfect, both pretty and too small to get lost in. Quiet, lush, and green, it looked as if someone had folded a cottage garden into a linen closet. And, bless Lady Kate, there were paths that wove through and around the beds of foxglove and oxeye daisies and delphinium in case someone needed to walk off strong emotion.

Olivia tried so hard to outrun her feelings. Arms wrapped around her waist, chest heaving with the effort to keep from shrieking like a banshee, she marched through those flowers like a fusilier, sending them waving after her as she fought against the shock and despair and rage. Especially the rage.

Those women. Those small-minded, self-righteous, hypocritical shrews. How dare they judge her? How dare Jack accuse her? How dare she let him?

She'd tried so hard. Five years ago, she'd walked away, just as they'd all demanded. She had disappeared as if she'd never been born and kept away, each rejection she'd faced another step in the descent toward oblivion. She'd carried the mantle of shame on her back when she'd done nothing shameful and had paid the price for crimes never committed.

And now those women had come to chase her away again. And Jack had listened to them.

How could he have sneered at her? How could he have taken the malicious word of two bored society matrons at face value? Had she really begun to believe that just because she'd saved him and cared for him and loved him he would change enough to turn to her for the truth?

She laughed, the sound harsh and abrupt. Yes. She had. And how bloody stupid of her. It was, she thought, pressing her hands against her burning chest, the last straw.

She would have to find somewhere else to go. No matter how kind Lady Kate was, it was unfair to expect her to bear the burden of Olivia's infamy. She would have to hide as well as she had the last time so Gervaise couldn't find her. So no one could recognize her and cost her another position. She would have to find another way to survive.

Oh, God, she couldn't bear it.

As if hitting a wall, she skidded to an abrupt stop.

No. She *could* bear it.

Jack wasn't coming back to her. After this afternoon, she wasn't sure she'd let him. But damn him if she let him shatter her again. Damn them all.

"Olivia? Is there anything I can do?"

Olivia jumped at the sound of Grace's voice. She looked up to see her friend standing at the library windows. "I wouldn't be seen talking to me, Grace. I'm afraid my alias has been exploded, and I am once more persona non grata."

Grace tilted her head, as if giving grave consideration. "You know, Olivia, I have spent my entire life assiduously avoiding such notoriety. I'm beginning to believe that I've missed out on quite a lot. If you don't mind, I'd like to stay."

Olivia walked up to her friend and folded her into a tight hug. "I should be noble enough to tell you no," she said. "But I have had only one friend as good as you and Lady Kate, and I know what I'd say if she tried to send me away for my own good."

"Excellent. Lady Kate wanted me to tell you that there are some particularly ugly bibelots in the morning room that have just been begging to be destroyed. She believes they would make a most satisfying noise against the fireplace."

Finally, Olivia smiled. "I'm afraid Lady Kate's bibelots will live to appall another visitor. I'm not a thrower."

Grace patted her on the back. "What are you going to do?"

Staring off into the late afternoon shadows, Olivia shook her head. "Is Jack awake?"

"And very quiet. I think he's trying to understand."

At that, Olivia's head came up. She considered Grace's words for a very long moment. With a grim nod, she pulled back her shoulders as she'd seen the Highlanders do before they'd marched down the Rue Royale on the way to war. "Well, Grace, I think it's about time he did."

Grace nodded. "His head was aching abominably, so we gave him a tisane. Finney said you had the dispatch bag."

Olivia rubbed at her eyes. "Yes. When I heard Lady Kate's guests, it occurred to me that we had run out of time. I would need to present it to Jack. I just didn't realize I would be using it quite that way." She shrugged. "It was the only thing I could think to do to stop him from leaving."

"Are you sure this is the time to confront him?"

She shook her head. "He already thinks he knows the worst about me. I don't believe we have the time to let him come to the correct conclusions on his own."

"What are you going to do?"

Olivia instinctively looked up to Jack's window. "You might as well mix him some more headache powders. It's time the Earl of Gracechurch found out what really happened five years ago."

And quiet, loyal Grace, smiled. "Oh, good. May I watch?"

Olivia strode past her into the house. "If you stand out of the way. Unlike me, Jack *is* a thrower."

Now that she'd made her decision, she thought she would have felt relief. After all, she would finally be given her say. But it seemed that one decision didn't have the power to defuse the emotions that had been waiting so long for release. Like thick, hot purulence, they pressed against her chest, up her throat, in her ears. She seethed with them, astonished that such a force had been contained inside her for so long.

Grace followed her up the stairs, and Olivia thought she heard staff scuttle out of sight as she passed. She gave them no thought. She marched into Jack's bedroom and faced Harper.

"Have we done any damage?" she asked.

"Ah, no. Sure, isn't he stronger than he looks?"

"In that case," she said, amazed at how controlled her voice sounded, "he won't need you for a bit. But you might advise Mrs. Harper to prepare some tisanes, just in case."

"Ah, that's grand." Harper flashed her a big grin and

gave her a pat on the arm on the way by. "A touch of the home brew never hurt a soul."

"What is this all about, Livvie?" Jack asked from where he sat in an armchair by his bed.

Olivia expected to see the cost of his fall on his features. Instead, he just looked impatient and angry. It made what she had to do that much easier.

"What else have you remembered, my lord?" she asked, keeping a careful distance. She clasped her hands at her waist to prevent them from giving in to overwhelming impulse.

"Don't you think I am the one with the right to ask questions?" Jack demanded.

"You'll have your turn. But it will help to know what you remember."

He didn't look any happier, but he answered. "My sisters warned me," he said, looking beyond her. "Well, everybody but Georgie. She always sided with you. My mother reminded me that blood would tell."

Olivia flushed, struggling to hold herself still. How odd that even this old insult could still affect her. "I'm sure she did. But as little as she respected my father, he is the brother of a baron. Not exactly the chimney sweep."

Jack's face screwed up. "A blatant toady."

"Indeed he is. If he hadn't been, you never could have married me so quickly."

"Was it all planned, then?"

For a moment, Olivia stood there, too stunned to speak. Then she burst out laughing. She laughed so hard, she had to bend over to breathe. Seeing the shock on Jack's face, she plumped herself on the other chair and wiped her eyes dry.

"Oh, Lord, Jack, even when you hated me most, you never resorted to that old chestnut. It was *you* who first approached *me*. You followed me into town when I gave out poor baskets. You trailed me through the market and demanded you carry my parcels. You helped me pick flowers and even put on an apron to help Maizie and me make plum pudding. You terrified me with your attentions."

"I'm sure you'd like to remember it that way." He shook his head, his face looking pinched. "I've changed my mind. I don't want any answers from you."

"Then I guess it's a good thing Harper's around to keep you from running. Because this time, you have no choice."

She stood again, the strength of that old outrage propelling her. He watched her as if afraid she would strike. He should, she thought, and tightened her hands to keep from lashing out.

"I truly thought you'd changed," she mused, looking out the window onto Lady Kate's fine little garden. "You were never cruel, Jack. Just impulsive. Prone to believe the wrong people." She rubbed at the ache in her chest that never seemed to die anymore. "You've been so different these last weeks. Still the Jack I loved, but wiser, more thoughtful. Stronger. I began to hope that this time you would weigh all the evidence before making a judgment."

"Then the memory is false? I didn't find you in the cottage with your cousin?"

The sudden pain was crippling. "The memory is absolutely true. You found us where your sisters had told you we would be, and you accused me of every faithless act imaginable. Those were the last words you ever spoke to me."

"And then?"

She paused for a steadying breath, the memories dripping like acid. "Your father filed for a divorce for you. You couldn't be there when the case went before Parliament, of course. Your family had long since shuffled you off to the West Indies to avoid prosecution for the duel. But your father represented you brilliantly. By the time he was finished with my name, I couldn't secure a position on a street corner in Covent Garden."

Then his family had seen Jamie. That had been the first time she'd gone into hiding.

"I kept waiting for you to contact me," she said, knowing she sounded bemused. "To at least demand your ring back. I kept thinking that even an angry man would have made sure his wife wasn't cast off without a ha'penny."

He snorted. "Of course I settled something on you, Liv. And you had a perfectly good family. You make it sound as if you wandered the streets in the snow."

Her smile was twisted. "Oh, Jack. You had the measure of my family. They were angrier than the marquess. Do you really imagine they would keep me close enough to constantly remind them of their losses? I think they would have forgiven a sin. But to forfeit that lovely patronage? My name was cut out of the family Bible in front of my father's congregation. My sisters were told I was dead. I wasn't even allowed to go to Tris's funeral, and I...I was his only friend in the family."

"It would have been unseemly." His voice sounded less assured, as if he were trying to shore up his outrage.

"Indeed, yes. And if I hadn't known, there were

certainly enough people to remind me. As for a settlement, my lord? No. You made it very clear to your solicitors. An unfaithful wife deserved nothing. I believe that outraged my father most of all."

There was silence for a time. "But how could you...?"

She shook her head. "Another story for a different day."

He didn't deserve the truth.

"And yet you haven't denied you were in that cottage with your cousin," he accused. "Not only that, but also you have given me no explanation."

She closed her eyes, struggling against the rancor. "Not for want of trying. You were the one who barred me from the Abbey."

Facing him, she braced herself. "Listen and listen well, Jack. I am tired of begging you to listen. So I'm simply going to tell you. I went to the cottage that day to say good-bye to Tris. He had decided to leave the country. It was the only way he and his lover could be together. I snuck him my pin money to help him reach the Continent, where I'd hoped he'd finally find some peace. I had just forced the money on him when you burst in like a two-penny actor."

Briefly he closed his eyes, as if avoiding her. He had one hand on his forehead and his other fisted. Her instinct urged her to go to him. To soothe him.

"Name his lover," he ground out.

She shook her head. "I will not."

His lip curled. "After all this time, it can hardly matter."

"After all this time, my lord," she said, "his lover could still be hanged."

There was a charged silence, the kind that pulsed against the ears. She could see Jack begin to assimilate the facts.

"Yes, Jack. Tristram's lover was a man. I knew it, but it was not my secret to tell. Lady Kate also knows who it is. I'm hoping you'll trust her word more than mine, or you put a grieving man in terrible peril."

For what seemed an eternity, Jack stared at his clenched fist, as if, Olivia thought, it could divine the truth. "If you were so innocent," he said, "why were you in dishabille?"

Which meant they had finally come to the crux of the matter. The point on which her defense would either succeed or fail.

"Because your cousin Gervaise tripped me on the way to the cottage. At the time, I thought it was an accident. It was only later he made it a point to disabuse me of that rather naïve notion."

That was what brought Jack to his feet. "Don't be absurd."

She faced him eye-to-eye so he could never say she'd lied. "Who told you about my fictitious gambling, Jack? Who gave you my pearls and said he'd recovered them from the moneylenders? Who whispered warnings in your ear that I was just a bit too close to my cousin for comfort? Your sisters might have directed you to the cottage, but they were just willing accomplices. Gervaise orchestrated everything. Even my 'dishabille.'"

She hadn't thought his eyes could grow any colder.

"Tell me you're lying," he grated, his eyes betraying fear.

She didn't hesitate. "I'm telling the truth."

He slumped back into the chair, his elbows on his knees and his head cradled in his hands. Olivia tensely watched and waited. She might have even prayed.

Finally, he raised his head. "No. I won't believe it."

And just like that, all her rage died a terrible death. It was as if a great, gaping hole had opened up inside her. There was so much more she had to say to him, so much he needed to know. There was no way she could do it now. She could only thank God she hadn't told him everything.

"All right, Jack," she said, and heard the despair in her voice. "It's your choice to make. But I won't wait around for you to destroy me again. Once we learn what you were doing on the battlefield, you'll never see me again. That should make your life much tidier."

He huffed impatiently. "Don't play me a Cheltenham tragedy, Liv. If I want to find you, I will."

"Gervaise hasn't. Not for three years. It's the only way I've been safe."

He shot her a skeptical look "You're saying he persecuted you?"

"I'm saying he has never stopped hounding me to become his mistress. I'm saying that it is only Lady Kate who saved me this time. That is what I'm saying."

Jack shook his head again. "He's my cousin. I've known him my whole life."

Olivia sighed. "Actually, I don't think you have. But"—she shrugged—"that is no longer my affair. I'll leave you to Harper now, Jack. Tell him if you need more headache powders."

She turned, feeling as if she were wading through water, and walked to the door.

Suddenly, behind her, Jack spoke. "You were breeding."

It stopped her cold. Ah, and she'd thought she couldn't feel any worse. She squeezed her eyes shut, desperate that he should never see this new anguish. "I was."

"You're going to say the baby is mine."

She opened her eyes then and stared at the blank yellow wall across the hall. "Was, Jack. He *was* yours. But you don't have to believe it. It doesn't matter anymore."

She started walking again.

"Livvie, wait!"

This time she didn't stop.

Lady Kate was waiting downstairs in the foyer. "You didn't tell him about the dispatch bag."

Olivia had no time for this. She had to get away before she disgraced herself. "Finney can tell him if he'd like. I think I'm finished."

She couldn't bear the sympathy in the duchess's beautiful green eyes.

"It was a lot to take in all at once," Lady Kate suggested.

"I'm sure it was. I'm just tired right now. Would you mind if I sat in the garden again?"

"Of course not. In fact, some of my ugly bibelots have somehow found their way onto one of the stone benches."

Olivia managed a smile. "Thank you." She knew, though, that she would be throwing no ornaments. Suddenly she didn't have the energy. "Oh, and, Lady Kate," she said, stopping in the library door. "I think we need to get Kit Braxton over here as soon as possible. Jack is bound to begin remembering something now. It might help us solve our mystery. After I know you all are safe, I will take my leave of you." She turned but couldn't see the expression in Kate's eyes past the hall shadows. "I know it sounds melodramatic, but you did save my life. Now it's time to pay you back."

"You're certain?"

Olivia fought the familiar pull of despair. "I am."

It seemed it was once again time to start all over again.

Chapter 20

He had to get out of here. He had to find Braxton, get to Whitehall, speak with his family. He had to locate Gervaise and discover what was true. Olivia had looked so desperately sad, and he knew that wasn't right. She had sounded so sure, but that couldn't be right either.

Not Gervaise.

He rubbed at his aching eyes. He felt as if the earth had tilted on its axis and was spinning off into oblivion. He felt as if his heart would explode in his chest and his brainbox split wide.

It couldn't be true. Not Gervaise. Not smiling, funny, harmless Gervaise.

But not Livvie either.

She had no sooner left him than the memories had begun to return, disjointed and often meaningless. Him dancing with Liv at the Harvest Festival, her hair falling down her back and her eyes alight as he spun her about the big barn. Livvie ministering to any of the cuts or bruises he seemed to collect, her hands as soft as sunlight.

Her patience when he'd come home late. Her delight when he'd brought her the silliest gifts he'd picked up on his rambles, like a schoolboy bringing birds' nests to the little girl down the lane.

He could see the hallways of his home, softened by the passing of a thousand feet, worn by time and attention. Not so much a grand estate as a jumble of mismatched wings. He had a favorite, the old Jacobean with its coffered ceilings and linenfold paneling. He had a flash of Livvie there with him, laughing. She had always been laughing.

Not like now. Now she looked worn and sad and empty.

And the babe. She'd lost the babe? She must have. He couldn't imagine any other reason for such a look of unspeakable loss in her eyes.

He looked down at his hand, to see that it was shaking. He'd laid that hand against the subtle swell of her belly, her hand covering his, her eyes brilliant with awe and delight.

"Can you feel him move?" she'd asked. "Can you?"

He had. He'd never had another moment to match it.

And now their baby was gone.

Then, oddly, he saw himself seated atop a magnificent bay horse, looking out to the sea. But it wasn't the sea he knew from Yorkshire. It wasn't Scarborough or Ramsgate or Bristol. From flat dunes, he had watched the gray sea and waited. He didn't know what for; he didn't know why. He only remembered the feeling of anxiety. Impatience. And underlying it all, a profound despair.

He remembered family and friends and places he couldn't name, voices speaking English and French and Spanish.

Mimi. Laughing, happy Mimi.

And again, Livvie. He saw her, suddenly, standing tear-stained and rigid on the Abbey drive. He remembered the satisfaction of slamming the door in her face and then hurrying to the front salon window to watch Rogers, the gamekeeper, escort her off the property at the business end of a Purdy. He remembered the acid taste of betrayal that had fueled him as surely as steam, and how satisfied he'd felt at the pathetic look of her.

And who was that behind him? He didn't see, but he heard.

"Maybe next time she'll think twice before betraying her husband."

"Next time it will be her protector she'll betray," he heard himself say, and was ashamed.

And he heard the other person laugh. Gervaise's laugh.

The memory spun away, and Jack was left with the bitter dregs of self-loathing. Had he really been that brutal? Had he truly never listened to her explanation?

Had he been that sure, or had he let them all convince him? Especially Gervaise. Leaning close, looking so regretful, so embarrassed, just as Livvie said, hesitantly relaying—for Jack's own good, of course—another rumor of what Olivia had done while Jack had been gone somewhere.

Could Gervaise truly have been the monster Livvie said he was?

Rubbing at the headache the memories incited, Jack got to his feet and wandered to the window that looked down over the garden. It was late now, the moon silvering the nodding foliage. She was still there, as motionless as a statue. She'd been that way all afternoon. Jack had seen people come and go, mostly just standing in the library doors to watch her, sometimes speaking to her. Once Lady Bea had just sat next to her, not even touching. He thought he saw Olivia shake her head once. Other than that, she simply hadn't moved.

Why should that hurt so badly? Why should he feel so fearful for her? Even if she had spent that morning in his arms telling him how much she loved to watch the first sun wake him. Even if he could still smell her and hear her gurgling laughter as he nuzzled her neck. Even if he couldn't quite imagine how a woman who trusted so wholly could seek to betray at the same time.

He had been unable to imagine it before, though.

He could remember his father now. Red-faced, thumping the desk, flinging accusations at Olivia like mud. But was that memory of his decision to marry or his decision to divorce?

He had to find out. He had to return to Grosvenor Square and hope his family was in residence. First, though, he had to make sure Livvie was safe. Reaching for his coat, he turned for the door.

"Ah, no," Sergeant Harper said from the hallway. "You'll not be wanderin' the streets this night. Sure, wouldn't you bash y'r head on the cobbles, and we'd be right back to where we started?"

Jack stopped in his tracks. He hadn't even realized that the bandy-legged soldier had been waiting out in the hallway. "What makes you think I'm trying to leave?"

Harper, bold as brass, grinned and pushed himself away from the pale yellow wall. "Sure, haven't I seen that very look on raw recruits before? One good skirmish and all they want is to go home to their mam. I'm afraid it's somethin' you can't do, if you'll pardon my sayin' so."

Jack was flummoxed. "And just who are you to stop me?"

Harper was still grinning. "One who's got a good two stone on ya and steadier legs... well, now, leg, anyway."

He seemed to find that hysterical. Jack felt as if he were trapped in a cage.

"Well, if you're all that able, why aren't you down making sure Livvie is safe? She's been out there too long. Someone could see her."

Harper tilted his head. "What should you care?"

He flushed with shame and looked away. "You don't know the manner of enemy after me. They wouldn't think a thing of hurting her."

"And is it somethin' you're rememberin', now?"

He could only shake his head. "A feeling. Stay with her, even if I can't."

"Ah, now, don't fesh y'rself. That nice Major Braxton sent some people around to help fill in the staff. We're watchin'."

Jack's head came up. "Braxton? He was here?"

"Nothin' more than a note one of the men carried."

"Ah." He fiddled with his button. "Good. Well, if you have help, then you won't need me."

"And you think you should spend y'r time askin' y'r family for the truth?"

Jack startled and looked over to see the most knowing blue eyes he'd ever seen beneath that red mop of hair. "How do you know?"

Harper shrugged. "Y'r rememberin' things you can't reconcile, and you're thinkin' y'r family'll be happy to help you. Oh, lad, don't I think they just would? But I'm also thinkin' they wouldn't have the charity to piss on my poor girl if she was on fire."

Jack frowned. "You mean Olivia?"

"I mean that poor lost lass who thought she could trust you. I've seen a lot in my time, but nothing as bright as her eyes when she thought you loved her or as empty as her eyes when she found out the truth. Faith, you didn't see her starin' at nothin' as if she didn't have a tear left in her to shed."

Jack glared at the little man. "She said she'd been acquainted with you for no more than two months. What could you possibly have to say to the matter?"

Harper nodded, as if considering the question. "Did you ever ask just how it was Miss Olivia found you, y'r lordship?"

Jack felt a wisp of dread snake through him. "What do you mean? Chambers found me."

"And brought your wife to rescue you. Sure, wasn't her ladyship in Brussels fetchin' and humblin' herself for a pittance as a companion to some bold-as-brass old trout who wasn't fit to shine her shoes? When the battle started, your lady could have stayed safe, gone home to England like all them other English ladies. Not her. Didn't she walk right into the tents with my Miss Grace and wear herself to shreds tendin' the wounded? And if you think you know what that's like, m'lord, I'd have to call you a liar, all right, and take the consequences."

The tough little man shook his head, as if he saw that day right before him. Jack swore he could see them, too, and it was horrific.

"But even that wasn't enough, now," the sergeant

continued. "Didn't your little lady climb right up on a carriage with Miss Grace, lay a gun across her knees, and go with us right into the battlefield to turn over dead bodies so she could help my girl find her da? It was there she found ya, on a battlefield, my lord. A *battlefield*."

Jack felt as if he'd been lashed with the man's words. His Livvie? How could that be?

How absurd of him to question it. The Livvie he knew wouldn't have hesitated.

He couldn't look at the sergeant. "And you think that alone proves that she couldn't have cuckolded me."

"I think that I've never seen a truer child in all my life and that you have to be the thickest Englishman I've ever met not to know it. And if you'll pardon my sayin' so, after thirty years in this man's army, haven't I met a world of thick Englishmen?"

Jack walked back to the window to look down again. She was still there. Still not moving. He kept shaking his head.

"I need to talk to my cousin."

"Ah, now, I'm not thinkin' so, sor. Not 'til you talk to the duchess anyway."

Jack turned around. "Why?"

"Well, I'm thinkin' as how she'll tell you who it was cost Miss Olivia her job with the trout. Who made sure she had nowhere else to go until the duchess caught wind of it."

Why couldn't he breathe? Before he realized it, he was sitting down.

"Ah, damn me," Harper mourned, limping in. "I've gone and kilt ya."

"No such thing," he managed, his head in his hands. "I just need a minute. Would you send the duchess to me?"

"Soon as she's finished helpin' the staff ready another room for Miss Livvie. Sure, didn't we think she was settled?"

And with not another word, Harper stumped out.

"Keep Livvie safe," Jack called after him.

The words alone incited a new memory. But it wasn't a memory of Livvie.

Blond hair. Big blue eyes. Breasts like pomegranates.

Mimi.

She was laughing, catching the sound behind her hand, her big blue eyes twinkling. It was evening, and they were strolling back to their hôtel. She smelled of lilies and coffee. It must have rained, because there was water on the cobbles. Music drifted from a cafe, a scratchy fiddle and a badly played accordion. He smiled down on her, even though his mind was a hundred miles away.

Tomorrow, he thought. *It will all be over tomorrow.*

And from one moment to the next, his world disintegrated. Mimi stumbled alongside him and whimpered. He heard something behind him, a pop. He turned to see that blood had suddenly blossomed across her chest. She had such a look of surprise as she raised her hand and looked down, as if to find out what had struck her. And then her knees gave out, and she was pulling him down, down onto the glistening cobbled streets.

Was he screaming? He couldn't tell. He didn't remember any more. Only her surprised, falling face. And the blood.

"My God," he groaned, shutting his eyes. "She's dead."

"Who's dead?" the duchess asked as she strode in.

Distractedly, Jack looked up. "Mimi. I saw her die."

Lady Kate nodded. "I'm sorry. But not as sorry as I am that you have once again hurt my dear friend. I thought better of you, Gracechurch."

He blinked, not certain he had any words for what he'd been remembering. All he knew was that his memories had begun to hurt too much. And that the memories of Liv hurt the worst.

"I was in France," he said baldly.

"Yes," Lady Kate said with disconcerting frankness. "We thought so."

That brought him to his feet. "You thought so? What do you mean?"

"Oh, sit down. I'm too small to pick you up off the floor."

He did and she pulled another chair over so that they sat with the window next to them, as if each wanted to keep an eye on Livvie where she still sat in the garden.

After she'd arranged herself like a deb at tea, Lady Kate lifted the bag Livvie had held earlier. "Recognize this?"

He stared at it. "They're looking in the wrong direction," he insisted. "I need to tell them."

"Tell who?"

If he'd expected startling insight, it still didn't come. "I have no idea."

"And you were in France."

He could no longer argue the point. Hadn't that been a Parisian street he'd been walking with Mimi? He remembered Paris from when his father had taken him there during the brief 1804 peace. There was just something distinctive to the city—the architecture, the smell, the flow of that musical language.

And he'd been wearing a French uniform.

He began rubbing at his head again. It seemed the headache never left anymore. "In Paris. And at the shore waiting for someone."

"And there's nothing else you remember?"

"Mimi. I saw her die in front of me. Poor girl..."

"Yes, I'm sure."

Jack actually found himself smiling. The duchess didn't look as if she cared at all. "You might at least express regret at the passing of a soul."

A laughing girl who pulled him away from despair. Who told him...told him what?

The duchess didn't seem impressed. "You'll understand that our first consideration must be for Livvie. And until you can remember just what you were doing in a country we were at war with, and how you managed to appear on a battlefield in a French uniform carrying French dispatches—"

His head shot up so fast, he thought it might snap off. "What do you mean?"

Her face folded into chagrin. "Oh, blast. And I was going to be so careful."

"What dispatches?"

"To General Grouchy. Does that ring a bell?"

"Yes. He commanded reserve troops on the right flank."

"The left flank, Jack," she said. "If you were looking from the British lines. And General Grouchy isn't that well-known."

He felt the blood seep out of his face. "Are you telling me I'm a traitor?"

"I'm telling you we don't know. Well, Livvie doesn't believe it, but she has been a bit prejudiced when it comes to you. But until we're sure, we cannot let you out of this house. And until we can let you leave, Livvie will continue to be miserable. So we've asked Kit Braxton to return tonight."

Jack wasn't sure what it was that caught his attention out the window. He'd been thinking that the duchess had bats in her cockloft to think he could possibly betray his country, when he turned to instinctively check on Livvie.

But she wasn't there.

"She must have gone in," he said inconsequentially. "Call Marcus Belden."

The duchess frowned. "Earl Drake? Whatever for?"

But Jack wasn't attending. He couldn't seem to look away from the empty garden. It was all shadows and half-light down there. How could you really see anything amid those flowers?

But he did.

Suddenly he was on his feet. Livvie *was* still down there. She was struggling with someone, a man, and Jack could see the moon glint off something in his hand.

"Get help!" he snapped, jumping to his feet. "Livvie's being attacked."

Before the duchess could even get to her feet, he was running out the door.

"Goddamn you," he hissed in her ear. "Where is it?"

Olivia frantically pulled at the arm that was wrapped around her throat. She couldn't breathe. She couldn't get away. He had a knife in his other hand, and he had it pointed right at her eye as he dragged her backward through the flowers.

She heard the scrabble of her slippered feet on the gravel path and smelled tobacco on his breath. She smelled something else...something...Sweet Jesus. He was aroused. The first bite of terror sank into her chest.

"Where. *Is*. It?"

He'd eaten onions. What an odd thing to think when struggling for air. Shouldn't her life flash before her eyes?

The only thing she saw was Jack. And Jamie.

Dear God. Jamie.

"I can't..."

Her attacker must have understood. He loosened his hold just enough to give her air. They had reached the far corner, deep in the thickest shadows. He still had the knife. He lifted it just to remind her.

Sucking in a desperate breath, she tried to get her feet under her. "Where is what?"

She felt so stupid. Even after the fire, she really hadn't expected this. She'd been certain that it would be Mrs. Drummond-Burrell's tongue that would destroy her. Not a bully with a knife.

"Don't play games, Countess," he cooed, tightening his grip on her throat until she saw stars. "I know you sent for Braxton. So you must have found it. Now, I know you don't want that handsome husband of yours to be hanged for a traitor, and he will be if they find it before we do. But if you give it over to me, I'll have no reason to stay."

She struggled to stay calm. Her heart was thundering, and she couldn't get a good breath. "He didn't have anything. Just a message for General Grouchy. That was it. I swear!"

"He had a list!"

Desperately, she shook her head. "No. No list."

She had to make him believe her. The minute he didn't, he would lose his use for her. Except maybe as a threat. A well-placed corpse with her throat gaping from ear to ear to let the others know the price of intransigence.

She couldn't let that happen. She had to get back home. She'd never said good-bye. She'd told them she'd be back.

She'd promised.

Oh, why hadn't she told Jack already? What if she died and left Georgie alone to fend off Gervaise? Would Gervaise still go after them if she were dead?

She couldn't take that chance.

"Where do you . . . think . . . the list is?" she asked, fighting for breath. "I can look."

"And why would you do that?"

She knew her laughter sounded desperate. She was clutching at his arm, trying to ease the pressure on her throat. "I don't want him to . . . hang. Please."

Instead he shook her like a terrier taking a rat. "I don't think I believe you, Countess. I think you want me to convince you to tell me the truth. I think you want me to let my knives speak for me." Pulling her as close as a lover, he whispered in her ear, "And they so love to speak."

She shook with revulsion at the sensual tone of his voice. She struggled against his implacable hold.

"Yes, do," he murmured, resting the edge of his knife along the side of her throat. "Fight me. It makes such better sport."

And before she could answer, she felt a slice of pain open up along her neck.

It was like a fuse being lit. Suddenly, rage flooded through her. That white-hot fury she'd spent the afternoon trying to quell spilled through her, and she welcomed it. She felt it rekindle her resolve. Her energy. She knew, finally, what she could do with all the resentment and hurt and indignation she'd been storing up.

She would get away from this madman. She would warn the others. She would tell Jack the whole truth, and then she'd walk away.

For the first time, she thought she could do it.

Focus, Livvie, she said to herself. *Assess.*

"I'll look for it," she whimpered, trying to sound more vulnerable than she was, even as she felt blood seep down her neck. "I promise."

She had had to protect herself before. She could do it now. Her eye on the lethal sweep of moonlight that reflected off that knife, she let herself sag, as if frozen in panic. She measured the distance from that deadly blade to her hands.

Please, God. Don't let me fail.

"And just why would I want to believe you?" he asked.

She wanted to gouge his eyes out. But she had to get to that knife before he could use it. She had to stay calm. Taking short breaths, she slid her feet under her.

Oh, Jack...

"I don't want to die," she pleaded.

Wrapping a hand around his forearm, she let her knees buckle. She curled her other hand just out of his sight and sought her balance. That blade was so close. If she could only surprise him. If she could at least knock the knife away.

Light winked to life in the library windows. Her captor

turned to look. It was Olivia's chance. Giving a huge push straight up, she slammed the top of her head right into his nose. Ignoring the crack of pain, she grabbed his hand and bit down hard. He howled. She stomped down on his foot and whirled to slam her knee into his crotch.

"You *bitch!*"

Livvie heard the bushes rustle. She heard footsteps. Her saviors were coming. "Here!" she yelled. "Help!"

She turned to run.

She never got the chance. Her captor grabbed her by the hair and yanked her against him. "Bad choice, Countess."

He still had the knife, and he was laughing.

"Livvie!" she heard Jack yell. He was calling to other people, directing them. She had to gain them time.

"Here, Jack!" she cried.

She fought and scratched and pushed, but her attacker was too strong. He clubbed her on the side of the head, which stole her legs.

He laid his mouth right next to her ear. "You should have listened to me, sweetheart."

She could hear people coming. She saw the knife glint. She raised her arms to protect her neck. He started dragging her toward the back gate.

"Just kill her," she heard behind her, and thought she knew that voice.

"There are two of them!" she tried to shriek.

Her attacker punched her hard in the mouth. She fought to regain her balance. Her ears were ringing, and her jaw screeched with pain. It seemed to take so long for Jack to reach her.

She saw the knife rise and thought that Jack would

be too late, and oh, God, she hadn't told him. She hadn't kept the most important promise she'd ever made.

Suddenly the moon was blotted out. She heard a primal roar, and her attacker stiffened. The knife began its descent to her throat, when Jack ran full tilt into them and she was slammed to the ground.

She vaguely saw the knife lift again and then sail, a bright, glinting arc into the night. She felt a searing heat against her throat and then a jarring impact as her head slammed hard against the stone wall.

But she was free. She could get away. She heard feet pounding through the garden. She vaguely saw lights wobble toward her, carried at a run. She heard hollow thuds nearby and the awful crunch of bone against bone. She was kicked a couple of times as her attacker struggled to get free. She could hear his frantic panting and Jack's curses. And just for a moment, she thought she saw the man by the back gate.

Desperate to get away, she scrabbled to her hands and knees. She wondered why she felt rain on her hands. She thought the sky had been clear.

"The other one's getting away," she warned, but wasn't sure anyone heard her.

"Not for long," Jack answered, and she thought she'd never heard such a steel-hard sound before. "Go after him!" he yelled to someone. "And find out what happened to Braxton's guards."

Was it Harper who bent over her? No, Finney. Harper was next to Jack.

"Time to lay off now, y'r lordship," he was saying. "You want him alive to question, now, don't ya?"

"Not... necessarily."

"Jack?" she whispered, terrified he'd be hurt again.

"I'm here, Liv." Then his hands were on her, and they were shaking. "Are you hurt?"

She let herself briefly lean against him. "I'm all right," she whispered, tears burning her eyes.

Her knees hurt from where she'd fallen. Her face hurt. Her head hurt. She was dizzy and nauseous, and she couldn't seem to get to her feet. There were suddenly many hands helping her up.

"Get that bastard into the house," Jack snapped to somebody. "I want to question him."

"Not for a while yet," Finney said. "You proper milled him down."

"Hey!" she heard Thrasher cry. "That there's the Surgeon!"

"We'll take care of him," Harper said. "See to your lady."

Jack seemed to be back in command. "Send someone for the Earl Drake. He'll know what to do with our surprise guest." And then he was gently lifting Livvie into his arms. "Come on, love. Let's get you inside."

She knew she should correct him. She should shake him off. But she was so cold. She was feeling lightheaded and wobbly. And his arms were so comforting.

She couldn't seem to keep a thought in her head except that he sounded so different, so certain. And that she needed to tell him after all. He would know, she thought, what to do to protect them from Gervaise.

"I have you now, Livvie," he said. "I won't let you go."

"No, Jack," she begged, searching his face. "You're hurt."

He didn't even look down at her. "I'm better."

She'd thought she would be too drained to weep. But the front of her dress was wet, so she must have been wrong. Then Jack carried her into the library, and Olivia realized that she didn't have rain on her arm. She had blood.

She looked at it distractedly, wondering what it meant. "Jack?"

For some reason, that made him look down. "Oh, my God. Liv."

She looked up to see stark distress in his eyes. "What?"

"Oh, hell," the duchess said from the doorway. "Get her to the couch. Grace, send someone for Dr. Hardwell. Bea, get us some brandy."

"A round for the house," the old woman announced.

They were all moving so fast, but it seemed to take forever.

"What's wrong?" Olivia asked, seeing how upset everyone looked.

"Are you hurt anywhere else?" Jack demanded as he settled her on the brown leather sofa and yanked off his neck cloth.

"My arms are red."

"I know, sweetheart. You need to lie down."

He was pressing it against her face. It hurt.

"The cut goes all the way down her neck," the duchess was saying. "You'll need to get her necklace off."

Olivia lurched up, yanking her hands free. "No! No, you can't take it off."

"We have to, dear, or the doctor can't patch you up."

Olivia felt tears welling in her eyes. "I've never taken it off. Not once."

"You can hold it in your hand. Is that all right?"

And Jack's hands were at the back of her neck. Somebody was pressing a pad to her cheek and she remembered. Oh, yes. The knife. The man had cut her. He'd wanted a list. He'd almost killed her.

Jack was staring down at the locket where it lay in his palm. "But I gave this to you."

"Give it back!" she pleaded, knowing how shrill she sounded. "Give it to me!"

She saw the confusion in Jack's eyes, the pain. She didn't care. She had to hold her locket, or . . . or . . .

She sobbed when Jack slipped the little chased gold oval into her hand. She clutched it as if it were her only link to life. As it was. As it always had been.

"It's all I have," she sobbed again, and was surprised that she'd said it out loud.

"Of course it isn't," Jack soothed. "You have all of us."

She jerked back from him, and this time she faced the sorrow in his eyes. "No," she said definitely. "I don't."

"Jack," Lady Kate murmured, "she'll do herself damage if she doesn't settle. You might want to help the men."

"No, wait, " Olivia said, grabbing his arm in her anxiety. She knew she might not ever be able to return to him, but she could do this one thing, no matter what it cost her. She had to do this. "Not yet. Jack, you have to promise."

He looked frightened. She thought he was trembling. "Anything."

"If something happens to me, you'll find Georgie. You'll go to her. Promise me, Jack."

"Find Georgie? What do you mean?"

She was shaking again, but she felt better. He would

protect them if she couldn't. She at least knew that much. "Promise me," she begged, clutching his arm. "You'll find her."

"Of course."

She nodded. Good. If he found Georgie, he would learn the truth.

"Oh," she muttered. "My head hurts."

"What did he want, Livvie? Do you know?"

"Not now, Gracechurch," Kate said. "Let her rest."

"No," Olivia disagreed. "I need to tell you."

Grace appeared in her sight. "And you will, dear. After we fix you up. Jack will be in the next room, won't he?"

Livvie heard them all shuffling around. "Don't let me forget. He wanted a list. I need to tell Jack."

And then Grace was kneeling next to her, gently dabbing her face with something cool and sharp.

"He heard me, didn't he, Grace?" she asked, suddenly afraid she'd only thought it all.

"Of course he did, dear."

She sighed and closed her eyes. "Good. Then it will be all right. He'll protect him for me."

"Who, dear?"

"Jamie. Jack will see that Jamie is all right if I can't."

"And who is Jamie?"

She smiled, but tears continued to slide down her cheeks. "Our little boy."

Chapter 21

Jack had been about to walk out of the library when he heard what Livvie said. Stunned, he whipped around.

She was just lying there, her eyes closed, her poor, hurt face hidden beneath a cloth. Grace, her eyes a bit wider, was looking at him in warning. *Not now*, she was trying to say.

Yes, now. His *son*?

But Lady Kate had him by the arm and was dragging him out of the room. "She'll tell you when she trusts you, Jack."

"When she *trusts* me?" he demanded, turning on her. "Did you hear her? My son is alive, and she hasn't thought to even tell me, and you say I need to wait?"

Lady Kate leveled him a steely glance. "Oh, really, my lord earl? You've decided without proof that it is indeed your son? What exactly has changed?"

She stopped him right in his tracks. She was right, of course. It had been the last and worst accusation he'd leveled at Olivia.

Suddenly, like a knife slicing through his heart, he remembered the glow in her eyes the moment she'd whispered the wonderful news. They were to have a child. She'd been feeling ill, she said. She'd suspected, of course, but she'd wanted to give Jack this present on his birthday. They had laughed and danced around that old parlor like a pair of gypsies, parrying ridiculous names and planning futures.

Three months later to the day, he'd forbidden her his front door with the words "let your lover raise his brat."

Had he really done that to her? Could he truly have been so cruel to the woman he'd sworn to protect? Could he have honestly trusted anyone more than his Livvie?

He didn't remember everything, but he remembered this much. He had been a coward. He'd failed her.

"You knew?" he asked, his anger shriveling into misery.

Sadly, Lady Kate shook her head. "We all thought the babe had died. As frightened as Olivia is of Gervaise, I wonder if she hasn't spread that tale to throw him off."

"And just left her child with my scapegrace sister?"

Lady Kate shook her head. "Oh, you do have a lot to catch up on, don't you, my dear?" Leading him inexorably along, she continued. "We might as well share some Madeira over it."

She settled him in the Chinese sitting room and plied him with wine. "Are you all right, by the way? You were getting quite physical out there."

He'd damn near pummeled the bastard to death. "I'm fine."

"Can you tell me why you called for Earl Drake?"

He looked blankly up at her, then managed a small

grin. "Because it's all his fault, of course. He's the one who recruited me."

Her eyebrow lifted. "Recruited you? For what? You remember?"

"Some of it. But that can wait. Tell me of Livvie."

For a moment, he thought she might deny him. She simply sat on her settee sipping at her wine.

"My poor Olivia," she finally said with a slow shake of the head. "Can you imagine what these last years must have cost her? In the time I've known her, she has never once betrayed that baby by so much as a whisper. She had to be so afraid."

He couldn't take it all in. A son. He had a son. That babe who had once been no more than a flutter beneath his hand was now four years old. And Livvie was acting as if he didn't exist.

He remembered the sheer panic in her eyes when he'd tried to take away her locket. Was Lady Kate right? Was Olivia so afraid that she kept herself isolated even from her own child? Could there be any threat so awful? Dear God. He had to find him. Jamie? Why had she called him Jamie? There was no one in his family named James.

He knew why, of course, and the anguish of it seared him. Exactly why should she name her baby after him? He'd thrown her out with no more thought than that it served her right.

Where had she gone? How had she survived?

"Georgie must have found her," Lady Kate mused, as if hearing his question.

He lifted his head. "Then she must have rebelled against the entire family."

He saw the quick anger in Lady Kate's eyes and knew he wasn't going to like her answer.

"She didn't have to," Kate said. "They threw her out too."

He could only stare. "No," he said, the idea incomprehensible. "Not Georgie. She's everybody's favorite."

"Yes, Georgie. About four years ago."

"But why? What could she possibly have done?"

"She fell in love with a naval captain."

He frowned. "Was he unacceptable?"

"You mean a commoner? Heavens, no. He was Cox's youngest."

"Then why?"

"Because he wasn't the Earl of Hammond."

Jack knew he was gaping like a fool. "They were going to marry Georgie off to that doddering fool? He's sixty if he's a day."

"And already buried two wives. But he also had ten thousand a year and a title."

He couldn't seem to breathe. "But Georgie..."

Lady Kate sneered, and Jack suddenly remembered about her marriage. "Do you really think they cared any more for Georgie's wishes than they cared for yours?" she demanded. "Coming so close on the heels of your misalliance, they were out of patience. Not only did they disown her, but your father also convinced Cox to do the same."

"But a naval captain isn't exactly destitute."

"He was killed two years ago while on blockade."

He closed his eyes, the revelations of the last few minutes collecting like sins in his chest. "Do you think Georgie and Livvie have been supporting each other?"

"I think that your wife has been supporting all of them and that I don't pay her nearly enough."

He couldn't breathe. He couldn't think past the fact that he'd done this to Livvie. She should have been running across the back lawns of the Abbey, laughing and chasing her lively son. She should have been holding Jack's hand as they watched their little boy sleep.

He had sent her into exile.

He had sent her into hell.

"Do you really believe Gervaise is capable of what she said?" he asked.

There wasn't a moment's hesitation. "Yes."

He looked up again to see a sympathy he never thought to find in the eyes of the sharp-tongued duchess.

"Oh, I didn't when she first told me," she said. "It makes me realize why she chose to hide. Gervaise is such a charming character, not a care in the world. The perfect dinner companion. But...I've seen him watch her, and I think she's right. He's always wanted what you have, and he figured out how to get it."

Jack blinked. "What do you mean? He can't be earl."

"Of course not. But what about your reputation? Your friends and your lovely young wife? Your child? You have to admit that if he did orchestrate Livvie's downfall, he did it brilliantly. Not only was she left with nowhere to turn but him, but also you were no longer the golden boy. It's been Gervaise who has been your stepmother's escort. Gervaise who helped pop off the twins. I assume if you'd been here, it would have been your task." Slowly she shook her head. "I think it would take an exceptional woman to keep him at bay."

For a very long time, Jack could only sit there staring

at the thick red liquid in his glass. Absently, he noticed that the blood Livvie had spilled on his hand was much the same color. He wondered what color redemption would be.

"How do I make it up to her?" he asked.

And heard only silence. When he looked up, he saw that the duchess was thoughtful. "I don't know if you can. I don't know if Livvie will ever be able to truly trust you again, Jack."

"But I didn't know!" he insisted. "How could I?"

He thought her smile was the saddest thing he'd ever seen. "Oddly enough, women expect trust to be based on faith. Not evidence. She'd hoped you loved her enough to take her word."

"How could she?"

"Need I remind you that she took you in and cared for you when all she knew was that she found you on a battlefield in an enemy uniform?" The duchess shrugged. "She chose faith over evidence."

He'd thought the pain of memory was too sharp to bear. It was nothing compared to the despair that followed. He had forsaken his own honor. He had condemned an innocent woman and killed the man he blamed. And by the time he'd realized it, Livvie had disappeared. His work in France had been nothing more than his own purgatory.

He wasn't certain how long he sat there, the empty goblet clasped in his hands. He knew the doctor was seeing Livvie. He'd wanted to go in and hold her, but she wouldn't let him. Harper had come to report that he'd found their guards unconscious. Livvie's attacker was still in the same condition.

"Thrasher says he's the Surgeon, all right," Harper said. "Won't be doin' much surgery soon, the way you left him."

The second attacker, unfortunately, had escaped, although he'd lost a ring in the fight. Harper laid a signet in Jack's hand. Jack looked down at the ruby that glinted from a field of old gold and knew that he could feel worse after all.

It came to him then. That moment sitting on his horse on the beach, looking out over the water. And he knew why he'd forgotten. Why, rather, he'd refused to remember. He could so vividly feel that grim taste of betrayal, of shame, of despair. He'd believed the wrong person, and it had cost him everything.

He remembered too late what it was he'd been carrying.

"You know the ring?" Harper asked.

He nodded and slid it into his pocket. "I'll deal with this myself."

"You might want to wait a bit. I'm to tell you that your lady is anxious to talk to you."

The goblet fell to the carpet as Jack sprang to his feet. He was wobbly, and he hurt all over. He thought maybe he'd broken a rib again. He'd deal with that later.

"You'll be kind to her," Harper warned.

Jack glared. "Get out of my way, you redheaded lump of potato, or I'll show you exactly how I left the Surgeon the way I did."

The Irishman gave him a huge grin and stepped aside.

Jack ran into the library as if his life depended on it. Livvie still lay on the couch, her skin a sickly gray, her hair matted and damp. A line of stitches ran from her right ear all the way to the neck of her dress. His insides twisted. How could she have borne what that doctor had just done? He hadn't heard a whisper during those long, awful moments.

He knew someone else was in the room, but he saw only Livvie as he dropped to his knees beside her. "Oh, Liv," he managed on a thick whisper, taking her hand. "I'm so sorry."

"It's all right." She flinched from him, and he tried to ignore the stab of pain.

He kissed her bloodstained hand. "No, it's not. You were almost killed, and it's because of me."

"Because of a list," she said.

He felt a faint shudder in her hand and wanted desperately to pull her against him. To feel her heartbeat and know she was safe. To be allowed to keep her protected and happy.

"She's afraid she looks a sight," Grace said behind him.

He saw Olivia shoot her friend a glare. He lifted a hand to trace the ragged cut on her poor, bruised cheek. "You're lovely," he whispered. "Nothing can ever change that, Liv."

She gave a weak tug on his hand. He refused to let go.

"My God, Liv," he continued, lifting that hand for a kiss. "You were so brave. I have a feeling if I'd been awake while being stitched up, you would have heard me a mile away."

She gave her head a small shake. "I had quite an example set for me in Brussels. Couldn't shame myself in such company."

Tears he hadn't remembered weeping in years crowded the back of his throat. He didn't deserve her. Not his brave, beautiful Livvie. How could she talk of shame, when it was he who had let her down?

"He was looking for a list, Jack," she said.

"Yes," he said, nodding absently, focused more on the tangled hair he was stroking. "There is a list. Of lions. But that can wait, Liv. You can't."

"I'm afraid I have to disagree with you, my friend," he heard from behind him. "That list can't wait at all."

Turning where he knelt, he beheld Kit Braxton standing in the doorway. But he wasn't the one who'd spoken. That had been the man standing behind him: tall, brunet, wickedly elegant Marcus Belden, Earl Drake.

"About time you got here," he snapped, struggling to his feet. He didn't let loose of Livvie's hand, though. He had the most irrational fear that if he let her go, he'd lose her altogether.

"The doctors told us to leave you alone, old son," Marcus said quietly. "We thought it was safer that way."

Jack's temper flared. "Really, Marcus? To whom? My wife, who just came within amesace of having her throat slit?"

Drake strolled into the library as if entering a ballroom, but Jack saw real distress in his eyes. "My sincere apologies, ma'am," he said, bowing. "This isn't the thanks we should offer a lady of such courage. We did have people watching the house, but they were...disabled. Did you see your attacker?"

"Her attacker is in the wine cellar," Jack said. "He was looking for the list I carried back for you."

"You remember?" Drake asked, his eyes lighting.

He shrugged. "Bits and pieces. You, certainly."

"And you're going to tell us what this is all about," Lady Kate said from the doorway. "Why the head of Drake's Rakes would be responding to an attack at my home?"

"Trojan horse," Bea offered in a disapproving tone.

Lord Drake chuckled. "I'm afraid so, Lady Bea. I know you will keep this confidential, but I spend some of my time doing some small services for the Crown. Jack has been helping."

Lady Kate frowned. "In France."

"When needed. Some of us weren't lucky enough to don a uniform. We do what we can."

"I assume you know what Jack was doing there," she said.

Marcus smiled. "In fact, I do. I'm the one who sent him."

Olivia scowled. "And you couldn't have told us before now?"

Jack found he could grin. "How could he, Liv?"

Drake nodded. "Until you contacted Braxton here, we didn't even know that Gracechurch had survived. We lost contact with him a good four months ago." He flashed Jack a grin. "Good to see you, old man."

"I was in prison." Jack stopped, overwhelmed suddenly by that memory of cold. Of hunger. Of desperation. "They caught me when Mimi was killed."

Lightning sheared through his head, and his stomach lurched. He so wished he could regain his memories all in a lump instead of this haphazard fashion. It would save so much time and discomfort. And he could get on with making amends with Liv.

"Oh, Jack," Livvie murmured, looking sincerely distressed. "Prison. And after all that, you were too late. Napoleon was defeated without you."

"I did escape in time to intercept those dispatches," he said. "But it wasn't really Napoleon I was trying to stop."

Drake stiffened. "I beg your pardon?"

This time Jack did smile. "You've been looking the wrong way, old man."

Lady Kate shook her head. "My, you do make up for lost time. Just think of all the effort we could have saved if we'd just told you the truth right away."

All Jack could think was that if they had, he would have had no time at all with his Livvie.

"I believe you need to explain," Marcus said.

Jack tamped down a flash of irritation. "Can't this wait?" he demanded. "Livvie needs to be taken care of."

Truly, he just wanted to shove everyone else out of the room so he could talk with her. Hold her. Beg her forgiveness.

It was ironic, really. He'd devoted almost four years to collecting this very information. He'd suffered jail for it, torture, isolation, the deaths of those around him. And right now he couldn't care less. He just wanted to make Livvie understand that he would do anything to redeem himself in her eyes.

Olivia lurched up into a sitting position. "You try leaving, Jack Wyndham," she warned, poking a finger in his chest, "and I'll personally drag you to the floor and sit on you. If anyone has a right to the truth, it is we four."

Jack went right back down on his knees next to her. "You're going to hurt yourself, Livvie. Lie down."

Her glare should have frozen him. "Not until we know exactly what you've been up to."

Marcus considered the usually calm Olivia. "It's actually very simple," he said, flipping the tails of his coat as he took one of the Sheraton chairs. "Jack has spent the last few years infiltrating the highest levels of French society in an effort to uncover the English traitors who have been aiding Napoleon."

Olivia nodded graciously. "Thank you."

Now Jack stared at her. "You don't seem surprised."

"Of course not." She didn't look at him. She didn't pull her hand away either. "I was only afraid you'd be accused of treason before you could prove your innocence."

Trust.

Jack swallowed his shame. He looked at her battered face, at the locket that symbolized every hurt he'd served her, and he couldn't understand how she could still believe in him.

Why didn't she batter at him? Why didn't she pour vitriol over his head, as he deserved? Even when she'd faced him up in his bedroom, she'd kept such an icy control. Where was her rage?

And now she faced him without a hint of doubt in her eyes.

"I don't deserve you," he said.

"No, you don't," all four women answered at once.

He couldn't help smiling. He noticed that Livvie didn't answer. But she didn't turn away.

"Is that what the list is?" she asked him, as if he hadn't spoken at all. "The traitors?"

God, he wanted to kiss her. He wanted to fold her up into his arms and carry her away where they could be alone. "Yes," he said instead, because that was what she wanted. "They call themselves the Lions. The British Lions. But they weren't working for Napoleon. He was just a tool. The Lions have far bigger plans."

"Than *Napoleon*?" Drake demanded.

"I had trouble believing it too. But the proof was irrefutable. These Englishmen seek to overthrow the throne."

"God's teeth," Marcus breathed. "Why?"

Jack opened his mouth, but there were no words. His memory had just slammed shut again. He didn't know whether to feel frustrated or frantic.

All he could do was shake his head. "I don't know. I know it will come to me. They tried to recruit me, after all. I just know that they're extremely well organized. And they probably considered Waterloo no more than a setback."

Marcus was looking far less sanguine. "And you have a list of their members?"

"As complete as I could under the circumstances. I hid them where no one would think to look." He turned to Livvie. "No, Liv. Not the dispatch bag. That was just a serendipitous opportunity to help disrupt the French. I was still in a French uniform when you found me, though, yes?"

Now it was Olivia's turn to look distressed. "Yes. Why?"

"I sewed the list into my jacket lining. Unless you ripped it up for bandages, it should still be there."

"I'm sure it is," she said, her voice suddenly sounding

small. "Right next to Château Hougoumont, where we found you."

He could almost hear the sigh of disappointment in the room.

"I'm so sorry," Livvie whispered, and he knew she was devastated.

So he reclaimed her hand. "Oh, Liv. How can you apologize to me? You saved my life. You made it possible for me to warn the government. I can't imagine you would have had much luck carting me through British lines in that coat. Besides, I'll remember the names. I spent too long collecting them to forget for long."

Drake nodded briskly and clapped his hands. "In that case, we'll be off, shall we, Jack? We have work to do."

Jack climbed slowly to his feet again. "No."

Drake frowned. "National security, my son."

"Can wait until I have a few moments with my wife."

"No, Jack," Olivia demurred. "Really."

He turned to see outright fear in her eyes. "They'll wait, Liv."

She looked, if possible, paler.

"See us off, then, will you?" Drake asked. "We'll take your prisoner with us. Braxton will bring you along later."

Jack didn't waste his time on his superior. He brought Livvie's hand to his lips. "I won't be long."

He wasn't entirely sure she'd still be there when he returned.

Exhausted beyond bearing, Olivia lay back down and closed her eyes. Her face felt as if it had been stretched and set afire. Her head throbbed, and several of her ribs protested breathing. And she knew that tomorrow she'd feel worse.

Jack was remembering. That was good. He had taken control of the situation like a leader born. He'd saved her life.

And still she hesitated to tell him the truth.

She'd held it to herself for so long. She'd had to, locking and double-locking her little Jamie behind impenetrable walls in her mind so that she could keep him safe. So she could open her eyes each day without wanting to die.

It was so hard to let go of that caution. Gervaise was still close by. Jack's family would want their heir more than ever, and they had proved even more ruthless than Gervaise. Could she trust Jack to act any differently?

She had to. Those long, terrible moments in the garden had made her see that. She had to believe that he would protect her child as fiercely as she did. She had to hope he could love his little boy half as much.

But she was still so afraid. She couldn't seem to make the tears stop.

"Olivia?"

Jack. She took a breath and opened her eyes to discover that everyone else had deserted her. Jack settled himself next to her on the couch and reclaimed her hand. He looked as stretched as she felt and was moving stiffly.

"Are you all right?" she asked.

His quick smile unsettled her. "I'm fine. Will you talk with me?"

She studied his face and saw how tormented he was. She knew she had to finish their conversation. She just wasn't sure she had the strength.

"We can continue later, if you want," he offered, and bent to wipe her tears with his handkerchief.

She closed her eyes. "I might not have the courage later."

She wanted to run away. She was so afraid, and the familiar comfort of having her hand in Jack's was only making it worse.

Don't leave me.

She stiffened, hearing the sobbed words again in her head. She had run after him. She'd grabbed at his coat, only to be thrown off. She had begged and pleaded and negotiated, offering anything if he'd just listen to her.

She had only humiliated herself.

She was stronger than that now. Wasn't she?

"May I put your locket back on for you?" he asked quietly.

Tears scalded her throat. She nodded. She unclenched her hand and felt him lift the locket away. She waited to feel it around her neck. Instead she heard a *snick.*

She lurched upright. "Don't..."

But it was too late. He was already staring down at the open locket.

She wanted to snatch it back. She wanted to scream at him, to hold that precious image close against her heart where she'd kept it so carefully for these last years.

"Is this me?" he asked, running his finger down the tiny miniature that lay beneath the curl of sable hair.

She saw the impish light painted into those huge sea-green eyes, the way that wispy mahogany hair curled over his little head. She felt her heart break all over again.

No box was strong enough to save her from that kind of pain.

"No, Jack. It isn't you."

He looked up at her, and there were tears in his eyes. "Is it Jamie?"

She lost her breath entirely. "You heard me."

"You weren't ever going to tell me." He looked so hurt.

"You wouldn't have believed me."

She saw the shaft pierce home. "He looks just like me at that age," he said, sounding awed.

She moved a bit away from him and braced her feet on the floor. "I know," she said, turning away. Testing him again. "It's why your father tried to take him from me. It's why Gervaise tried to murder him."

She said it deliberately, daring him to scoff. Wanting her hopeless wishing to be over once and for all.

"Why would Gervaise hurt a baby?" he asked, but it didn't sound as if he doubted her. It sounded as if he were appalled.

She couldn't help the hard smile. "Because he saw Jamie. He knew that the minute you saw him, you'd know the truth and accept him as your son."

As if in pain, he drew a ragged breath. "Do you think I wouldn't have?"

She shrugged. "How could I know, Jack? Would you have believed me if you hadn't seen the proof?"

He bent his head, both hands now holding on to hers. "You have every right to doubt me," he said. "But I did believe you. Finally." When he raised his head, she saw the grief in his eyes. "God, Livvie, can you ever forgive me?"

She felt so utterly weary. "I already did, Jack."

He gave her a tentative smile. "Will you take me back?"

She could only stare at him. She didn't want to hurt

him. She never had. But she didn't know how many more times she could face devastation.

"Why?"

He looked surprised. "Because I love you."

She shrugged. "You loved me before."

She saw the impact of her words and would have once apologized. She couldn't now. There was far more at stake now than ever before. And she was much, much harder. She'd had to be.

"I was wrong to ever doubt you," he said. "I will never be able to atone for that. But let me try. Let us try together."

She looked up at his dear, funny face, and she saw the sincerity shining in his eyes. The remorse and regret. She knew he meant every word. Now.

"Last time, I lost only you," she said. "But if you left again, you could take my child. You could decide that anything I've done in the last five years makes me an unworthy mother and keep me from ever seeing him, and I would have no recourse. Worse, you could let Gervaise close enough to him to finally kill him. He's tried twice already, you know." She shook her head, all that old pain bubbling up again. "I might survive losing you again, Jack. After all, I have before. But I would never survive losing my Jamie."

"*Our* Jamie," he corrected.

"No, Jack. You didn't want him. You didn't raise him or protect him or sacrifice everything for him."

"But I want to be part of his life. I want to be part of *your* life. Tell me how I can make it up to you, Livvie. Tell me how I can convince you I've changed. That the boy who did those terrible things to you died in France."

She heard the wash of blood in her ears. She could smell the brandy the doctor had used, and she could taste the foul remnants of bitterness on her tongue. She could see how the shadows had settled in Jack's eyes and made him sad.

"I don't know, Jack." She sighed, knowing she was breaking her own heart. "I just don't know."

At first, his only response was to just watch her, her hand caught tightly in his. "I understand. But I can't bear to leave you again. If you wish it, I want to marry you again and give Jamie back his rightful name." She meant to object, but he held up his hand. "I know I have a lot of work to do, love. But one thing you will not argue with me about is caring for Jamie. I will no longer allow you to live so far away from him. Please say you'll at least let me settle you somewhere while you decide your future."

Now her heart was skipping, stealing her breath. A home again. All the time in the world to hold her baby in her arms, to watch him discover the world without fear or want or insecurity. To be able to give Georgie back what her dearest friend had given her—support and solace and friendship.

"Georgie is Mrs. James Grace now," she said. "He died two years ago on blockade. He was a fine man."

"He would have to be if you named your baby after him."

"James is only Jamie's second name," she admitted. "His whole name is John James Arthur."

She saw the shock settle in Jack's eyes. "You named him after me?"

She looked away for a moment, her throat thick with

old regret and older hope. "He is your son. But James is the one who took him in and raised him with his own child."

Jack grinned. "Georgie has a child?" He shook his head. "Good Lord. England is no longer safe."

Olivia managed a smile. "Your family will not be happy."

"Be damned to my family. If it weren't for them, you and I would have already been a family, and you and Georgie would have been safe."

Wishes she had never allowed herself. He would not seduce her with them now. Words were easy.

"Your family wasn't alone in their actions," she had to say.

She could have just as easily stabbed him. His eyes were desolate. "I know that, Liv. And I can't make up for these last years. But I hope to make it up to you from now on. At least let me do that."

She saw the naked pleading in his eyes and couldn't refuse. "Thank you," she said, barely keeping from stroking his hair. "I want you to know Jamie. I need him to be safe."

"Believe me when I tell you that Gervaise will never hurt our son again."

"An honorable sentiment indeed," Gervaise said from the doorway into the garden.

Olivia jumped as if he'd struck her.

Jack just scowled. "I don't suppose we could have just a few more minutes of privacy."

But Gervaise stepped all the way in and closed the door. "Sorry, old man. No time."

"Indeed there isn't, Gervaise," Jack said, standing.

Olivia felt the sudden tension in the room. Gervaise was smiling like the cat with the canary in sight, but Jack looked completely unconcerned. She didn't overlook the fact, though, that he reached down to hold her hand again.

"In fact"—Jack tsked like a nanny—"you're a bit worse for wear, dear boy. I can't imagine you presenting yourself so."

That was when Olivia finally took in the fact that Gervaise, usually neat to a fault, looked…rumpled.

"Ah, well," Gervaise said. "I do hope Livvie forgives me for appearing in all my dirt, but I was so anxious to see you both."

"If you were hoping to see me named traitor, Gervaise," Jack said, "you're too late."

Gervaise smiled. "The minute I saw Drake here, I figured as much. So he's your contact, is he?"

"You think I'm going to tell you?"

But Gervaise's attention had already wandered. Olivia felt his gaze crawl over her skin. "Ah, me, Livvie," he said with patently false sympathy. "I'm afraid your looks have suffered a bit. Might prove inconvenient, don't you know. Especially when you are in the hunt for a new protector."

She saw then what he meant to do and felt a cold resignation settle over her. She should have known she would get no reprieve.

"I'd appreciate your not slandering my wife, Gervaise," Jack said.

Gervaise pulled out his snuffbox and flicked open the lid. "She got you to buy her story, did she? The baby was yours? I wonder, Jack, if you've considered who else looks like you."

Olivia held still, her pulse thundering in her ears.

Jack just shrugged. "Diversion is always a good tactic," he admitted. "But this time I'm afraid it won't work." Reaching into his pocket, he pulled out a ruby ring. "Lose something?"

Gervaise just looked disappointed. "Ah," he said, taking a pinch of snuff. "It always was just a bit too big. I imagine it was stolen. Say, this evening?"

Jack shook his head. "How could you? With everything you've been given, you have the gall to betray your country?"

"Oh, come, Jack. I did no more than most. Passed a bit of gossip. Listened in on a few conversations. Tell me who in the *ton* does not."

"But they do not sell those secrets to the French. You sup with traitors, Gervaise; you cannot claim innocence."

"Oh, my dear, no. Really. Not sup. Merely shared a sherry or two. Besides, what do you know about what I have? Why, I've been forced to scrabble around just to pay my tailor, uncaring creature. In fact, I can't tell you how much I appreciate your letting me administer Livvie's trust fund. Admittedly it wasn't much, but every little groat helps."

Livvie found herself gaping. Gervaise. Dear Lord, she should have known. Jack might have been impetuous and easily led, but he had never been dishonorable. He would never have left her and the baby without funds. She at once felt the lifting of an old rage and the settling of a new regret.

"You bastard," Jack growled. "I should call you out."

Livvie jumped to her feet. "No, Jack."

Jack laid a hand on her arm. "Don't worry, Liv. He's not worth it. And I vowed a long time ago that not another human would die by my hand on a field of honor."

Gervaise just smiled. "Oh, Jack, you always were too easily led. But, then, so is most of the *ton*."

"Did you lead that man tonight to us?" Olivia had to ask, even knowing it would put her back in Gervaise's notice.

But he was too well pleased with himself to let her distract him. "That is the most brilliant part of the entire escapade. I only mentioned Livvie in an effort to force her hand. And voilà. Suddenly the world is abuzz about Jack, and everybody and his Aunt Maude is looking for him." He actually giggled. "It was positively delicious."

"Why are you here, Gervaise?" Jack asked. "You must know that your story is blown. I can't imagine you'd try and kill us now. Not with the house this busy."

"Good Lord, no. It might as well be Almacks on Wednesday. No, Jack, I'm leaving. But I had one final gift to give you."

Olivia took an instinctive step forward, as if she could stop him. She should have known he wouldn't have forgotten. It was what he'd come for, after all.

Five years ago, she might have begged. She knew better now. Her future was sealed, and Gervaise would take immense pleasure in accomplishing it.

"A gift?" Jack asked, his arm now around Olivia's shoulder. "I'd be delighted."

She almost shook him off. Better now than after Gervaise told the rest of the story.

"I just didn't want to leave you with a misconception," Gervaise said, carefully inspecting his nails. "The one about how you'd found two true women, your wife and your mistress. And how you couldn't wait to get back to pure little Livvie. You shared the information with me, when we met last year. When you told me what it was you were doing in France." He raised his head, smiling. "Ah, what a bit of gossip that proved to be."

"You were the one who sold me out."

"Indeed I was. But here's the best part, Jack. No one has been true to you. No one. Remember Mimi? The girl who helped you forget Livvie? The one who made you rediscover life?"

"What of her?"

His grin grew. "Why, she isn't dead at all. In fact, I'm off to meet her now. As for being true, she helped set up your capture. With me, as a matter of fact. She was my mistress long before she was yours. And she was my mistress again after you."

And now, dropping his venom into the breathless silence, he turned deliberately to Olivia. "Just like your wife," he said, his eyes hard and bright. "Isn't that right, Livvie?"

Chapter 22

Olivia felt the life draining out of her. So it all came down to this.

"No, she wasn't," Jack said, his hold on her even tighter.

Gervaise's smile grew. "Do you want me to tell you about the lovely birthmark she has beneath her left breast?"

Livvie desperately wanted to defend herself. She wanted it not to matter. But it did. It sealed her doom. Knowing she had no alternative, she braced herself for Jack's rage.

Instead, he stared at Gervaise as if seeing him for the first time. "You may have seen her birthmark," he said, "but you were never Livvie's protector. She has more respect for herself and for our child."

Livvie felt the earth shift beneath her feet.

"But I *have* tupped her, Jack. I tupped her well."

Olivia tried so hard not to react. Not to give Gervaise that satisfaction.

But again, Jack surprised her. "You took advantage of her; I have no doubt at all. I'm just sad I was the one who put her in that position. I'm even sadder she hasn't been able to trust me enough to tell me about it so I could have told her that it made no difference."

Olivia felt oddly frozen. Jack's words seemed to bounce off her like pebbles, not able to break through her growing shock.

Gervaise began to laugh. "Oh, please. No man is such a saint that he will put the horns on his own head."

Jack turned to Livvie then and, smiling, gently closed her gaping mouth with a finger beneath her chin. "I know, my love. You have no reason to believe me. But I've remembered some lessons I learned in the last years. One was that you are, indeed, as Sergeant Harper said, the truest lass I've ever known. I'm just sad I didn't remember that lesson sooner. The other is that trust is based on faith. Not evidence. And, oh, Livvie, how could I ever have mislaid my faith in you?"

Livvie could barely see him through the tears that filled her eyes. "It was a month or so after the duel," she said, trying so hard to sound unaffected. "You had disappeared. My parents had disowned me. I had . . . no one. He acted so"—she spit out the last word—"*concerned.*"

She still expected Jack to vilify her again. She was overwhelmed when he wrapped her tightly in his arms and kissed the top of her head. "Oh, Livvie. How will I ever forgive myself for putting you in such a position?"

A small sob escaped. "He couldn't wait to tell you. I can't believe he didn't."

"Shhh," he whispered, rocking her a bit. "It doesn't matter. *He* doesn't matter."

She heard Gervaise sigh, as if in disgust. "Ah, Jack, you're no longer fun to play with."

Jack dropped one final kiss on Olivia's head and turned to his cousin. "I'm afraid this time you've tried to diddle the wrong man, Gervaise. You're officially under arrest and will be transported to Newgate."

Gervaise laughed as if Jack were the funniest man on earth. "You won't do that. Think of the scandal for the family."

And, amazingly, Jack grinned right back. "Sod the family. Sod you. Sergeant!"

Gervaise spun around to flee, only to run right into the solid wall of Sergeant Harper, and behind him half a dozen other military men, all with weapons.

"Really, Gervaise." Jack tutted. "Did you truly think I'd let you go?"

Caught firmly in Harper's grip, Gervaise blinked. "Yes." But then he saw Drake, and his insouciance was back. "Excellent," he crowed, slipping his snuffbox away. "It is far too fatiguing to be forever avoiding the law. I'm certain I have a few names you'd like in exchange for a comfortable life for me elsewhere."

Drake didn't bother to answer. He just waved his hand, whereupon Gervaise was escorted out.

"Au revoir, old lad," Gervaise said to Jack on the way by. "Places to go, traitors to name."

As he passed, Jack lifted his head. "One more thing, Gervaise. If you ever so much as mention my wife or son again, I won't waste my time with a duel. I'll strangle you with my bare hands. And, Gervaise?" Jack's smile was wolfish. "You wouldn't be the first person it's happened to."

"Your son?" Gervaise gaped at Livvie. "Well, I'll be damned. He's not dead after all."

"No, Gervaise. He isn't."

Instead of railing at Livvie's perfidy, Gervaise laughed all the way out the door.

He was quickly forgotten as Livvie lifted her face to a smiling Jack. "Ah, my girl," he said. "What troubles I have set upon you."

She knew that fresh tears slid down her cheeks. "I told you," she said. "I've forgiven you."

He shook his head, lifting his hand to cup her face. "I wouldn't be quite so quick with your forgiveness, if I were you. I'd make me work hard for it."

Olivia knew Jack felt her stiffen. She wanted so desperately just to love him and let the devil take the hindmost. But her experience had come at too dear a price, the life she had to protect far more precious than her own.

Jack rested his forehead against hers. "Let me make a start, Liv. Please. Let me resettle you somewhere safe and visit. Let me woo you all over again."

The tears were running unchecked down her face now. "I'd like to try."

Slowly, so very slowly that she all but lost patience with him, Jack lowered his head until his lips touched hers. His arm tightened around her, and he spent the next minutes kissing her as if she were the most precious thing on earth.

"And now, my girl," he said, gently setting her away, "it's to bed with you. Alone. I'd appreciate it if you'd at least dream of me, though. I'm off to do battle with the Wyndham griffin. After that, I believe I am much overdue in making the acquaintance of a very small boy."

Livvie could barely sit still. She and Jack had been traveling all day toward Shoreham so they could save time by sailing to Devon, and she was out of patience. She wanted to see her son, and he was still at least a day away.

They had stopped at one of Jack's homes, Oak Grove, a lovely redbrick Queen Anne estate on the slopes of the South Downs. Any other time, she would have loved to tramp across the manicured lawns or wander farther afield up to where she could see to the coast. But she could think of nothing but how far she still was from Jamie.

She was so afraid. She had had no contact with Georgie for seven months. Were they all right? Was Jamie growing and healthy? Would he know her? Would he run to her, just as he had every time before, as if he'd been waiting for her by the window? Would he shriek when she lifted him up and swung him around, and would he still have that wonderful little-boy smell?

Oh, God, she couldn't bear the wait.

Squeezing her eyes shut, she prayed for patience. For wisdom. For judgment. She had finally opened that special, well-locked box that held all her love for her little boy, and the sweet agony of it flooded through her.

That left only one box to sit alone on that far, top shelf, and it held a long-ago dream she still wasn't quite ready to examine. The dream of her family. Jack and Jamie and her together. Possibly other children. Breathless days keeping up with their little boy. Quiet evenings spent curled up by the fireplace, nights lost in love.

It was a wish too fragile to take down and examine yet. An old dream that had been shattered and waited in the dark to be mended.

"You're supposed to be eating something," she heard.

Startled, she turned to see Jack walking into the room.

Just as she did every time she saw him, she felt her heart stumble and lift. His tobacco-brown Bath superfine jacket still hung a bit loosely on him, but otherwise he was beginning to look so much healthier. His face was certainly looking better than hers.

Would she frighten Jamie? She was black and blue, and her scar was pink and puckered. She'd never had any claim to beauty before, but now...she'd seen women turn from her in one inn.

And here was Jack, smiling on her as if she were his first sight of home.

"I can't eat," she said, looking down at the muffin she'd picked apart. "I want to go."

"Soon enough," he said, stepping up to the table. "Sam's fixing a broken trace on the harness."

She almost got up to pace. Then she saw that Jack was holding something in his hands and staring at it as if afraid of it. Suddenly it occurred to her he was as nervous as she.

"Jack? Is something wrong?"

He looked up to flash her a chagrined smile. "I need to speak with you."

That quickly, her knees gave out from under her. "Something is wrong."

"No." He pulled out the chair kitty-corner from her and sat. "I, uh, was going to give these to you sooner. And then later." He laughed like a green youth trying to hand a girl a bouquet of wildflowers. "I have something for you, Livvie, and I want to give it to you before we meet Jamie. I think it's important."

"What?" she asked, suddenly afraid. "Is it your family? Your father? Is he objecting? You promised that they were...were..."

His smile was gentle as he laid a hand over hers to calm her. "They would like to know Jamie, too. But they will not interfere. I told you I'd protect you from powerful marquesses and I will. No, Liv. This is between you and me."

She struggled to slow her breathing. She was so close to home. But she'd been disappointed before.

"What is it, Jack?" she demanded. "Please. I've lost my taste for surprises."

When he looked up, it was with a shy smile that caught her heart. "I know this is unwieldy, Liv. I've been arguing with myself all the way here. But I've thought of what I could do to ease your fears about Jamie and your future. Even if we don't end up as a family, I don't want you to ever again be afraid."

Livvie saw now that it was documents he held. He looked down at them a moment and then, abruptly, handed them to her.

Suddenly nervous herself, she picked up the first. "It's a deed," she said, looking up to see the uncertainty in his eyes.

He nodded. "To this property. You seem to like it here, and it's mine to give. I have deeded it to you and Jamie, free and clear. No matter what happens, it is yours. And it will support you. It is a very profitable little place."

She looked down at the deed that was suddenly trembling in her hands, then back up to Jack. "But why?"

He took her free hand in his. "I took everything away from you, Livvie," he said, and suddenly there were tears in his eyes. "I never want that to be possible again."

She felt answering tears burn her chest. She didn't know what to do. What to say. It was too much. She thought her heart might shatter with it.

"There's another document," he said, nudging the second paper forward.

She swiped the tears from her eyes and picked it up. Jack let go of her hand and rose to his feet, as if he couldn't watch while she read. She realized that he'd gone dead silent, and it made her even more afraid.

The document was thicker than the deed, and it bristled with seals and tape. She opened it as if it were one of her boxes, barely overcoming the urge to close her eyes before she saw what it was. But she smoothed the pages and began to read.

Then she read them again. She checked all the signatures, but they didn't help her understand. She looked up at Jack to see him standing utterly still.

"Can you do this?" she asked, her voice hushed and raw.

"I can. I did." His quick grin was so like the Jack grins of old, brash and bright. So like his little boy's. "Although I had the devil's own work to accomplish it. As you can imagine, the marquess was not best pleased. But I told him that if he ever tried to interfere in Jamie's life again, he'd never see either of us as long as he lived. The pater might be a tartar, but he does bear a certain fondness for me."

She was surprised by a sob. "But, Jack..."

He knelt by her and took her free hand. "I love you, Livvie. I always will. But in the end, we might not marry again. You need to know, no matter what, that you're safe. This document appoints you sole guardian of Jamie until such time you choose to change your mind."

"But you're his father."

He shrugged. "We're divorced. This way, even my father

has no rights to Jamie unless you say so. No one will ever try and take your child again, Liv. On my honor."

She was weeping in earnest now, great, gulping sobs that only made him smile. "Here," he said, taking the documents and slipping them into his coat pocket. "We don't want the ink to run."

He took her into his arms then, and suddenly she was on her knees, too, her head buried against his chest, five years of grief and sorrow and loneliness pouring out of her like old poison. He stroked her hair and rocked her and murmured that it was all right, that she was safe now, that he would never desert them again as long as they lived. And deep inside her heart, the tiny kernel of hope she had cherished for the last week began to grow.

"I never cry, you know," she gulped, laughing. "You're making me a wet goose."

"As long as these are happy tears," he murmured.

"I think, Jack Wyndham," she managed finally, smiling up at him, "that you have become the man I knew you could be when I fell in love with you five years ago."

His eyes were as sweet as dawn as he wiped her tears away with shaking fingers. "Could you love me again, Liv?"

She smiled and knew that her heart lay exposed to him. "Love has never been the problem, Jack. I've always loved you desperately."

"And you won't mind being wooed?"

"Properly."

He groaned, but he was smiling. "You could well kill me," he admitted. "But you have a deal."

And then he was kissing her, his hands in her hair, his heart thundering to meet hers, his mouth so gentle she thought her last dream might well be mending. She closed her eyes and sipped at the unfamiliar taste of happiness.

And then, as if he had choreographed it, Jack dropped one final kiss on her nose. "If what I'm hearing is what I think it is, I may have one more surprise for you, Liv."

Still lost in the sweet delight of his kisses, she couldn't quite keep up with him. "Another surprise?"

But he was looking over her head, and then, with a big grin, he pulled her to her feet.

"My Lord," Harrison, his butler, solemnly intoned, as if in High Mass, "your visitors are here."

And suddenly, like a miracle, there he was. Taller, a little broader, with his baby fat sadly gone. But his eyes, his daddy's beautiful sea-green eyes, were happy, and he was laughing.

"Mama!" he yelled, and ran for her.

"Jamie!" she cried, and opened her arms.

"Mercy," Georgie said from the doorway. "What happened to you two?"

But Olivia was too busy to answer. She was whirling her son around, smelling his little-boy smell and thinking how precious his weight was in her arms, how she had been gray and silent without him, how she had lived only days in the last years—the days she'd been able to see her beautiful boy.

And then she was on her knees before him, swiping his hair back off his forehead and listening to his excited babble about the boat he'd just been on and the storms they'd had and the letters Aunt Georgie was teaching him, and dash it, where had she been?

"I've gone to bring somebody home for you, love," she said. Leaning close, she whispered in his ear. "Do you see that man behind me?"

He looked up with wide eyes. "Who is he?"

"He's your daddy."

Much, much later, she would remember that this was the moment she finally pulled that last box off her shelf. The moment when Jamie, wide-eyed and serious, took the measure of the man who claimed to be his father.

"And just where have you been?" he demanded.

His voice suspiciously gruff, Jack knelt before his son. "Trying to get back to you and your mother."

"Why did it take so long?"

"Because I had to learn how to be a good father first."

And Jamie, hands on small hips, leaned his head back and frowned. "Well," he said. "I suppose we could let you try."

"It's all I can ask," Jack said, his eyes glinting with tears. "It's more than I deserve."

It was finally, after five long years, a reason for Olivia to hope.

It could have been worse, Gervaise thought. At least he was on the state side of Newgate until he finished negotiating with the government. They knew he would talk. He just had to convince them that the information they received would only be equal to the compensation offered, which shouldn't be difficult. In the meantime, he could make sure he had more aces up his sleeve.

He was doing that now by writing one last letter when the door swung open behind him. "Be with you in a moment. I'm in the middle of suggesting my uncle, the marquess, afford me an allowance in exchange for keeping the family name off the scandal sheets."

"Oh, I don't think that will be necessary."

Gervaise turned with a huge smile of relief. He hadn't wanted to admit how anxious he'd been here, where the wrong people could find him. "Ah, good. It's you." His chuckle was a bit forced. "Then they're going to pay me more for my silence? Excellent! I admit I'd half expected to turn around to see that rogue Surgeon looming over me." He shivered. "Chap has no sense of humor, you know?"

"I do, Gervaise. I do. Fortunately for you, though, he is still safely imprisoned. So I come to see you instead."

Gervaise's laugh was strained. "Good. Would you like the West Indies, do you think? I hear it's lovely there."

"Oh, yes. This prison, it does not agree with you, I think."

"It's all right. I won't be here long."

"No. No, you won't. But here, close your eyes and let me make your time a bit better."

Gervaise chuckled. "Ah, you make me feel better, and I'll make our friends feel better. I have a special bit of information I believe they would pay dearly for. Quite enough to see us to Barbados."

Giving a sly wink, he leaned back a bit, spread his legs, and closed his eyes as commanded. He shouldn't have. Before he could even cry out, his throat was sliced open from ear to ear.

His eyes flew open in surprise, then bemusement. He looked down at himself, as if confused by the sight of all that bright red blood pumping down his pristine clothing and splashing onto the floor. Looking up at his attacker, he slowly collapsed like a discarded rag doll until his head rested against his half-finished letter, his eyes clouding over in an odd expression of amusement, as if he were thinking, *Ah well, the joke's on me*.

And so it was, Mimi thought as she wiped the knife off on his biscuit pantaloons and slipped it back into her thigh sheath. "Ah, *mon pauvre*," she said softly to his dimming eyes. "It is too bad you did not know that the Surgeon is not the only one with a love for knives, him. In fact"—she leaned close to whisper in his ear—"he learned this from me."

Dropping a parting kiss on Gervaise's forehead, she pulled up her hood, stepped carefully over the gory wooden floor, and knocked on the door.

"All finished, then?" the warder asked, carefully averting his eyes.

She tapped him on his chest with perfectly manicured nails and sauntered by. "But of course."

And then, knowing she wouldn't be questioned, Mimi simply walked out of Newgate and went home.

Epilogue

It was just as Jack had envisioned it. The morning was bright and clear, the sky that sharp blue of early autumn. The trees had begun to turn, but the weather was still warm enough for Jamie and cousin Lully to be chasing his new puppy across the back lawn. The house rang with workmen who were helping Olivia and him to transform Oak Grove into a home where children could grow in safety and comfort. Where, if nothing else, he could watch close by.

His family had reacted as he'd feared, showing not an inch of remorse or regret for what they'd done. No, that wasn't exactly true. They bitterly regretted not originally being successful in kidnapping Jamie so they could raise him in the Wyndham image.

They had also reacted to Gervaise's murder. Not with shame at his treacherous behavior but with fury at Jack for revealing it. Grieving for the butterfly they thought Gervaise was, they let Jack say nothing bad about him.

Which made the decision to raise his little family as far as possible from the Abbey much easier for Jack. After what his family had put Olivia through, he had no intentions of exposing her, Jamie, Georgie, or her little Lully to their poison.

The only exceptions he'd made had been for his younger brother Ned, who he'd learned had spent two years searching for Livvie so he could help her, and the twins, who had helped.

The more he heard about those terrible days, the more he loved his Livvie. The more she humbled him. His colleagues at the War Office had been telling him of his alleged acts of heroism while in France. He didn't remember more than one in five. He'd remembered only two names besides Gervaise's on the list, low-level government employees who had been dealt with. He did remember, night after night in his dreams, his callous behavior toward the only woman who would ever hold his heart.

He spent every day trying to mitigate his sins. It was why he lived in the Oak Grove dower house, much to his father's outrage. It was why he spent his days helping restore a dormant estate so that it would be a gem for his son to inherit or, God willing and he won back his wife, a daughter.

Watching now as Jamie tumbled over his own feet to roll, laughing, down the slope of the lawn, Jack knew it didn't matter that his family didn't understand. He would live out under a tree if it was the only way he could spend time with Jamie and Olivia.

Even if Livvie never let him closer. Even if she could never quite bring herself to trust him. He had five terrible years to make up to her. He had a son to acquaint himself with. He had a sister who had become even more beloved to him as he witnessed the grief that still shadowed her smiles, and a niece with the most impish green eyes he'd ever seen. He would make it up to them all, and be damned to the stiff-necked, holier-than-thou Wyndhams.

As if called, he heard Livvie's brisk step in the hallway.

"Oh, good, Jack," she greeted him, stepping into the room. "I don't have to go searching through the entire house for you."

He looked up to see that she grew more beautiful by the day. Finally out of those horrid grays, she was instead clad in a lovely blue dress with long sleeves and a ruffled neckline that enhanced her soft blond beauty. He was so relieved to see the weariness easing from her healing face.

She didn't look up to see his examination. Her focus was on the small gift-wrapped box she held in her hands.

"I hope you don't mind my breakfasting here, Liv," he said, standing. "I want to get an early start on the roof."

She waved off his query. "Don't be silly. There's nothing to eat down at the dower house. Besides, you shouldn't have to eat alone on your birthday."

"You remembered," he said, unaccountably uncertain.

She looked up and smiled, her soft, sherry-brown eyes gleaming. The happiness he saw there seemed to be genuine. "Of course I remembered. I'm not the one with amnesia."

Setting her burden down, she took the time to load up

her plate, pausing by the back windows to look out over the view that had so captivated Jack.

"You're going to spoil them," she accused gently, although her smile had grown, and Jack saw tears well briefly in her eyes. "Ponies *and* a dog, all in one week. And you realize that beast is going to grow taller than Jamie by Christmas."

"He's an Irish wolfhound. They're reported to be protective."

"Very true," she agreed, finally pulling her gaze from where Jamie and Lully lay on their backs shrieking as the gangly dog enthusiastically licked their faces. "In fact, he almost didn't let me into Jamie's bedroom last night."

Jack held out her chair and accepted another quick smile from her before reclaiming his seat. "I'll have a talk with him."

"That you will," she said, then tapped the box before her several times, as if assessing it. "After I give you your birthday gift...well, my..." Impatiently, she shook her head and pushed the box over to him. "With all my heart, Jack."

Jack looked up at her. He couldn't remember Livvie ever looking this blatantly anxious. "Should I open it?"

"If you don't, I'll never speak to you again."

So he did, pulling a lovely gold ribbon free and carefully lifting away the pretty foil paper to find nothing more than the box his boots from Hoby had come in. He looked up to see Livvie biting her lip. Now really intrigued, he lifted the lid.

Trash. There was nothing but ripped up papers inside.

For a second, he couldn't make any sense of it. Then he saw the ribbons. Red ribbons. And seals, all crushed, as if their power had been shattered. Suddenly he wasn't sure he could breathe. Tears he thought he'd done with thickened his throat, and his hands shook.

Carefully he looked up to see that Livvie looked as unsure as he felt. "This is your guardianship of Jamie," he said.

She nodded. "You said until I was ready. I'm ready."

For a second he couldn't get sound past his throat. "You're very sure, Livvie? I'm not giving you another chance to say no."

And then, like day breaking, a look of such pure love radiated from Livvie's face that Jack felt awed. "I'm sure. I would like to invite our friends to celebrate with us, Jack. Is a month too soon?"

He almost groaned. He'd deliberately kept from her bed these last two months, knowing that a child would only provide him with blackmail over her. "It's too long, but I'll cope. I'd like a real wedding, Liv. To make up for the last time. To show everyone I mean it. Do you mind that I've been checking with the chancellery courts about Jamie's status? Even if we don't marry, I can claim him as my son and legal heir, since we were legally married when you conceived. But, oh, Livvie, I want it all."

Her smile was shy and sweet. "So do I, Jack. I'm tired of being afraid. Of being careful. I want to try again."

She didn't have a chance to say anything else. Dropping the box, Jack swept her up in his arms and kissed her thoroughly. So thoroughly, in fact, that neither one heard the intruder until she was tugging at Jack's coat.

"Are you listening to me?" Georgie demanded, waving a letter. "Let her go for a moment, Jack, and pay attention. Livvie, check your mail. You have to see if it's true."

Jack saw that Livvie had to blink a few times before being able to attend his sister.

"Oh," she murmured vaguely. "Has the mail come?"

He grinned. "What's true, imp?" he asked his sister, never looking away from Livvie's languorous eyes.

"I got a letter from a friend," Georgie said, bouncing a little on her toes. "It's about your friend Grace, Livvie. She got married."

She even had Jack's attention now. "Really? Who to? That Braxton chap?"

Georgie looked between them. "Diccan Hilliard."

"What?" Olivia demanded, grabbing the letter.

"Oh, no," Jack disagreed with a grin. "Not Hilliard. That would be the greatest *misalliance* since Prinny and Princess Caroline."

But Olivia was shaking her head, her expression blank. "Diccan Hilliard. Oh, Lord. I have to see her."

Jack lifted the letter from her fingers and handed it back to Georgie. "Nothing you can do now, my love," he said, pulling her back to him. "Besides, we'll see them in a month anyway."

It took a second to get Livvie's full attention, but in the end, she melted back into his arms. "You're right. We'll see her in a month."

"What's happening in a month?" Georgie asked, her chestnut curls bouncing as she looked from one of them to the other. "Happy birthday, by the way."

"Thank you," he said, focused completely on the well-remembered joy in Olivia's eyes. Never, he vowed to himself, would she lose that joy again. Not as long as she lived. "It seems that Livvie has accepted my hand in marriage. Again."

Georgie jumped up, giving a shout. "Finally!"

"Yes," Jack said, saying everything he needed with his eyes to his precious, dauntless Livvie. "Finally."

More stunning
historical romance from

Eileen Dreyer!

Don't miss the breathtaking
second book in her
Drake's Rakes series.

Please turn this page
for a preview of

Never a Gentleman

Available in August 2011.

Canterbury
September, 1815

Grace had had dreams like this before. Vague, anxious fantasies in which a man would make love to her. Where, for once in her life, she was beautiful enough to incite a man's hunger.

Usually her dreams were indistinct, more suggestion than fact. After living with the army her whole life, she knew what copulating looked like. Her knowledge of lovemaking, though, was vague at best. So, too, were the images in her head, not much more than a lot of kissing and fondling.

This time was different. In this dream, her lover lay tucked against her back like spoons in a drawer, waiting for her to open her eyes. He was nuzzling the base of her neck where the most delicious shivers lived, exploring her body with a callused hand. All of her body.

The scrape of his palm ignited her skin like too-dry

tinder. His scent filled her nostrils. Her insides felt as if they were melting, and she couldn't seem to hold still.

She smiled in her sleep, where it was safe to dream a bit. Just enough to remind her that beneath the gray dresses and pragmatic mien everyone saw, she was a woman. A woman who wanted the same things other women took for granted. Touch. Comfort. Pleasure.

She stretched, a cat in the sun, to arch closer to his hard, lithe body. She gasped at the feel of his hair-roughened chest against her back, at the surprisingly hard shaft that nudged her bottom. Such an alien pleasure, so intriguing. So deeply erotic.

Her breasts filled; her nipples pebbled. Her body opened to the heat he trailed from his hand, a heat that pooled, settled, sank so deeply into her it touched her very womb, like the sun warming a dormant seed.

In her head, she pleaded with him to hurry. To stoke the fire, to ease it. To pull her closer, closer yet, so she could claim this man who fit so perfectly against her. So she would never again have to be alone.

Then she heard it. A moan. A gravelly, low threnody that resonated right through her. His hand slid lower, spreading such heat her body should glow like a torch. Her heart was pounding; her skin was damp. She heard another moan.

Abruptly she stiffened. Her eyes popped open.

She really *had* heard a moan.

She tried desperately to think. She could see the early morning light seeping into the inn room. Yes, that was right. She had stopped at the Falstaff Inn at Canterbury with Lady Kate the night before. She took a careful breath, expecting to smell woodsmoke, fresh linen, her own rosewater scent. Instead she smelled brandy and tobacco and a subtle scent of musk.

Her heart seized. Her brain went slack. She had dreamed him; she was certain. Why could she still smell him?

Then she felt his hand move toward the nest of curls at the juncture of her legs, and she knew. He wasn't a dream at all.

Shrieking, she lurched up. The bedclothes were tangled around her feet. She yanked at them as she pushed with her feet, trying hard to get away. To at least gain a few feet of space. She pushed too hard. Suddenly she was tumbling off the side of the bed, arms flailing wildly for balance. She might have shrieked again, just as she landed with a thud on the floor.

For a moment she lay where she was, eyes closed, pain shooting up her leg, her stomach threatening revolt. She was dizzy and dry-mouthed and confused. And, evidently, lying on the floor of a strange man's bedroom trapped by his sheets. Christ save her, how could that be? She had to get away before worse happened.

"Bloody hell!" she heard from the bed, and knew that it was already too late. Worse had happened. No, the worst. It wasn't a stranger at all in that bed. It was Diccan Hilliard, the single most elegant man in England. The one man who never failed to turn Grace into a stuttering fool.

In the months since Waterloo, Grace had seen him frequently in Lady Kate's drawing room. He had always been unfailingly polite, the perfect gentleman. But Grace had never felt anything but large and ungainly and unlovely in his presence. The last thing she wanted now was to see his honest reaction to finding her in his bed.

Still cursing, he sat up. The early morning sunlight gilded his skin like a Rembrandt painting, limning muscle and sinew and bone with molten gold, revealing the intriguing shadow of new beard on his cheek and the dusting of dark hair across his chest. Grace wanted to groan. As if she needed any greater illustration of the absurd disparity between him and the horse-faced beanpole who sat on his floor.

Worse, much worse, she saw the exact moment he realized who it was he'd been fondling.

She could still feel his hands on her skin, the unbearable pleasure of his body against hers. His expression of horror made her want to shrivel with shame.

"Miss Fairchild, isn't it?" he drawled, his voice like ice. As gracefully as a god, he climbed out of the bed and walked around to stand spread-legged before her, his glare formidable. "If I might be so bold, what the deuce are you doing here?"

She was too shocked to answer. Dear God, he was magnificent. He had solid shoulders and arms that had worked hard. His chest was taut and lean, shadowed with curling dark hair that arrowed down his torso right to... She flushed hotly. She had felt the curious spring of that hair against her bottom. That intriguing shaft. He was an ancient statue come to life... well, except for one small difference.

Well. Not so small at all. It wasn't as if she could miss it. He was stark naked. And, if she knew anything about men, magnificently aroused. Just the sight of his shaft, jutting straight up from that nest of dark hair, made her shiver.

Of course, the minute he got a good look at her, his

erection wilted like warm lettuce. Grace couldn't really blame him. No man of taste would have reacted any differently.

"I'm still dreaming," she muttered, shamefully unable to look away. "That's it. A nightmare. I should never have had that second piece of pigeon pie last night."

She should shut her eyes. She should make a grab for her clothes and run. She should at least defend herself. She couldn't so much as move.

Grace thought she had never seen a man look so cold. "I expected better of you, Miss Fairchild," he said, his voice dripping with disdain. "Never did I think you'd be the kind of scheming, brass-faced hussy who'd force her way into a man's bed. Just what did you slip into my drink?"

Suddenly furious, Grace clambered to her feet, grabbing a bedpost to steady her when her leg cramped. "What did I slip into *your* drink?" she demanded, outraged. "Why, you insufferable, self-centered, overweening park saunterer. You're the last person on earth I'd let near me—"

Instead of apologizing, he squeezed his eyes closed. "For the love of God, madame, cover yourself."

Grace looked down and squeaked in dismay. She hadn't considered her state of undress when she stood up. She'd grabbed the covers because it was frigid in the room. Not because she was . . . oh, dear sweet Lord. She was as naked as he was, providing him with an unblocked view of her bony chest.

She couldn't help it. She shrieked again and whipped around, struggling to adequately cover herself with the voluminous blanket.

"Where are my clothes?" she cried, mortified that he should see every unlovely jutting angle of her. Especially her leg. Even her mother hadn't been able to tolerate the sight of that leg.

"At least you are covered," he said, not moving. "Thank you."

They were still both naked. In the same room. Alone. Grace felt panic closing off her air. Her head hurt. She felt sick.

Suddenly the door to the room slammed open and bounced against the wall. In a flash, Grace saw a crowd of people in sleepwear, crowding the doorway like gawkers in a theater pit. Gasping, she dropped to the floor and yanked the covers over her head. If they didn't see her face, they wouldn't recognize her.

"Isn't that General Fairchild's daughter?" a woman who sounded like Lady Thornton demanded from the doorway, and Grace shrank down even more.

"How delicious," another woman answered with a delighted giggle. "The horse-faced hussy obviously thinks she's nabbed Diccan Hilliard."

Grace heard laughter and wanted to die. There must be a full battalion of social gossips out there.

"Good to see everyone," Diccan was saying, as if they had come to tea. "My apologies for presenting myself to you in *dishabille*."

More salacious laughter. Grace squeezed her eyes shut, the thundering of her heart almost drowning out the wags who could be heard taking bets on her future. She was terrified she was going to disgrace herself. Her stomach was lurching as if she were back on the channel packet.

"Well, well," she heard a new and welcome voice intrude. "Mrs. Maxwell, I had no idea that this was what you wore to bed. Amazing color, really. And, Tommy, what an...interesting nightcap. You all must have been dragged right from your sleep. Which, I'm afraid, isn't the most attractive time of the day for any of you."

Lady Kate had arrived.

If this had been happening to anyone else, Grace might have smiled. Leave it to Kate to send the cream of the *ton* scurrying away like embarrassed debs. But it was happening to *her*. She was the one crouched on the floor, naked beneath a blanket as an audience laughed.

She must not have heard the door close, because suddenly she felt a gentle hand on her shoulder.

"Grace?"

If it could be possible, she felt worse. She had so few female friends. Only three, really—Olivia Grace; Lady Bea; and Lady Kate, who had taken her in after her father had died at Waterloo. It had been Lady Kate who had seen her through those terrible days. Lady Kate who had provided safety and support as Grace adjusted to civilian life. She couldn't betray her friend this way. Even a notorious widow had no business associating with a ruined spinster.

"Grace, tell me you're all right," Kate said, sounding distressed.

"I'm fine," Grace managed, huddled miserably on the floor.

It didn't occur to her to cry. Soldiers didn't cry, her father had always told her. At least not after their seventh birthday.

"Is this some joke of yours, Kate?" she heard Diccan demand, sounding like a petulant child.

Lady Kate huffed. "Don't be demented. I'm even more stunned than you are. I know for a fact that Grace has better taste."

"Why, you repellent *brat*," he snapped. "Your *friend* just arranged to make an appearance in my bed before half the *ton*. Naked."

"Really, Diccan? She must be amazingly sly, then, since neither of us expected to see you or them here."

"She *must* have, damn it! They're here. And *she's*... here."

Lady Kate sighed. "You might want to get your clothes on, Diccan."

"What about *her*?"

Still crouched beneath her blanket, Grace sighed. Her leg hurt. The blanket was beginning to feel scratchy. And a draft had found its way inside to bedevil her. And yet, she couldn't gather the courage to move.

"Grace can dress after you leave," Lady Kate was saying over Grace's head. "From *her* bedroom, by the way."

"Hers?"

"Indeed. I accompanied her to this very door last night."

That helped Grace a bit. Diccan had been the one to mistake bedroom doors. Not that it mattered now. The damage had well and truly been done.

She heard the rustling of clothing. He must be dressing.

"What *are* you doing here, by the way?" Lady Kate asked as if she were addressing him over tea. "We were supposed to meet you in Dover tomorrow."

There was sudden silence. "This isn't Dover?"

"Canterbury," Grace answered before she thought of it.

"Canterbury?" Diccan echoed, the sounds of movement ceasing. "Deuce take it. How the hell did I get here?"

"Well," Kate said, sounding absurdly amused, "once you're both dressed, that is certainly one of the topics we'll need to address. Are you still all right under there, Grace?"

Grace felt another miserable blush spread over her. "Do you see my clothes?" she asked.

"Strewn over the floor as if they had been on fire," Kate informed her. "Which is another reason I know you aren't the culprit here. Even during those awful days we spent caring for the wounded from Waterloo, you never once failed to fold your clothing like a premier abigail."

"She could have been anxious to get into bed," Diccan suggested dryly.

"Not with you, she wouldn't," Kate said, sounding supremely delighted. "She doesn't like you."

Grace made a sound of protest. It wasn't polite, after all, even if it was true. She didn't like him. It didn't mean she was immune to him.

"Don't be absurd," Diccan was saying. "Everyone likes me."

"Would you *please* get your pants on and leave?" Grace demanded, finally losing her patience. "I'm about to catch the ague down here."

And damn him if he didn't chuckle. "Anything you say, Boadicea."

Which made Grace feel even worse. A month or more

ago, Diccan had nicknamed her after the English warrior queen, undoubtedly because he couldn't think of another female tall enough to look him in the eye. Which, as Grace well knew, was not necessarily a compliment.

"I reserved a private dining room for breakfast," Kate was saying to him now. "Why don't you meet us down there?"

Grace heard some inarticulate grumbling.

"Oh, never fear," Kate answered. "You'll only have to get past half a dozen witnesses. Be forewarned, though. One of them is Letitia Thornton."

This time it was Grace who groaned. The most sharp-tongued shrew in the *ton*. The news of her ruination would be all over London before dinner.

Diccan, it seemed, had no more to say. Grace heard the door open and close, and knew without being told that he'd left.

"Come out, little turtle," Lady Kate said, her voice too gentle for Grace's mood. "I'll turn about while you dress."

Diccan Hilliard was in a rage. No one could see it, of course. Diccan had long since perfected the mask of insouciance that was his trademark. But his mind was seething with outrage. How could this have happened? He was always so careful. So alert to attack. And then, in a matter of days, he had suffered two spectacular setbacks.

Instinctively, he looked down at his hands, as if expecting to still see young Evenham's blood on them. He'd tried so hard to reach the lad before he'd put that gun to his head. But he hadn't reached him in time. He hadn't reached him until the only thing he could do was cradle that poor broken body in his arms, drenching his hands in the boy's blood. Now, like Lady MacBeth, he wasn't sure he'd ever get it off.

Which was why he couldn't let what happened this morning delay him. He had to get back to London before they found out that Evenham was dead. He had to be the one to tell them, or any information he'd gleaned would be lost to the scandal.

That was, if it wouldn't be lost to *this* scandal.

Well, he thought, still looking at his empty hands, at least he hadn't brought Miss Fairchild to suicide. He looked back up to see the avid interest of a dozen hotel guests, and sighed. Correction. He hadn't brought her to suicide *yet*.

Of course it was Thornton who was the first to speak. The pig-faced peer wasn't any fonder of Grace than was his knife-thin wife. "Wasn't there anything better in town to entertain you, old man?" Thornton asked with a simper as Diccan passed him in the half-timbered hallway. "Thought you had better taste than to dally with the Praying Mantis."

The malice in those words brought him to a halt. "I beg your pardon?"

"Oh, come now." The overstuffed peer chortled, poking him in the ribs with an arm like a sausage. "You're the one who came up with the handle. I imagine that now you know better than anyone how appropriate it is."

Diccan deliberately slowed his breathing. He would deal with his own sense of guilt later. He might be furious at the Fairchild chit, but it didn't justify what he'd once called her in a drunken moment. Or how viciously pleased this worm was to fling it about.

"Thornton," he said calmly. "My friend. I know that you're sensible."

Suddenly Thornton looked a bit less assured. "Why, of course."

Diccan nodded. "Good, good. Then you would never do anything that might cause you to find yourself across a dueling ground from me. Knowing, of course, that I have already stood up four times." He leaned a bit closer. "And walked off alone each time."

He thought Thornton might have gulped. "Naturally, Hilliard. Naturally. Didn't mean any insult. Just...well, you must know."

"Actually, no," Diccan said softly enough that Thornton's face went chalk white, "I don't. I do know that I would find it...unpalatable to hear any slander spread about Miss Fairchild. No matter what else she is, she's a lady, and, according to my cousin, related to half the aristocracy."

"Of course," the peer said, by now nodding so hard he knocked his cravat askew. "Excellent. I'll just toddle off. Busy day today. Looking over a new property with the wife. Don't wish to be late."

Jerkily tipping his hat, he lurched off, which left Diccan with only five more witnesses to intimidate. He he realized as he continued on to the breakfast room that he simply didn't have the energy. He was still feeling nauseous and wobbly, and his head was throbbing like a broken foot. He needed coffee, he needed silence, and he needed answers.

Grace Fairchild.

Bloody hell, couldn't it have been any other woman in existence? Grace Fairchild had to be the most honest, honorable, well-thought-of spinster in England. She was also the most unfortunate. She couldn't even walk without lurching like a sailor on shore. Whoever had named her Grace must have had a grim sense of humor.

Plumping himself down in a chair, he drank cup after cup of coffee until the cobwebs began to clear in his head. He had been set up. Drugged, shanghaied, stripped, and left to be found naked in bed with the most notorious virgin in the realm. He knew he was the target. With all the will in the world, he couldn't imagine one person who would consider Grace Fairchild an enemy. But those same people would know just how Diccan would react to finding himself shackled to the tall, gawky, almost colorless female. They must have known that his first instinct would have sent him running faster than a felon.

The frustrating thing was that he loved redheads. He couldn't think of any more exotic treasure than that burst of fire right at the juncture of a woman's legs. It was more promise than color, a hint of the delights that lay beneath, a flash of whimsy and heat and lust. He loved every shade of redhead. He loved their milky coloring and their vivid personalities and their formidable tempers. He even loved the smattering of freckles he sometimes found on their more intimate places.

Except for the freckles, Grace Fairchild could boast of none of that bounty. To call her a redhead was to exercise unforgivable license. Her hair was virtually colorless, the kind of faded, dismal hue one might see on an old woman. Her skin was almost swarthy from all her years spent under the Iberian sun, and her blushes were unfortunate at best. She had no shape to speak of, no temper, no spark.

The sharpest reaction he'd ever gotten from her had been the day he had dubbed her Boadicea. For just a moment, he'd caught a spark of fury in her eyes, a spirited defiance in her posture. But as quickly as the fury had risen in her, it had dissipated, almost as if there was no place on her to gain purchase. Word was that she had never even wept when she carried her father's body back from Waterloo.

Grace Fairchild was eerily even-tempered. The antithesis of everything Diccan Hilliard loved in a woman. If only Kate's animation could have rubbed off on her. Kate was the only woman Diccan could ever imagine himself married to. Kate was spirit and challenge and sharp intelligence. And Grace Fairchild was no Kate.

Groaning, he poured out the last of the coffeepot. He had to figure out how this had happened. He had a suspicion of who was involved. After all, Evenham hadn't killed himself over nothing. What he'd told Diccan could topple great families. Did someone hope that involving Diccan in a scandal would diminish the weight of his accusations? Or did they simply mean to delay him long enough to counter the damage of Evenham's death?

Whichever it was, he wasn't about to let them succeed. Pulling out his pocket watch, he checked the time. He needed to be on the road to London today. But before he could leave, he had to deal with Grace Fairchild.

As if called, the door opened and in she walked, clad

in one of her ubiquitous gray dresses. Diccan wasn't surprised that she couldn't quite look at him. He was still trying to understand it all himself. How could he have gone so hard tucked up behind *that* body? Climbing to his feet, he gave his best bow as Kate followed and shut the door behind her.

"Kate. Miss Fairchild. Let me ring for breakfast."

Miss Fairchild went almost chalk white. "Not for me, thank you. Some tea and toast."

Diccan tilted his head to assess her. "Stomach a bit unsteady?"

"A bit."

"Muddled head? Dizziness?"

She looked up briefly as she reached the table. "Indeed."

Diccan held out her chair and waited for her to sit. "I thought so. I have the exact same symptoms. I don't know if you tipple to excess, Miss Fairchild, but I rarely do, and never on a packet boat. So in the absence of other evidence, I believe we were both drugged."

He was disappointed when Miss Fairchild failed to react. "You're not surprised?" he asked.

She looked calmly up at him. "It would explain why I can't remember anything."

He shook his head, a bit disconcerted by her poise. "Kate," he said, turning back to his cousin. "Who sent you the message to meet me?"

She sat down. "You did. Didn't you?"

"As a matter of fact, I did not. Where did you receive it?"

"We were at a country weekend at Drake's."

That brought Diccan's head around sharply. "Drake?

And you received mail there? Who knew you were there?"

Kate gave him a grin. "Undoubtedly everyone in town. Word of the house party was in the society page of the *Daily Mail*."

Even so. Marcus Belden, Earl Drake, was the one who had asked Diccan to meet with Evenham. Could he somehow be involved in this latest debacle? Diccan just couldn't figure out how. Or why.

"The note did look to be in your hand, Diccan," Kate said, bringing his attention back to the matter. "Who do you think sent it?"

He rubbed his thumb against his temple. "Someone who does not wish me well, obviously. I don't suppose you know why most of the worst gossips of the *ton* had also bedded down here last night."

Kate shook her head. "Why would someone go to all this trouble?"

"I don't know." He hoped he looked convincing. "I have been involved in some delicate negotiations. The postwar map of Europe and all."

Kate raised her head. "They finally gave you a real job?"

Diccan flashed her a smile. "Purely by attrition, my dear. The usual suspects are simply too busy. I offered to help."

She gave him a brisk nod. "About time you got off your proverbial arse."

Diccan couldn't help but laugh. "Impudent baggage." Sucking in a breath to settle his fresh nausea, he steeled himself to get on with business. "Our first order of business, of course, must be to make plans. Propitiously we're in Canterbury, and the good archbishop is one of those ubiquitous cousins. I should be able to obtain a special license by the afternoon. Do you wish to stay here or repair to London for the ceremony?"

Kate looked toward Miss Fairchild, who sat stonily silent. "Oh, London. It will make it look less like a hole-in-the-wall event."

Diccan nodded absently, beginning to pace. "I'll have to find a town house, of course. My wife couldn't be expected to bunk down at the Albany." A sudden dread had him eyeing his cousin with disfavor. "You don't expect the pater to preside over the nuptials, do you?"

Kate sighed. "It would look odd if your father were excluded, Diccan. He is a bishop, after all."

That was the last straw. All he needed right now to complete this farce was to see his father in one of his bouts of self-righteous indignation. When the maid returned, Diccan would ask for hemlock in his coffee.

"Excuse me," Grace spoke up.

Diccan stopped. The deuce, he'd all but forgotten her sitting there. "Yes?"

"Am I involved in these plans?"

He blinked. Surely she wasn't that dense. "Of course you are. What did you think?"

"I thought you might have consulted me."

The expression on her face was serene, but Diccan could see the pulse in her neck quicken. "What? You'd rather be married in Canterbury? Don't blame you. The pater is a regular tartar."

"I'd rather not be married at all."

And without another word, she stalked out of the room.

Finally, Kate, too, got to her feet. "Well," she said,

sounding suspiciously amused as she settled her primrose day dress about her. "Now I understand why you are thought to be the suavest man in England."

And she walked out too.

Diccan was still standing slack-jawed when the maid finally came to answer his call. He slumped back into his seat and dropped his head to his hands. "Coffee," he growled. "And see if you have any hemlock."

THE DISH

Where authors give you the inside scoop!

♥ ♥ ♥ ♥ ♥ ♥ ♥ ♥ ♥ ♥ ♥ ♥ ♥ ♥ ♥

From the desk of Eileen Dryer

Dear Reader,

Blame it on Sean Bean. Well, no, to be fair, we should blame it on Richard Sharpe, whose exploits I followed long before I picked up my first romance. If you've had the privilege to enjoy the Sharpe series, about a soldier who fights his way through the Napoleonic Wars, you'll understand my attraction. Rugged? Check. Heroic? Check. Wounded? Usually.

There's just something about a hero who risks everything in a great endeavor that speaks to me. And when you add the happy bonuses of chiseled features, sharp wit, and convenient title, I'm hooked. (For me, one of the only problems with SEAL heroes—no country estates.)

So when I conceived my DRAKE'S RAKES series, I knew that soldiers would definitely be involved: guards, hussars, grenadiers, riflemen. The very words conjure images of romance, danger, bravery, and great posture. They speak of legendary friendships and tragic pasts and another convenient favorite concept of mine—the fact that relationships are just more intense during war.

So, soldiers? I was there. I just had to give them heroines.

That was when it really got fun.

My first book is BARELY A LADY, in which a companion named Olivia Grace recognizes the gravely injured soldier she stumbles over on the battlefield of Waterloo. The problem is that this soldier is actually her ex-husband, Jack Wyndham, Earl of Gracechurch (You expected a blacksmith?). Worse, Jack, whom Olivia hasn't seen in four years, is dressed in an enemy uniform.

Jack and Olivia must find out why before Jack's enemies kill them both. Did I mention that Jack also can't remember that he divorced Olivia? Or that in order to protect him until they unearth his secrets, she has to pretend they're still married?

I didn't say it would be easy. But I do say that there will be soldiers and country estates and lots of danger, bravery, chiseled features, and romance.

It certainly works for me. I hope it does for you. Stop by my website and let me know at www.eileendreyer.com. And then we can address the role of soldiers in the follow-up book, NEVER A GENTLEMAN, not to mention my other favorite thing—marriage of convenience.

Happy reading!

Eileen Dreyer

♥ ♥ ♥ ♥ ♥ ♥ ♥ ♥ ♥ ♥ ♥ ♥ ♥ ♥ ♥

From the desk of Dee Davis

Dear Reader,

I have always loved run-for-your-life romantic adventures: *King Solomon's Mines*, *The African Queen*, *Logan's*

Run, *Romancing the Stone*, and *The Island*, to name a few. So when I began to conceptualize a story for Drake Flynn, it seemed natural that he'd find himself in the middle of the jungles of Colombia. After all, he's an archeologist when not out fighting bad guys, and some of the most amazing antiquities in the world are hidden deep in the rainforests of South America. And since Madeline Reynard was involved with a drug dealer turned arms trader, it was also easy to see her living amidst the rugged beauty of the high Andes.

There's just something primal about man against nature, and when you throw two people together in that kind of situation, it seems pretty certain that sparks will fly. Especially when they start out on opposite sides of a fence. It's interesting, I think, how we all try to categorize people, put them into pre-defined boxes so that we have an easy frame of reference. But in truth, people aren't that easy to classify, and even opposites have things in common.

Both Drake and Madeline have had powerful relationships with their siblings, and it is this common bond that pulls them together and eventually forces Madeline to choose between saving herself or helping Drake. The fact that she chooses him contradicts everything Drake thought he knew about her, and the two of them begin a tumultuous journey that ultimately breaks down their respective barriers and leaves them open to the possibility of love.

So maybe a little adventure is good for the soul—and the heart.

For a little more insight into Madeline and Drake,

check out the following songs I listened to while writing:

"Bring Me to Life"—Evanescence
"Lithium Flower"—Scott Matthew
"Penitent"—Suzanne Vega

And, by all means, if you haven't seen *King Solomon's Mines* (with Stewart Granger and Deborah Kerr), Netflix it! As always, check out www.deedavis.com for more inside info about my writing and my books.

Happy Reading!

Dee Davis

♥ ♥ ♥ ♥ ♥ ♥ ♥ ♥ ♥ ♥ ♥ ♥ ♥ ♥ ♥

From the desk of Amanda Scott

Dear Reader,

Lady Fiona Dunwythie, the heroine of my latest book, TEMPTED BY A WARRIOR, was a real person, the younger daughter of fourteenth-century Lord Dunwythie of Annandale, Scotland. She is also the sister of Lady Mairi Dunwythie, the heroine of SEDUCED BY A ROGUE [Forever, January 2010] and cousin to Bonnie Jenny Easdale, the heroine of the first book in this trilogy, TAMED BY A LAIRD [Forever, July 2009].

Writing a trilogy based on anecdotal "facts" from an unpublished sixteenth-century manuscript about events that took place two hundred years earlier has been fascinating. From the manuscript, we know that Fiona eloped with a man from the enemy Jardine clan, and as I learned from my own research, the Jardine lands bordered Dunwythie's.

We also know that Fiona's sister inherited their father's title and estates, and that Lord Dunwythie died the day Fiona eloped, while he was angrily gathering men to go after her. Since we know little more about her, I decided that Fiona had fallen for her husband Will's handsome face and false charm, and had ignored her father's many warnings of the Jardines' ferocity, lawlessness, and long habit of choosing expediency over loyalty.

To be sure, she soon recognized her error in marrying Will. However, when she meets Sir Richard Seyton, Laird of Kirkhill, she is not interested in romance and is anything *but* eligible to wed. Not only is she married to Will and very pregnant with his child but her father-in-law is dying, her husband (the sole heir to the Jardine estates) is missing, and his father believes that Will must be dead. Worse, Old Jardine believes that Will was murdered and is aware that Fiona was the last person known to have seen him.

Old Jardine has summoned his nephew, Kirkhill, because if Will *is* dead and Fiona's child likewise dies, Kirkhill stands next in line to inherit the Jardine estates. Old Jardine has therefore arranged for him to take them over when Jardine dies and run them until the child comes of age. Jardine also informs Kirkhill that he has named him trustee for Fiona's widow's portion and guardian of her child. Jardine dies soon afterward.

Kirkhill is a decisive man accustomed to being in charge and being obeyed, and Fiona is tired of men always telling her what to do, so she and he frequently disagree. In my humble opinion, any two people thrust into such a situation *would* disagree.

The reactions of a woman who unexpectedly finds herself legally under the control of a man she does not know seems consistently to intrigue writers and readers alike. But in a time when young women in particular were considered incapable of managing their own money, and men with land or money were expected to assign guardians to their underage heirs and trustees for their wives and daughters, it was something that happened with regularity. I suspect, however, that in many if not most cases, the women and children did know the guardians and trustees assigned to them.

In any event, I definitely enjoyed pitting Kirkhill and Fiona against each other. The two characters seemed naturally to emit sparks. I hope you enjoy the results. I love to hear from readers, so don't hesitate to fire off a comment or two if the mood strikes you.

In the meantime, *Suas Alba!*

Sincerely,

Amanda Scott

http://home.att.net/~amandascott
amandascott@worldnet.att.net